Half of Faith

Rod Johnson

A Josh Morgan Publishing novel.

ISBN: 0578414007
ISBN-13: 978-0578414003

DEDICATION

For Amy & Allie

ROD JOHNSON

"PATIENCE IS HALF OF FAITH."

Attributed to the Prophet Muhammad

ROD JOHNSON

PROLOGUE

Patience is an aggravating virtue, especially to its victims.

An animal goes into hiding for any number of reasons. Battered, it runs off to lick its wounds. Beaten, it sometimes moves timidly in the background, relegated to second-tier status by a new alpha male.

But occasionally it retreats to merely recover and lie in wait. Circumstances may change and another opportunity present itself, if only the animal has patience.

For years the Islamic State, al-Qaeda and their brothers around the globe unleashed a campaign of attacks with varying degrees of success. While provoking terror throughout the world, the results were lacking any significant accomplishments until various factions combined in an unprecedented campaign against the Saudi royal family. The attacks were in part retribution for Saudi cooperation with the Great Satan in the first invasion of Iraq, which many jihadists viewed as the beginning of all-out war with the infidels. And though the Saudis had outwardly refused to cooperate with the infidels in the second Gulf War, the royals had still voiced only token opposition, and this was, in the minds of extremist Muslims, equivalent to tacit approval. Real cooperation had to be discouraged.

So, a secondary purpose of the early attacks was to warn the royal family from participating in the US war against al-Qaeda and the emerging Islamic State.

The intimidation of the royal family through small terrorist acts had successfully halted any real cooperation with the United States except in economic trade. In the several years following there was relative calm with regard to al-Qaeda but that changed in a dramatic way. The emergence of

ISIS as an entity capable of seizing large pieces of geography inspired the radicals to launch a united, focused attack against the Saudi Kingdom.

One possible outcome of the conflict would be the outright executions of the crown prince of the Royal Kingdom of Saudi Arabia and his family. However, he was offered the choice to escape that fate by stepping down. In the end the crown prince accepted the lesser of the two disasters and fled with his family's heads and his riches intact. His abdication of royal power brought about a government of the people and of Allah, into which, of course, the al-Qaeda Party stepped.

The resurrection of al-Qaeda in Saudi Arabia would have pleased bin Laden. This nation of such wonderful history, once soiled by the presence of the infidels, blasphemers, and harlots that comprised the American military had savaged Iraq during their first assault against Saddam. But now this holy land was honored by patriots of Allah.

Historically the Great Satan winked at whatever Saudi Arabian activities displeased it, preferring petroleum and pragmatism to confrontation and coercion. Turning a blind eye was more difficult now, however. Suspicion and wariness had not totally disappeared from the American psyche but much of the nationalistic fervor that surfaced as a result of the attacks on the twin towers of the World Trade Center and other targets on September 11, 2001 had faded, exponentially so as each year passed. But the new Holy Islamic Republic of Saudi Arabia currently elicited more suspicion than most other countries, taking the place of Iraq in the minds of most American as the chief terror villain.

Sanctions were put in place at the time the royal family relinquished power; sanctions that still remained. However, over the years the ruling al-Qaeda political party seemed to be a kinder, gentler incarnation of its former self. The government of the former Royal Kingdom of Saudi Arabia had by all appearances divorced itself from terrorism, but the very name al-Qaeda still stirred deep-rooted hatred and bitterness among all Westerners. And for al-Qaeda those feelings were mutual.

Most Americans viewed the current Saudi al-Qaeda Party as all bark and no bite.

But animals can go into hiding for any number of reasons. And sometimes, they're simply being patient, lying in wait.

CHAPTER 1

DAY 1 – FRIDAY

Even for those who had visited Cozumel before, the approach to the airport on the Mexican island was often unsettling. The Boeing 737-700 fell nearer the water until it was scant feet above the crests of the waves. Then *terra firma* rushed into view beneath the plane to the quiet relief of all onboard. The aircraft landed with a thud and the brakes were applied so forcefully that the passengers' torsos pitched forward with the abrupt loss of speed.

Veteran flyer that he was, the passenger in seat 9C still let out an almost audible sigh as the *AeroMexico* plane touched down. It slowed sufficiently, negotiated the turn at the end of the runway, and began the brief taxi toward the tiny terminal. Once inside, he proceeded to the lines of people awaiting entry through Customs.

Though jet-black hair, dark skin, and moustache were shared by most of the male inhabitants of the island, nobody would confuse him with the Mexicans. In fact, Fadi Al-Majeed stood out noticeably from the mostly whites and Latinos in the airport. Middle Eastern tourists were rare here.

◆

The Cuervo Gold had worked its spell. After making a substantial dent in the almost full bottle, Josh Morgan had lain practically comatose on the sofa for a couple of hours. But the pounding on the door brought him marginally – and reluctantly – back to life. Morgan couldn't describe his experience as a nap; there had been nothing restful about it. What it did do was allow him to close his mind, however briefly, to the tornado of memories ripping through him.

He forced one eye open, then the other, not quite sure whether the clamor that had roused him was real or imagined. But as he slid his fingers through his brown, matted hair, the knocking resumed. It was a gentle, almost apologetic rapping. Still, in Morgan's current state, it sounded like a jackhammer.

With a moan he propped up on a single elbow, allowed himself a momentary pause from the effort, then sat up, eyes alternating between strained wideness and forceful squinting. A coarse grunt filled another pause until finally, not entirely drunk, nor entirely sober, he steadied himself against the back of the sofa and slowly navigated the few steps to the entryway.

As he neared the front door, through the leaded glass window he made out a familiar silhouette.

"Shit."

◆

Al-Majeed's real name on his passport would have triggered red flags, even in Mexico. However, despite the fictitious name on it, in the present global environment the passport he held, merely identifying him correctly as a Saudi Arabian would likely generate some level of unwanted scrutiny.

Like many of his generation Al-Majeed had left Saudi Arabia to join the jihad against western devils at any place and in any form in which they appeared. Kept on the run by his own quest to fight for his religious beliefs in whatever arena possible, the Saudi found his place among a group of holy warriors that had arisen as a splinter of the ISIS faction and which had ultimately displaced the Saudi Crown Prince, building a sanctuary for the al-Qaeda remnants. Fighter that he was, Al-Majeed despaired at the mostly passive nature of the al-Qaeda Party as it ruled the Holy Islamic Kingdom of Saudi Arabia. Timidity had no place in the heart of a soldier, he believed, and many like him felt ill-suited to stand idly as the Party had done in recent years. But that was about to change, Fadi Al-Majeed knew.

Even to the Arab it was a remarkable path that had brought him to where he was today. While Muslims rarely conceived of miracles in the same way that Christians did, instead believing that miracles of Allah were simply the result of zealous obedience to his will, Al-Majeed nevertheless concluded that his present circumstances were indeed a miracle – a reward for his faithfulness. His submission to the teachings of the Quran had brought abundant blessing – his survival of the massive firepower launched against Bin Laden and his brothers in Afghanistan, his participation in the conversion of Saudi Arabia to a national refuge for the faithful, and now his role in bringing the judgment of Allah powerfully to the Great Satan.

A miracle indeed!

◆

It occurred to Morgan to pretend he wasn't home. It would be a tough sell, though. Maggie would know better. Both his vehicles were parked outside the house and besides, she knew he hardly left his property anymore. So he urged himself forward, plodding along on reluctant feet, straining just for the energy to stand upright.

His head felt as though it were filled with mud, thick, damp, trying its best to seep through his ears and eye sockets. His mouth, on the other hand, felt as if it had never known moisture, and tasted so extraordinarily foul that it offended even Morgan. He paused and rubbed his eyes with the heels of his hands forcefully enough that it hurt before he realized it. Then, his forehead against the doorframe, the man turned the handle weakly and coaxed the wooden door open.

Maggie Loughlin gazed at the disheveled figure barely standing at the door.

"Be still my heart." The smile started first in Maggie's deep blue eyes before spreading to her lips. She pushed past Morgan as she always did, laughing, and tossed her purse onto the table in the hallway. Flopping back in Morgan's easy chair, Maggie kicked off her shoes and pulled up her knees, resting her chin on them exactly as she had the first night she had visited Morgan's home.

She widened her eyes, leaned her head forward and chuckled again. "Yikes, Morgan. You look like shit."

Morgan's nose wrinkled and the corners of his lips rose ever so slightly. He remained frozen against the edge of the open door, eyes closed more from embarrassment for forgetting that he and Maggie had plans to go out than from the growing queasiness that his mobility had created. Collecting himself, he pushed the door to – quietly – and turned to face Maggie. What small reservoir of energy he had was fading rapidly and Morgan sagged against the wall behind him and raised vacuous eyes toward his visitor. He could only grunt.

Maggie shook her head as she arched her eyebrows and performed another up and down survey of the disheveled figure standing before her. A slight giggle added the exclamation point to her assessment of her friend.

◆

"Red," observed the dark-skinned tourist with annoyance. In the Cozumel airport "traffic lights" determined which travelers' bags the Customs officials searched. Green for "go." Red for "stop."

In contrast to the huge bags of dive gear, golf clubs, and other vacation toys being dragged by most of the tourists, Fadi Al-Majeed carried only a small suitcase. The obvious contents of the bag were of no consequence and he was confident that the hidden objects would escape any search short of ripping the entire exterior apart. The contraband possessed no scent for the drug dogs being led about by their handlers. Nor did it have an unusual shape or metallic parts that would appear in an airport x-ray. Still, Al-Majeed thought, the inspection was a concern.

The attending airport agent leisurely unzipped the cloth front of the bag. The fact that there were two planeloads of passengers backed up in the area apparently created no obligation on his part to expedite the process.

"Number of bags?" he inquired in accented English.

"One."

The agent cut his eyes upward without raising his head. "You travel light."

"I am only here for a long weekend." He offered no more information than was required. He knew better than to volunteer answers to questions that weren't asked. Al-Majeed was a veteran agent – and no fool.

Another Customs Agent joined the uniformed attendant. He held up the tourist's passport, alternating his eyes between the photograph on the document and the man it represented. The first agent removed the entire contents from the suitcase's main compartment, as well as from every zippered section as the second agent looked on.

Al-Majeed wondered at the attention but remained expressionless. The original agent picked up the bag and turned it about, inspecting it from every angle. Next, as if to validate the findings, the second man performed an identical examination. He tapped on the sides of the bag, then gathered the Arab's belongings in a wad, paused to stare at the traveler several seconds, and stuffed the aggregation of items back into the luggage. The first agent closed the top of the suitcase roughly and slid it to Al-Majeed unzipped.

A perfunctory "*gracias*" ended the inspection and the duo turned their attention to the next red-light victim as though the Saudi no longer existed.

Experienced or not, it was a tense moment for an intelligence professional to receive such attention. He wiped a trickle of sweat from his brow and, though not out of place in the warmth of this tropical haven, the perspiration wasn't from the heat.

Outside, there was no need to hail a cab. A number of Mexican men and boys assailed Al-Majeed, imploring his patronage. In Spanish or broken English each urged him to what they insisted was the only taxi that could deliver him quickly to his destination. As the Saudi moved to one of the waiting Chevy Suburbans, the driver reached for his bag.

"No, *gracias*," came the reply with a forced smile. Al-Majeed took the seat in the front while six more tourists took their places on the rear bench seats. Two hotels and several minutes later the last three, including the Arab, exited the cab at the Cozumel Palace and tipped the driver. While the other passengers gathered their luggage, Al-Majeed took his sole bag, checked in and made his way to his room.

◆

"The willingness to die for the Lord is certainly evidence of ultimate commitment for any Christian. But the true measure of discipleship is the willingness to live for Him. Not 'live' in the abstract sense where the bottom line of our lives tips the scales slightly toward righteousness…"

Everson Blake's hands flew about, pointing toward his listeners, to the heavens, to himself, thrusting the Good Book skyward for emphasis. His brow glistened despite the air conditioning in the banquet hall and an occasional spray of spit baptized the people unfortunate enough to occupy the front row. His voice rose and fell with the fervor of an old-time evangelist. It was rather high-pitched, incongruous with its owner's rough complexion and a face marked with the results of years of harsh necessities. Blake's fit, muscular build only underscored his height, undersized by proportion, about five-feet-ten. If one closed his eyes and listened, he heard an accountant or perhaps a librarian. But opening the eyes revealed a man capable of brutal action and who had no doubt seen much of it in his day – and who had likely initiated a great deal of it.

The contradictory nature of the man's countenance with his message enthralled his friends in the audience. A man's man who loved the Lord! It just didn't get more inspirational than that.

The Deputy Director of the nation's most secret agency paced energetically behind the podium, practically sprinting the span of the room. The distance his movements placed between him and his notes was irrelevant. He was well past reliance on his script and was speaking from his heart. And he had many minutes earlier exceeded the allotted time for his mini-sermon.

"No, brothers, the essence of 'live' is to give substance to our salvation in the context of practical, everyday devotion. It is moment-by-moment obedience to God's Word. It is choosing to do the unpopular thing – the godly thing – in the face of extraordinary opposition. 'Live' means making the constant daily sacrifices that give testimony to the world that, not only do we rely on God for our eternal salvation, but we also surrender every aspect of our existence to Him. Ultimately it is demonstrating that He may in turn rely on us to give witness through everything we say and do that He is indeed the Lord of our lives."

Blake continued on for a few minutes more. A small number of the listeners fidgeted and glanced at watches, though most hung on every word the lay preacher spoke. The air filled with "amens" as Brother Blake concluded the protracted testimonial to the monthly meeting of his church's men's fellowship.

He smiled with satisfaction.

◆

Morgan's eyelids strained to squeeze out excessive daylight as he calculated how to deal with Maggie. While he detested the thought of adding to the long list of disappointments he had caused her, he was sure his stomach wouldn't allow him to stray too great a distance from the bathroom. His mind was in even worse shape but found its way nevertheless to a sudden recollection of the way in which he and Maggie had met.

In Josh Morgan's days at CIA, he had, in spook parlance, non-official cover, or NOC, meaning he wasn't assigned to an embassy or consulate. Instead, the cover for his real job was as a photojournalist and, over time, he had gained a deserved reputation as a world-class photographer, one who would go fearlessly into any global flashpoint to cover a story. However, in his real job, NOC exposed him to the greatest of risks, for it offered no diplomatic immunity from prosecution. Discovered, he would be arrested, tried, convicted, and jailed. Spies were rarely executed because there would be political consequences. And besides, it would take months, if not years, of debriefing to determine the full scope of his crimes. Only when that process was complete would his captors repatriate him in exchange for one of their own. But in the end, it wasn't detection by the counterintelligence forces of some foreign land that led to Morgan's departure from CIA. The Agency had dismissed him for his part in an unauthorized operation.

When he left, though, Morgan did so with a talent and a reputation that could have opened a number of lucrative doors. But aside from some freelance work, Morgan did little more with his expertise than to teach a couple of community education courses in photography offered through the Jackson, Wyoming Independent School District. Maggie was a student in the first session he taught.

What he noticed first was her shimmering auburn hair. It had an untamed look, but not unkempt. He would later tease her that it looked like she cut it with a weed trimmer. Short on the sides and back, it was almost longest at the front, strands dancing delicately over her blue eyes. She must have brushed it back a dozen times during the first class, he remembered.

"You're not Andy Jones."

There was no disputing the accuracy of those first words Maggie spoke to him, but Josh couldn't grasp the nature of the accusation they seemed to contain.

"Beg your pardon?"

"I took this course specifically because they told me Andy Jones would be teaching it and that he was the best photographer in town." Her voice was low, but not too low, with an occasional lilt that sang in concert with her eyes.

"Really cute, but a bit of an attitude." Those were the first conscious thoughts Morgan had about Maggie.

"No. No, Andy wasn't able to make it for the course after all, so they called me in at the last moment," he told his tentative student. What he didn't say was that Andy Jones was a hack and a lush. He worked for the local paper until his fondness for alcohol finally got him fired, whereupon he had packed and disappeared into the night for parts unknown.

Furthermore "best" was a phrase the organizers of these courses used to promote them. It was just good marketing to characterize the instructor for the next course to be the "best," regardless of the truthfulness – or lack thereof – of the claim.

Morgan continued, "If you aren't satisfied with the course after tonight, the school district will give your money back."

Maggie waited silently for a moment, staring back at Morgan. She tried desperately to look menacing, he thought, but was unable to manage it.

"We'll see," she challenged as she moved to take a seat, shooting one last glance as she did.

Over the next eight weeks Maggie captivated Morgan. They became fast friends during the photography sessions. She had a natural eye for camera work and pursued it with a passion he had long since lost. That was what it was about Maggie, he thought; her unbridled energy and enthusiasm for anything she did. And she was so… wholesome.

"Really, wholesome?" he asked himself. "Of all the adjectives I could have come up with, and I picked wholesome?" But it fit. With a freshness that was contagious his student was passionate about the smallest of things. Everything was a cause for her – her love of animals, her devotion to her friends. And she had a killer body, he noticed frequently. And that was a much more characteristic observation from Josh.

Just about the time Morgan began to think their friendship was evolving into something more, Maggie dropped in unexpectedly at his house one night. Oddly, to that point in their relationship, neither had been to the other's home. On this night Maggie had marched in with the same boldness she exhibited for everything else and offered a simple, "Hi, Josh." Stunned, but delighted, to see her standing at the door, Morgan did little else than stammer.

"Great house," Maggie continued. "Got some pics I want you to look at." And with that, she began to open her laptop and access the photo files.

Josh silently congratulated himself, thinking this could be his chance to "make his move." But after showing some exceptional photographs she had made up the road in Grand Teton National Park, his guest abruptly announced, "I'm moving to Dallas in a couple of weeks."

Maggie's job took her to Texas for over three years. During her absence Morgan became increasingly withdrawn as his disenchantment with life swelled. Despite the fact that he rarely replied, Maggie emailed Morgan regularly. Her first day back in Wyoming, she called him and left a message. She followed with two more calls over the next week and, excited though he was to hear her voice, Morgan never returned her calls.

So, one day Maggie showed up unannounced at his doorstep. He opened the door and, belying the joy he actually felt at seeing her, simply said, "You're back." Bewildered at the tone, she hesitated in coming in for the only time that Morgan recalled.

"Yep, that was really me leaving all those messages."

"Your hair's longer."

"I hardly cut it the entire time I was gone."

And at that point Josh Morgan became Maggie's latest project. For Morgan, looking for some measure of logic in how their lives were intertwined was like trying to complete a jigsaw puzzle without the box's cover photo to tell him what it was supposed to look like – and with some of the pieces missing. They seemed to be perpetually on the periphery of becoming lovers, always a strong physical connection, but never consummated. Yet in spite of the absence of sex, their intimacy ran much deeper than that of many "couples."

And, most importantly, they were, at the end of the day, friends.

"Hello? Earth to Morgan!"

"Huh?" Morgan murmured as Maggie's remark forced him abruptly from the past and into the fog of his present.

"I said," and she cupped her hands to her mouth, "you – probably – don't – feel – like – going – out. Of course, that's only a guess." Another smile. "Right?"

"Uh, yeah… No."

Springing out of the chair, Maggie headed for the refrigerator. "Then I'll whip up something… Whacha got in here?"

"Nothing. There's nothing in the fridge." Morgan always got pissed when Maggie just took over, but she always ignored his protests. But he managed to keep his voice calm, more for the sake of his pounding head than to avoid escalating the tone.

"Oh, sure there is. I'll find us someth…"

"Screw lunch."

Maggie looked over her shoulder from her search of the refrigerator, eyes wide with feigned hurt and lower lip extended in a pout. "Aren't we the Grumpy Gus today?"

"Listen. I'm sorry that I forgot our plans, but I don't want to go out… I don't want to eat in… I… I just want to be left alone, so please just go home… go the hell somewhere. I don't care where." He closed his eyes and massaged his throbbing temples. "Just go… please!"

Maggie closed the door and leaned against the refrigerator. "Please, Josh. Don't hold back." Sometimes, when Morgan was in one of his "moods," as she politely thought of them, sarcasm would disarm him. His silence, though, told her that this wasn't going to be one of those occasions. With a shrug, she offered her "you win" smile and walked over to pick up her purse and shoes. "Okeydokey, sweetie. But you need some serious cheering up," she said, flirtatious blue eyes accenting the diagnosis.

She stood on the toes of her bare feet, and placed a deliberately noisy kiss on Morgan's cheek, from which he turned away.

"God, Maggie. Just listen to yourself. Don't you get tired of being so sappy?" He hated himself instantly, but the words fired out with a life of their own. He searched her eyes for the hurt he knew he would find there.

After an awkward, questioning silence, Maggie broke the tension. "Asshole," she laughed. "You can't fool me. I know you love me." With that she skipped down the steps to her pickup. She flung open the door and stepped onto the running board, looking over the cab at Morgan. She tilted her head, flipping her now more than shoulder-length hair to one side, and brushed it from her eyes out of habit, though there was no longer a need. She smiled at Morgan and lingered a moment before taking her seat in the truck.

"Talk to you tomorrow," she promised.

Morgan couldn't hear it, of course, but the slight quivering he saw through the red Ford's window made it clear that Maggie was chuckling again. To get in the last word — Maggie always got the last word, whether verbal or not — she leaned toward the window nearest Morgan and blew him a kiss with an exaggerated wave of her hand.

The only thing that surpassed his irritation at being laughed at was the relief he felt that she had summarily dismissed his sorry behavior. She was irrepressible and brash, and he loved it.

But just for show, he slammed the door anyway.

CHAPTER 2

President Wendell Mercer stood with both hands resting on his desk, scanning the briefing handed him by his Secretary of State. It was mid-afternoon, far too early in the day to feel this tired.

"Sue, what's it going to take to get this done? Hell, we're practically giving them the keys to the store and we can't close the deal?"

Secretary of State Susan McGregor flinched at the candor of her boss' remark. At sixty-one and a career Foreign Service professional, she was accustomed to the oratorical ballet of the diplomatic world, to the special language that only ambassadors truly understood. She was practiced at communicating through subtext and innuendo – through body language, insinuations, implications, and undertone – through every form of communication imaginable except saying exactly what you meant.

"Sir?" she queried in her trademark New England accent.

The president maintained his fixation on the short stack of papers bound in the "President's Eyes Only" folder. Without looking up, he rubbed upward on the back of his neck at the red hair and clarified, "I don't know how much more we can move. I'm already going to be in deep political do-do for this, but in the long term, I'm convinced it will be the right thing to do for the country. It's just that there are simply no more concessions left to offer." Finally cutting his eyes toward the SecState he repeated, "So what will it take to get this done?"

"Sir, I appreciate the precarious nature of your position in this matter publicly, and I can assure you..."

"Sue," he interrupted, waving both hands, eyes wide with impatience. "Sue, it's me."

The portly woman stiffened with an accompanying wince that was similar to what you would expect from a teenager who was about to tell her dad that she had wrecked the car.

"I… Well, I really don't know, sir."

"You don't know. What the hell do you mean, you 'don't know.' It's your job to know."

"Yes, sir. If I can speak frankly?"

President Mercer managed to stifle a small smile in spite of his frustration at the situation. He knew that direct, frank talk was an occupational anathema for people like the Secretary. But her attempt at it would be interesting, he thought, so he motioned her to one of the chairs in the sitting area in front of his Oval Office desk.

"Please," he encouraged as his guest moved to the seat.

"Mr. President, I know Saudis don't think like we think, but, for the life of me, I don't know what they want. I would agree with your assessment that we are giving them the store. Furthermore, I think they know that.

"For all their public posturing about serving Allah and despite the fact that they are, figuratively, descendants of bin Laden, these aren't your father's al-Qaeda… so to speak. Certainly, elements in the country are responsible for some of the terrorism that still exists in the world, but they're committed to maintaining a viable government in Saudi Arabia. They've found heaven on earth there. It keeps them protected and rich. It gives them at least some aura of legitimacy and a platform for their religious rants. They don't want to lose that. But behind the bluster they are skilled negotiators who know when it's time to close the deal."

McGregor folded her arms uncharacteristically and shook her head almost imperceptibly from side to side, moving the still black hair that was longer than usual for women of her age. She exhaled and looked skyward.

"Were they uncertain as to the limits of our concessions," she continued, "I would understand their reluctance to conclude negotiations. You know – fear of leaving money on the table and all that. But I'm convinced they know we've extended our – shall we say – 'generosity' as far as we can. The framework for an agreement is in place. We have received tentative approval from their negotiating team. They insist they are merely waiting for President al-Hashimi's approval. They also assure me that this is simply a formality and that his consent is certain and imminent."

"But they've been saying that for months now. What the hell is the holdup?" the World's Most Powerful Man bellowed.

McGregor literally wriggled in her seat, a move so incongruous with her temperament and reputation that it secretly delighted Mercer that he could intimidate this fearless woman.

"Then what?" he asked again.

"Sir, I believe al-Hashimi is enjoying the idea of making you wait – of making you…" She paused. "Of making you squirm, sir." She cast her eyes downward.

Mercer rose to his full six-foot height and put both hands on his hips.

"Goddammed prick." His voice was measured as he repeated, "Goddammed fucking prick."

The President of the United States paced to the window, leaving one hand on his hip, placing the other against the glass, and gazed out. He exhaled a muted sigh and folded his arms across his chest.

"Oughta blow the fucker's ass to hell. Then just march into Riyadh and take the damned oil."

◆

Reverend Earl Gaston shook his deacon's hand vigorously, then doted on the Deputy Director of the National Security Agency for several minutes, holding him up as the perfect example of the Bible's admonition that Christians be "in" the world, but not "of" the world.

To serve one's country, as Everson Blake did in the Navy, Reverend Gaston said, then at the NSA, he continued, while keeping his faith intact and his life on the straight and narrow... well, that was the very definition of discipleship in a topsy-turvy, sinful world that challenged Christianity at every turn, the minister maintained.

Blake maintained his image of contrition, but in his mind, he agreed with every word that his pastor spoke. Modesty and humility were traits the NSA officer aspired to, but generally fell short of. He took great spiritual pride – was that an oxymoron, he wondered? – in the deep and abiding faith he had maintained despite the often spiritually trying nature of military and intelligence work. And Blake was further convinced that God looked upon him with tremendous favor. He was certain that God understood the demands of his careers and granted wide latitude with regard to his behavior.

Reverend Gaston concluded, "Thank you again for your message, Brother Blake. It's an inspiration to see a devoted Christian and family man in such a place of influence regarding our nation's security. It's a comfort to know that at least one part of our government is under the direction of one so morally and spiritually committed as you."

Another round of amens, then the guests surged forward to shake the hand of their honored speaker.

◆

The crunching of the gravel on the driveway grew fainter as Maggie's truck receded. Morgan collapsed onto the couch, immediately regretting both the sudden motion and the abrupt stop. He ran the fingers of both hands through his tousled brown hair. A groan escaped, barely audible, but deeply felt, as he mustered himself to a sitting position. Morgan's fingers pressed on the magazine that had incited this mini-binge and slid it toward himself across the aspen wood that formed the surface of his coffee table. The photo on the open page looked exactly as it had earlier that day.

"Everson freaking Blake." The name dripped from his mouth. "Bastard hypocrite," muttered Morgan.

He flung the magazine across the table and leaned back again.

He wondered at times if he had become what shrinks would diagnose as manic depressive. He cycled through episodes of anxious despair and – well, the manic part wasn't really all that manic; it just seemed so in contrast to the increasing fits of despondency.

When his life had taken its unexpected detour, Morgan anticipated that his bitterness would diminish with time. But the truth was his anger had become an abusive companion and often the only emotion in an otherwise impotent life. She mocked his inability to shake free of her spell.

For Morgan most days were merely tolerable. Almost none held true happiness. And the number of days given to whining and self-pity – days like this one – were increasing in both number and frequency. The native Texan only occasionally left his home near the Snake River, most often to visit the liquor store or to fish. And therein lay the disparate sanctuaries from the demons that haunted Morgan's life. He seldom drank to excess, at least not so that it was a serious problem. But drinking was his way of escaping the panic attacks and fits of anger. At the other end of the emotional spectrum, depression and disillusionment dominated idle days. And he exorcised those ghosts by fishing. It was an activity that fellow Texan George Strait might sing was time well-wasted. Morgan felt most at peace during the time he spent casting about for trout in the various rivers near Jackson Hole. Flyfishing required patience and concentration. And while those attributes were in short supply in his non-fishing life, Morgan managed to rediscover them on a mountain stream. His time there was peaceful and uplifting. Morgan's spirit seemed to rise with the rhythm of fishing. To him fishing was less about catching fish than about casting off the disappointments of the real world. He needed to think about nothing more than selecting the right fly, making an accurate cast with a good drift, and, if he was lucky, lifting his rod at the proper instant to hook a fish. But the last part was not essential to his fulfillment.

Recently he almost always fished alone, as was the case with most things in his life after leaving the Central Intelligence Agency in disgrace.

All Josh Morgan wanted was his old life back. Not that the life he had lived for the last six years was completely without appeal. It was just that Morgan increasingly felt the same lack of purpose and growing resentment that many retired people suffered after a lifetime of work.

But Morgan was only thirty-two.

Technically speaking, he had a job. He was even listed in the Jackson, Wyoming, Yellow Pages and on many online references under Photographers, Commercial. But in truth Morgan was a mostly-fisherman, sometimes photographer. His refusal to accept that there were indeed things in his life over which he had no control had shaped a passivity to those things that he could change.

"Everson freaking Blake," he spat again.

The former CIA officer understood that he had been his own worst enemy in the downward spiral that was his life. The combustive mixture of arrogance and naiveté that Josh Morgan had as a younger man had made him a prime candidate for his rapid fall from grace. Mostly Morgan was exhausted by fear. This timidity angered Morgan the most. And it was what he was most in denial about.

But he also knew that Blake had set the scheme in motion that ruined his career. Blake had serious connections and because of that Morgan had known little peace in recent years. For the first eighteen months after being booted from CIA he lived in outright fear – justifiably. There were people in powerful places who wanted parts of their old lives back as well, and the knowledge that Morgan possessed held them at bay. Ultimately, he managed an uneasy recognition that what existed was, for all intents and purposes, a stalemate. Perhaps his life was no longer in danger, he speculated. And it certainly never hurt that he had a former president of the United States as an insurance policy.

Yet despite the relative safety that Morgan now felt, he still lacked the courage to take even the most inconsequential risks in life. He realized that what he missed most from his old life was not the job, but the fearlessness with which he attacked life. The younger Morgan had been relentless in pursuing anything he wanted, either personally or with regard to the demands of his job. He wanted to recapture the enthusiasm and addiction to life that he once had. Josh Morgan's life was stagnant. It was as if he had developed multiple personalities, not in the clinical sense, but in a Walter Middy sort of way. It was only in Morgan's mind that he lived out most of the possibilities that life held. In the real world there were alternate Josh Morgans who reported for duty as circumstances dictated.

At CIA Morgan had accepted too much at face value. He trusted the system too readily and thus found himself in a sensitive situation not of his own making. Yet when judgment fell, there had been many inequities. The greatest injustice of all, the one that still caused barely containable rage and resentment in Morgan, was that not only had Blake survived with his career intact, he had moved to NSA where he rose rapidly through the ranks. He was on track to become NSA Director.

So, as was common in life, there were survivors and there were fall guys.

Morgan had taken one for the team. Everson Blake had walked.

Furthermore, high on Morgan's list of things he despised about Blake was his professed faith. Not that faith was a bad thing. Though hardly measuring up in recent years to Christian ideals, Morgan himself nevertheless had a deep and sincere faith in God that was borne of the influence of a strong and loving Christian mother. But Blake? Well, Blake was a hypocrite. Morgan knew it would be difficult to find many others who shared this view of Blake because his public persona seemed so genuine. But Morgan had seen up close and personal what Blake was capable of. He was ruthless in a way that only those who have justified their actions in the light of some deluded concept of righteousness can be. He was much like the jihadists that required so much of Blake's organization's focus.

And it was Ev Blake's mug that stared back as Morgan reached again for this week's issue of Time.

"Deputy Director of the National Security Agency! Shit!" Morgan shook his head, his lips pursed. The muscles in his jaws flared as he ground his teeth. He glared at the magazine. The left crease of Blake's lips still had that slight upward skew that made his coarse moustache appear as a theatrical prop that had been pasted on crookedly. His hair was different now, slicked back, Morgan observed. It looked as if whatever he used on it could be wrung out and refined.

"Who told you that looked good?" Morgan taunted the two-dimensional Blake. "Just makes you look like the snake you are."

Just the thought of Blake always kindled a quiet fury in Morgan. But at actually seeing his face again, Morgan bit at his lower lip and shuddered. His left hand moved to his face. His thumb and middle finger stretched outwardly across his face at the corners of his closed, dark brown eyes. His entire hand moved slowly downward, massaging his unshaven face before squeezing his chin. Finally, and for reasons somewhere in the recesses of his subconscious, Josh Morgan turned to look behind him.

The awakened memories renewed their assault on his mind and though he was conscious of the thoughts, Morgan could isolate none of them nor apprehend their meaning.

After some minutes in numbed silence, he finally rose, stalked the half-empty bottle of tequila on the counter and poured himself a taller drink than he should have. The anticipated burn in his throat was welcome as he returned to the escape he had begun at eleven that morning.

The westward-facing rooms at the Cozumel Palace commanded a spectacular view of the Caribbean waters that separated Cozumel from the Yucatan peninsula. The richness of the blues amplified as the distance from the shore increased. Just off the beach, the sea was a pale turquoise with the sun reflecting from the sand beneath the shallow depths. Pockets of darkness littered the sandy bottom indicating stands of coral. The following band of blue was deeper and held a hint of dark green over the coral wall to which thousands of scuba divers flocked each year. From there to the horizon the color was the intense blue of water of seemingly infinite depth as it plummeted to the abyss beyond the nearly vertical reef. The afternoon sun's reflections shimmered on the water like millions of diamonds surfing the waves. And at the point where the curve of the earth claimed the images of anything beyond, there was the just-visible sliver of darkness that was the Mexican mainland. So, given the inspiring nature of the view, it was likely that, of all the guests to arrive at the seaside hotel that day, Al-Majeed was the only one whose first task was to close the curtains.

Al-Majeed moved about the room in routine fashion, checking behind this picture, under that desk, removing and replacing light bulbs, unplugging lamps, unscrewing the ear- and mouthpieces of the room's phone. Satisfied, the Saudi agent opened his bag and removed its contents. He had two changes of clothing, a small bag of toiletry items, a medium-sized, blue rumpled backpack, and little else. Al-Majeed unzipped the smaller bag and emptied the contents onto the countertop by the bathroom sink. He took the clippers and unfolded what was usually a nail file. On this one, however, it was a small blade with a highly sharpened tip. Returning to the bed, he pulled back the top of the suitcase. The Samsonite had a gray fabric exterior that covered walls of a plastic hard enough to protect the bag's concealed contents from the airlines' baggage mishandlers. Al-Majeed began to cut away the zipper from the bag's main compartment. The outer barrier of this suitcase was actually double walled. From between the two layers he lifted stack after stack of US-denominated twenty- and fifty-dollar bills, shrink-wrapped with thin plastic instead of held together with paper bands. He removed the soft material lining the bottom of the case next, exposing even more of the currency. He stuffed all the green pieces of paper into the blue backpack and closed the knife.

The Saudi reflected that one hundred thousand American dollars seemed like a paltry sum for the purchase it would make. Of course, he reminded himself, in the minds of his – what do Americans call them? – contract laborers, this was just the down payment.

Having finished the task at hand, Al-Majeed opened the curtains to his balcony and slid open the glass door. Setting the backpack by the inside edge of the exit to the terrace, he stepped outside and straddled one of the chaise lounges. Finally lying down, Fadi Al-Majeed assumed the role of vacationer for a couple of hours and simply enjoyed the view.

CHAPTER 3

DAY 2 – SATURDAY

President Mercer was in uncharted waters. Acts of terrorism had gone through cycles since George W. Bush launched the war on terrorism a few administrations earlier. Surges in Afghanistan and Iraq seemed to quell the terrorists, only to see the rise of ISIS and more attacks on US soil by both foreign and US-born individuals and groups. Finally, there was the overthrow of the Saudi government and a subsequent lull in violence again.

Mercer's predecessor, President Trenton Weston, had adopted a hardline approach to the shakeup in the Saudi Arabian power structure, refusing to recognize the government that replaced the ousted monarchy and using his political muscle to put into place economic sanctions in the hopes of weakening the new regime. However, those acts were the limit of what the country would tolerate. Weston's constituents no longer had the stomach for a seemingly perpetual war. Weston remained convinced that Saudi Arabia now fell into that category of nation that President Bush described in his famous position that if you harbor a terrorist, then you are a terrorist. And while some in the US government maintained a high level of rhetoric against the "evildoers," the truth was that most Americans now seemed to view occasional attacks as normal but largescale terrorism as an almost nonexistent threat.

Mercer took pride in his ability to navigate seemingly impossible circumstances and succeed where less committed and creative men would have failed. Through months-long overtures to his own and the opposition party the president prevailed, and by the narrowest of votes, Congress passed a resolution supporting recognition of the current Saudi leadership yet refused to remove the sanctions.

That was in his first term. But today was different. President Mercer was for the first time speaking directly with the first President of the Holy Islamic Republic of Saudi Arabia. It was probably a historic moment, he realized, but not the type he cared to have plastered on the front page of the New York Times. Therefore, this historic conversation occurred by phone rather than in person.

There was the usual lag in the conversation owing to the interpreters. In addition to the practical requirement of making the two presidents understood to one another, interpreters created breathing room in sometimes tense situations. Any blips in the dialogue, any verbal missteps by the leaders could be attributed to inaccurate translation.

Though on the other end of the telephone conversation al-Hashimi insisted that only he and his interpreter were present, President Mercer suspected otherwise. The American chief executive had himself lied to the Saudi leader when he said that the only person with him was his interpreter. In truth, other of his aides, along with Secretary of State McGregor and her aides were in the Oval Office, listening to the conversation on headphones.

"President al-Hashimi, I am anxious to continue the progress between our nations. Though relations have been greatly improved during my administration, there is, I feel, some remaining distrust and uneasiness. These are contributing to a continued state of tension that is unhealthy for our nations and for the entire Middle Eastern region. I believe the tentative agreement we have before us is a significant step in moving that process forward. I felt that a direct conversation between the two of us might lead to a finalization of this undertaking."

What the US President really wanted to say was, "I wanted to see if I could get you off your sorry ass, you two-bit street thug. I need to get gas prices down and you're jerking my chain." However, he was sure his counterpart wouldn't appreciate such candor.

A moment passed while his words became Arabic, and the reply became English.

"I, too, am anxious to bring to an end once and for all the atmosphere of hostility that has existed between our countries…"

"And so on, and so on," Mercer thought. "Blah, blah, blah. God, I hate this two-step shit." His mind wandered during the translation process and he wondered just how much of what each man said was being accurately passed along. Hell, he mused, these interpreters could be making it up as they went, creating foreign policy on their own.

◆

Anytime in Cozumel would be wonderful, thought the Arab spy.

Summer was a little hotter, he was sure, but it was probably little different than fall, winter, or spring here. The island's location meant that the weather varied only within narrow ranges throughout the year, and today was one of those glorious days, even by tropical standards, that made the words paradise and Caribbean synonymous. The turquoise waters surrounding the tiny Mexican island of Cozumel had long attracted scuba divers, but over the last several decades the added commercial developments and improvements in infrastructure had made the resort more accessible, comfortable, and therefore increasingly popular with the more generic fun-in-the-sun vacationer as well.

The Saudi strolled along the road from the hotel among the multitudes of sun-seekers toward the heart of the island's only town, San Miguel. It was a walk of maybe ten minutes and Al-Majeed had plenty of time before his meeting. He strolled casually past the assorted shops, glancing in the windows, ostensibly to survey the wares, but in actuality, indirectly surveying his surroundings by checking the reflection in the glass for anyone showing undue interest. Resorts were at once both the easiest and most difficult of places to conduct intelligence business. Because of the masses you could easily blend in, lose yourself. And people rarely gave you a second look except in the shallow assessment of your appearance and whether you would be a suitable companion in fact or fantasy. But for all the same reasons it could sometimes be difficult to ascertain when you had been made, versus just being looked at.

As the Arab got closer to the village, the number of shops increased, and, since it was after ten o'clock, most were open. The owners or workers mostly stood in the doorway, assessing the *dinero* that approached them in the form of tourists. They began their pitches long before Al-Majeed reached their storefront and continued well after he passed.

The main square of San Miguel was teeming with people. Al-Majeed made a couple of unnecessary blocks, doubling back on occasion. He scanned for recurring faces, endeavoring to determine if anyone else was following his unusual route.

No, it still looked okay.

With the blue backpack slung casually over a single shoulder, his white pants, tropical shirt, and sunglasses made the Arab looked every bit the vacationer. He sat on the sea wall and rested momentarily, looking again at the faces of the passersby. Standing and stretching, Al-Majeed reversed his previous direction, and walked south along *Avenida Rafael E. Melgar*. A few blocks later he arrived at *el Café Cuzamil*, which he had identified on his first pass. Ascending the whitewashed staircase to the veranda, the man took a seat at the northernmost table nearest the patio's wall. The waiter hurried over with water and toasted bread. He placed an open menu in front of Al-Majeed, then retreated to his usual place near one of the arches that led to the interior of the small *café*.

The Arab was at *el Café Cuzamil* for about twenty minutes before a short Mexican man walked to his table.

"It is a beautiful day here in *paraiso. ¿Si?*"

"*Si*. It would be wonderful to live in such a place," confirmed Al-Majeed.

Identities established through the prearranged dialogue the Mexican asked, "May I join you, *amigo*? It is sad to dine alone."

Lunch overlooking the gin-clear waters that lay between the island and the Yucatan peninsula was a decidedly tourist thing to do, but the two men dining at *Café Cuzamil* had more serious matters to discuss than coral reefs, mariachi bands, or the proper strength of sunscreen. The agreement they sought to finalize could alter the courses of three nations. It would exalt one country to its rightful place of power in the world, while bringing another to its knees. In the third nation, power would shift and indigenous peoples who had been bypassed by the growing prosperity of their country would resume the fight to claim the heritage of their ancestors.

Suddenly multiple pairs of eyes in the Oval Office locked on one another as Mercer, McGregor, and everyone else in the room struggled to digest what had occurred.

al-Hashimi had himself begun speaking in English, an ability that had gone undetected by every intelligence agency in every nation of the world.

"President Mercer, may we have a private conversation? Just you and I?" President al-Hashimi spoke serviceable, if not altogether fluent English.

The US president's speech faltered and, stunned by the unexpected revelation, he stammered, "Why, uh, yes. I mean… certainly, President al-Hashimi."

"May I suggest that everyone leave your office? I will order the same thing here."

"Of course." Mercer looked at his companions, shrugged in genuine bewilderment, and flicked his head toward the door.

Secretary of State McGregor removed the headset and could do little but sit for a moment as she tried to comprehend the significance of the improbable disclosure she had just witnessed. Finally, she gathered her papers in an untidy bundle and headed for the exit.

"The horse's ass speaks English," an astonished POTUS said to himself. Probably a "know your enemies thing," he speculated, and he was at once impressed and wary.

"I am alone now," he confirmed to his Arab counterpart after the others had left, though he had little confidence that the man on the other end of the telephone had likewise complied. "So, what's on your mind?" he wondered

◆

Trenton Lewis Weston belonged to an exclusive club. There had been few presidents, so consequently, few ex-presidents in the history of the United States; even fewer still alive. The five years since he left office, or more precisely, since the voters kicked him out, were a study in contradiction. He had rediscovered himself in the context of life outside the Beltway, but he regretted the loss of the opportunity to accomplish all the things he had gone to Washington to do.

On the other hand, Weston delighted in the reprieve from the 24/7 demands of being president. And he was astonished to discover just how many little pleasures of life he had sacrificed throughout his public life. Things that real people took for granted were impossible for the leader of the free world, things like driving your own car, or popping out for a meal at a fast food joint. As president, when he just wanted a Whopper with cheese, the trip to Burger King disrupted the traffic and the lives of every other person trying to accomplish the same thing at that particular place at that particular time. Every movement by the president was an event. It was hard to be spontaneous when you dragged a huge contingent of Secret Service Agents everywhere you traveled.

Now, though, Weston had standing security of only two agents for routine days, and an expanded number for special events and journeys. The smaller detail was still an impediment to a normal lifestyle, but manageable. The ex-president had seriously considered following the lead of President Carter, who refused Secret Service protection altogether upon leaving the White House. But at the urging of every one of his advisors, chiefly his wife, Alicia, he relented. The former First Lady resented the intrusion into their lives more than her husband, but she understood the necessity. Weston had made a number of enemies, domestic and international, and, well, you just never knew, Alicia had told him.

What Weston missed desperately was the sense of giving to his country. It was difficult for many people to believe that there was a genuine desire in most politicians, he was sure, to serve the people. This longing coexisted with the myriad of other less appealing ambitions, such as for power and prestige, and was too often buried under the heap. But the former president was certain that, at heart, most of the men and women in elected office in D.C. were well-meaning patriots, even if many were idiots.

When voted to the highest office in the land the former Senator from Texas held the same lofty goals that he suspected every other first-term president aspired to. He would, he promised his party, control the agenda and facilitate the fulfillment of the mostly conservative promises he had made to the American people. But quickly he was beset by the true nature of the beast. The president and Congress butted heads over who would set the agenda, preening and posturing to create the public perception of who was in charge. It was an immediate lesson to the new president that, in reality, you don't manage the agenda; it manages you.

World events and international conflicts dominated most of Weston's single term. Promising to continue to prevail against terrorists that many believed to be relics of the past was the requisite campaign starter, but the real thing everyone wanted to hear was: would Weston continue and build upon the economic prosperity of his predecessor?

After the November election but before the president-elect assumed office the following January terrorists launched the attacks that deposed the Saudi royal family with the instability causing a dramatic rise in oil prices. Elections were held in the new Holy Kingdom less than three months later, confirming the roles of the interim leaders who had led the coup. Withholding recognition for the new Saudi Arabian government, the American administration saw its economy begin to falter rapidly as the Saudi oil spigots were closed to the US. Of course, the result was a renewal of drilling in the US after a long period of minimal domestic production. During a time when oil prices were low, it became cost prohibitive to pump the black fuel from US land. Plus, during that time severe limitations had been placed on drilling within the US out of environmental concerns.

So, elected on the promise of safety and prosperity, Weston moved to Washington in the midst of world events that would severely impact his chances for a second term before he even had all his belongings unpacked. The worst of the economic fallout came near the middle of his four-year term when Weston should have been hitting his stride as chief executive for the programs he had advocated in his campaign.

But the president astounded everyone by fully digging out from under the disaster that was Saudi Arabia. The economy rebounded to a surprising, if not completely stellar, extent – with the exception of gas prices. Closer ties were forged with Mexico, from where some of foreign replacement oil came. And with oil prices on the rise, the domestic wells were pumping at near full capacity again. Petroleum achieved sufficient quantities to keep overall prices at the pump to manageable levels. Even more important was the fact that the new Saudi regime seemed to have divorced itself from overt support for terrorism. It had never resurfaced on any significant scale.

So, with surprising progress on all fronts Weston's team dedicated itself to the one thing that most first terms are about in today's politics – getting a second term.

President Weston was determined that his second four years in office would bring about the accomplishments he felt were so critical to the justice and prosperity he wished for his nation. But the stunning Election

Day upset denied him the second term, sending him to his new home in Frisco, Texas with more than desired time for golf and memoirs.

Former President Weston gazed at nothing in particular out the window of his home in an affluent area north of Dallas and considered the political climate in Washington now. His successor's first term had been flooded with the scandals that seemed to be an inevitable component of any administration. But the man was a political survivor and had narrowly won re-election. The second term was as trying as the first. The Saudi situation may have preceded Mercer's administration but the impact to the US economy rose and fell in relation to other issues and the degree to which petroleum voids were filled by imports from Mexico, Venezuela, and other oil exporters. Currently energy needs had arisen as a crisis again. With environmental restrictions being increased on domestic production of oil, prices had soared.

Partisanship had reached new heights – or depths, Weston reconsidered – and new allegations of misconduct were surfacing at the White House. It was difficult to not feel at least some sympathy with the current president. Weston knew that the unrealistic degree of scrutiny by the press and watchdog groups made it all but impossible for any president to emerge unscathed? Even Weston's staff committed what, at best, would be called indiscretions and the press nailed them. In most circumstances, he thought, it was the typical badgering of the incumbent by political foes. But on one occasion a top political adviser had taken the fall for Weston himself for the sole skeleton in the man's political closet.

But now the practically bullet-proof Wendell Mercer was suffering in the approval polls and the scuttlebutt was that he was frantically looking for some point of redemption that would appease his constituency, silence his adversaries, and solidify some sort of legacy in his remaining time in office. In such a context Weston believed that the voters had actually done him a huge service in forcing his retirement.

Still, Weston felt the political scene cried for an opposing voice, the one he had until now failed to provide as the elder statesman of his party. He had remained in virtual seclusion since his defeat. But in a matter of days, that would change.

Watching the hummingbirds hovering at the feeder outside his study's window, he contemplated the upcoming event that he hoped would resurrect his public service. He wondered, would his excursion into the public eye be seen as a sort of triumphant return? Or would people see him as just another has-been politician trying to capitalize on the misfortunes of his successor to regain some of the limelight he desperately missed? "Nobody likes a loser, Trent," the former chief executive reminded himself. "And they hate the loser who refuses to go away even more."

◆

The meeting between the Saudi and the Mexican would mark a transition. Plans and schemes were giving way to actions, to the unavoidable reactions, to events that had roots in deeds occurring years earlier. *Subcomandante* Geraldo Morales wondered if he and his new patron had anything in common. Perhaps there was a mutual heritage of persecution dating back centuries in each man's respective country, he supposed. But no, he decided. The difference was that he was among the oppressed; his new benefactor and business partner was an oppressor. Their only common ground, he realized, was that each felt that his destiny lay in the outcome of the cooperative effort they were giving birth to. God, each was sure, though they knew him by different names, was giving him a sacred responsibility in vindicating the sins committed against his people and their forefathers by powers that were as evil as they were strong.

As they spoke Al-Majeed assessed his short dining companion whose torso inspired the image of a square with arms and legs dangling from it. The khaki pants wore the stains of infrequent laundering. The brushy black moustache drooped over his lips far enough that it blew gently forward with the peasant's words. Disgusted with the careless appearance of the Mexican, the Arab resumed his discrete surveillance of the people passing the *café* on the *avenida* below, ever alert for the possibility that someone was observing the meeting. Perceiving the lack of Arabs, he mentally noted, "I would have blended in more easily in America." In most large US cities Middle Easterners were common and their national origins indistinguishable to an untrained eye. "Yes, I would be safer in the very belly of the beast."

Morales felt equally exposed, though hardly because of any physical distinctions from the inhabitants of the Mexican island. He was himself a Mexican, more precisely a Mayan, and therefore a true native of this country now called Mexico. With an ancestry dating to the early cultures of the lower portions of North and Central America, Morales, in fact, viewed "modern" Mexicans with a measure of contempt. They were impure, interlopers produced from interbreeding with the Spanish invaders of earlier times.

But on this island, he felt a connection. The Mayan influence was strong on Cozumel. It was his people who settled the island in 300 AD. The island's name was derived from the Mayan phrase *"Ah-Cuzamil-Peten,"* or "place of the swallows." Not only an important Mayan trade center, the island was also a holy site, drawing worshipers from throughout the Mayan empire to the more than thirty shrines of Ixchel, the Mayans' only goddess, and the mother of their many gods. The religious significance of the island, the *subcomandante* felt, added a sense of divine ordination to the business he had come here to conduct. It was as if the gods of his people's past and the God of his present were at once lending their blessings to his efforts.

Morales remembered a story of how, in the early 1500s, eighteen Spanish survivors of a shipwreck washed up on the eastern shore of Cozumel. Inhabitants of the island sacrificed almost half of them to Ixchel and feasted on them. "If they had known what the future would bring them, they would have eaten all of them," he assumed. The subcommander smiled at the thought. He wished that the onslaught of the Europeans could have been prevented, but he could not change the past. He could only help write the future. And that was why he was here.

While ancestry allowed Morales to blend with the residents of the island, it did not put him at ease. Less trained than his counterpart, he moved his eyes transparently. He was an outlaw to the government of Mexico as well as to the *Zapatistas* of Chiapas from whom his faction was re-forming all these years after the rebellion effectively ended in 2003. When pursuing activities in Chiapas his face was always covered with the black ski mask that had come to be a symbol of the *Zapatistas'* struggle. Still, he always suspected the government authorities knew but little cared of the identities of many of the rebel leaders. And as the commander-in–waiting of a long-dormant movement, he assumed that he was of interest to the powers that be. Even here, he feared his face was not totally unknown to Mexican *Federales*.

"Stop fidgeting, *amigo*," lectured Al-Majeed. "The kilometers between you and your home almost certainly make your recognition unlikely. But who would not be suspicious of you even if you wore the clothing of one of your priests – just because of the way you act? The holy prophet Mohammed said that patience is half of faith. If you believe in the undertaking we have agreed upon – if you have faith that it is just and that it will be accomplished as Allah, or god, wills – then you must demonstrate this faith with patience, with calm."

Morales knew the Saudi was right, but stiffened at the rebuke, nonetheless. It occurred to him that the man across the table had perhaps dealt with people in his own country in the way that the *Federales* might deal with him. If identified, Morales might disappear at their hands, a practice that had become rare, but not yet abandoned as a way of dealing with rebellious citizens.

His eyes hardened further when he considered the inequity of his situation with this foreigner's. Morales had traveled alone and by land, not just because it was more discreet, but because his small revolution had few resources. He journeyed the first couple hundred of kilometers to this meeting by auto with two of his lieutenants to *Minatitlán*, in the state of Tabasco. From there the rebel traveled alone on a bus to Playa del Carmen where he finally boarded a ferry for the final 19 kilometers to Cozumel. As soon as he concluded this meeting, he would immediately board the ferry to begin the journey back to Chiapas. No overnight stay; no rest. Hardly fitting transportation for the leader of such a noble cause, he complained to himself.

Yet opposite him sat this serpent, with all the resources in the world at his disposal. But that was the reason for the alliance with this pagan, Morales admitted. The Arab had agreed to pay the subcommander three hundred thousand US dollars in exchange for the delivery of a single piece of merchandise. The money was necessary to fund the fledgling revolution, but, ironically, the boldness of the act required to secure the commodity would itself endow Morales with the credibility and air of invincibility needed to secure his position as rebel leader in the eyes of his countrymen. He would have almost delivered the item for free. Almost.

"I am sorry if I am less able than you to conceal my anxiety," he stated in a too-loud voice. "I am not a spy; I am not a politician. I am a warrior for my people. I do not prefer to dance about with deceit. I prefer to meet on the battlefield with honor."

The Saudi's thought was instantaneous. "You self-exalting infidel." Now Al-Majeed was the nervous one. This Mexican fool might as well be broadcasting over a loudspeaker, he raged to himself. His eyes flitted about the restaurant. Most of the patrons were absorbed in other things, so probably had no interest in the conversation.

After a moment he spoke reassuringly. "My apologies, *amigo*. I only wished to offer my help in putting you at ease. As you say, I am trained, and am conscious of what is going on around us. You can trust me." The unfinished part of the thought: "I would just as soon slit your infidel throat, but you are my means to an end. Perhaps later."

"I would rather trust a rattlesnake," Morales wanted to bark, sensing the contempt of his lunch companion. But instead, "I, too, apologize, my friend."

The idea was almost humorous to the Mexican. Friend! He could never be friends with such a man. He would not be here at all except that this pagan could provide what he needed – what his cause needed, he corrected. A revolution costs money, and money from the devil himself spends as easily as from an angel. While each man sat quietly, attempting to lower the tone of the exchange, Morales considered the arrogance of the man sitting across from him. He detected more than a hint of condescension piggybacked atop even his friendliest words. And he wore his costume of a vacationing capitalist like the robes of a prince. "He knows nothing of being poor and struggling for a good life," the *subcomandante* judged. "But I am a patriot, like Zapata and Guevara before me, and will lead my people to *libertad.*" The rebel leader couldn't hold back the sigh accompanying that thought. His leadership was in dispute among the faction that had split from the *Zapatistas* of Chiapas. The situation was no different than in most revolutions. Until victories solidified his status among his people, there would be other ambitious young men ready to take his place. They were already nipping at his feet like playful puppies, but soon they would grow into the wild dogs that would rip at his throat, Morales worried.

No, you could never be my friend, he thought again.

As the quietness lingered Morales contemplated the strange symbiotic relationship between them, between their countries. The association was solely a business transaction. The Arab's mission was against an international enemy. His greatest need was to keep his operation against the "Great Satan," as he referred to his adversary, covert until the proper time. The Mayan did not fully understand or care about the politics surrounding his associate's hatred for Mexico's neighbor to the north. But he did know that Al-Majeed had virtually limitless resources – for travel, for technology, for anything he wanted. And, most importantly, to pay Morales and his army for their assistance. This monster's *dinero* would provide desperately needed financing for arms, for training, for the myriad of logistical needs for Morales' fledgling uprising.

The aspiring rebel leader had no qualms about the task he was to perform though, for his part, the Mexican had no real grievances against the United States. In fact, the American poor were not poor when measured against the lower class of any other nation. Furthermore, they seemed to have at least some advocates representing their interests both socially and at the governmental level. By contrast, Saudi Arabia's poor were generally the ones suffering as a result of their leaders' greed and repressive governmental policies. The Saudi lower class was victimized in much the same way as the Mayan people were in Mexico. It made dealing with these Arabs almost intolerable. But *Subcomandante* Morales was a practical man.

Morales' fight was not international. It was not even national – yet. It was at best a regional revolution, but opposed not just by the Mexican national authorities, but his former *compañeros* as well. A single bold act might energize the whole of Chiapas behind him to complete the rebellion begun many years ago. "Then," Morales thought, "the nation will unite behind me against the oppression and corruption that has smothered the hopes of my people like a fog."

So, putting aside any personal animosity he might have for the man and his country, Geraldo Morales resumed his gracious attitude toward Fadi Al-Majeed while the pair completed their business. During the course of the conversation Morales occasionally glanced at the blue bag that almost certainly contained the down payment that would finalize this alliance of convenience.

◆

President of the United States Wendell Mercer sat in his chair a full ten minutes after hanging up with the Saudi president. The pallor that had taken hold of his tanned face could not have been more severe had he just seen the specter of Lincoln in the bedroom named in honor of the long-dead president. The proposition laid out by the Saudi leader transcended anything imaginable.

Mercer recognized that this was no longer just an exercise aimed at easing years-long tensions in exchange for petroleum to ease the critical shortages in the US. al-Hashimi had practically guaranteed he could usher in a lasting peace and promote stability in the Mid-East. And, most importantly, he indicated he would attribute the results largely to Mercer. Further negotiations could lead to even more oil, he had promised, but peace in the Middle East! Mercer understood the implications of the prospect. Untold lives would be saved if the centuries-old conflicts came to an end. al-Hashimi assured his American equivalent that every Arab nation in the world would be on board with him if the United States would allow certain unspecified events to unfold with only token interference.

The potential rewards – political, socially, internationally, personally, Mercer thought – in the current scenario were infinite. So were the risks but the president, consistent with public perception, was courageous and tough as nails.

"Peace in the region." Mercer echoed the Saudi president's promise again, aloud this time, testing it for believability. "But at what price?" The Saudi Arabian leader had not provided details of the "events" in question.

God knows what the son of a bitch has in mind, Mercer could only speculate. He had asked his prospective partner pointedly if the "events" – god, how sinister that sounded, the president warned himself – if the events had anything to do with terrorism. The reply had been an instantaneous laugh from the dictator and Mercer wasn't sure what to make of that. The president had a gift for reading people and exploiting their weaknesses. But the bizarre revelation of al-Hashimi's ability to speak English had unnerved the American chief executive and thrown him off-balance. Had it made him vulnerable? It didn't take a genius to recognize that a snake was a snake was a snake. They just couldn't help acting like snakes. His instincts told him, though, that al-Hashimi was telling the truth when he declared that the actions involved nothing that would occur on American soil. It wasn't exactly a resounding denial of terrorist intents but with that meager assurance President Mercer, for all his political courage and aggressiveness, had elected not to pursue the matter in more detail.

So, with the range of ominous possibilities that existed, despite the extraordinary uncertainty of what the Arab was going to attempt, the most frightening, implausible part of this scenario was that Wendell Mercer was considering complying.

◆

Avenida Rafael E. Melgar was always crowded, running as it did along the western shore of San Miguel, Cozumel. It was a seemingly endless lineup of T-shirt stores, dive shops, drugstores, markets, and restaurants. In this hustle and bustle it was likely that hundreds, if not thousands, of photographs were made daily. A young tourist, American, wearing a shirt that said "Divers Do It Deeper" peered through the viewfinder of his camera at his friend and the two young ladies standing in front of the *Café Cuzamil.* The long-haired twenty-something year-old raised the camera angle slightly, framed the shot, and pressed the shutter. The finished photo would show, in the foreground, three friends having a wonderful vacation, and, in the background, two men speaking across a table during lunch.

The two men finally rose and shook hands. Al-Majeed continued practiced, casual glances. Morales' eyes darted about. As the Saudi took his seat again and the Mexican departed, the young photographer snapped his tenth shot of two ambitious and desperate men.

Subcommander Geraldo Morales now carried the blue backpack as he descended the restaurant's steps. He crossed the street and walked rapidly north to the dock where the ferry was already boarding. His journey back into the heart of his tiny revolution, he thought, would also begin the fulfillment of his destiny and carry him into the pages of history.

Fadi Al-Majeed could not prevent his gaze from following his luncheon companion down the street. He delayed his departure for ten minutes or so. He shook his head as he thought about the man upon whom everything rested. The man was fairly educated but not intelligent, verbose but utterly without eloquence. Al-Majeed had hopes for Morales because he sensed in him a rage and a daring that would propel him into action. But the hope didn't necessarily translate into confidence. Leaving the *café,* the Arab knew he had plans to change.

◆

Regardless of what time he went to bed Josh Morgan rarely slept in. Perhaps because he didn't make it to his bed at all last night, he slept on the sofa until nearly ten. The unwelcome memories still hounded him, though he tried to distract himself with the previous morning's paper. His Golden Retriever Biscuit slept on the couch beside him and, as Morgan shuffled through the pages containing briefs of national news, the headline of a short article about a tiny Central American nation seized his attention.

"Terrador," Morgan said. "Every shitty thing in my life seems to be resurrecting itself right now," he told Biscuit, who, like any good dog, seemed to understand and care.

The transplanted Texan skimmed the two-paragraph summary about the island country that few people even knew existed, but which Morgan knew intimately. He tilted his head back against the sofa and closed his eyes. Immediately the disturbing image of Victor Palacios rushed to his consciousness.

"Jeez," he complained.

The ex-spy would never forget Victor or the friendship that developed while Morgan was on assignment in Terrador. But in spite of the many pleasant memories he had of his Terradoran *amigo*, whenever Morgan thought about him the picture that always surfaced was of Victor lying on the ground dying.

Morgan considered with the detachment that comes with the passage of time how he had gone to Terrador to act as a liaison between American intelligence agencies and local resistance who were planning to assassinate the president of that country. He remembered the circumstances under which Miguel Salinas assumed the leadership of his nation's government in its first free elections, held after the people of Terrador deposed corrupt dictator Juan Castañeda in a peaceful coup. In contrast to the image in the minds of his countrymen as a savior, the portrait painted of Salinas by Morgan's handlers was of a T-rex in sheep's clothing. He was a madman of terrible proportions, they coached. Charming and slick, he was, they insisted, duplicitous and calculating.

But in the course of pretending to be a journalist Morgan had learned to really think like a one. He recalled the anxiety he suffered as his instincts and then his own investigation into the plot in which he was involved began to raise doubts about his associates' portrayal of Salinas. The resistance leaders, troubled at Morgan's obvious misgivings, decided he had to go and set a meeting with him that was in reality a trap. The sight of Victor's rushing into a blind alley to warn Morgan and being gunned down was as vivid as ever even seven years later.

The Terradoran officer lay on the ground with wounds in his chest and neck, staring up at Morgan, smiling and knowing he was about to die. Morgan could still almost feel the bullets that flew by as the men who had laid the trap for him blasted their way to cover. Watching as Victor fell limp Morgan grabbed his friend's M-16 and dashed behind a wooden trash container and began to return fire. The former spy remembered how, at one point while looking for a way to escape, he had been startled by the sight of Victor, who was not only still alive but raising his sidearm to fire in Morgan's general direction. When he turned toward where Victor aimed, Morgan saw a pistol pointed directly at him. He fell frantically backward, and the attacker's shot flew by and struck the brick wall beside him. The memory of Victor firing at the man, hitting him in the stomach, was still fresh but the horror was in recalling the assailant spinning and firing at Victor. The bullet entered through his chin and went through the top of his head carrying bits of bone and flesh and a massive spray of blood.

That was the image that always came to mind whenever the thought of Victor Palacios came up: lying on the ground, already dying and a bullet ripping through the top of his head.

Nearly seven years after that gun battle Morgan sat in his Jackson Hole home and said aloud, "Pretty shitty way to remember you, *amigo*. I'm sorry."

Picked for the Terrador op specifically because of his inexperience Morgan's intuitive skills altered not only the course of the operation but the rest of his life. And the incident set him on a collision course with a very dangerous man.

"Blake and Terrador."

Morgan shook his head as a tiny unfelt smile made its way onto his face. "I need some coffee."

Among the people strolling along the avenue were two American couples. The Saudi operative's glance lingered as he watched the unrestrained physical contact. Like the whores he knew they were, the young women in shorts and bikini tops showed more skin in their everyday dress than Al-Majeed had seen on his wedding night. The men's hands were all over the girls. The decadence was disgusting, but the Saudi was unable to break his gaze. As he listened to the flirtatious laughter, his pulse quickened. He had stared down armed enemies and not had blood rush to his face like this. But it was not entirely in disdain. Even this hardened intelligence officer wasn't immune to the sensuous display. Women around the world all had the same parts, but he was sure that the abandon with which American sluts serviced men would surely be exciting.

As the Arab assumed the deliberate pace that would return him to his hotel, one of the young men in the quartet peeked at Al-Majeed over his companion's delicate shoulder. He squeezed her waist with one hand and clutched his camera with the other. His gaze followed the Arab and he smiled.

"Gotcha!" he said, just under his breath.

CHAPTER 4

Inside his room at the Cozumel Palace the Saudi government's intelligence officer called an AeroMexico agent. Once he had changed his flight reservations, he began to place the clothes he had bought during the walk back to the hotel along with a small suitcase to replace his now destroyed one into the dresser drawers. That done, he relaxed a moment and allowed himself a look at the clear ocean waters.

"Allah be praised!" the Muslim proclaimed. At last there would be judgment for the sins committed against his country, his people, and Muslims throughout history, he felt. An enemy would pay. He had all but given up faith that Allah would will it so, but today's meeting had set the events in motion and his righteous God would vindicate every evil of the Great Satan. In the years since they wrested control of the country from the royal pigs, Al-Majeed had viewed the current Saudi government as less than the force for Allah that it should have been. But this bold plan would reinvigorate the spirit of al-Qaeda that coursed the veins of the leadership. It would give hope to Muslims everywhere. And, he relished, his own agenda of personal revenge would be fulfilled.

Yet, as he lingered, staring toward the Mexican mainland, he experienced a twinge of uncertainty tugging at his gut. Man of faith and of action, Al-Majeed still trusted his instincts. The serene smile gave way to a sneer as the skepticism of the competence of his surrogates returned.

The Arab had intended to go to the Saudi Embassy in Mexico City but now it was necessary to travel to the northern part of the country. And it might be less noticeable to begin the trip from somewhere other than Mexico City. He would remain in Cozumel a few more days.

◆

Alicia Weston looked at her husband napping in his favorite chair. She loved the soft snore as he slept. Through her eyes he was still the boy she had married forty-four years earlier. Just out of West Point he had swept her up into a world of ambition and love of country. Trenton – she was the only one besides his mother to still call him that – was a little softer around the middle, she knew, but when he walked, he stood to the full measure of his six-foot one-inch height. He was unbowed, still proud and hopeful, despite the disappointments and personal setbacks.

It occurred to the former First Lady that his hair was much grayer than when he left office five years ago, but not as streaked as you would expect for a man of sixty-six. He wore his glasses almost all the time now. She recalled that when he was President, he had permitted himself the one bit of vanity of not wearing them in public. And now he seemed to always be just on the verge of needing a haircut. She chuckled softly. He always hated haircuts, and when you were the Chief Executive of the United States, a trim was at least a weekly occurrence. Alicia often joked of her surprise that the demand for constant grooming hadn't prevented him from seeking the job in the first place. Post-Washington, her husband allowed himself the luxury of putting off visits to the barbershop until he darned well felt like it.

Alicia had worried about him during the first year of his life as a civilian. He left the White House with honor and grace, but he withdrew from public life almost totally. She was initially concerned that he was in denial, or perhaps suffering from depression, but she learned in time that he was simply tired of the games. She scowled that his successor, Mercer, never asked for his advice, or consulted with him on matters of international importance, as most presidents did with their predecessors. This increased her resentment because Trenton would have done whatever was asked of him. Despite the extreme bitterness of his campaign for reelection, her husband was a man who put aside personal matters for the good of his country.

The former First Lady sat on the arm of the former President's chair. She lightly touched the peach fuzz on the back of his neck and leaned over and kissed him gently on the forehead.

"Your country still needs you, you know."

"Hmmm? What'd you say?" Her Prince Charming opened one eye.

"I was just saying how you're going to have to start getting haircuts pretty often if you're going to get out more."

"Hmmph!" Weston stretched both arms behind his head, arching his back so that his shoulders and butt were the only point of contact with his La-Z-Boy. Then with the speed of a cat – an older cat – he grabbed his wife around her waist and spun her into his lap.

"Then I might have to reconsider."

They smiled, and kissed, and sat together in silence several minutes until Weston cooed, "Honey...

"Yes, sweetheart."

"My leg's going to sleep."

Alicia Weston tweaked his nose between her thumb and forefinger and stood up. "There are cookies and milk in the kitchen."

In an effort to push aside the current intrusion of Terrador and Everson Blake into his psyche, Morgan spent the rest of the morning taking it easy. He felt surprisingly good – considering. The only pain he suffered was guilt about his behavior toward Maggie.

He did wonder why they were still friends, whatever that meant for them. He knew he neglected her and at times his behavior bordered on abuse. But somehow, she saw through his blustering and insults. She simply chose to tough it out and forgave him, he knew, without his ever asking her.

Around noon he had breakfast, and throughout the afternoon he did a few chores before relaxing on his front porch.

His property sloped away from his house to its boundary with Moose-Wilson Road. The photographer spy sipped at his Diet Coke and accused himself, "Josh, you're falling apart over this thing." He knew he was letting the memories of Blake and his recollections about Terrador affect him far more than it should, but Blake and Terrador were why he was where he was at this point in his life – in Wyoming in forced retirement instead of spying on unsuspecting nations.

The ex-intelligence operative turned his thoughts to Terrador again. He knew he had been a fool to have been taken in so easily by the plot hatched by Blake and his associates in the insignificant Latin country.

Its lack of visibility and proximity to a number of Central American hotspots had made Terrador the perfect jumping off point for a number of covert operations by US intelligence and special operations units into sites in Central and South America. Self-appointed *El Presidente* Castañeda found himself the beneficiary of extensive aid from the United States. Uncle Sam's investments in massive infrastructure were for the express purpose of developing the logistical requirements for a base of operations.

Morgan smirked as he recalled how Castañeda had shrewdly put the improvements to use for his more lucrative personal agenda as well. The dictator had turned Terrador into a safe haven of sorts for international drug traffickers, providing offshore banking and vacation retreats for cartel leaders. Morgan still marveled that the United States government, for its part, totally ignored the situation because the *Generale's* activities didn't affect US operations or policy in any way. And besides, as long as Castañeda was happy he would allow the Americans to operate freely from his nation.

The memory of the puppet dictator growing wealthy through the use of assets provided by the US still bothered Morgan. And he became absolutely livid in recalling how the situation had proved so alluring that a number of intelligence operatives insinuated themselves into the operation. Castañeda had hardly been receptive to his uninvited partners but when they began to provide intelligence and other support for his personal initiatives, his riches increased so dramatically that he was glad to share some of it with the Americans. The resulting organization grew exponentially and so did the profits, with everyone getting a share. A number of important US officials became wealthy in their own rights and Morgan remained certain to this day that Everson Blake was at the top of the food chain.

But when the shit hit the fan in the US about covert operations in Central and South America, official support for Terrador – for Castañeda – was withdrawn. And without the American presence it proved impossible for the dictator to maintain control over his people. They overthrew him without firing a shot.

With General Castañeda gone and Salinas in his place, a fledgling democracy was born. And Blake and his associates were out of business. The plot to kill Salinas was all about money, about getting him out of the way and reinstalling Castañeda, who had fled to Columbia where he was later killed in a dispute with cartel heads.

Morgan ultimately uncovered the truth about the plot and foiled it. But he paid the price for his involvement, though unwitting, in the assassination plan when he knew it was in direct violation of US laws.

Morgan looked across his acreage, past Moose-Wilson Road, to the groves of trees that traced the Snake River in the distance.

"Josh, you've got to get a grip on this," he warned himself. But the truth was he didn't know how. He hadn't thought much about Blake and Castañeda, about Terrador and Salinas for some time now. But he knew it had always remained just below the surface of his awareness, gnawing at his spirit and sapping him of any resolve to actually have a life. How else could he explain his perpetually shitty disposition and sorry outlook on life?

◆

Maggie was true to her promise of the previous night. But instead of the phone call Morgan expected, she showed up at his house to collect on her rain check from the night before.

"I don't remember anything about a rain check," Morgan protested.

"You probably don't remember a number of things about the last twenty-four hours," she bluffed.

So, about an hour later, sitting in the restaurant where she had dragged him, they talked little. Maggie knew that Morgan was usually quiet for a while after his demons had overwhelmed him, though she had no inkling of the source or nature of those demons. She also knew he was embarrassed but to avoid having to admit it, was acting upset with her to keep the talking to a minimum.

"That's okay, Morgan. I got you figured out," Maggie thought. She honored his moratorium on talking and only looked at him and grinned.

"What?" quizzed Morgan through a mouthful of ribeye.

"What 'what?'"

"You were smiling at me."

"No, I wasn't"

"Yes, you were smiling," he repeated with the cocked head and raised eyebrows he used when he was insisting on being right.

"I didn't say I wasn't smiling. I said I wasn't smiling at you."

"Sheesh!" Morgan stabbed another bite of his steak and poked it in his mouth.

With the quiet game ended, Maggie decided to probe for answers. "So, what had you so bent out of shape yesterday?" She usually got right to the point.

"Don't want to talk about it." Maggie noticed he cut his next bite of steak a bit more forcefully.

"Okay," she relented.

A few seconds passed. Morgan lowered his head momentarily, then set his fork down and whisked his napkin across his mouth. He laid it beside his plate just as the waitress came by to refill his iced tea. He managed an obligatory "thank you" and then looked Maggie squarely in the eyes. She leaned back a bit.

His voice was quiet. "When I was a kid growing up in Texas, I spent a lot of time on my grandparents' farm. There was this old forgotten cemetery near their house that I stumbled onto – literally – one day while I was out hunting. I found it by tripping over a fallen grave marker. When I realized what it was, I looked around. There was a couple dozen of them, barely visible only if you knew what you were looking for. And it seemed that every covered-up tombstone had a small path to it. They were actually trails to where rabbits or rats or whatever lived under the stones, but I didn't figure that out until later. I was just a snot-nosed kid – about thirteen, I guess – and to me they were trails of the spirits that lived there. Anyway, it never failed, that whenever I found myself back there, even as a young man, the hairs on my neck stood up like they did that very first time I saw them."

Maggie knew when to just listen.

Morgan went on. "The point was, logic didn't matter. I just got used to being afraid there. My mind told me there were no such things as ghosts. But my emotions didn't buy into that."

Maggie's dinner companion pursed his lips and tilted his head back. When he leaned his head forward again his eyes locked squarely onto Maggie's. The silence stretched into several more seconds, virtually screaming for someone to speak. Finally, Morgan spoke again. His voice was barely audible.

"Yesterday I saw a ghost. Not a real one, of course, but someone that I've just gotten in the habit of being afraid of. There is probably no good reason to be afraid of this guy, but I honestly didn't expect to ever see him again. So when I saw his picture in this magazine, it was as if I had walked into that old cemetery, and actually saw the ghosts that I had feared but had decided weren't there."

Over the years that she had known Morgan, Maggie never once considered that there might be anybody he was afraid of. She had seen him become more distant. And his belligerence, his pettiness — well, she knew there were things he was afraid of, like taking chances, of failure. But afraid of a flesh-and-blood, human being? It had just not occurred to her.

She remembered meeting Morgan and thinking he was bigger than life. She never told him, but she knew who he was the very first time she met him at the photography class. She had taken a couple of journalism classes at USC where his name and his work had come up. From the time she was a child she had dreamed of travel and excitement and here was this guy that had photographed some of the most important recent events around the world. He had lived the life Maggie lusted after. Maggie never understood why he had given it up. She figured that he just burned out, but seeing how he had changed during her time in Dallas, she decided that he had seen things or experienced something that had shaken him up. He had observed and photographed famines, revolutions, terrorism, wars. Any one of those things could have lasting effects, she supposed.

"I understand," she finally said.

"Do you?" he doubted, now looking everywhere but at Maggie, finally resting his eyes on the floor beside their booth.

"I think so, Josh. I understand that there are people or things that we are all frightened of. The ghosts that haunt us aren't the invisible spirits that go bump in the night. They're the evil we have seen, or even people who have hurt us, or someone who has some kind of power over us…"

She noticed that Morgan looked up at the last comment.

"I'm tired of being afraid all the time, Maggie."

CHAPTER 5

"I don't give a rat's ass!"

Everson Blake had been around rough language too much in his life to be offended by it, but he still thought it a flaw of undisciplined men. In this case, though he kept a straight face, he was amused that the President of the United States could utter the words with such intensity and never raise his voice above a whisper. It was equally remarkable that he would often string together such a vile cascade of invectives while keeping that "genuine" smile on his face. He had been caught with his pants down, so to speak, many times early in his first term by television crews. But he learned quickly. Now he maintained that practiced, duplicitous smile so that someone observing them from across the room might just as well think he was commenting on his latest round of golf.

"Mr. President, I just meant that this might not be an appropriate place to have this discussion."

"Those bastards are about to get a gift from this administration," President Wendell Michael Mercer went on, "and there will be conditions attached. So, if they have a problem with this, screw 'em. Furthermore, if they are up to something, as the email you copied me on suggests, I don't freaking care about that either." And with those parting words, the President of the United States seized Blake's hand warmly with his right, patted his shoulder with his left, and told him again at a now normal speaking volume how glad he was to see him. Then POTUS, the consummate politician, moved away to greet others at the reception.

"God forgive you," Blake whispered at his back.

President Wendy. My, how Mercer hated when people used his childhood nickname, which made it even more amusing to Blake to think of him in that way. His now ex-wife had let it slip in an interview that his childhood friends had called him that. He was about to take one of the biggest political gambles of his administration and was a little edgy. You would never know it by looking at him right now, Blake thought. A handsome, energetic man, the President had charisma in spades. And not just the political kind, the sort that is inherent with his being the Most Powerful Man in the World. No, he just had that natural spark. He lit up a room in a way that women virtually swooned and men wished they were him. Blake watched him work the room and it was obvious that this man loved his job. And though Mercer was a year into his second term, Blake saw that he looked as youthful and fit as the day he took his first oath of office. His advisors had suggested, Blake had heard, that Mercer actually dye his hair gray at the temples to add a bit of gravitas, but he refused. You don't rise to the highest office in the land without at least some degree of vanity, but this President raised the bar. And impressively, at age fifty-four, he had hardly a gray hair on him and barely a wrinkle on his face or brow. No, Blake saw – and permitted himself a bit of envy – that there was just none of the normal wear-and-tear that you expected to see after five years in his position.

Blake took another sip from his glass of water and placed it on the tray of a waiter who was passing by. Then he noticed his own image in one of the large ornate mirrors in the banquet hall. Unaware of the narcissistic appearance of the act, he turned to face the mirror squarely, straightened his tie, assessed his reflection, and smoothed his hair with both hands. "Goodness," which for Blake was tantamount to cursing. "I'm the same age as 'Wendy,' and my face looks like a prune." Of course, that was an exaggeration, but there was no denying that he was indeed showing the mileage of his years in intelligence. Or was it raising three daughters that had done this to him? He smiled. He again examined his new hairstyle and was pleased at how it seemed to add a touch of mystery to him. A slightly ominous look was fitting for a man on the fast track at the nation's most secret organization. His eyes then focused on the substantial gray in his black hair. Definitely his girls!

Blake raised his wrist so that the Timex watch stared back at him. Another fifteen minutes he thought, and it would be acceptable to head home. Throughout his adult life he kept eternally long hours at work, but still somehow found the time to be a devoted husband and good father. And the NSA's Deputy Director never worked late on Saturday nights. Blake would have normally been home by now. His wife had trained him well, he thought. Since Sunday morning church services were mandatory in his family, Saturday nights were normally reserved for reading the next morning's Bible lesson. But, of course, you don't turn down invitations to the White House. And this was his first time there.

Blake had been in a few working meetings with the President by teleconference, but never to a social function, and never to the White

House. Senator Ralph Burroughs, Chairman of the Intelligence Oversight Committee had announced his intention to retire at the end of this term a few days before and Mercer had decided to hold an informal – by White House standards – reception for the man. Burroughs was one of the President's most vocal supporters during the numerous scandals plaguing the White House and it had not gone unnoticed – or unrewarded. It was said that President Mercer had a special connection with the Senator. They had both attended Princeton, though a couple of years apart. And they had become fast friends immediately upon the new President's arrival five years ago. They were kindred spirits in their devotion to liberal causes and public opinion polls.

Blake watched the President and Senator Burroughs laughing. The chief executive, whose Secret Service code name was "One Iron," was pointing out flaws in his friend's simulated golf swing. "Burroughs goes to my church. How can a decent man like him be so close to a scoundrel like the President," thought the Deputy Director, NSA? He had approached Burroughs on the subject once and his fellow church member had said that it wasn't his place as a Christian to judge. And besides, he said, he thought the president could use some friends. But Blake wasn't buying it.

Blake rolled his wrist over to check the time again. Yes, a few moments more and it would be proper to excuse himself.

CHAPTER 6

DAY 3 – SUNDAY

Geraldo Morales sought to displace Subcommander Marcos as the man associated in the minds of people worldwide as the leader of the Chiapas *Zapatistas*, whose movement had stagnated after perceived betrayal by the Mexican government and the suspension of dialogues between it and the *EZLN* in 2003. Little had transpired in the intervening years and Morales believed it was past time for a revival of the rebellion. But as the presumptive *jefe* stood, or more precisely, posed before his small army at their camp in the Lacandon Jungle of Chiapas, one distinction was apparent. Whereas the intellectual who had organized the rebellion that began in Chiapas in 1994 had a natural charisma and authoritative bearing, Morales' demeanor was strained. He thought himself a poet in the mold of Marcos but while his command of his native language had a certain eloquence, his lack of both style and insights into the human spirit exposed his pretense. He had correctly reached one conclusion, though. Marcos had achieved legendary status that extended far beyond the borders of the state of Chiapas so any appearance of attacking the man personally would destroy his efforts at assuming leadership and reigniting the movement on a large scale. Morales knew he must avoid portraying Marcos as a failure. Instead, he judged, he must position his own leadership as an evolution of the *Zapatista* rebellion, as a logical next step. At the same time, he would have to point out shortcomings in the revolt's past to legitimize his own proposals. Morales had a delicate task ahead of him. He knew he had to give the speech of his life.

"*Amigos*," he began, looking out over the almost one hundred and fifty men. "January 1, 1994, gave birth to new hopes and dreams for us in

Chiapas. We cried, 'No mas! No mas!' and the world heard us. With *Subcomandante* Marcos we renewed the cry of Emiliano Zapata, 'Land and Liberty," and the government took notice. We have succeeded; and we have failed. We triumphed in many battles; we have also suffered many defeats at the hands of our oppressors, betrayed and ignored. Our enemies are powerful and many and they have largely forgotten us, but our spirits still rise to the challenge, and we will resume our cause and prevail." The speaker felt an intense gratification at the shouts of agreement that began throughout the mob.

"The *Ejército Zapatista de Liberación Nacional* is one cause. But while we are one body, the *Zapatista* National Liberation Army has many faces, and so must have many voices. Though we are united in purpose, we must be diverse in tactics.

"*Subcomandante* Marcos has led us from these very jungles and these very mountains. He has correctly said that 'ideas are weapons, too.' But ideas must have substance to realize victory. Words become powerful through action.

"It is good that we had dialogues with the government. It is good that we sought to open doors. But the same deceit that assassinated Zapata will lead to our destruction if we trust too blindly, if we yield too generously. The great Zapata himself said, 'It is better to die on your feet, than to live a lifetime on your knees.'"

Morales surveyed the looks of approval among his soldiers and felt his confidence and courage swell.

"And so, we must now fight our battles on two fronts. We must demand dialogue for peace, but at the same time we will pursue justice with gun and sword and sweat and blood. Today we give birth to a new chapter in the life of our movement. We branch out and act independently to complement the battle of words. Today we form our army to take up the fight of our brothers and sisters of the *EZLN*. Today we are the *Soldados Nuevos de Zapata*. The *EZLN* ultimately gave up their fight with force to arm themselves with ideas and principles. The New Soldiers of Zapata will arm ourselves for deadly combat. We will add power to any new dialogues. There will be two edges of the same sword – the honor and influence of ideas, and the might and urgency of action."

The *subcomandante* paused and the silence prompted more shouts of approval from the listeners. He paced regally for a moment, then thrust his fist forcefully toward his God for effect. He knew that his words held no risk of objection so far, but the ones that followed would introduce a new element into the rebellion.

"In the world, many others share our plight. We do not stand alone in our quest to have control over our lives. Like us, *compañeros* in other countries are rising to challenge those who would litter their farms with their remains. They, too, have been betrayed by those who would lead. And as they have been bold in their actions, so must we. We must find allies wherever we can. It is time for us to move beyond the borders of our state and even our nation. We must find friends who share our struggles and will support our cause. And we must return their friendship by being their eyes and ears and hands and feet in Mexico. We must cultivate these new friendships; we must join them against their enemies."

Morales' wait was unrewarded this time as he surveyed the confused looks of the *Zapatistas* who were hearing the first mention of a partnership. He dared not let the silence linger into a sense of disapproval.

"The United States of America has given much to Mexico, but it requires much in return. *Si*, it has given to us, but for its own benefit. The United States has assisted in bringing much prosperity to our country, but they have guaranteed that it stays in the hands of the powerful. The authorities have much while we have little. Chiapas has more resources than any other state, but they serve only to fill the chests of our government and the American capitalists with *dinero*."

Heads began to acknowledge agreement again.

"*Amigos*, the Mexican government is a puppet that will continue to perform as long as the puppeteer has breath. We have an opportunity to strike out at this puppet, while our new allies fall upon the puppeteer. We will gain much money to buy our voices. With a bold act we can make those voices heard – voices of bullets and blood."

The assents began to rise in volume as Morales paused again and examined the impact of his declarations on the army. Suddenly, unrestrained cheers and rebel cries exploded into the jungle, assuring him that he had accomplished his intentions. With great ritual the rebel laid out the details of the plan to his men. With their support – and the money the bold act would bring – his revolution would grow, and his place of leadership solidify.

◆

"It's a lot smaller than it looks on TV," Blake noted mentally. "Lots of patriotic paintings, too."

Each president changed the decor of the Oval Office to suit his taste and his desired image. Wendell Mercer had selected a number of works of art depicting moments from the American past. Probably thought they would lend a bit more dignity to the man who used the office, guessed Blake. He had half expected to see nude portraits or dogs playing cards. His snicker escaped with a snort, bringing eyes his direction.

The Deputy Director of the National Security Agency and his boss had waited for the President for nearly forty-five minutes. When he had finally arrived and invited them into this famous room, he promptly got on the telephone.

Blake looked at his watch for the fifth time and twisted the corner of his moustache between his thumb and finger. His church service would have ended thirty minutes ago, and it was only a few minutes from the White House. He let his eyes wander around the remainder of his surroundings, and then clasped his hands together in his lap. It did not come as a shock that church was not on his host's schedule for the morning. Neither did the delay in beginning this impromptu meeting surprise him. The President had a reputation for being undisciplined in many areas of his life; promptness and regard for others' time were among them, the Deputy Director recognized.

"Gentlemen. Ladies." POTUS rose and walked from behind the desk to shake the hand of each of his guests warmly, motioning them to return to their seats. "You honor me by your willingness to come here on such short notice. I, myself, canceled my plans for church this morning so we could have this meeting," he lied.

"Deputy Director Blake, let me apologize for my remarks at the reception for Senator Burroughs last evening. You were right on the money when you said my concerns would be better discussed elsewhere."

"Not at all, Mr. President. I regret that I may have sounded disrespectful." Figures – you apologize for the location of the conversation, but not the coarse language, was what Blake didn't add.

"Nonsense. You made a valid point." The smile vanished and Mercer pursed his lips and bobbed his head almost imperceptibly as he surveyed the guests in his office. This was his usual manner for indicating that business was about to commence. "You all know that my administration hopes to make a major announcement soon with regard to the Holy Islamic Republic of Saudi Arabia. That is the reason behind the requests coming out of the West Wing recently for the special intelligence assessments. I applaud your cooperation and rapid response."

Everson Blake smiled, not to be gracious, but because of the thought that had occurred to him. President Wendy was proof that sincerity was the most important thing there is, as he recalled a journalist or somebody had once stated. If you can fake sincerity, there's no end to what you can do.

It was uncommon for Blake to be included in a meeting such as this. Around the room were most of the top intelligence professionals in Washington. In the chair to his left was his boss, NSA Director Stanford Grayson. To his right was Director of Homeland Security Anson Larson. Next to him sat Director of Central Intelligence Christopher Donleavy. CIA Deputy Director for Intelligence Elizabeth Parnell and Mercer's National Security Advisor Edgar Templeton were on the couch across from him. The President's Chief of Staff Henry James, and oddly, thought Blake,

Secretary of State Susan McGregor were on the small love seat facing their boss. "Why is she here?" he wondered of the SecState. Beside the President was Vice President Sandra Melton-Hendrickson.

"There seem to be a number of issues in play, some apparently at cross-purposes, with regard to our initiative with Saudi Arabia," POTUS continued. "Underlying all of this is that my administration has concluded that it is time to end the unofficial economic sanctions against that country. We feel that it is in the best interest of stability in the Middle East if we begin moving toward Most Favored Nation status in an evolving manner. This is not going to be a popular move with some of our citizens, but it is the right thing to do."

Plus, we need their oil, almost everyone in the room recognized.

"I have asked Secretary McGregor to give a brief update regarding the progress she and her staff have been making behind the scenes. Madam Secretary."

Susan Leigh McGregor began in her Bostonian accent. "When the United States plots a course of action, we are not only concerned with the implications to our nation, but must consider the impact on our allies and the world at large."

Blake could hardly refrain from rolling his eyes. Give the diplomacy-speak a rest, Sue, he wanted to urge. Occupational hazard, he supposed, to never take less than twice the amount of time practically necessary to say what was on your mind.

"Initiatives such as the one we have been exploring are not to be taken lightly. The risk of any courageous act is the possibility that the motivations will be misunderstood, at best, or exploited for political gain, at worst. There will be fallout, both at home, and abroad, if – or should I say – when we announce that we favor a phased movement to MFN status for the Holy Islamic Republic of Saudi Arabia. We will be hailed by Russia, France, Arab nations, and other governments. We will be vilified by conservatives at home, vis-à-vis their continued assertions that we waffle on commitments. We will cause some consternation among some of our allies who will feel that we have given in to the blustering of President al-Hashimi. The danger is that they will view our progressive position as a lack of commitment to the remaining requirements put into place when the Saudi royal family stepped down."

"Are we to understand that the MFN is a done deal?" DCI Donleavy inquired.

SecState proceeded as if oblivious to the question. Donleavy and the DDI exchanged a bemused glance.

"The President has instructed me to…"

It was the President that interrupted this time. "Chris, the answer to your question is a qualified 'yes.' We are prepared to make an announcement as early as next week that we will immediately lift remaining trade restrictions with the Saudis and relax some of the other sanctions, both economic and military, against that nation. There are two preconditions. The first is the completion of our dialogue with the United Kingdom. As our strongest ally, the UK is also the one that might have problems with this.

"The second factor will be the nature of the information you are prepared to share with us today. But I'm getting ahead of myself. Sue, please continue."

Blake noticed that every guest in the Oval Office shuffled, as if synchronized, everyone but himself.

"The status of our discussions with Saudi Arabia is that we have reached an agreement in principle regarding several matters. We will initiate a six-month long schedule to remove our military presence in Iraq along its Saudi borders. Secondly, we will..."

"What if the Brits don't buy in?" queried NSA chief Grayson.

"They will, Stan," answered the President. "But in the very unlikely event that they balk, we are prepared to act unilaterally."

At that point everyone in the room representing the intelligence agencies realized that whatever they said today was, in reality, irrelevant. "You've already made up your frigging mind," thought the DCI.

McGregor resumed her summary. "Secondly, we will immediately lift the embargo of all technologies, and basically, all imports, with the exception of any military items of an offensive nature."

"Defensive weapons?" posed DDI Parnell.

"I see no reason to restrict them," responded POTUS.

Blake noticed the Veep glancing down at her nails. As she shifted in her chair, Blake realized that she had remained oddly silent during the entire meeting. Even President Wendy's Chief of Staff, Hank James, had been fidgeting noticeably. "Not on board with this, Hank?" Blake wondered.

"The third major foundational piece of the agreement is that the United States is prepared to resume limited trade with Saudi Arabia. Though the Islamic State remains a particularly nasty thorn there in that it still controls a large swath of the country geographically, it appears that the government has largely solidified its control of the economy. I see no reason that we cannot be pragmatic. Their primary product is crude oil and since that is a current need in our country, it is the most logical place to start." McGregor looked around the room. Everson Blake was the only one nodding agreement, a detail that didn't go unnoticed by Mercer.

"Mr. President," inquired Donleavy, "may I ask what concessions al-Hashimi has agreed to? I apologize for such an elementary question, but some of us are disadvantaged in not being privy to the details." The rebuke wasn't as veiled as he had intended.

The Chief Executive's teeth ground and his brown eyes hardened as he paused before speaking. Blake wondered who was going to reply, the schmoozing, syrupy sweet politician, or the volatile "I'm the darned President" Mercer.

The pause was palpable. "Peace in the region," the President recited to himself. "If only you morons understood what I am about to achieve, you would understand the magnitude of this initiative." But Mercer knew he had to keep the off-the-record agreement with al-Hashimi to himself – at least for the foreseeable future. Until he understood the *quid* for his *quo*, he would keep his private conversation with the Saudi President close to his vest.

Finally, "Good point, Chris."

One corner of Blake's lips curled up faintly.

"Certainly that is the question that must be on everyone's mind. Saudi President al-Hashimi has agreed to a total renunciation of terrorism and support for a new round of talks between Israel and the Palestinians."

"That's it? Words?" blurted Parnell aloud.

"Hell, did Mercer carry a white flag into the negotiations?" she asked herself, as her lips pursed and the interior ends of her eyebrows dropped. And while that observation remained unspoken, its implication in her remarks touched a nerve in Mercer.

"Uh-oh!" the Deputy Director, NSA thought. "Here it comes."

The President leaned forward in his chair, forefinger of his left hand wagging at the DDI. "Listen, Betsy. There are times to take a hard line on things, but at other times alternative interests demand a more moderate approach. This is one of those fucking times."

Heads wavered and eyes dropped around the office.

"And as for your observation about being in the dark," he blasted, turning to Donleavy. "You're the goddammed king of 'need-to-know,' aren't you? Well, you didn't frigging need to know." There's a lot you don't know, smartass, the President delighted in thinking.

When the President spoke this way, it wasn't so much that his voice got louder, just more intense, Blake observed. Maybe it's just the language, or the contrast from his normally patronizing manner, he thought.

Mercer went on. "These are political issues and the policies will be formed by politicians. When one of you gets elected by the nation to make these types of decisions, then have at it. Right now, every damned one of you was appointed to your job by me, or by someone who was." This was, of course, not true of the Vice President, an elected representative of the people, who was the only one looking directly at her running mate.

"This is not an intelligence issue. It is not a national security issue. It is only about what is in the best economic interests of this country." Hank James turned sharply toward his boss, eyes squinted as he determined to

49

make sense of what the man had spoken. Mercer immediately realized the foolishness and contradictory nature of what he had said.

Seven or eight seconds passed, which were filled with people once again shifting in their chairs and continuing to gaze anywhere but at POTUS.

When he resumed, President Mercer spoke in a tone that was not exactly conciliatory, but at least mellower. "I recognize that we cannot break down the 'best interests of the country' into categories. We can't separate economic issues from security issues, from defense, from social issues. They are all unalterably intertwined. My point is that each situation requires – no, demands," – he was wagging his finger again – "that these needs be weighted, with each being considered in relation to its importance. There are certainly intelligence and national security issues here," he said, talking slowly now as his smile returned and he surveyed the group assembled in his office. He would have made eye contact with each individual, except no one was looking back. "Hell, if that weren't so, I wouldn't have asked you here for your counsel."

The President returned to his chair and leaned forward with his elbows on his knees, his hands opened toward his guests. "The importance of this initiative transcends our national boundaries. It is about restoring peace to the region. It is about reaching out to other Middle Eastern nations by reaching out to Saudi Arabia. This is about what is ultimately and undeniably right." And about the oil, he didn't say.

Though relations were strained nearly to the point of collapse when the al-Qaeda remnant and ISIS offshoot brought about its coup of the royal family, Washington and Riyadh never broke off diplomatic relations. And it was certainly no small matter to the US administration that the terrorists, no matter how inactive they might appear to be, gained some degree of legitimacy and had set up diplomatic shop almost exactly one mile due west of the White House. The Embassy of the Holy Islamic Republic of Saudi Arabia occupied the same facilities as it had when it was known as the Royal Embassy of Saudi Arabia, located at 601 New Hampshire, NW, across the street from the Watergate Hotel complex.

But however great the disdain for the new leaders, the US government had at least outwardly, accepted the changes in the former monarchy as a result of the democratic process. Behind closed doors, though, the policy was more a wait and see approach. In the world of nations and politics, practicality required that the two countries, however strong the animosities, preserve lines of communications.

In a secure room on the second floor the Head of Mission to the United States and the Station Chief for the Saudi General Intelligence Directorate, the men in the agency responsible for security, anti-terrorism, and foreign liaison functions, were discussing the unfolding plan that would elevate their homeland to a position of power and respect in the world. Of course, to these men and their countrymen, the two terms were synonymous.

"Al-Majeed has doubts about the successful completion of the mission," said chief spy Saadiq Nagim.

"His meeting did not go well?"

"In his words this Mexican rebel is a 'power hungry bastard.' The man portrays himself as some sort of idealistic revolutionary, but he is – again Al-Majeed's words – 'uneducated, pompous, and utterly lacking in self-control.'"

The mission's diplomatic chief Syed Abou-Shakra folded his hands as if in prayer and rested his chin on the tips of his forefingers. After a moment his eyes returned to his deputy. "If a man cannot control himself, how can he control others?" His eyes resumed their downward gaze.

Another few seconds passed. "What does our brother intend to do?"

The intelligence officer replied, "He has determined to travel to and remain in northern Mexico until the plan has been executed. He feels there may be a need to change some of the details. Worse, he fears there may be a mess to clean up."

"Keep me informed."

"As you wish."

◆

In his few experiences with President Mercer, Ev Blake had recognized one thing. The man could say and do things to make the people working for him feel like they had stepped in the biggest pile of crap – or worse, that they were the crap. Then, having said his piece, President Wendy, would simply be "over it" and wonder what was wrong with everyone else.

Smiling now, he said, "So, my friends, tell me what you've got."

Chris Donleavy handed a briefing folder to the President marked with the code name "Summer Storm." Then he passed folders to each of the other participants at the meeting. These had fewer contents. For the most part, they were only summaries of the detailed documents he had given Mercer.

"Mr. President," he began, 'Homeland Security, CIA, and NSA have received information, through independent sources, that has given strong indications of activity by the Saudis in our hemisphere. I would like to have Betsy explain the crux of the intelligence we have developed."

Parnell cleared her throat. "Sir, my Senior Intelligence Officer at the Saudi Arabia Desk at Langley, Ben Reid, has been doing a workup on an individual about whom we have been receiving intel. The intercepts and

HUMINT indicate he is a former Saudi intelligence agent, a troubleshooter of sorts. We actually hit on him while doing surveillance on a terrorist.

"What makes this unusual is that our source tells us the man is very close to President al-Hashimi. He was previously known to us as a high-level officer in the Republican Guard during the second conflict with Iraq. At the conclusion of the hostilities we lost track of him. There was no reason to track him further at that point. Because he was military, we have little hard information on him at all, other than his name, which is Fadi Al-Majeed. From a diplomatic viewpoint, he came out of nowhere to assume the post of what could best be called a roving ambassador for the al-Qaeda Party of Saudi Arabia, sort of a special envoy for al-Hashimi. It was, of course, a shock to us to have a spy posing as a diplomat," she said dryly.

Everyone laughed, including Mercer.

"Al-Majeed is in Mexico, I guess you would say he is using a Saudi legend, since he is in the employ of the Saudis now. He made landfall in Cozumel rather than going to the embassy in Mexico City. Mex City is the kind of place you might expect a new diplomat to get his feet wet. But it sounds like the subject is moving from one Saudi embassy to the next. So, if the man is so close to the Saudi dictator, why is he in Mexico?"

Parnell continued the briefing. "Under the royal family Saudi Arabia's intelligence agencies were very ineffective, mostly in place to gather personal intel for the Crown Prince. Since the al-Qaeda Party assumed control in Saudi Arabia, however, we have seen these services beefed up and become very active. Their Mexico City station is the hub of all western hemisphere espionage. That is in contrast to most of our friends and enemies who operate their organizations directly out of their embassies here in the District. But still, Washington would seem to be the assignment of choice for highly regarded diplomat spies. So again, the question is why a man with close personal ties to the leader of their Republic would be sent to the Latin country?"

"Even outside the US there would seem to be other posts more receptive and appealing to an al-Hashimi representative – Paris, Moscow… These places are more visible and would likely be disposed to exchange intelligence," said the President.

"Exactly," returned the DDI. "Those are the kinds of places you would think the dictator would send a personal delegate. They represent places where the al-Qaeda outcries against the perceived injustices against them, and so on, would get the most coverage – and the most sympathy. They offer the potential for greater political capital for al-Hashimi. But Al-Majeed is in Mexico. Perhaps there is something going on that requires a very trusted friend. And that is what our new asset in al-Hashimi's government says. We don't know exactly what, but something is afoot, and he thinks it may involve us."

Mercer began to feel a tightening in his gut as the realization gripped him that he might be about to hear from his own people details about the events to which he was to turn a blind eye.

Donleavy picked up the story. "The intel is from a source very high in the food chain in the Saudi government. I don't need to tell you what this new source means to our intelligence capabilities. The drawback is that it is a new, unproven asset, so we have low confidence as of this time. We have few sources in their government, none as close to President al-Hashimi as this one. This makes it all but impossible to validate the intel through second sources. We wouldn't be concerned at all, but no sooner did we get first mention of this Fadi Al-Majeed, than he showed up on the radar screen – very nearby. While I said we have no complementary human intel, there is additional data that NSA picked up, which, if it has to do with the same guy... well, there could be a problem." The DCI turned to his NSA counterpart. "Stan."

Mr. President," began NSA Director Grayson, simultaneously beginning the ritual of distributing his briefing folders, "we have picked up several transmissions originating from Saudi Arabia's US Embassy and directed to the Mexican Embassy and Riyadh. It seems to indicate that... Hell, Ev's sitting right here and it's his baby."

Blake's head turned quickly toward his boss, and then toward the chief executive. Sitting up a little straighter, he fumbled with his papers. "I...uh...well..."

He took a deep breath and began again. "Sir, our Directorate of Operations has intercepted several transmissions, as Director Grayson alluded to, going among three places – the Saudi Embassies in Washington and in Mexico City and Riyadh. The communiqués in question seem to link the Saudi Embassy in Mexico City with something that sounds like a potential revival of unrest in Chiapas. There are indications that the al-Qaeda Party is offering to provide financial support to them. Yet we have monitored transactions in the financial institutions and have seen no monies delivered to any of the organizations formerly tied to Subcommander Marcos and the *Zapatista* movement.

President Mercer's mind raced. It competed with itself in trying to listen to and digest what his advisors were telling him while also laboring to jump ahead in his understanding of what the conclusion of the summary would represent.

"The latest messages include the name of a new – apparently – faction of the *Zapatistas*. It is called the *Soldados Nuevos de Zapata*, the New Soldiers of Zapata. Sir, this is the first mention we have of the *SNZ*. It could be that it is a successor organization to the *EZLN*, some new group altogether. But the contents of the decoded messages indicate there may be a growing relationship between these guys and the Republic of Saudi Arabia. There must be some *quid-pro-quo*, but we haven't determined what it is. We have found nothing that the *Zapatistas* can offer in return. And not knowing what it is troubles us."

Mercer stood and walked to a window behind his desk. Everyone watched and waited as he folded his arms and gazed skyward. So al-Hashimi seems to be engaged with the rebels in South Mexico, he summarized silently. He processed scenarios as quickly as he could to try to determine what in hell that could possibly have to do with the US, or more pointedly, with his conversation with the Saudi President.

Finally, he said, "I've heard a lot of 'mights' and 'maybes' but very little, if anything, in the way of concrete facts." He turned to face his audience. "Let's summarize what you have said we know. We know that Saudi Arabia's western hemisphere espionage activities are being managed, at least in part, from Mexico City. But we are conducting negotiations with Riyadh. Doesn't it make sense that they would be coordinating with one another? You know, just wanting to keep an eye on what we are up to?"

"You make a valid point, Mr. President," said Donleavy. "In fact, we aren't surprised by that kind of activity. It's just when you tie in the Chiapas thing, the admittedly 'possible' exchange of money, and our source in Riyadh telling us that some op is being planned. Well…?" The DCI tilted his head and raised his eyebrows.

"Nothing," the President silently persuaded himself. "This has nothing to do with my agreement with al-Hashimi." Then aloud, "You're making several assumptions that all of these things are linked, and they may, in fact, not be connected at all."

"Sir, our analysts are paid to…"

"Of course, that's right," POTUS patronized.

DDI Parnell spoke again. "Mr. President, there are a couple of other things."

POTUS returned to his chair and let out an exaggerated sigh.

"First, we have an agent in place with intimate knowledge of former *Zapatistas* representatives in Mexico. That source says there are no indications of any contact with any representative of the Saudi government."

"Betsy, you make my point for me," the leader of the free world gloated.

"Not at all, sir. On the one hand, the intel could indeed indicate our analysis is wrong and there is absolutely nothing happening between the rebels and al-Qaeda. Adding to the argument that we should be skeptical is that we have never seen the *EZLN* work with outsiders before. And as you know, there have been a lot of meetings, several overtures that seemed to pave the way for a resolution to the conflict between the indigenous people of Chiapas and the government of Mexico. That petered out long ago. And now there's the new organization, the *SNZ*. President Portillo hasn't had to deal with this matter as a real problem. I mean, it basically fell off the radar in 2003. So why would Chiapas suddenly pop up out of nowhere? And, in light of the intel mentioning this new *SNZ* so prominently, where does that leave *EZLN*? What we believe is there is indeed a successor splinter group at work here."

Mercer asked, "What does your *EZLN* source say about the *SNZ*?"

"Never heard of it," answered Betsy. "But that makes sense. An association with another country is out of character with the *EZLN*, and they felt they got burned in peace talks. The only related violence in years was the murder of a teacher and wounding of a dozen or so more said to be involved with the *Zapatistas* around 2014, I think. In fact, the locals in the area have finally begun to realize some autonomy in recent years. Why would they want to upset that apple cart? My guess is a splinter group.

"Sir, Marcos was an educated, passionate man. There would be no logic for him to undertake any actions contrary to that image. In fact, if you'll recall, he announced in 2014 that he was stepping down, as it were – that the movement no longer needed him as a figurehead."

Mercer leaned toward Parnell slightly and displayed a "gotcha" smile. "Betsy, if you apply your same logic to the Saudis, what sense does it make for al-Hashimi to jeopardize the pending agreement he has with us." He leaned back and folded his arms in an overtly self-congratulatory gesture. "Seems like everyone in here," he said, glancing about his office, "thinks I'm giving away the farm. Why would he blow that?" The President felt increasingly comfortable that he was in the clear with regard to his discussion with al-Hashimi.

Donleavy intervened. "Forgive me, sir, but common sense has never been a strength of the man. Your administration has been conducting these talks for nearly five months now. But despite the overtures from Sue and her people at Foggy Bottom, there is no denying that al-Hashimi has still been strutting his stuff. If anything, the force of his rhetoric has intensified dramatically during these months.

"The guy – and this is my opinion – is feeling his oats. Just as Saddam did for a while after the first Gulf War, he has withstood all the measures we have thrown at him. In surviving our sanctions, he feels a certain amount of invincibility and in his mind that translates into an opportunity at vindication. The man has thumbed his nose at this administration, the UN, everyone."

Everyone in the Oval Office expected another outburst from POTUS, but his response, though measured, seemed genuinely understanding. "The sanctions, as constructed, were not the right approach. My predecessor let President al-Hashimi off the hook, in the same way as was done with Iraq after the first war with that nation ended. Our post-war approach didn't work then; it didn't work with the change of regime in Saudi Arabia. The

Saudi leadership must maintain the appearance of defiance to save face with their people. That's what all the muscle-flexing is about. Basically, al-Hashimi has achieved what he wanted to by his posturing. He has a public face; he has a private face – just like all politicians. To the world al-Hashimi is belligerent. Now, behind the scenes, he is thoughtful and practical and is pursuing this agreement with us.

"Sue, you never finished your update earlier. What is your take on the attitude of the Saudi government?"

"Mr. President, the bottom line is that we have had assurances that the conditions we have set forth to the Republic of Saudi Arabia are acceptable. And their foreign minister, Muhammed Ali Asaad, understands the need for us to consult with our allies and to prepare American citizens for what may not be a universally popular move."

Nobody in the room had ever heard Secretary of State McGregor speak so briefly and to the point. Perhaps she's tired and wants to go home, too, Blake speculated.

Donleavy outlined the possibilities. "I make three scenarios, and they all play out badly for the US. The first is that they are organizing a terrorist attack directly against us here inside our borders. Secondly, they could make a move against American interests elsewhere. The third possibility is that their plans involve an ally of ours – and by the looks of it, that could be Mexico – forcing us to act. If any one of these scenarios plays out, there goes the diplomatic initiative."

"Dammit, Chris! They would be nuts to pull a stunt like this with so much at stake. It just wouldn't be rational," Mercer reiterated – and he believed what he said.

"With all due respects, Mr. President, al-Qaeda and ISIS have always operated along a unique set of guiding principles; attacking the Twin Towers, the bombings in Iraq after Saddam's fall to destabilize the coalition, the insurgence in the Middle East, particularly in Iraq; these things would hardly be considered rational by our sense of morality, either. Rationality is not their long suit."

"What did you say your level of confidence is regarding this new asset?" The President swung a pointed finger at the NSA Deputy Director but maintained a direct gaze at Donleavy.

"Marginal, sir," Blake confessed.

"There is one last thing," the DDI offered, handing a series of photos to the commander-in-chief. "Based on the reports from our new asset in Riyadh, we opted to put extended surveillance on Al-Majeed. One of our case officers managed these photos of him meeting with a Mexican national in Cozumel. The Saudi agent gave the man a backpack. We have no idea of the contents. We don't know where the local went to, either, but after the meeting he boarded the ferry back to the mainland. We had a source waiting for the ferry when it arrived at Playa del Carmen and tailed him until he got on a bus – for Chiapas."

President Mercer granted a cursory look at the series of photos, then tossed them onto his desk. "So a Saudi stationed at the embassy in Mexico City meets with a Mexican…" He threw his palms up and shrugged.

"From Chiapas," Betsy interjected.

"Possibly from Chiapas," POTUS continued, "and that is supposed to be evidence of some terrorist conspiracy?" He recovered the photos and waved them in the air as Parnell and Donleavy cast a quick glance at one another.

With eyebrows arched, head leaning forward, Mercer pounded the edge of his right hand into the other palm like a knife blade, restating his assertion as though saying it a second time would somehow make it truer. "I still firmly believe that the Saudi government knows it would be shooting itself in the foot by pulling any stunt that would jeopardize this agreement. It is just too important to al-Hashimi politically, at home and abroad." And to me, he thought.

◆

Elizabeth Parnell flew by his desk so quickly that Ben Reid barely noticed her motioning at him with her head as she passed. He jumped from his desk and took a couple of long strides to catch up.

"Apparently it went really well." His laugh threw Betsy off her anger a bit. She wheeled about causing Reid to almost collide with her. Her mouth opened but no sound emerged. She wagged a finger. No sooner had Reid come to a stop than Parnell spun about again and resumed the dash to her office. Just as abruptly, she reversed course a second time and, this time as well, her subordinate hit the brakes to office a collision.

"The man is such a pr…" After a pause another sound escaped but Reid wasn't sure whether Betsy had said something or had simply let go with some sort of growl. She held her tongue until she entered her office. Ben shut the door. It seemed like the right thing to do.

Betsy laid her briefcase on her desk, but still clinched it tightly. She threw her head back and let out a muted, animated scream. She grabbed at her graying blonde locks, bit her lower lip, and turned her head to one side. Sitting on the corner of her desk, she leaned back and grasped its edges with her hands.

"The man is an absolute moron. President Wendy…" she said, looking around the room animatedly. She picked up the small lamp from her desk and spoke into it. "President Wendy, if you're listening, you are a moron." She replaced the lamp, smiled momentarily and then snarled.

Reid seated himself in the chair across from her desk. "That good, huh?"

"Ben, the man... I just can't believe he got reelected. He doesn't coordinate his various agencies and organizations. He sets his mind on an agenda, then expects everyone to make their information or advice fit that vision, whether it does or not."

Because of his work at the Saudi Arabia Desk at CIA, Reid was aware of the ongoing negotiations, at least to the extent that anyone outside of the West Wing and State was. He "needed to know" because it could influence his analysis of the intel he received.

"So he sees no conflict between our analysis and his dialogue with the Saudis?"

Betsy tapped the tip of her nose with her right forefinger as she glanced up at her subordinate. "Bingo!"

She walked behind her desk, sat, and propped up her feet on the trash can beside her desk in a decidedly un-Betsy like manner. She leaned backed in the swivel chair and ran her fingers through her hair. "Not only that..." She dropped her feet to the floor and leaned toward Reid. "Not only that, he is much further along than any of us imagined. He has McGregor ready to pass this by our coalition allies this week. Christ, Ben. This thing is a done deal.

"Of course, he'll have Hank James coordinate a few leaks, you, know, trial balloons, to the press. He can size up the public reaction and spin the announcement to the best effect. But, shit, Ben, the man is going to do this come hell or high water. He is going to threaten unilateral actions – threaten our allies, for God's sake – if they aren't on board with this. He is such a pig."

"Doesn't he listen to anything Donleavy says in their intelligence briefings? Does he read any of the reports we prepare?" Ben puzzled.

"I know that was rhetorical, Ben." Betsy said, rolling her eyes back. "Listen. What is the number one problem our President is facing right now? Energy; oil prices," she pronounced before Ben could give the same answer.

"He didn't say so in our meeting; hell, he would never say so, but he has this hard-on for better pricing on Saudi Arabia's oil. Everything else is secondary. Only an idiot could think of restoring full relations with those lunatics, even if they do have all the oil in the damned world. And you know, he'll get a lot of people thinking he's done the right thing when gas prices fall twenty or thirty cents. By the time it hits the fan, he'll probably be out of office and watching the next guy deal with the consequences."

"You show him the photos?"

"See, that's the deal, Benny. For Mercer, everything happens in its own little universe. Every bit of intel is viewed in a vacuum. Increasing communications throughout the Saudi government about dealing with a new organization in the state of Chiapas? No big deal. Photos from Cozumel of a new diplomat-slash-agent in the Saudi Mexican Embassy? What's the crisis? he wonders. He says, 'the man is just doing his job.' Oh, and so what if the man he met with is from Chiapas, probably just a coincidence."

Ben had seen her frustrated before, but not like this. Elizabeth Parnell had butted her head against the glass ceiling for years. She had tangled with people who resented her ambition and intelligence. Yes, Reid thought, she was one of the brightest people he had ever met. And her exasperation with the President was professional, even though she had a real reason to personally dislike the man.

About eighteen months into office, Mercer appointed Christopher Donleavy to head up CIA. Donleavy was one of the last of the good old boy network that had powered the Agency for so many years. But despite this image, what most didn't realize was that he was one of the most decent, fair men in the Company. To almost everyone's astonishment, he made Betsy his Deputy Director, Intelligence. The new DCI had fought off objections — even from President Mercer, the scuttlebutt was — to her ascending to this position. As a sign of independence, and in an act that would cause immediate and lasting tension between him and Mercer, he went to bat for Parnell in a very public way.

Shortly after his own confirmation, the new DCI mounted what was, for all intents, a PR campaign for his young protégé. He disregarded as nonsense arguments that she was too young. He joked to a Senator once — and Betsy got a kick out of it — that she wasn't as young as she looked anyhow. He had taken age away as an issue. He recited her resume on a number of occasions to fend off arguments about her experience. He stood up for her as no one had ever done.

On the first possible occasion after she assumed her new job, Donleavy took Parnell to a briefing with Mercer. He had her prepare a brief analysis about something — she didn't even remember now what it was — just something to give her an excuse to speak before POTUS. The man met her with the graciousness that she had come to expect from seeing him on TV.

His first words to her had begun innocently enough: "Congratulations, Ms. Parnell. We are thrilled to have you work on behalf of your country in your new position." Then he turned to Donleavy and continued, "I'm sure there has never been anyone so lovely in this job before. I can understand why she caught your eye." Betsy had been so stunned that she simply said, "Uh, thank you, Mr. Merc-, I mean, Mr. President." She was so ill at ease that she completely botched her briefing, insignificant as it was. Donleavy assured her that she read too much into Mercer's comment, but she had noticed the tiny flare in her boss' eyes, too, when he heard the President. It wasn't even so much the words as the demeaning tone.

But despite that and other encounters with the Big Man, Reid thought, Betsy knew how to keep professional and personal separate. For her to be this agitated, it must have really gone poorly.

"You know, Ben. There is a part of me, the dark side…," she intoned in a low voice that ineffectively mimicked Darth Vader. "I shouldn't say this," returning to her normal voice, "but there really is a part of me that wishes this whole thing would blow up in his face. But the sensible part of me knows that the consequences might very well be too grim."

There was silence for a couple of moments. The DDI gazed at her folded hands in her lap while Reid considered how to respond.

"Damn," Ben thought, "she really is worried about this thing."

"Anyhow," broke the silence. "It's Sunday and you should get home to the wife and kid. How is your little angel?"

The mood in the room swung a hundred and eighty degrees in an instant. "A little terror waiting to happen," grinned Reid. "She's just starting to walk a bit. But she is beautiful. Looks just like her mother. You should see the pictures of Becky at that age. It's amazing."

Betsy could feel the warmth from her analyst. She felt that occasional twinge of regret of never having married or had kids. But she had made her choices.

She stood and walked over to Ben as he rose. "Sorry to have brought you in. I thought we might have some analyses to churn out, but I guess not. Say 'hi' to Becky and kiss the little girl for me."

Henry Brian James sat across the Oval Office from his boss. While Mercer sat at his desk reviewing his schedule for the following day, his chief of staff considered other matters.

"You know, your old pal Weston is making an appearance tomorrow."

"Hmmph." Mercer didn't raise his head but looked over his reading glasses at James. "Really? What's the old goat up to now?" he asked, resuming his reading.

"He's taking a little trip with his *amigo*, President Portillo."

"Oh, yeah. The train thing."

"You know, we could issue a statement just before the scheduled departure." The twinkle in James' eyes was almost childlike.

The President leaned back in his chair, removed his glasses, and stuck the end of one earpiece in the corner of his mouth. Momentarily he smirked. "The old fart would shit a brick, wouldn't he?" The chuckle that followed was reflexive.

"This is his first foray into public life, at least in any meaningful way, since we kicked his ass six years ago. Maybe we could put him back into hibernation with nothing more than a press release recognizing the

60

important role he played in US-Mexican relations and wishing him well on his 'ambassadorial' trip. Then we go on to highlight some of our accomplishments we have had with our neighbors to the south and express our regrets that you weren't able to participate in the trip."

"Yeah, Hank? What have we done to improve relations with those assholes?" Mercer almost snorted when he laughed at that. But even in the privacy of the Oval Office, the chief of staff fidgeted a bit at the crassness of his boss that he never got used to.

"The only thing that sorry-assed country ever did for me was provide all the nice little boys' towns along their border with the United States. Went to a couple of 'em when I was in college. You know, Spring Break, down near Laredo, Texas. Or was it Juarez? Anyhow, that was my first experience with foreign relations, you might say."

The memories of his teen-aged adventures flashed through his mind. "Whew! I haven't thought about that in a while. Wonder if we should make a state visit to those border towns? Hell, I wonder if that's why Weston is going." Even James laughed aloud at that.

"No, let him have his day," Mercer permitted with a wave of the hand. "Besides, I'm not sure we want to call any attention to him at all, certainly not in any positive way. We're about to bury his ass anyhow. When we announce the resumption of relations with al-Hashimi, we'll do so in the context of the failed sanctions carried over from Weston's administration. We'll portray it as a foolish move to have even engaged in the strategy, that it was an effort to insert American power in a governmental change that didn't involve us. We'll spin it that he was trying to divert attention from his inability to resolve the Israel-Palestinian mess. Or better yet, we'll bring up his domestic failures. Shit, that's what they're always saying about us."

"Mr. President, Weston's position with respect to Saudi Arabia was incredibly popular."

"Yeah, well, that was a long time ago, Hank; a long time ago. People are paying over four bucks a gallon at the pump right now. It's killing them. And it's killing my popularity in the process. No, the people want relief from this energy crisis. They'll believe what I tell them to believe."

CHAPTER 7

DAY 4 – MONDAY

Alicia Weston assessed her husband's haircut. "Very nice!" and she pecked him on the cheek. "You are such a stud!"

The former President's cheeks showed the slightest reddening. "Aren't we a little old for you to be thinking of me in that context?"

"When you quit being one, I'll quit calling you one… stud." She slapped him on his butt as she started away. Turning, she came back and embraced him, burying her face in his chest.

"I am so proud of you."

"Alicia, I…"

"Trenton, I don't mean for taking this train ride. I just mean… I just mean for everything." And she left to resume her preparations to accompany her husband."

◆

Some six-hundred or so miles away, in El Paso, Texas, a Hispanic woman was turning eyes as she walked northward from Delta Drive. Raven-black hair, long muscular legs, high heels, sunglasses – all gave her an air of inapproachability that heightened the lust of every man – young or old – even more than usual. The rare gusts of breeze flared the hem of her barely adequate white skirt, offering tantalizing glimpses of bare cheeks only slightly separated by a thong. Mariana Lopez jaywalked briskly across Tobin and continued toward its intersection with East Paisano. She glided up the steps like a cat and into the Washington Park Station Post Office. When her turn arrived at the counter, she said in Spanish, "*Por favor.* Make sure this is postmarked today."

"*Si.*" The postal clerk fed it through the machine and between hardly concealed leers at his customer, he recognized the address: 1600 Pennsylvania Avenue, Washington, D.C. He wondered, "How does the President do such a thing? Gets in their pants even from two thousand miles away." He laughed and threw the letter in the bin.

Mariana boarded a bus, transportation incongruous with her looks, and began the journey to the border with Juarez, Mexico.

◆

There were certainly worse scenes to wake up to, Morgan told himself. He stood on his front porch watching the cow moose lumber across his acreage toward the road. He brushed through his short hair with his fingers. The steam from his coffee swirled up around his face, its warmth noticeable in contrast to the cool Wyoming morning, even in July.

He sat down on the wooden swing and just a touch from his feet started the slow forward-and-backward motion that was familiar from his childhood. Growing up in Texas, he had spent a lot of time on this swing. He had rescued it from the old home that was his grandparents shortly before the structure was bulldozed. After his dad passed away, when Morgan was eight, his mother had to work for the first time in her life. The first months were as frightening to Peggy Morgan as anything she had ever experienced. She and her son spent countless weekends at her parents' farm, trying to occupy the empty moments of their lives.

Morgan learned to shoot from his dad. He learned to shoot well at the hands of his grandfather. Silas Houston and Josh hunted deer and birds, fished incessantly. But what Morgan remembered most were the early mornings as Ellie Houston and Morgan's mom cooked breakfast. The smell of ham and eggs, and biscuits – god, Grandma made the world's best biscuits, Morgan recalled – filled the entire countryside, it seemed. And young Josh would have his milk in a mug just like the one Grandpa used for his coffee, whose steam curled up around his face.

Looking down into his very black coffee, Morgan inhaled deeply. "July mornings in Texas were a little hotter than here, though," he whispered aloud.

Morgan smiled. He generally rose about this time of the morning, but today things seemed a little less bleak.

◆

The flight to San Antonio from Dallas was a mercifully short forty-five minutes. The two additional Secret Service Agents assigned to Trenton Weston specifically for this trip had driven his Suburban down the previous evening and were waiting for him as his plane rolled to a stop. Rounding out the detail, Agents Daniel Pollard and Teresa Mendoza walked smartly down the ramp, scanning the entire area through the dark lenses of their glasses.

The former President and First Lady followed. Alicia grinned widely as she noticed the long-absent spring evident in her husband's step.

Weston himself was relieved to see that the two agents on special assignment for this trip were familiar to him. Neither the two on permanent duty to him nor the two tasked with his protection for this trip took their responsibilities less seriously because they were guarding a former President.

The couple walked to the SUV where the retired Chief Executive held his hand out to each of the agents in turn. This always made them uncomfortable, but quietly thrilled. It was just Weston's way. As he moved toward the door being held open by Agent Theodore Baker, Weston thumped him in the stomach. "Still pumping iron, I see, Teddy Bear."

As he closed the door behind his charge, Baker smiled what, for a Secret Service Agent, was a huge grin, but one which would have been hardly noticeable to anyone. "Teddy Bear" hardly fit the image conjured up in the minds of most people when they envisioned an agent on a Presidential security detail. At six feet four inches and barrel-chested, Baker had the physique of a professional bodybuilder. Despite this, he was quick and agile. He had the commanding presence of a bouncer at a topless bar. His nickname, though, came as a result of his tendency to cry easily at sad movies. But his tender sensitivities aside, he was as intense as any other when it came to his job. And Teddy Bear loved working for Weston. That was the way he always viewed him, not as a charge or responsibility, but as a boss to whom he was devoted. He climbed into the passenger-side front seat of the Suburban.

Agent John Johnston moved behind the wheel of the black truck. Jack, as he had been called since his days growing up in the Bronx, was not as imposing as Baker, but no less serious about his duties.

Alicia Weston lowered the window separating the driver's area from the passenger compartment, and leaned forward to sympathize, "Jack, I was very sorry to hear about your wife."

"Thank you, ma'am. The kids are holding up pretty well. It was great of you to send the card, and for the President to attend the funeral."

"I wanted so much to be there, too, but..." The woman reached to place her hand on the Agent's shoulder.

"Yes, ma'am, I understand. And the flowers were great, too."

He paused.

"Ma'am, I know I'm wasting my breath, but you really shouldn't distract me. I'm supposed to be on the lookout for bad guys. And if you do need to talk to me there is…"

"I know, I know. The intercom. I hate those blasted things. They're so impersonal. Anyhow, bring the kids to see us sometimes." She rolled up the window.

The two agents in the front seat glanced at one another and each smiled a real, normal-person smile. It wasn't just that the former First Lady had invited her bodyguard and his kids to her house. It was that she meant it. Mrs. Weston would love to have them come over for milk and the homemade cookies for which she was practically famous. Johnston and Baker couldn't sort out whether the affection they felt for this dignified couple interfered with their work or made them more diligent. But it didn't matter. They couldn't help it.

Pulling up to the depot, the former President's SUV, followed by the one containing Agents Pollard and Mendoza, had to negotiate a security nightmare. San Antonio police and Texas Rangers lined the street, while a Department of Public Safety helicopter hovered just a few hundred feet overhead.

Weston glanced out the window at the crowd of people pushing at the barricades, wondering what they were protesting. He was astonished to see that the signs they were waving carried messages of greetings and encouragement to… him. He rolled down the window.

The intercom objected, "Mr. President."

"Oh, hush, Jack."

In the vehicle behind the President's, Mendoza said, "This is really great for him. Really great."

The festivities were just over an hour away, yet over one hundred and fifty people were already on hand to see their former President and the President of Mexico, who would be arriving momentarily. A rousing cheer echoed off the train cars and the depot windows as Former President Trenton Lewis and Former First Lady Alicia Weston emerged from their vehicle. Alicia embraced her husband closely with her right arm while waving with her left. Her husband held both hands high in the air.

Looks like that scene from Rocky, she thought.

Knowing what would happen next, Mendoza and Pollard moved toward the barricade where the crowd was waiting. And, as was the ex-chief executive's custom, while they scanned the swarm of well-wishers, President and Mrs. Weston moved to shake hands with as many as they could reach.

At the same time, President and First Lady Portillo were arriving at the depot, virtually unnoticed because of the attention being given the American couple and because their arrival was partly obscured by the train.

Weston's aide, Julie Bishop, who had arrived a day earlier, waited a respectful distance while her boss basked in the outpouring of affection. After what she thought was an appropriate period of time, she came and touched the President's arm lightly.

"Mr. President? Sir?"

He turned, and without pretense or regard for appearances, he embraced Julie affectionately.

"Honey," teased Mrs. Weston, "one of your predecessors got in a world of trouble for that very thing."

The Westons exchanged a brief stare before erupting into laughter.

The husband leaned over and whispered to his wife. "You know how we 'studs' are!" And they laughed again.

Julie spoke loudly over the clamoring of the crowd. "Mr. President, we should head to the platform now," she urged, knowing it would take another minute or two before he actually moved.

Finally, Weston said to the crowd, "Well, this is a train ride and trains have schedules to keep. Better head that way, or they might leave me," he said, holding the backside of his open hand to the corner of his mouth.

And as he turned to go, he said, more to the onlookers than to his wife, "Honey, did you remember my toothbrush?" The crowd roared with affection.

◆

Morgan knew he watched too much television, but, he justified, it was mostly news channels and nature documentaries. And of course, all the Dr. Who episodes. Pouring himself another cup of coffee, he pressed the button on the remote. There was the brief, customary crackle, and a sound like a very tiny jet spooling up as the image sprang to life. He plopped into his La-Z-Boy, shuffled away newspapers and magazines from the last several days, and reclined his chair. He caught the Quantum News Network reporter in mid-sentence.

"…what was an estimated one hundred and seventy-five people as late as an hour ago, has swelled to an unexpected six- to seven-hundred now. The agenda calls for the Mayor of San Antonio to provide opening remarks. The presidents of the US and Mexican railroads participating in this venture will follow."

"San Antonio, huh? Bet they're already sizzling." One of the things Morgan most remembered about his home state was not just how hot it got, but how early it got that way, and how late into the evening the misery persisted.

Morgan recognized the reporter as Cameron Neal. "She's hot," and he didn't mean the temperature.

Neal continued, "After the railroad executives, we will hear from former

President Trent Weston, who will welcome President Francisco Javier Portillo of Mexico."

The QNN anchor inquired, "Cameron, will President Portillo address the crowd as well? His popularity extends well into this country. And San Antonio is considered to be a virtual Hispanic capital of Texas."

"Yes, Tracy, he will make a few comments. Many of these people" – she waved to the spectators with one hand – "would feel slighted if they didn't get to hear from the man who is leading his country's rapid progress out of third-world status.

"His remarks are expected to be somewhat brief here. He will take center stage when the train arrives at Los Mochis, Mexico, at the end of its journey. Remember, too, that a huge number of the Hispanic onlookers are just as eager to see the former US President, as well. The financial assistance and moral support provided by his administration are rightly recognized to have been the catalyst in Mexico's economic resurgence. So, he is an extraordinarily popular figure with Mexicans and Mexican-Americans. It certainly plays to the citizens of San Antonio that he is near-fluent in Spanish as well."

There was a pause in Neal's coverage as she put her right hand to the tiny earpiece in her ear as though offering a weird salute of some sort. "Tracy, I understand the mayor of the city is about to speak."

The camera angle changed to show a man, whose two hundred and twenty pounds were a mismatch with his five-foot seven-inch frame, stepping to the podium. To his right was the engine of a train that looked every bit as if it had rolled through a time warp from the nineteen-forties into the present, when, in fact, its construction had been completed in the last seven months. Banners draped the train, proclaiming its identity as *el Águila de la Amistad*, or The Eagle of Friendship. The use of the word "eagle" referenced the fact that the image of the large bird appeared on both the Mexican flag and the Great Seal of the United States. The bunting and decorations, like the train itself, were reminiscent of a time over three-quarters of a century earlier, and combined the red, white, and blue of the US with the red, white, and green of the Mexican states.

"Ladies and gentlemen, welcome. Welcome, all! We are here today to commemorate the friendship between the United States and Mexico." The mayor's comments went longer than expected. The people attending the festivities fanned themselves with anything at hand, their caps, the signs they had made for the occasion.

The president of *El Águila de la Amistad*/United States, Incorporated, held his address to a compassionately short five minutes, a time approximately duplicated by his Mexican counterpart, the president of *El Águila de la Amistad*/Mexico. The two gave a brief history of the train and the origins of the joint venture.

After the two businessmen concluded, the two politicians made their entrances. From positions offstage President Portillo, former President Weston, and their wives made their appearances. In a ceremonious display, the two couples began at opposite ends of the platform, waving to a cheering mob until meeting at center stage. The two men skipped the usual preliminary handshakes, beginning instead with the warm embrace of good friends. Each kissed the other's wife on the cheek in the way that relatives did after some period of absence. The four turned again to the people gathered there and waved enthusiastically. After the frenzy subsided, they turned to the railroad executives and other officials, shaking hands, and smiling warmly. Then all took their seats, except for Trenton Weston, who moved to the podium with long, energetic strides.

Finally, the first of the two men whom the spectators came to see began to speak.

"Wow, he looks good." Morgan was pleased to see President Weston getting such a spirited reception. "Good for him."

"Thank you for coming today, for braving this heat. Of course, we Texans are used to it." The crowd moaned its agreement.

"You honor me; you honor my very dear friend, President Francisco Portillo with your presence here today."

Weston paused to place his emotions in check.

"San Antonio is a city with a history inextricably linked with the history of Mexico. This wonderful city represents the best of what we pray for as residents of this planet. It is a symbol of the evolution of individual hearts and the spirits of nations – from times filled with war and adversity, through times of fragile co-existence, to, ultimately, an era of true friendship and cooperation, of shared goals and dreams.

"Before you is another emblem of the friendship between two neighbors. *El Águila de la Amistad* will begin a journey today. But it also continues another journey that has been in progress since time began. The journey of which I speak travels not across rails and bridges. Neither does it traverse the pastures or rivers, the deserts or the mountains of our two countries. It is the journey that moves through the hearts and minds of good men and women, not just in Mexico and in the United States, but indeed, in every place where people are present in this world. It is the journey toward that point in time when we put aside the bitterness that drives wedges between us, surrender the suspicions that divide us, and cast off the burdens that selfishness has placed there."

The crowd listened reverently as the former President spoke.

"It is true that this journey often progresses too slowly. But its perseverance is fueled by compassion and selflessness. It achieves momentum through our resolve to prosper together. Nations may be the vehicles through which peace is discussed, but it is the kindness and the strength of character of individual men and women, teaching our children wrong from right, and demanding honor and dignity from our leaders, through which peace will finally be achieved."

The cheers and applause echoed throughout the train station as if every person in San Antonio were present.

"And finally, *el Águila*, in a greater sense, is a celebration of the progress we have made in yet another journey. It is the journey of friendship between the United States of America and *los Estados Unidos Mexicanos*. We have persevered through conflicts in the past to find common ground in the present. We have replaced the ordeals of our ancestors with the ideals of our times. We have sown the seeds of peace and liberty in the hearts of our children. May they journey far beyond the borders of our two nations. Thank you for coming, and may God richly bless you, and the USA, and Mexico. Now let me welcome…"

President Weston's attempt to move forward with the proceedings was interrupted as the listeners sounded their agreement with riotous applause. Once there was quiet again, the former leader of the United States introduced his friend from Mexico City.

"The friendship between nations is only as strong as the friendship between the citizens of those nations. I am honored to say that President Francisco Javier Portillo is my friend. We are friends, not because of the successes we achieved for our two countries, but rather, I believe, we achieved successes for our countries because we became friends."

And it was true, Weston knew. The two men had bonded in a way that previous chief executives of the two countries had not. Weston would attribute this to the greatness of Portillo. Portillo would likewise contend it was the gracious way in which Weston treated him as an equal. Previous relationships between the heads of the two countries, while not quite contentious, were definitely carried out with a definitive sense of who was the alpha male. But for whatever reason, these two men became fast friends and labored tirelessly in an attempt to balance the inequities of their respective homelands' situations.

Morgan's Samsung flat screen displayed the hoopla as Weston continued for just a moment or two before giving way to his *amigo*. The former CIA officer listened to Portillo's closing comments, but when the talking heads resumed their commentary, telling viewers what they had just heard, he went outside, leaving the television on, as was his custom.

Morgan walked the short distance to the partially completed hole in the ground that was destined to become a trout pond. He started up his tractor and drove into the recessed area of dirt. "What a difference there is between President Weston and that pretender we have now," he observed. Then he lowered the oversized scoop on the front end of his John Deere and began to scrape out more dirt.

◆

The coverage of the inaugural run of *el Águila de la Amistad* continued until its departure. The train was a replica of the trains that crisscrossed Mexico and the United States in the middle twentieth century. Only this one ran on diesel instead of coal. And the cab of the locomotive was redesigned for the comfort and protection of the crew. Furthermore, in contrast to their ancestors, the cars themselves were air-conditioned in order to spare the passengers from the stifling summer heat of west Texas and northern Mexico.

There were ordinarily eight cars, but the executives had the foresight to build a special VIP car for this occasion and for those instances when they wished to provide special accommodations for other important guests. The VIP car, or "Railcar One," as the press had dubbed it for this inaugural run, owing to the dignitaries it carried, was the last car in the procession. As *el Águila* pulled out of the San Antonio train station, the Westons and Portillos stood on the rear deck waving to the lingering spectators. Children rode the shoulders of their fathers. Mothers held babies up. And each parent was certain that the two Presidents had smiled and waved specifically to their children. The platform on which the men and their wives were standing had been fashioned after the great whistle-stop trains of earlier days. It was spacious and secure enough to guarantee safety while the train was moving. Unlike its predecessors, though, this train had built-in loud speakers. And just inside the door to the car was a cabinet containing wireless lapel microphones for the addresses the designers knew might be given from time to time from the rear of this railway car. At the front end of the interior of Railcar One the builders had included a recessed closet that was capable of holding all manner of items, which on this occasion consisted of powerful weaponry.

Above the dignitaries and other passengers an MQ-1 Predator hummed in circular patterns, tracing the route of the rails. The Predator, an American unmanned aerial vehicle (UAV) built by General Atomics, served extensively in the war on terror in Afghanistan and Pakistan, primarily used by the Air Force and CIA. Though capable of carrying Hellfire missiles or other munitions, the ones used by the Border Patrol for this mission carried only real-time cameras for forward observation. The UAVs could fly for fourteen hours or so and had a range of a little more than 450 miles so one would run up to its limit and then be replaced by a counterpart.

With the last of the citizens of San Antonio receding into the distance, the locomotive took off its warm-ups and really began to accelerate. *El Águila* was capable of over seventy-five miles per hour, though she would normally cruise at only sixty. This train was not intended to get people from Point A to Point B in the shortest possible time. It was a tourist train. Its route would take it through the heart of the Chihuahuan Desert. From San Antonio it followed Union Pacific tracks due west, passing north of the small town of Eagle Pass until it reached the Rio Grande River, which constituted the border between Texas and Mexico. It turned to the northwest there, remaining in Texas, and passed through Sanderson on its way to Alpine.

At Alpine, Texas, *el Águila* intersected the South Orient Railroad tracks, which carried it southwestward and just north of Big Bend National Park. Under normal circumstances the train would spend a day in Alpine to allow the passengers to ride route buses into the National Park. On the inaugural trip, however, they passed on that opportunity. Finally, the processions of cars would reach the Rio Grande once again, crossing it this time at the town of Presidio, Texas, into the Mexican state of Chihuahua. The tracks became Mexican right of way at Ojinada, Chihuahua, the border village just across the river from Presidio. From this point until the end of the route into Los Mochis on the Mexican Pacific coast, the track belonged to the *Chihuahua al Pacifico* Railroad.

As the procession of engine and cars made its incursion onto Mexican soil, above them the Predator UAV turned northward, remaining in US air space and beginning its journey back to its base. Its mission had been solely to surveil the train's journey during its American portion.

The Presidential couples entered the plush confines of Railcar One. Its interior was also fashioned after its earlier cousins but contained all the luxuries and appliances of modern life – satellite phone service, computer hookups, refrigerators, and microwaves. And though they were called berths the sleeping quarters were four bedrooms that rivaled any number of luxury hotels' rooms in size and comfort.

"*Mi amigo*, it is so good to see you again," POTUS said to his Mexican friend. Each man placed his hands on the other's shoulders and looked squarely into his friend's eyes. "Three years, I guess?"

"*Si*, about that. I, and my country, owe you a debt of gratitude. Your successor has not been so forthcoming with his time and support. But fortunately, my country was on a solid foundation when…" The Mexican President's face flushed.

"When he defeated me? It's okay, my friend."

"I am sorry. It was as much a defeat for the people of my country as your own. But, of course, we are here to visit and to celebrate, not to discuss politics."

An attendant appeared and offered the men and their wives' champagne and orange juice mimosas. Each of the four VIPs raised their glasses. It was Portillo who offered the toast.

"To a wonderful journey, long life, and eternal friendship."

"Eternal friendship!" returned the chorus.

CHAPTER 8

DAY 5 – TUESDAY

"Hi, Mag."

"Josh?" The cell phone barely maintained contact with her ear as she lifted her head to look at the clock beside her bed. "Josh, it's six-thirty. Why is it still dark?"

"It's 6:30 in the morning."

"I, uh… I, uh, didn't know there were two of them," she said wryly. You okay?" At the possibility that he might answer 'no,' she summoned a bit more alertness.

"Yeah. I mean, yes, I'm fine. I'm going fishing. I was just thinking that maybe we could get together when I get back." Morgan waited a couple of moments without getting a reply. "Hello?"

"I'm here. Sure. I mean, I have some conference calls with a client in Hawaii, so I can't get free until nine tonight. Want me to call you?"

"No, just come on by. Deal?"

"Deal… Hey, Josh, you sure you're all right?"

"I'm fine, Maggie. Really. Sorry I woke you."

"It's okay. I'm glad you called."

Maggie pressed the button to disconnect her phone, and realized she was wide-awake. She knew she wouldn't go back to sleep, but bed still seemed like the best place to be. Pulling her pillow to her chest, Maggie clung to it with both arms and smiled.

Morgan poured the last of the coffee into his stainless-steel mug and picked up his daypack. Biscuit followed him to the door.

"Not today, fella." He shut the door and thought to himself that he had other things to do than go fishing. There was the home office he was remodeling for the specific purpose of holding the Apple computer on which he digitally processed his photos and the oversized Epson printer on which he made large format museum quality prints of his photos. There was also the room he was building in the garage attic. And the trout pond. He smiled, then reminded himself silently, "Shit, Josh. There are no more important things to do than fish.

"So many trout; so little time," Morgan quoted the commonly observed bumper sticker aloud. He thought his GMC Denali was a better choice for the long drive to his destination. The canvas top to his Jeep was in desperate need of repair. An unexpected rain shower pouring through the plethora of holes would make for a pretty chilly ride, even in the summertime. He started the engine and opened the window to his truck. The freshness of the morning air filled his lungs, and his spirits.

◆

Since the inaugural run for *el Águila de la Amistad* was largely ceremonial, the railroad had eliminated some of the stops that it would make on future treks. Since the day trip at Big Bend National Park was omitted, they were ahead of what would have been a typical schedule, but exactly matched the forecasted itinerary for this trip. There were many aboard for whom time was a precious commodity. For President Portillo, the trip meant several days of attending to governmental matters from the limited environment of the train. Despite the conveniences aboard the Presidential Car, including satellite uplinks and the sophisticated equipment his staff had brought along, it was no replacement for his office. Had he not been so looking forward to the time with his American friend, he might have forgone the trip.

One of the journey's normal stops, one that the corporation managing the train intended to keep in the inaugural run, however, was at the Mexico's Copper Canyon. The popular site was southwest of the city of Chihuahua. It was the highlight of the trip. Twenty-four hours into the trip, the train was making excellent time through the northern Mexican desert, well on its way toward the country's "Grand Canyon."

The reduced number of passengers were delighted to have the world leaders aboard. The former American President, his wife, the President of Mexico, and *Señora* Portillo had even elected to take breakfast in the dining car with the excited patrons of the first trip on the *Águila*.

After returning to Railcar One, Alicia Weston and Isabella Portillo were chatting enthusiastically about charities, cooking, movies. The twenty-something years of difference in their ages was a non-factor. And the content of their discussion never betrayed the fact that they were wives of powerful men and famous women in their own right. They were simply two good friends catching up after a long period since their last visit.

Weston and Portillo were drinking iced tea at the sofa in the center of the railcar. The American cast an envious look at the Mexican. Francisco Portillo was making history as the first Mexican President to occupy his nation's top office for a second term. During the administration of his predecessor the constitution of the United Mexican States was amended to revise the term of the office of the Chief Executive. Instead of a single six-year term, the law now called for four-year terms. And like their northern counterparts, *los Presidentes* were permitted to seek a second consecutive term. The economic boom had created a consensus among the citizens that a more frequent public referendum was appropriate to determine who should be their leader. The goal was to allow voters to retain a popular, effective President and provide an opportunity to more quickly remove one who wasn't. The amendment even established for the first time the office of Vice President of Mexico. Portillo was in his second turn as President. Weston had been denied that honor.

"So, Francisco, you're pleased with the progress of your administration?"

"Yes, my friend. The national prosperity and stability allow me to accomplish things now that I was not previously able to spend time on. My first years were occupied with attending to the economy and uncovering the corruption in my government. I found that the lure of money and power was an irresistible temptation among even lifelong friends, members of my own party. And then, the economy, *Madre de Dios*. It took years to realize the goals we set together when you were in power."

The former American President personally abhorred that term – "in power" – but he understood the pervasiveness of the expression and took no offense from his friend. "So, what occupies your time now?"

"There are so many things. Regulating the increased trade we have been blessed with. New oil discoveries. It is peculiar that President Mercer has not made more overtures to us, in light of the extreme nature of your country's energy problems. It is as though he is somehow opposed to continuing the relationship you and I established between our nations." Portillo shook his head and took another drink. "So does he even have an energy plan?"

"There are rumblings, you know, a few hints that a major announcement is coming soon. Hell, Francisco, I'm the former President of the US and what I know of his intentions is scarcely greater than anybody watching the television news shows."

"Well, our petroleum fields are growing in numbers. And while the quality may be slightly less than Middle Eastern crude, there is much of it, and we would be willing – no, eager – trade partners with the Americans. You already buy some. We would sell you much more." The Mexican took another drink.

"We are also considering renewing dialogues with the *Zapatistas*. There is the distinct possibility of some type of negotiated agreement with the Chiapas leaders before the end of the year. The dialogue has been dormant for some time. Like my predecessor, I am sympathetic with their grievances, at least philosophically. I am surprised that the discussion was abandoned. But though my representatives have made some initial overtures, the Chiapas leaders ask too much. Their demands are the virtual equivalent of becoming an independent nation. But as I learned at Harvard, negotiations begin with each side asking too much and offering too little. I am confident a compromise is possible."

◆

Everson Blake's eyes narrowed as he looked at the latest matrix of deciphered transmissions relating to the, until now, unknown operation. "God help me – with Blake this really was a prayer – I should have put this together weeks ago," he thought. He hoped sweat wasn't pouring from him the way he felt it was.

"Sir, I asked if you wanted me to prepare briefings for anyone."

"Sorry. Uh, no. No, thanks, I'll prepare them myself, Terry," he responded to the protégé in his office.

"There are references to some people, coded names, I guess. Anyhow, I was about to run this by analysts. It really sucks to translate this shit into English and still not know what it says most of the time." Henderson waited for direction.

The Deputy Director, NSA, knew what the communiqué said. "I'll take care of it, son. Probably gonna wind up just being filed. I really don't think it's much of anything, certainly nothing urgent. But I'll run it by some people here and over at Langley, just to be sure." He said this knowing the information would never leave a close circle of associates. "You did good, Henderson, bringing it to my attention first, though." Real good, he thought.

The junior analyst closed the door behind him, and Blake picked up the secure line in his office. The speed dial button ripped off the programmed series of beeps.

"Mark, it's me. Buddy, it's about to hit the fan. I don't know if it's a crisis, or an opportunity."

CHAPTER 9

Alicia Weston viewed Agent Mendoza from a few feet away as the woman gazed out the window at the passing landscape. At five feet, seven inches, the woman wore loose clothing that disguised the one hundred fifty pounds of rock-hard muscles. Her hair was the jet black common to her heritage. One hand hugged the bottled water that she carried during one of her infrequent breaks.

"Teresa, thinking of your children? I know these road trips are hard on your family life." The former President's wife brought a smile to the agent as she approached.

"No, ma'am. Actually, just daydreaming a bit. I grew up near here – Laredo. My parents still live there, and I was just thinking that this is as close as I have been to them in several years. Time just gets away from you. They've never been to see us in Dallas in the five years that we've been there. It's sad how we can say we're a close family, but rarely see each other. They hardly know Gabriella or Angelina."

The former First Lady startled her protector as she took her hand. "Oh, I don't think closeness is a matter of geography. It's more a level of consciousness – how often you think about people, the way you think about them. I think it's more about how much a part of your lives they are in spite of the miles in between."

"Yes, ma'am, I'm sure you're right. But death creates a divide that we can't cross with cars or telephones. I'm afraid it will be soon. They are elderly. Time grows shorter. I just pray they know how much they have meant to me."

The dark-haired agent was suddenly flushed with embarrassment at her openness with Mrs. Weston. "I beg your pardon. I shouldn't..."

"Of course, you should."

Dammit, the Westons made it hard to maintain your detachment,

Mendoza thought. They were too approachable, too open themselves.

Alicia Weston placed a delicate kiss on the agent's cheek. "Call them, Honey. You have a satellite phone." She squeezed her hand and walked away. Looking back over her shoulder, she smiled. "Call them."

Across the VIP car, two of Mendoza's counterparts were discussing life and protecting the ex-Chief Executive while moving along the windows.

"It's tough raising kids alone, Jack. You know, I've had my hands full with my little brother and sister since our folks passed on. Tommy's a good kid, but he's just so full of himself. Thirteen going on twenty. And jeez, Samantha..." Ted Baker rolled his eyes. "She's nine; she needs a woman to talk to. I don't have a friggin' clue what to say to her. I've thought about getting married just for her. I don't think they have a rent-a-wife."

"Sure they do. If they're for the men, they're called prostitutes. For the kids, they're called grandparents," Johnston teased. Both men laughed.

They looked at the car's protective detail again. Two of Portillo's men by the rear exit to the car. Another of the Mexican detail and Pollard near the front entrance. Mendoza had returned to the gangway between the VIP car and the car ahead, which contained journalists and paying passengers.

"I understand. I do. Ted, I don't know how my kids are going to make it without their mom. Me, either. Emily was just..."

"I know, pal."

"My sister is staying with them while we're on this trip, but I feel guilty being away so soon."

"It's what we do."

"Roger that. Could be a helluva lot worse," Johnston said, glancing over at the ex-President. "We could be guarding a prick."

"Amen, bro!" Baker agreed.

The festive atmosphere aboard the train among US and Mexican citizens was evidence of a narrowing of the gap that had separated the neighboring nations – economically, socially, and politically. The passengers were almost evenly split between US and Mexican citizens. And as the two guests of honor, accompanied by their security details, mingled throughout the cars, the enthusiastic support from the train's guests was almost tangible. There was no Republican Party or Democratic Party here, no *Partido Revolucionario Institucional* or *Partido Acción Nacional,* just citizens – albeit mostly very wealthy citizens – who were overwhelmed to be in such close proximity to these two powerful, popular men. It was a heady atmosphere. Photos were taken by the scores, hands shaken, and autographs signed. Both Portillo and Weston listened graciously as many of their traveling companions waxed philosophical and proffered their solutions to the problems facing their nations and the world.

Press coverage was extensive. Each of the major television networks had reporters on board the *Águila*. Quantum, Fox News, CNN, and MSNBC each had full contingents, traveling on the car just ahead of the two Presidents'. Along the way, through the small towns in south Texas largely populated by Hispanics and through every village in the Mexican desert, excited citizens waved and shouted to the passing locomotive and the one hundred or so travelers. And through most, the VIP guests stood on the platform at the rear of their car to return the waves and the affection, a scene eagerly recorded by the journalists traveling with them.

The ex-Chief Executive of the US veritably basked in the glow of the lights of the television cameras. Buoyed by the strong showing of public support he had received since the start of the train ride and by the presence of his good friend from Mexico, Weston falsely recalled how much he had enjoyed such public excursions with the press. In truth he had enjoyed meeting his constituents but had felt that largely ceremonial events such as this one had interfered with his job. And the press was, in his mind, a hugely unnecessary evil. Always dignified and ready with a smile, as President he nonetheless felt strained in front of the press corps, especially in the period leading up to his unsuccessful bid for reelection. Today was a different story.

"Yes, Cameron, it is a thrill to be on *el Águila de la Amistad*, but more especially so because of the opportunity to reunite with my good friend, President Portillo." President Weston placed his arm on the near shoulder of his *amigo*.

QNN reporter Cameron Neal was the network's eyes and ears for the inaugural run of the transnational train.

"President Portillo, what does this train symbolize for you and the people of Mexico?"

"Ms. Neal, *el Águila de la Amistad* represents a new symbol of an enduring friendship. The relationship between the United States of America and the United Mexican States has never been as strong as it is today. As much as anything else," Portillo continued in perfect English, "I believe it correctly moves the focus of the relationship from the realm of government and politics to that of individual Mexican and US citizens.

"The alliance of two nations can never be considered firm until it exists among the men and women whom the elected officials represent."

"Are you disappointed that President Mercer was unable to participate?" the reporter asked, wrongly assuming that he had been asked.

"Certainly it would have been wonderful if he had been able to be here" – even if the egomaniac has virtually neglected Mexico, he wanted to say. "But the trip could not have been considered complete without President Weston. His administration helped formed the foundation of the strong ties and mutual success we currently enjoy in the Mercer administration," Portillo graciously added.

"President Weston, you have made your home in Texas since you left office. You must be especially gratified at the role your adopted state plays in this endeavor…"

The interview continued for another fifteen minutes, with the two politicians giving canned, though no less true, responses to a reporter who smiled and nodded while ignoring the answers as she listened to the bodiless voice in her earpiece for prompts for the next question. Watching the scene, Julie Bishop smiled at her prospects as well. She loved the Westons. She loved working for them. But in the long term, being the aide to a hibernating former Chief Executive was far less beneficial to her career than holding the same position for a vibrant, visible elder statesman. All the while he responded to questions from the press and bantered with passengers, the former American President smiled. Just like the good old days, she thought.

To President Portillo the difference in security precautions for the former US President and a sitting President was extraordinary. His friend's detail consisted of four agents instead of the legions that had followed him around while he was in office and the countless more that preceded him to every destination he would visit. There was, however, no doubting that they were armed for violence, if it ever became necessary. The arsenal at their disposal would outfit a small – maybe not so small – army. Through the US portion of the trip, outside the train, while it passed through populated areas, there was a greater presence by US Secret Service. Oddly, though, it was for the benefit of Portillo rather than Weston. It could not be allowed that a sitting foreign leader suffered harm while on American soil.

But the reduced number actually in his company was just fine with Weston. He had told Portillo more than a couple of times during the train ride, that he would just as soon be rid of the lot, but that, if he had to have the escorts, there were none he would rather have than these.

Portillo reflected on how he had first been impressed with that characteristic in Weston. Even while in the White House, there was a total lack of pretense. He never thought of himself as superior to anyone and was not afraid to get close to the people surrounding him. It was obvious in the affection he had for his agents. Portillo had seen both former President and Mrs. Weston chat with the individuals charged with their safety. The couple knew every detail of the agents' personal lives, even the two that were temporarily assigned to them.

However, though the presence of US security agents might be lacking, the United Mexican States' effort more than compensated. The country was providing additional security forces, not just for the protection of their

President, but also because of the responsibility they had as host to a foreign dignitary. The Mexican military and executive protection details provided agents in numbers appropriate for the circumstances. All but a handful were scattered throughout the other cars. Weston's contingent of four and a detail of four of Portillo's guards were in the Presidential Car. In spite of the added protection provided by the Latin country, the United States Secret Service was unwilling to completely entrust the security of even a former commander-in-chief to any other country's security forces. An advance team of two agents was sent through most of the villages along the train's route to make sure the way was clear. Thought had been given to sending a US helicopter ahead of the train to check throughout the countryside for any suspicious activity. But like many other things in governmental affairs, costs were cut in this area where obviously they should not have been. The Mexican government, however, deployed a McDonnell Douglas/Hughes MD500 light utility helicopter for forward reconnaissance ahead of the train while south of the border.

The Mexican protectors approached their responsibilities with tremendous gravity aboard the train as well. On the VIP car they had heavier arms than even the Americans, including sniper rifles and grenade launchers, mostly purchased from the United States. Oddly not a single member of the detail assigned to the car with Portillo was qualified on the specialized weapons.

Throughout the trip the tactics of security personnel in the US cities and towns and that in the Mexican villages were a study in contrast. With only a few exceptions the American Secret Service Agents and SWAT teams were discretely positioned, most of the former mingling covertly among the crowds of people and the latter positioned on rooftops. In the Mexican *ciudados*, though, the presence of security was highly visible by intent. Armed police and soldiers were on every street corner to deter any hint of violence or political demonstration. Between the villages, however, throughout the desert through which the train would pass, security was virtually nonexistent. The two Presidents joked that there was apparently a rule, known to terrorists and security teams alike, that it was unfair to attack outside of a populated area.

As the two VIP guests and their wives continued to mingle with other passengers, in the Presidential Car two of the men charged with their safety discussed mutual concerns.

Dan Pollard felt the little tingle that had served him well in his twenty-four years in law enforcement as he surveyed the landscape speeding past the windows.

"Miguel, I just don't like all the open spaces during this trip. They provide too many gaps in our coverage. When we're in or near a city of any size, it's obvious the security is adequate. But there are simply places we can't access in this terrain – not from the ground, at least."

Miguel Sanchez's accent was thick, but his English was passable. "It was our understanding that the US Secret Service would be providing air coverage by helicopters alongside ours."

"Hell, Miguel, budget cuts. I don't know how it is in your neck of the woods…"

"Excuse me?"

"Sorry. In your country. In the United States we are seeing a real drop in resources available to us."

Unaware that US overhead surveillance had ended at their border crossing, he continued. "But we do have a couple of Customs Services' Predator drones taking turns watching over us from around 20,000 feet, but no support of any other kind."

"I am confident our air surveillance will be sufficient, Danny."

"Of course, it will. I'm just the nervous type," Pollard conceded, but the subtle electric charge traveling his spine was saying something else.

Still, there was a trace of logic in the planning. There were few places to hide in the northern deserts of Mexico. The Mexican government believed the soldiers accompanying the dignitaries aboard the train were of sufficient numbers to forestall any problems that might occur along the route. The UAV flying above the route could theoretically identify any potential aerial threat to the safety of the important passengers traveling on the train long before it could realize that potential.

◆

In Jackson Hole, Maggie Loughlin sat at her desk, head rested on her hand, tapping her pencil rhythmically. She looked out the window at nothing in particular and wondered how Morgan's fishing was going.

There was no shortage of work to do. Since graduating from USC with double majors in Public Relations and Political Science, Maggie had had only three jobs. A time with a small public relations agency in Jackson led to an offer to join a large consulting firm in Dallas. She excelled there, becoming the go-to person for political image consulting. Maggie possessed a keen sense of what the public wanted to see in those in leadership roles in both private and public institutions. She had commanded immense respect and raised the bar in her firm for billable hours – and the associated rates – for her area of expertise. Ultimately, the longing for her home state prevailed over the professional success she was enjoying.

When Maggie announced her intentions to return to Wyoming to open her own image consultancy, her employers pulled out every device at their disposal to tempt her to stay. They ultimately offered to put Maggie on an accelerated track to a partnership, but the ploy failed. The lure of returning

home was too great. Yet in spite of her refusal, the senior partners all held
the young consultant in such high regard that they promised to send
business her way. And they were true to their word. Their referrals and
Maggie's own considerable aptitude for attracting prestigious clients made
Image Quest perpetually overwhelmed with new and repeat business. The
situation was exacerbated by the fact that the growing company was a two-
person operation. Since her administrative assistant left four months earlier
to be a stay-at-home mom, Maggie had run every aspect of her agency with
only her junior associate, a protégé she lured from Dallas with the appeal of
career potential that only a small firm can offer.

The travel demands were becoming more considerable as her business
grew, but she was in the midst of a stretch of over a month that included no
out-of-town trips. There was plenty of work on her plate, but today Maggie
felt no guilt about her lackluster approach to the tasks.

"Maggie? Yoo-hoo! Calling Maggie Loughlin!"

The boss turned toward her assistant. "Hmmm. Oh, yes, Curtis."

"I was wondering if I could use your brain today. It's apparent you
aren't going to need it." Curtis Jones let loose an almost impish giggle as he
swung a chair toward himself, straddled the seat, and rested his arms atop
the back. The paper sacks' contents strained at the containers as Jones set
them over the antique chair's wooden back and onto his mentor's desk. He
announced, "Lunch is served." He tore at the bags and lifted the enclosed
wrappings.

"Not quite with it today, huh?"

Maggie felt a small smile creeping onto her face and squelched it before
it fully manifested itself. "What'd you get us?"

"Well, the choices were prime rib, duck *al'orange*, pheasant under glass,
or hamburgers. I went with the burgers."

"Very funny. Thanks a lot." She twisted one corner of her mouth and
her eyebrows slanted below the auburn wisps hanging over her forehead as
she looked into the bag. Lifting the Styrofoam containers from the sack, she
turned her attention to her associate.

"So how are you and Tim doing?"

A red warmth emanated from Curtis' face and he shifted his eyes away
from his boss. "We're fine. Never better."

Maggie flipped on the small TV behind her desk. As the brightening
glow formed a picture, the image displayed two world leaders laughing and
gesturing in front of a train.

Seeing the former President Maggie said through an unladylike mouthful
of French fries, "You know Josh Morgan?"

Curtis dipped his head to one side trying to catch Maggie's blue eyes.
"Yeeaah?" His voice lilted as he smiled.

Now it was Maggie's turn. The red burst into her cheeks as she ducked her head to avoid the inquiring glance. She finally threw a fry at her subordinate. "Turd," she mumbled and faced him with a smile.

Jones cackled proudly upon provoking the embarrassment.

"Anyhow," she finally continued, pointing at the small TV, "I think Josh met him once."

"Who?"

"Weston."

"While he was the Prez?"

"I think. I don't know for sure."

"So how is... Josh?" Curtis' almost sang the name with two distinct syllables.

"Fine... I suppose." The flush returned.

◆

Isabella Portillo and Alicia Weston charmed their way through each of *el Águila's* passenger cars long after their husbands had retired to the haven of Railcar One at the rear of the train. Each woman served their country alongside their spouses beyond just their roles as confidants and fountains of endless moral support. The gracious ladies had inspired attention to charities and worthwhile causes. They had both impressed political pundits with their independent thinking. While philosophically in tune with their husbands, there were some differences and neither gave the impression of being mindless parrots simply regurgitating administration policies and doctrine. Many had observed that either Mrs. Weston or *Señora* Portillo might be able to mount a successful run for the Presidency in their respective nations because of their immense popularity.

Chatting amiably with every person aboard the train, they worked in concert. To the passengers aboard *el Águila* they were far more approachable than the politicians to whom they were wed. There was no mistaking who the real VIPs were.

Throughout history, despite intense precautions, threats occasionally penetrated even formidable shields around important persons. Sometimes it was mere luck, the sheer boldness of violent action provided a momentary advantage. For democratic nations it was impossible to totally prevent an evildoer from gaining a measure of proximity to leaders who mingled with his constituents. There were other times when an organized effort was simply able to move without detection.

In the sparsely inhabited Mexican state of Chihuahua, farmers and ranchers occasionally still rode horses and carried weapons. Those rare few that could afford them utilized four-wheel ATVs in place of living conveyance. So it was not unusual to see the occasional man alongside the tracks aboard one of these mechanical means of transportation. But the minimal attention given to securing the vast open stretches between towns in Mexico had allowed fifty men riding a combination of ATVs and horses to gather in one place.

Approximately halfway between the United States-Mexico border and the city of Chihuahua, very near the small Mexican village of *Cuesta de Muñiz*, at one of the beautiful vistas along the journey, the Mexican security forces' helicopter meandered above the terrain. Two Mexican federal security agents manned the craft, the Mexican pilot and a Secret Service Officer with binoculars. Passing over one of the many small, nondescript hills near the railroad tracks the eyes of the operation noticed, without the need of his optics, a band of onlookers approximately one-half kilometer from the right-of-way. He directed the pilot to approach the group slowly and to otherwise stand by. The MD500 drifted slowly toward the group of maybe ten mounted men, in the process skirting a bluff against which another forty were huddling undetected. Four aerial eyes were fixed through dark sunglasses on the more obvious group of men, who were now waving excitedly and smiling.

"What is happening?" the pilot inquired.

"*Nada.* Another group anxious to see *el Presidente*," the passenger misjudged.

"Call the train?"

"No. No, these people just wish to show their support for their leader," came mistake number two.

The chopper crew failed to detect the smoke trail of the FIM-92A Stinger. Streaking to a speed in excess of Mach Two it rose toward the exhaust of the chopper and struck it at the rear of the cabin. The destruction from the American-made Stinger missile was as instantaneous as it was unexpected. The Mexican helicopter crumpled into a heap as it hit the floor of the Mexican desert. The smoke was dark, though not extensive.

Two kilometers to the east *el Águila* cruised along the track. In the cab with the engineer and the rest of the train crew another pair of security agents scanned the horizon, focusing their attention almost exclusively on the lateral landscape, trusting the surveillance helicopter to assess conditions ahead of the train.

Over a small hill ahead rose a thin black column of smoke. The engineer driving the train observed the wisps but assumed that the observer on the helicopter would be aware of any risks from that area.

The locomotive neared the summit of one small mountain that opened into a flat valley before giving rise to another mountain. The train climbed the first gradient at nearly full speed. At almost the crest the Mexican security agent in the cab turned his attention forward. He saw the black smoke, which he traced to a smoldering heap of twisted metal on the ground as the valley floor came into view.

Over the smooth summit lay a long straight section of track, followed by a large curve in the tracks where they would begin the ascent of the second, slightly larger mountain. That the curve demanded a slower speed for safety made it necessary for the train to decelerate in the first section of the straightaway to a suitable pace through the valley as it headed to the pass. The engineer throttled back as his engine topped the hill to avoid gathering too much momentum going into the curve preceding the following hill.

At approximately the same time the Presidential Car completed the train's climb up the mountain, two sets of binoculars trained on the same point on the landscape below. The American of the pair raised his walkie-talkie to his mouth.

"Shit! Eagle's Nest," he called to the VIP car. "We have a situation. It looks as though the recon bird is down. I repeat: recon bird is…

"Look!" screamed the Mexican guard.

"Shit! Shit! Shit! Eagle's Nest, we have subjects approaching on the north side of the train!" He spun around to the southern window in the cabin. All clear.

"North side only!"

Just as the train had settled completely onto level ground, a band of about thirty men appeared alongside the string of cars making up the train. A handful rode ATVs with engines screaming as they advanced parallel to the cars. The remaining banditos galloped at full speed aboard their horses, moving to flank the car at the end of the train. Two-way radios crackled as alerts of the attack circulated among the security details throughout the train. Presidents Weston and Portillo were pushed to the floor by their guards. Agents and soldiers moved to windows in every car.

In the next-to-last railcar television photographers jockeyed for positions to record the unfolding event. And security agents pushed the two wives of the political leaders to the floor.

"Get down! Everyone get down!" yelled the agents.

Alicia Weston and Isabella Portillo peeked at one another through the arms that held them down. Their eyes mirrored the nausea and weakness racing through their bodies. Neither made a sound, either holding their breath or simply incapable of breathing due to the weight of the two men shielding them. Finally, hurried gasps exploded from each and the pressure of uncontrollable moisture erupted from their widened eyes.

Members of the security teams bolted through doorways to the open spaces between the cars to repel the assault.

"O, Madre… Madre de Dios!" came the high-pitched cry from the train's driver. "Jesucristo!" he continued, frantically crossing himself with one hand and pulling the throttle back with the other to slow the train. Lunging forward, a Mexican agent intervened, slamming the throttle forward in an attempt to distance the train from the approaching assailants.

The engineer fought off the visitor to the cab, again pulling the lever back. "Too fast! Curve!" he threw his hand at the bending tracks ahead. "Too fast!"

The two men settled into a stalemate. The train was traveling slower than desired in order to safely negotiate the tracks, and therefore too slow to separate itself from the bandits.

Its momentum now stalling the locomotive engine struggled in vain to accelerate. Suddenly it was the train's quivering driver who thrust the throttle lever forward to propel the now too-slow string of cars into a charge up the mountain. As the train lurched up the increasing grade one of the members of the Mexican security detail exited the railcar immediately in front of Railcar One onto the platform at the rear. He halfheartedly raised his weapon in the direction of the raiders; the real object of his attention was the metal coupling between the cars. Crouching and placing a hand on the lifting pin he attempted to sense the rhythm of the cars' movements. The irregular surges of the train as it struggled for constant speed up the incline tightened and slackened the space between the couples of the coaches causing them to continually bump into one another. At a moment of slack, the conspirator yanked the uncoupling lever.

At the same time Mendoza emerged from the Presidential Car and braced herself on the front gangway, placing herself nearly side-by-side with her Mexican counterpart. Suddenly the US agent realized that she was the only one firing. Agent Mendoza turned to look at the Mexican agent, fearing that he had been hit. Instead what she saw both confused and terrified her. Just a few feet away the security agent had removed the pin that would separate the Presidential Car from the rest of the train.

Mendoza did not waste time shouting to the man. Two shots in rapid succession felled the traitor, but the damage had been done, as the coupler sprang open. The US agent lunged to try to lock the cars together, but her efforts were in vain. As the engine pulled the rest of the train up the incline, gravity seized control of Railcar One, and almost instantaneously stifled its uphill progress. Agent Baker witnessed the situation and his associate's futile efforts on the gangway and yelled into his microphone for the team occupying the locomotive cab with the engineer to stop the train. Sparks flew as the train wheels locked up, throwing passengers, train personnel, TV crews, and security agents and soldiers off balance and to the floor. Agent Mendoza, distracted in trying to deal with the uncoupled cars, failed to see the rider move beside her, and was felled with two blasts from a shotgun. Teresa Mendoza felt her life slip away. Her last conscious thoughts were of her children, and her mother, whom she never called.

Another attacker aboard a four-wheeler sped westward and positioned himself between the VIP car and the train. The locomotive had ground to a halt and was beginning to reverse direction. The attacker flipped a switch activating a timer and dropped the bag he was carrying onto the tracks. He was just beginning to accelerate away when he was killed by a single shot from a Mexican sharpshooter's rifle. But he had accomplished his mission. Mere seconds after activation, the timer reached zero. The explosion shook the train and the now-detached Presidential Car. In deliberate overkill an unnecessarily large amount of explosives ripped apart the track. On each side of the three-foot deep, eight-foot diameter crater mangled ends of railway track stretched upward like skeletal fingers. Unaware of the damaged track, the engineer struggled to accelerate the slow- and backward-moving train until the final car drove into the crater. The car listed as it dropped, again throwing all on board to the floor, but somehow it managed to remain upright as the front end buckled with the car ahead of it. Reacting to sight of his train derailing, the engineer shut everything down and the entire string of cars and the engine came to rest.

Radio messages were flying among the train, the city of Chihuahua, Secret Service command posts, and Mexican security details. Time became as much an ally of the Americans and Mexicans aboard *el Águila de la Amistad* as it was an enemy to the small army assaulting them. The passenger car carrying former President Weston and Mexican President Portillo finally succumbed completely to the pull of gravity, stalling in its upward climb of the hill. As it did so, the entire gang of banditos moved rapidly to a safe distance from the security personnel's gunfire, whooping and hollering. Half the men set up a skirmish line far behind the section of train comprised of the engine and the remaining passenger cars. The destroyed section of track prevented the train from backing down the hill, but the security details would pursue on foot. The mobility given the attackers by their horses and vehicles should guarantee that they would buy the necessary time for the mission to be successfully completed.

Six attackers were killed during the initial assault. The remaining men rode at an angle away from the tracks to the bottom of the small valley where the car and its occupants would ultimately rest. The VIP car gained speed rapidly in its reverse flight downhill toward the bottom of the valley. The high rate of speed provided enough momentum to carry the train nearly one hundred meters up the other mountain, before gravity reasserted its grip. The car stopped and reversed course yet again, gaining speed as it moved westward on its original course. The battle between momentum and gravity sent the train in alternating directions. The shifts in inertia created another several passes back and forth through this small valley in the northern Mexican desert until the lone car came to a stop at the very bottom. With the attackers outside of effective gunfire range the three remaining US Secret Service Agents and four agents in the Mexican President's detail moved into strategic positions to defend against the attack that would come at any moment. Frantic calls to the US Customs office flying the drone above continued to demand help. However, help was already on the way. Two F-16s were scrambling from Holloman Air Force Base outside Alamogordo, New Mexico. Two helicopters with Army Special Forces A-Teams were taking to the air from Biggs Army Airfield at Fort Bliss in El Paso, Texas.

Of the original thirty attackers, eight now lay dead. Twelve of the survivors were engaged in a firefight up the tracks, holding off reinforcements that would try to reach the railcar where the prize lay waiting to be collected. An additional twenty men joined the other attackers remaining from the first wave at the bottom of the valley as they waited for the car to come to rest.

Despite their sophisticated weapons, the security forces knew the number and mobility of the assaulting force made the outcome inevitable. The best they could hope for was to hold off the attackers long enough for help to arrive. But even that held little comfort. They were quite literally in the middle of nowhere.

"What's in your arms locker?" Johnston demanded. The Mexican agent seated nearest it reached up and slammed his key in and twisted. A quick push released the spring-loaded lock popping the door open to expose a pair each of Swedish-made AT4 anti-armor rocket-propelled grenade launchers and M40A1 sniper rifles. The US Agent pointed and said, "Rifle." His Mexican counterpart thrust one of the 7.62mm weapons at him.

Johnston's time in the Army had given him exposure to a wide range of weaponry, but he was a truly gifted marksman with a rifle.

The Mexican banditos were cocky as they sat aboard their various mounts, waiting for the conclusion to the assault to unfold. But a pair of rapidly-fired shots from the Remington Model 700-based rifle in the VIP car brought their number down by two and sent the others scurrying in surprise. They regrouped and moved to relative safety behind the only small mound nearby. A combination of fear and rage overtook *Subcomandante* Morales' face. He nodded at one of the ATV drivers, who responded by pulling a transmitter from his pocket. The rebel flipped a switch and pressed a button. The ground shook from the ensuing explosion. This blast, by design, erupted a mere fifteen meters from Railcar One. After exploiting the ensuing silence for dramatic effect, Geraldo Morales raised a white cloth and rode ceremoniously aboard his brown mare to within one hundred and twenty meters of the car. He paused, lifted his head, and placed one hand on his waist. With his other he raised a bullhorn and spoke in Spanish.

Agent Johnston summed up his impression from his view out of one of the car's windows. "That little prick could strut sitting down."

"*Presidentes* Weston and Portillo. Your car has come to rest on a section of track that we have lined with explosives. The truth of my words was demonstrated a moment ago. We have no desire to kill anyone aboard but will if we must. We want only the American President. We will have him, or we will detonate the explosives and destroy the car and kill everyone inside."

Heads exchanged incredulous glances throughout the car. The former President spoke fluent Spanish, so he needed no interpreter. "I'll go," he immediately said to the Mexican leader.

"Out of the question, sir" corrected Agent Pollard from where he now crouched at the rear of the railcar. "Mr. President, if we can hold off these guys for another ten to twenty minutes, there will be two Air Force birds on the scene to blow their asses to hell."

"And as soon as the guys outside see it is hopeless, they will detonate the charges under this car anyhow. Son, it is time to cut our losses."

"I am waiting for your answer," came the voice outside. "And I am not a patient man." Morales knew that, despite the desert setting, they were not far from the city of Chihuahua and smaller towns. They had only minutes to complete their mission and make good their escape.

"*Amigo*," said Mexico's President, "this is not your decision. It is mine and I cannot let you do this. This is happening in my country on my watch." Weston tried to object, but Portillo waved him silent. "It is not simply one friend protecting the other. It is a matter of the ability of my people to right the wrongs that occur here, of our ability to defend our destinies from those who would take them. We must not let this succeed."

"*Señor Presidente*, we may have one chance to get you and the American President to safety," said Agent Miguel Sanchez. "The attackers have gathered on but one side of this car. Their overconfidence has left an opening. If we create a diversion, we may distract them long enough to get the two of you out of the car and run for the small mound about a hundred meters behind us. We would at least free ourselves from the threat of the explosives under the tracks. Perhaps then our superior weapons and training can enable us to hold them off long enough for the American fighters to arrive. And who knows, perhaps God will grant that the device to detonate the charges may itself be destroyed."

The former President spoke. "And they will kill us all there. We can't..."

"Trent, my friend. We will do as my agent recommends."

Agent Baker agreed. "Sir, ordinarily the train would be the safest place. But we know they aren't bluffing about having fireworks. We'll create some cover fire, then get you guys out."

Heads all around nodded agreement. Finally, President Weston consented.

Agent-in-charge Johnston spoke. "We need a diversion." He turned again to the arms closet where his eyes settled on the grenade launchers. "Sanchez, take one and give me one." The agent complied and Agent Johnston gave him the ten-second course in how to fire the AT4. He informed the rest of the security force of his plans.

"These things won't do much damage unless we hit someone dead on. They're designed to penetrate tanks before exploding, not blow huge craters. But they'll get some attention. We lob a couple of rockets, and then open up with everything else we have. Sirs, move to the door at the back of the car. Pollard, Martinez, get them out when you can! We'll give the bastards something to worry about!"

Jack Johnston watched the two dignitaries crawl to the exit. When the two reached the end of the car the agent paused, his smile reflecting his resignation, and winked at Pollard. Moving back to a window he examined the grenade launcher. The US Agent-in-charge looked at the remaining six agents as they prepared their weapons. Two Americans moved to a pair of windows broken during the initial attack. They prepared their RPGs, while their Mexican counterparts held automatic rifles. Johnston issued a warning, "Nobody stand behind the RPGs or you'll get fried when they launch."

Sanchez cast a sideways look at Pollard. The word was formed with his lips though the sound was never made. "Sorry." Pollard winked and shrugged.

Johnston looked at Teddy Bear Baker, and merely said, "It's what we do."

Baker announced, "Get ready, guys. As we stand to fire..." He looked at his associates, "Gentlemen, let's make this count. On three – go...go...go!" As he stood, he whispered, "Here's your frigging answer."

The rebel leader was astride his horse facing almost directly away from the railcar, speaking to a subordinate, when he saw the other's eyes widen and then tug frantically at his steed's reins. Morales could only turn enough to catch the sight of two smoke trails unfurling toward him before the first of the rockets landed scant meters from him. Though they were partially shielded by the small hill to which they had escaped after the earlier sniper shot, they had exposed themselves slightly while making their demands to the occupants of the car. The second rocket hit further away and did little but disorient some of the men, but the concussion of the closest one knocked Morales from his horse dazed. Two other men were killed and three wounded, each falling from his animal or mechanical mount. Almost simultaneously to the explosions of the grenades, the air was filled with the reports of automatic weapons, and the thuds of the bullets hitting all around the men held them in place behind the small mound. Only a handful of them had the presence of mind to raise their weapons and return fire. Several fled.

At the railcar Agent Pollard stood on the platform on the east end, firing his Uzi at the mostly-concealed band of attackers. President Portillo pushed President Weston through the doorway to give him the earliest opportunity for escape. The former President scrambled down the steps to the sandy soil and began to run for the tiny mound that he hoped would provide some measure of protection. Behind him President Portillo was exiting the doorway when a single bullet cleanly passed through Agent Pollard's chest and slammed into the left shoulder blade of the Mexican leader. His foot slipped from the top step of the car's platform and he fell backward, only partially catching himself on the metal railing alongside the small stairs. Portillo lay looking upward, desperately trying to summon the strength to move on. His American friend was some forty meters away from the car before he glanced back and saw the fallen leader clutching his shoulder with one hand and the small banister with the other. He turned to face the car, continuing backward up the terrain a few feet before stopping. He began his charge to help his *amigo*.

Behind the hill, what remained of the rebel band was beginning to summon its collective wits. Their leader disabled, many broke ranks and began to make a hasty retreat. For all their preparation and commitment to the cause, the thought of a battle with highly trained government agents offered little confidence of a victory so many fled. Some stood their ground. For these faithful, this mission offered the last hope for resurrecting their cause, and they would fight to the death. To them the only successful conclusion to this fight would be the capture of the American leader for their employer. The threat to blow up the entire railcar, though possible, was never a real option unless American planes and soldiers arrived on the scene.

The rebel in charge of the demolition had dropped the detonator when the exploding rockets threw him from his four-wheeled motorcycle. Gonzales lay quivering on the ground behind the overturned vehicle. His eyes searched for a route to escape. His ears listened for a lull during which to make his move. If the opportunity arose that he could safely run, he would. While the man considered his options, his eyes fell on the tiny transmitter on the ground. Gonzales reached cautiously and successfully for it. He looked about and, seeing dead and injured *amigos* around him, began to feel unquenchable panic overtaking him. "Mission be damned," he thought, and flipped the selector switch, then pressed the button.

President Portillo managed to rise weakly to a seated position and waved urgently and shouted, "No! No!" to the approaching figure of the American. He was attempting to rise when the end of the car on which he was standing was catapulted skyward. Ground zero for the detonation had been just forward of the end of the car through which they were escaping. The force lifted the entire car from the track, with the east end rising nearly a dozen feet in the air. The energy threw the Mexican leader upward from the platform an additional three meters and sent him laterally a dozen more. The American was approaching the car when the shock wave thrust him violently backward and to the ground, stunned by the concussive force. His Mexican peer fell just to his left.

As the end of the railroad car was settling back to earth, it landed askew of whatever remained of the tracks. Railcar One teetered momentarily before it finally succumbed to its off-balance position and fell on its side with a ferocious crash. Pieces of rail, the car, ties, and soil rained down for several seconds. Receding echoes bounced through the desert's hills and arroyos, punctuating the clatter of falling debris before giving way to an eerie quiet. Even the rebels who had been engaged up the hill with the forces from the train, and those forces themselves, turned in their confusion and gazed at the Presidential Car.

Morales, who had risen to his knees, spun his head to the man who had set off the explosion. Simon Guerra, a lieutenant to Morales, also glared at Gonzales. "*Estupido*," he shouted. "It is for nothing now." He turned and with one shot to the head ended the life of the imbecile whose actions had likely compromised their mission. Rising cautiously, Guerra stared at the train, fearing that all aboard were dead. He had no real concern except for their prize, the former US President. Though Morales was certain his plans lay in ruins along with the railcar, he had to know for sure. He motioned his lieutenant toward the train.

Summoning what bit of courage he still held, Guerra called to the other rebels, "*Muchachos, andale!*" He and the eleven or so remaining attackers in the group nearest the VIP car charged aboard their assorted mounts toward the smoldering heap of metal and wood. They received no fire from the overturned car and only token response from the train several hundred meters up the hill. The dozen that had survived the firefight at the skirmish line had broken ranks. Momentarily armed defenders would emerge from the cars and head to the assistance of their fallen leaders and comrades.

As they reached the overturned railcar two of the rebels jumped from their horses and climbed up the exposed bottom of the car onto its now upward-facing side. "Carefully," urged Guerra. "We must salvage whatever is left of our efforts. No more foolishness!"

The two men peered cautiously into the cabin of the car through the windows that now faced skyward. No movement. What had been the back of the car was totally destroyed, and pieces of the mangled undercarriage had pushed into what was the previously exquisitely decorated interior. The point man, Garcia, walked with great care along the side of the car. Continuing to gaze through shattered glass, he saw several bodies, some of which lay in carnage; others might for all the world simply have been sleeping. Garcia could not be sure that he had looked at every body in the car, but he could be certain of one thing: none of those he had seen was the American, or the Mexican *Presidente*. Then as he stood to indicate to the others that they may approach safely he noticed two additional bodies lying outside the car. He waved frantically to Guerra and to Morales, who was just now arriving at the car. The attacker scrambled off the car and there, a few meters from the distorted rear end of the Presidential Car, lay both Presidents.

While he gazed at the fallen Mexican leader it was obvious that he was seriously, perhaps mortally wounded. Blackened from the blast and filthy from the loose sand of the Mexican desert, he was barely recognizable as the vital, forceful President who had led his country for the last seven years. There was no regret tearing at Ernesto. Though he had no personal animosity toward this man – and Portillo seemed like a courageous man – he represented all against which he and others like him had struggled. Certainly the plan had never been to eliminate him, not with the multitudes of problems that would come with such an event. No, he was meant to live. Yet, there he lay, eyes dulled with pain disclosing only a glimmer of consciousness.

A few feet away, Morales beheld the man around whom this was all planned. There in the dust and dirt lay the man who had at one time been what people called "The Most Powerful Man in the World." As Morales reached the American, so did his companions. Guerra walked carefully, with a fair amount of fear, toward Weston. His fear was no less from the intense realization of what he and his men had done, than from the possibility that the man was dead, that everything that they had planned and attempted might be for naught. The implications of being hounded by authorities for murdering the man until he himself was caught and executed was only slightly less terrifying than being unable to deliver him to their sponsor. Guerra watched anxiously as Morales prodded the American with the end of the barrel of his rifle. From behind he heard a screaming proclamation. "*Terra y libertad!*" The crack of a gunshot echoed off the top of the car facing them, and both Morales and Guerra spun around in a crouch, their weapons at the ready. They saw Garcia, gun still pointed at the head of Portillo, smoke curling around its barrel. The blood from the *Presidente's* head mixed with the desert sand to form red mud. Morales rushed to Garcia and spun him around by his arm. He grabbed him violently by the throat, then glanced down at the now ex-Mexican President, who lay in the creeping red pool, his face a mishmash of tissue, skin and bones. Returning his attention to Garcia, the *Subcomandante* bellowed, "Is every one of you an idiot? The entire world will come down on us now!"

Morales was raising his pistol to the assassin's head when he heard Guerra behind him.

"Geraldo. *Amigo.*"

The angry subcommander held his glare on Garcia for another five seconds before lowering his weapon. He looked over his subordinate's shoulders at his lieutenant and was astonished to see him smiling. Guerra gestured to the fallen American.

Morales followed his pointing hand and, with incredible relief, saw the American's lids beginning to open, and then his head lifting tentatively from the ground.

CHAPTER 10

Today he was about one hundred miles from home fishing at the Henry's Fork, the southern fork of the Snake River that ran through eastern Idaho near the border with Wyoming. It had been a slow day. Henry's Fork is a notoriously tough place to catch fish, but Morgan had become an expert fisherman, and was almost always able to catch fish anywhere he went. Today had just been slow, with few fish presenting themselves as opportunities to be caught. But Morgan was a firm believer in the adage that "a bad day fishing was better than a good day working." And for about six years his life had progressively involved significantly more good or bad fishing days than good or bad working ones. And the beauty of the area and the tranquility of flyfishing made actually catching trout secondary to the activity itself. This late-July day, mild by even Idaho standards, had been picture perfect, fish or no fish.

Morgan was a familiar face around Last Chance, Idaho, often fishing Henry's Fork. The morning ritual was a stop at a local fly shop. Here he got the scoop on where and what the fish were biting.

At the other end of the day, the Texan religiously ate dinner before heading home. The photographer/spy turned fisherman generally stopped in to grab a burger at a small combination motel/restaurant, just across the highway from the fly shop. Occupying an older A-frame building, it served up some good grub. It was also one of the few places to grab a bite before hitting Highway 20 to head home. The evening's plans with Maggie preempted that ritual but he stopped in for a quick drink and a "hello" to the restaurant staff. Morgan was on a first name basis with most of them

96

due to the frequency of his visits. Most of the workers at the grill were avid flyfishers, too. They were fishing bums in the mold of their snow skiing counterparts. They worked at whatever jobs they could find to support their reason for living in Last Chance.

Morgan walked into the restaurant with a conflicting mixture of fatigue and refreshment and sat down at one of the tables.

"Hi, Josh. Do any good today?" Rick asked, sliding his customer the beer he knew to open for him.

"Hardly," he regretted. He raised the beer toward the waiter. "Thanks."

"Pretty weird about the President – well, former President, I mean," said the waiter as he laid the menu in front of Morgan.

Morgan pushed it aside and took a drink. "Come again."

"You know, the thing in Mexico. The kidnapping or whatever it is."

Morgan offered a blank stare to the young man. "Kidnapping? I'm afraid I…"

The waiter interrupted, "It's been all over the TV and radio. I guess you haven't heard. Anyhow, President Weston was on some train in Mexico or somewhere and some guys grabbed him. And the President of Mexico was killed."

"Portillo?" came the reply. Morgan rushed over to the bar for a better look at the obligatory TV. He glanced around until he saw the remote and turned up the volume. The television was tuned to the Quantum News Network. Tracy Adams, primetime anchor for QNN, was recapping the day's events.

"… of course, with his whereabouts unknown there is no way to speculate as to the condition of the former President." The anchor was in mid-sentence when Morgan began to comprehend the words. "At this time all indications point to a kidnapping. Certainly President Weston's body was not found at the scene, but the extensive amount of damage to the train car would seem to make it likely that he would have received at least some injuries."

"Holy shit!" whispered Morgan.

Rick stood behind his customer. "Say, you used to travel around all over taking pictures and stuff. Did you ever meet Weston?"

"Quiet!" demanded Morgan.

"Let's go live now to the scene for the latest information we have about this unfolding story," the anchor went on. "Here is Cameron Neal, near *Cuesta de Muñiz*, Mexico. Cameron was on the train when the events transpired. Cameron, what is the latest there?"

"Tracy, there is little more in the way of hard information surrounding what happened here, or why." The picture changed from a close-up of the reporter to an overhead view of the scene.

"Jesus," Morgan uttered, as he saw a railcar lying on its side. At one end of the car was a crater about twenty feet in diameter. As the camera aboard the helicopter panned about the area, what was obviously a number of covered bodies lay scattered in various places. Another crater was evident some distance away. A locomotive engine rested just ahead with several cars trailing, the final one leaning partially into a third hole.

Neal continued, "It has been confirmed that Mexican President Francisco Javier Portillo is dead. Again, it is official now – President Portillo of Mexico is dead. We have unofficial reports that only one member of the US and Mexican security details in the VIP car survived. The source goes on to say that, while in serious condition, he has been able to shed some light on the events of the day.

"Even for those of us on the train the details of the attack are sketchy. What we do know is this. President Weston, a near-recluse since losing his bid for reelection five years ago to President Wendell Mercer, had joined President Portillo on the inaugural run aboard the *Águila*. These two leaders had formed not only a strong political bond, but a close friendship during Weston's administration.

"Portillo credited the strong support received from the United States and from Weston personally for his success in supercharging the Mexican economy and starting his nation on a road to prosperity and a stronger standing in the world community."

Morgan listened impatiently as Neal continued to recite background material about Mexico's economic recovery, the two leaders' friendship, the symbolic nature of the train, and so on. "Crap. You were on the train when it happened. Get on with it," he urged through the television screen. What he wanted to hear were matters of substance.

"At around 3:40 p.m. Central Standard Time, a band of men attacked in what I can only liken to a train robbery in a western movie. Estimates of the number of attackers have ranged from twenty to about fifty. I saw around fifteen men during the brief time I had a clear view of the assault. While there is disagreement about the total number, we all agree that an initial group attacked the train and was later joined by reinforcements."

Morgan was dumbfounded at the description of the events.

"The attack was carried out aboard horses and four-wheeled all-terrain vehicles, used recreationally in the US, and by affluent ranchers here in Mexico. The Presidential VIP Car, seen in this overhead shot, was the last of the string of cars making up the train. It is not known how – even those of us aboard are confused as to the details – but it was separated from the rest of the train. Some have speculated that an explosion disengaged the car from the one I was on. However, complicating that theory is the fact that President Portillo's body was found outside the train."

The camera image changed from aerial back to ground level, showing the mangled VIP car from some distance away. Neal continued her narration. "There are two additional craters from explosions. One is up the hill – Barry, can you pan the camera up... yes, there it is... you can see it now. The end of the remaining string of cars rests in the second crater. Whether that explosion was meant to destroy the rest of the train is not known. Finally, one additional crater – Barry, yes, thanks – as you can see the final crater is quite some distance from the tracks. Early speculations were that these craters were from some form of launched explosive devices, such as rockets or grenades. Neither Barry nor I can confirm the method, but our experts have looked at our overhead views and stated unequivocally that they were formed by planted devices. So, the reason for a device so far from the tracks is unknown.

"You can also see that there are a number of bodies lying about the area. So far President Portillo's body is the only one to have been removed. Unofficial sources say he was pronounced dead at the scene by a gunshot wound to the head, though he reportedly had suffered other injuries as well. We also have unconfirmed reports that the lone surviving security agent from the Presidential Car is a US Secret Service Agent. While his condition is not known, he has apparently told authorities that President Weston had left the railcar prior to the explosion beneath it. One other item of note. QNN cameraman Barry Dement recorded some of the episode, including the explosions. All of us on the car just ahead of the Presidential Car, including the news crews were forced to keep low because of the gunfire being exchanged. However, Barry laid his camera in the open doorway and left it running while security agents ordered him to cover. The Mexican government has taken custody – temporarily, we hope – of the recording for its investigation. It's a little different environment here. But we have been assured that as soon as they have made a copy, the recording will be returned, and we will be allowed to air it. So at least for now, not much information at all, and very little sense from what we do have. Back to you, Tracy."

"Cameron, what have we heard from some of the other passengers traveling on the train?"

"Tracy, officials have prevented the passengers and crew aboard the other cars from speaking among themselves or with anyone else, including the news crews aboard the *Águila,* until they have been thoroughly debriefed. This has seriously limited our ability to report the story to you. Their accounts would be enlightening as to the nature of the explosions, and so forth. As soon as we are able to speak with other passengers we will be on live with that update. This is Cameron Neal, reporting live from northern Mexico."

"Thank you, Cameron," replied the anchor. As he spoke the "Breaking News" banner splashed across the television screen with the synthesized crescendo of the accompanying sound. Momentarily the news anchor reported.

"We have breaking news. Quantum News Network has just learned from a source who spoke on condition of anonymity that the US leg of the journey was monitored by an aerial drone, but that surveillance was discontinued once the train was on Mexican soil. I repeat, aerial drone surveillance was in place while the train was in the US but, unfortunately, ended at the border with Mexico. This certainly could have aided the search for President Weston. This is a developing story and we will provide more details as they are learned."

"What kind of boneheaded decision was that?" Morgan observed.

"We are maintaining uninterrupted coverage of this story. Certainly, nothing of this nature has ever occurred to a former President of the US. And even with Mexico's often volatile political history, it is unprecedented in the modern era…"

Morgan turned toward the door. "Gotta go, Rick." And with that he placed a ten-dollar bill on the bar and headed to his truck.

◆

The nearly two-hour drive seemed longer than usual. Morgan had indeed met President Weston. He had a history with the man, though the two had met only once. He owed the current life he enjoyed – hell, his life itself – to the integrity of this fine man.

Rounding the curve in the road to his house Morgan wasn't surprised to see the bright red Chevy pickup in his drive. Maggie had a key to his house for the rare times he traveled out of town and she had checked his mail and taken care of his dog. The last such occasion she had simply kept it.

The tired fisherman opened the door and said with a humor he didn't feel, "Loo-see, I'm home."

"Lucy" was walking toward him with an already opened bottle of Shiner Bock. Biscuit bounced over to him and received an affectionate pat on the head. Taking the beer from Maggie, Morgan simply raised his eyebrows and shook his head quietly. He threw back a long draw of the instant relief and walked to the couch in front of the muted TV. Maggie followed and sat down as Morgan turned the volume up.

Morgan's friend watched his reaction to the broadcast. "Pretty incredible, huh?"

He only nodded and took another drink. Finally, he managed a weak smile. "Yeah. Pretty incredible," he replied somberly. He reached down and slipped off his boots, then pitched his cap onto the coffee table.

The pair leaned back on the sofa in unison. Morgan resumed staring at the television, Maggie resumed staring at him.

"So, what do you think? Who's behind it?"

She received a shaking head and a shrug in reply. He held up the bottle and turned it absent-mindedly, gazing through its half-full liquid at the screen. "Could we have some coffee instead?" he asked, setting the bottle on the end table.

Maggie popped up and headed toward the kitchen. Morgan was never one to put things into the context of "woman's job" versus "man's job" so she understood he was just asking a favor. She measured the scoops of ground and sat on the floor with the Golden Retriever that had followed her into the room. She glanced over her shoulder at her friend mechanically surfing channels for information before finally settling on his customary channel.

The images were essentially the same on all the networks. None of the reporters was being allowed near the train, so most were standing alongside the barricades so that the cameras framed not only their faces but the overturned VIP car as well, lit by floodlights erected to facilitate the ongoing investigation and recovery operation. There was little new to the report and scant detail could be gleaned from the hotspots of light.

Maggie returned to the couch with Biscuit and sat down. She offered Morgan the steaming cup she cradled in her hands. Taking a drink from her own cup she slumped into place, leaned against her friend, and propped her feet on the coffee table.

Several minutes passed, each of the two companions blankly taking in the regurgitation of the limited facts about the tragedy. Biscuit dozed beside his master.

"It's a great night. We can go sit out on the porch."

Morgan's face turned only momentarily to hers before returning to its former position.

"Or not," Maggie sighed to herself. The soft light from the screen –

Morgan often watched TV in the dark – revealed a tiny bit of mist in his eyes. She wondered whether to speak, though not doing so was inherently against her nature.

Finally, "You're pretty upset with this."

"Yeah. Pretty."

"Wanna tell me about it?"

Just silence.

"Want me to take off my clothes and dance naked for you?"

At last, a smile.

Morgan rested his head against the sofa's back. He took a long, deep breath, and turned his eyes squarely on Maggie.

"Maggie when… Shit, I can't believe I'm about to do this.

CHAPTER 11

Morgan rested his elbows on his knees and propped his chin on his folded hands. He bit the corner on one side of his lips and gazed at Maggie for several moments. He considered asking her to promise that she would never repeat what she was about to hear, but if he didn't already trust her implicitly, he wouldn't be sharing this with her. He noticed Maggie's face; only her eyes held the faintest hint of emotion. There was a dampness forming in the deep blueness that Morgan didn't know how to interpret.

Finally, it was Maggie who spoke. "Josh, I'm not sure I want to hear what you're about to tell me."

Morgan reached for Maggie, took her hands and pulled her more closely beside him. He rested his forehead against hers. Finally, he leaned back yet again, still holding her hands inside his, as though trying to draw energy from her. He gulped in a lungful of O-two, flashed an inappropriately large grin, and began.

"The story you are about to hear is true. No names have been changed to protect the innocent," he said in an attempt to lighten the tension. Seeing that his attempt was fruitless, he continued.

"In the few years since you have known me, you have seen my life evolve, or I guess, devolve into a pretty big mess. You've been my best friend; you have strengthened me when I was in danger of self-destructing. Jeez, Mag, you even ignore me when I'm a jerk. I think you've earned the right to hear this." Morgan smiled again, but this time his eyes sagged at the corners and looked as if a film had formed over them. "Most of what I am going to tell you I know firsthand; the rest I have pieced together over the years.

"Before I came to Wyoming, I lived in Washington."

"I know that. You worked out of D.C. as a photojournalist."

"That's just it. I wasn't just a photojournalist. I worked for CIA."

"As a photographer?" The words came haltingly, and really sounded to be more of a statement than a question.

"As a case officer – a spy."

Maggie Loughlin leaned back in her chair, eyes widened. Morgan rose and stuck his hands in the pockets of his fishing pants. Walking a few steps, he scratched at the mortar between some of the huge stones that formed the fireplace. He stared at the mantle with the look of a boy whose mother had banished him to the corner for some misbehavior.

"I thought that was illegal. You know, using journalists as spies."

"Normally it is, but there are ways around it. The Richardson Amendment to the 1997 Intelligence Authorization Bill made it illegal, but another one called the Murtha Amendment provided some exceptions…" He waved his hand. "Doesn't matter.

"At college I satisfied my foreign language requirements with courses in Russian."

"I thought you took Spanish."

"I took a couple of semesters of that, too. My Spanish mostly comes from all the time I spent on my grandparents' farm. They had a lot of Mexicans working there, and I used to tag along behind them.

"Anyhow, I assisted my Russian professor as student advisor, and we got to be pretty good friends. He would invite me over to dinner at his home. A lot of times his wife would go to bed early and Dr. Crenshaw and I would sit out on the porch and just talk, often for hours. One night over some really good brandy, he filled me in on some of his life story. Turns out he had worked for the Agency; he was even stationed in Moscow. I was pretty impressed. He was the closest thing to James Bond I had met.

"Well, when I graduated, I got a job with a small magazine that was owned by the same company that owns Newsweek. I had a couple of photo essays get into Newsweek, wound up quitting my job about a year later to freelance.

"Dr. Crenshaw called me one night and asked if I could come back for his retirement party. Said he was hanging up his spurs at UT. He asked me to fly in a couple of days early and stay with him and his wife. My first evening there this other guy, a recruiter for CIA, came to their house. To make a long story short, the talk turned to me working for the Agency. After a rigorous interview process, I packed up and headed to the Farm. That's the CIA training facility at Camp Peary, Virginia. It seemed like the perfect solution for a guy like me who had no idea what he wanted to do when he grew up. I mean, with all the changes in majors, I wound up with a degree in journalism, a minor in psychology, and eight semesters of foreign languages.

"My Company career began as a NOC officer – Non-official Cover. Means I didn't work at an embassy or consulate. I was sort of a troubleshooter. It was pretty unusual for a rookie case officer, pretty heady stuff."

Morgan felt Maggie's presence behind and turned around. She took his hand and pulled him down to the hearth.

"You may not know much about a tiny Central American country named Terrador...," he began. And for the next half hour he provided his best friend with all the details about Terrador, about Victor, the overthrow of the dictator, and the rising of an opposition leader.

"So all those stories about our intelligence agencies' involvement with drug trafficking are true?" Maggie interrupted at one point.

"No. Not at all. At least I don't believe they are. I think they're largely overblown. But occasionally 'outlaws' in the community cross the line. You see, part of the deal in intelligence is that getting the job done means working with individuals on both sides of the line that separates good from bad. Largely, though, what we did fell in that in-between area, which is enormous and gray. Intelligence officers must come to terms that they will condone, even encourage many things they find morally appalling. Some people, after they've been around it long enough, simply find it less repulsive. It can be seductive, I suppose."

Maggie rose and went to the kitchen and poured two glasses of water. Morgan followed and sat on one of the barstools at the counter and continued his tale.

Maggie sat on a barstool beside Morgan's. "So, what has this all got to do with you? Or President Weston?"

"The bad guys in the US began to plot to get Salinas out of the way. He was intent on eliminating the last vestiges of involvement in drug trafficking in Terrador. There were hundreds of thousands – hell, probably millions – of dollars slipping away because of the man. They needed someone to act as the liaison between them and the insurgents they were trying to organize. They were going to assassinate Salinas. So yours truly was sent back to Terrador to act as a liaison between our bad guys and their bad guys." Morgan paused and turned to face Maggie squarely.

She looked at him, tilting her head to one side, her eyes slightly squinted. After the brief silence, they widened, and Maggie leaned abruptly back on the stool. "Jesus, Morgan. You were involved in this? You were helping to assassinate Salinas? I can't... I... I don't know what to say."

"Neither do I, Maggie." Morgan lowered his eyes.

"Shit, Josh, it's not just immoral. It was illegal then, wasn't it, for the US to try to assassinate a foreign leader? You had to know that, Josh."

"I did. But I was pretty green. I mean, that's why they picked me. Maggie, there are rules for public consumption; then there are the real rules. I figured this fell into that category of things you tell citizens you don't do, when really you do. There is the term – I know you know it – plausible deniability. No US resources were going to be directly involved in the hit."

"Dammit, Morgan. That's shit, and you know it. And this Salinas guy was trying to be friends with us. You knew that, too."

Morgan's head jerked up and to one side. His eyes flashed. "That I didn't know. You've got to believe me when I tell you that I believed it to be a legitimate operation." He stroked his face and let out a deep breath. "Listen, they had me convinced that Salinas was not what he appeared, that his intentions were entirely different than what he was saying. And that…" Morgan stopped and collected himself.

"There was this guy in NSA, Everson Thomas Blake." Morgan almost hissed the name. "Ev Blake was a career analyst there, after a short stint at CIA. He set up the alliance with Castañeda in the drug thing and the money laundering. He had a couple of guys working under him; they were falsifying intelligence and surveillance reports, covering up what was really going on in Terrador. To tell the truth, Terrador was such a piddly-assed country in the grand scheme of things, I don't think anyone would have really given a shit about what Blake was up to, as long as it stayed out of the press. But it was, after all, something he could go to jail for. And I'm sure he was involved more than just superficially.

"He had to have some guys at CIA in on it. I still don't know who they were. Nobody very high up ever got prosecuted, or even fired, on that side of the op. Just the grunts. The crux of the matter is that my handlers had me convinced that Salinas was about to reestablish the drug flow big time." Morgan chuckled. "Ironically, they convinced me that we were fighting the drug flow, but we were really just trying to facilitate it. They told me a resistance force had been organized to overthrow and eliminate Salinas. My cover allowed me to move freely in Terrador and liaise among the various players and find out what support they needed from the US."

Morgan gulped down the last of his ice water.

"So, what happened, Morgan?"

"He turned to Maggie again. He laughed, "Why, I screwed up the whole op, of course!"

"How did you know? How did you figure out that…?"

"What I was seeing just didn't mesh with what I was hearing from the guys at Langley, you know, through our embassy in Terrador. I mean, first of all, they told me I wasn't to discuss any of this with the diplomats there, not even the Agency's Station Chief. It just didn't feel right, you know."

For the first time since she assumed the role of priest to Morgan's confession, Maggie smiled. Josh Morgan, she thought, had better instincts that anyone she had ever met. He had this x-ray vision that saw right through to the heart of everything. With intuition like that, he must really be in touch with his feminine side, she joked to herself.

"Did you tell them that… that something wasn't right?"

"Hell, yes, I told them. I had some real problems with this op. But they told me, basically, that I was not to question why; mine was just to do or die." He halted abruptly, and then smiled at how corny that sounded.

"They said this was approved at the highest levels of the Agency and the government. The implication was crystal clear. Weston was President then. You know he had once served as Director of Central Intelligence, right? As President, he was known to immerse himself in intelligence matters more than any of his predecessors. So I figured he had signed off on this and I pressed on.

"What I didn't know was that, in Blake's plan, not only must Salinas be eliminated, but it must be obvious that Americans were behind it. This would guarantee that the US would never again interfere in Terrador's, or in other words Blake's business. It would even make it difficult for Weston to get the support for anti-drug operations anywhere. Blake and his gang would be back in business. Weston would be ruined. As DCI, Weston was very popular at operational levels within the agencies. But he was persona non grata with much of the management. His tenure at CIA had consisted of a massive effort to transform the Company. He wanted to make it more efficient, more accountable to the people. But there were a lot of hard feelings among the top spooks. So then Weston becomes President and pledges the same sort of overhaul as he wanted as DCI. At CIA Weston was a nuisance to Blake, but from the Oval Office he had his sights set on the NSA as well, and that was personal. The President had other things to worry about when the whole Middle East environment blew up – again. But there were no doubts the man had his sights on the Agencies. He had to go."

Morgan's eyes rolled back and he shook his head in a sort of self-indictment.

"So Ev Blake had this raw field officer – me – to run the American side of an op to assassinate President Salinas.

"It would probably be leaked that I was with CIA, and that responsibility for the act lay in the White House itself. Fabricated information – shoot, some of it wouldn't even be fabricated – would be given to the Intelligence Oversight Committee. There would be fallout within the agencies, sure, but that would pass, and things would return to normal for Blake."

Maggie was leaning forward, listening intently now, as though to an audio tape of a Nelson DeMille novel. "So how did you stop the thing?"

"It hit me, finally, that there were two ops being run – the one to implicate the country and the President through me. The other, to make sure that the hit was successful and that my side of the story was neutralized. After it was all done, it occurred to me that the only way out for them was to neutralize me, too.

Maggie's shiver was visible.

"I developed a source... It was luck, Maggie, pure luck, but he found out that I was being set up to be eliminated earlier than originally planned. You know, because of my snooping around." The next several minutes were a play-by-play of how he was set up for ambush, how Victor Palacios gave his life to save him.

Morgan's voice was barely audible to Maggie now. He rose from the stool and walked to the large window overlooking the hill sloping from his house toward the road. The almost full moon lit up the landscape in a surreal way that matched Morgan's story. Maggie, still seated, simply waited until Morgan was ready to resume his revelation.

"Sirens had begun to wail and the remaining attackers got the hell outta there. I stooped down to look at Victor, but there was... It was no use. I sat on one knee, and then all of a sudden, police were everywhere. I went over to the bastard that had shot at me. The hole in the rear of his head was massive, but the entry wound was small, and, Maggie," – Morgan turned to face her now – "I recognized the man. He was American. He was another CIA officer that had been seconded to NSA. Maggie, he reported to Blake."

"So you nailed Blake?"

"Hardly. I was taken in for questioning. I had friends on the police force who vouched for me, so they ultimately accepted my story and let me go. My first conclusion about the American was that he was working for the wrong team, that is, for Salinas. Almost immediately I had to face the fact that the guy wasn't working for Salinas at all but for Blake. I think he was supposed to be there just as an observer, to make sure it got done, and maybe a backup. I don't know. Maggie, I've been in dangerous situations in my cover as a photojournalist. I've even nearly been shot on a few occasions. But this was the first time I had been shot at. The gun was aimed at me personally. I wasn't just in the line of fire. You know, it's kind of sobering to know that someone in your own government wants you dead. And of course, there was evidence beyond any doubt that I was being played.

"I decided that the best course of action was to go right to the target. I knew that I was on a short timetable because the hit on Salinas was scheduled for the next day. Some friends of mine got me a meeting with the man. Maggie, I was pretty well-known in journalistic circles."

"I know," Maggie reminded.

"After talking with Salinas personally, I was convinced he was a man of honor, so I spilled my guts. The attempt was made on his life. In fact, it still almost worked. Blake's guys changed the plans after I survived the attack in the alley. But what I knew was enough and, for the most part, it was Salinas' own security detail that prevented him from being killed."

That was not exactly the truth, but Morgan didn't think Maggie needed to know every detail about the way the episode played out. "I helped in a plan to assassinate a foreign leader, a man who, as you said, Maggie, was a friend to the United States." He turned to stare out the window again.

Maggie was behind him now and reached around him with both arms and eased herself to him. She laid the side of her head gently on Morgan's back.

"Josh, you saved the man's life."

"Maggie, the plan almost worked."

"If they hadn't picked you, they might have chosen someone who didn't put it together. It would have worked. Think about it."

From anyone else those words would have sounded hollow, but from his best friend, they made sense. He turned to embrace her, the drops from his eyes dampening her auburn hair.

It was after a long period of silence, the two standing by the window, that Maggie spoke again.

"What about Blake?" Morgan took Maggie's hand and led her to the sofa, where they sat down. He only pointed at the issue of Time, as though touching it would cause some sort of allergic reaction. Maggie picked up the magazine. It was opened to a picture of several men. She recognized the primary subject as the National Security Advisor. She looked at Morgan and shrugged.

"Read."

She commenced reading the half-column article in Time. "'National...'"

"The caption," Morgan interrupted.

"'National Security Advisor Templeton meets with NSA Director Stanford Grayson and Deputy Director Everson Blake...'"

Maggie's eyes blinked and her head flinched backward. She looked at Morgan, then back at the picture before her. She dropped the magazine on the coffee table and sagged back into the cushions of the couch. "I don't understand, Josh."

"Simple, Mag, he skated. In spite of what I think, and other things I know to be true, there was not one shred of hard evidence against the son of a bitch. People who worked for him were fired. One of them is in jail now, but even his testimony didn't convince anyone that Blake had done anything besides cover up some misrepresented security documents. Several low-level people were let go at CIA. Their names were never made public. But Blake – he got a letter of reprimand placed in his file. Somehow, he even made it look like he had a hand in exposing the assassination plot. They had picked up some communications intelligence, he said. That was what he had planned all along. The story would work either way, whether Salinas was killed or not. And CIA – I know there's gotta be at least one person there that was involved, but everyone thinks I'm full of shit."

The light clicked on. "Everyone but Weston! That's why you're taking this train thing so personally."

"Right. But it goes deeper than that. The day before I left Washington, I got a call to show up at the White House. Never been there; ordinarily would have been thrilled at the invitation. But you, know, it was like taking the fall for this thing wasn't enough. I was going to get reamed by some mid-level bureaucrat whose job it was to put the fear of God in me, lest I disclose what I knew about something that was, for the most part, a pretty insignificant news story.

"So, I show up as scheduled – you don't just not show up at the White House – and I'm ready to hold my ground. But I arrive at the guest entrance and they escort me to the West Wing. They seat me at this little waiting area. I don't even know where I'm at. Finally, a door opens and out walks Stan Grayson. He was already NSA Director at that time. A man I didn't know was escorting him. A Secret Service Agent goes with Grayson and the first guy comes to me and says, 'Mr. Morgan, the President will see you now.' My knees are so weak I can hardly get up. The guy leads me into the Oval Office. 'Shit,' I'm thinking. Now I figure Weston was really involved in this thing, and he wants to know first-hand what my intentions were."

"So, what did he want?" Maggie was holding her breath.

"He started off with 'Son,' so I figured it was gonna be the soft, patronizing approach that you expect from politicians. And that really disappointed me. I had really liked the guy, voted for him. So I brace myself and he says, 'Son, I'm convinced our nation owes you a debt of gratitude we can never repay.'"

Maggie's jaw dropped, "What!"

"Really. But he told me that there was no way he, or anyone, could overlook the fact that I had acted illegally. He said he was convinced that I believed I was acting under legitimate orders, but that I knew the laws relating to my job. But then he said he understood how, for a young intelligence officer, the world is often gray. President Weston told me to take some comfort in the fact that I had exposed the op for what it was. He said he believed I was acting out of patriotism, and in the best interests of my country."

"So, what do you think his meeting with Grayson was about?" Maggie asked.

"Oh, he told me what it was about. He told me he thought Blake was up to his neck in this thing and wasn't sure how he walked. And he said he told Grayson as much. Then he went on to talk about something that I knew but hadn't quite wanted to face, that my life was in danger."

Maggie squeezed her friend's hand more tightly now.

"I told him that I was a pretty well-known guy and that I thought my visibility would protect me. He assured me that it wouldn't, but that he would. Maggie, these are some very powerful, very dangerous men. They have the will and the resources to protect their interests. I knew far too much for them to ever feel safe. Plus, it was very personal for them. At that time, I was going quietly, you know, love of country and all that."

Despite the off-handedness of the remark, Maggie knew he meant it.

"But they weren't likely to leave anything to chance. Fear of a professional journalist digging around and all. President Weston made two promises to me. One was that he would get to the bottom of all this in his second term. He intended to have the necks of everyone involved.

"The second promise was that nothing would happen to me. He said he asked Stan Grayson if he knew anything else about the Terrador op. He said Grayson's denials were 'thicker than a vanilla shake' – his exact words – but he told him, in no uncertain terms, he said, that if anything happened to me, no matter how accidental it appeared, no matter how attributable to natural causes it might seem, their collective asses were his. He said that Grayson began to speak in the hypothetical, suggesting that, if my accusations about Blake's role in this whole fiasco were correct, it would be political suicide for the President to make public what had happened. An attempted assassination of a foreign leader authorized under his watch. Weston said he told them directly that he didn't give a rat's ass – and I believe he did, too – about politics when this type of injustice is being perpetrated."

"I'm speechless," Maggie stated.

"The President said it might take time; that his attention was going to turn to his re-election campaign, but that he'd take care of me. He said I would never again get back into CIA, but I could rest a little easier. He arranged for me to get a full pension just like I had been with the Company for thirty years. But the main thing was that he was going to be my insurance policy."

The light bulb clicked on for Maggie, "But then he lost the election for a second term."

Morgan nodded, "When that happened, I began to have a more difficult time with things. I mean, I think he's still taking care of me. Shoot, there is less political risk to him now if he publicizes the whole Salinas thing. And I believe him to be a man of honor. Why else would he have met with me, or care what happened to me? It's just that…"

Maggie completed her friend's sentence. "It's just that now he can't clean house and get the a-holes who started this whole thing."

Josh Morgan's nod was almost imperceptible.

"I can understand why this is so hard on you now – this whole train attack, the kidnapping. I don't know what to say, Josh."

"I owe him a huge debt and there's not a blasted thing I can do to help him."

So that was it. The "Most Powerful Man in the World," Maggie realized, had, in effect, Morgan's back. Even if he was no longer President, he was still the man to whom Morgan felt he owed everything. And now he was kidnapped, or worse. She rose to get Morgan another cup of coffee.

She returned to the man who had just bared his soul to her and sat beside him. There were a few token words, but it was apparent to Maggie that Morgan had concluded his confession. The talk turned to the television reports, and the scarce comments by the former spy held a different perspective for her now. She pulled her legs underneath her, took his arm, and laid her head on his shoulder.

The light emitted by the television provided the only illumination in the otherwise unlit room. The volume was low; there seemed to be little point in hearing the mindless repetition of unimportant facts. Nothing in the way of new information had been related for some time. So the pair sat entranced by the mind-numbing glow. A while later, after deciding that disclosure was the act du jour, Maggie whispered, "I've loved you for a long time, Josh."

The silence was awkward. Maggie had feared this uncertain response more than outright rejection. She had just exposed long secret feelings, but nothing in return. She pushed herself to an upright position, unsure of what to say and turned toward Morgan.

Then she smiled and gently exhaled. She guessed it was the hypnotic effect of the late-night TV. Or maybe the unburdening nature of his revelation had woven a spell. But whatever the cause, Morgan was sound asleep.

CHAPTER 12

DAY 6 – WEDNESDAY

In the city of Chihuahua, in the Mexican state of the same name, two friends had spent the night embracing and holding hands. One knew she was a widow; the other could only wonder. Despite the buzz of activity and the presence of security agents, both Mexican and US, Isabella Portillo and Alicia Weston were isolated by their feelings from every other person in the world.

El Presidente de los Estados Unidos Mexicanos Francisco Javier Portillo's body had been cleaned and subjected to the acts of indignity inherent in an autopsy. The Mexican equivalent of Air Force One had arrived to return the murdered leader to Mexico City. On her first day as former First Lady, *la Señora* Portillo had temporarily emptied herself of the tears that had marked the passing of the night. She clung to her American friend.

The new President of the United Mexican States José-Eduardo Herrera had called to express his shock and condolences to Mrs. Portillo and assured her that he would prefer to be there with her. She knew, of course, that, like all democracies, Mexico would not place a leader in an environment of violence, current or recent. The new leader of Mexico promised *Señora* Portillo that he and his wife would be at the airport to meet her on her arrival. For now, Mrs. Portillo could only wait for the preparation of her husband's body to be completed.

"*Amiga*, I am so sorry we have brought you and your husband into this." Her head never rose as she spoke to the former American First Lady. "You should not have been on the train with us."

Alicia Weston dismissed the apology as the illogical comments that people often expressed in the confused moments after a personal tragedy. "Trenton would – no – we would not have wanted to be anywhere else," she replied to her friend.

Unlike her Mexican counterpart, Mrs. Weston had shed few tears through the night. Her response had been the addled quietness of disbelief. Now the liquid emotion began to fill her eyes and stain her cheeks as much for her friend as herself. "I don't know how to help you." The words somehow penetrated the heaving sobs. "Oh, your precious children…" She pulled her Mexican friend to her.

"*Señora*, time will help us. You must not concern yourself with me. You must pray, as we do, for your husband. Mexico will work with your country to find Trenton and return him safely to you. I know that President Mercer will use every resource at his disposal to rescue your husband."

Now both women's eyes became fountains. The shared grief continued until one of the Mexican Secret Service Agents intervened.

"*Señora* Portillo, we are ready."

Two former first ladies rose and walked to the secured passageway leading to the waiting aircraft. Passing before them was a coffin draped with the flag of the United Mexican States. Members of the military, law enforcement, and other agencies, many shedding tears of their own, stood reverently as the casket carrying the remains of their leader was ushered up the ramp.

Nearby, with no less reverence, though without the same formality, three coffins, each covered by the Stars and Stripes, were being loaded onto an American military cargo plane. Inside lay the bodies of fallen American Secret Service Agents. Teresa Mendoza, Daniel Pollard, and Theodore Baker were also going home.

A final embrace between the two friends, smiles, and they separated, one to mourn, one to wait. First Lady Portillo moved to the awaiting Presidential airplane; First Lady Weston was escorted to the US government Gulfstream that would carry her to Dallas.

◆

The blindfold was removed roughly and even though the light was minimal, Trenton Weston's eyes winked shut. He had been handled roughly but was uninjured except for the scrapes and bruises from the train attack. He tried to turn his head toward the presence he felt behind him, but a hand forcefully spun it back around.

First a crease of light, then a fully opened door appeared before him. The opening revealed the silhouette of a man, small in stature, but stocky, legs spread slightly, hands folded behind his back.

The figure strode toward him at a firm, even gait. The olive drab of his camouflaged military-style garb was interrupted by patches of dirt and stains. Rips in the fabric of his jacket exposed a dingy undershirt.

"I am *Subcomandante* Morales," he said in Spanish. "I know you understand me, so do not pretend that you do not. I wished you to see the man who has conquered you."

"You have kidnapped me. You have not conquered me," the former leader of the free world returned in perfect Spanish.

The left side of Morales' moustache rose significantly as he circled his captive, hands still behind his back, black eyes remaining fixed on the American.

"We will see who has been defeated."

"Where am I?"

"You are on the brink of your judgement. You are going to face the verdict for your country's evils against the world."

"I wasn't aware we had committed any 'evils' against the Mexican people – or any part of the world."

Morales halted his pacing directly in front of the former American President. He placed his hands on the knees of the seated hostage and moved his face to within inches of Weston's. In spite of the other demands the circumstances placed on his senses the sixty-six-year-old Weston still recoiled slightly at the mixture of tequila, tobacco, and dental neglect that assaulted him.

"Your government has helped the Mexican officials in their cruelty to the indigenous people of my country. You gringos have assisted them in stealing from us. Your trade treaties let them rob us of our resources and justify it to the world."

Morales stood and lifted his head as he snapped around and marched away from his hostage. "You Americans are rich enough, but you want to take from us."

"So why have you taken me?"

"You are a prisoner of war. You are a war criminal," shouted the self-proclaimed Subcommander.

◆

"Let's get out of here. Let's go do something today."

Maggie's eyes struggled to open. Morgan was sitting on the edge of the bed, handing her a mug. Only her left eye opened at first and when it finally focused on the images around her, the sight caused her right eye to pop open. Instantly "on," she lurched up on her elbows and surveyed the room. She was in Morgan's room, in Morgan's bed. "Oh, God."

CHAPTER 13

Shit, this guy's diatribe sounds more Middle Eastern than Mexican, Weston observed. "You will put me on trial?"

"I will be paid by someone who will, *señor*. I have no use for you, no use at all," growled Morales with a wave of the hand. He turned away from the American. "I have enemies more important than you, but I need money to fight them."

"You use the word 'I' a lot. Is this your own private war?"

Morales spun around and took two quick steps toward the taunting specter, jamming his finger forcefully against his chest. "I am a patriot, you insolent pig!!"

Taking a cue from his *jefe* the guard behind Weston thrust the butt of his shotgun in the rear of the seated man's head. Recovering his senses, the ex-President saw the rebel leader kneeling before him, inquiring with his eyes whether his hostage was injured. The Mexican leader's eyes flashed upward toward the guard.

The former President mumbled, switching to English. "I, uh… I think I'm…" Then feigning greater difficulty than he really experienced, he returned to Spanish. "I think I'm going to pass out. I… uh, I need water."

Morales complied quickly – too quickly, Weston thought. So, I'm not supposed to be harmed, Weston realized. That might be helpful later, he hoped.

He watched as his captor opened the door and heard him shout for a canteen as he exited. During the delay the American surveyed the single room of the shack in which he was being held. There were two men besides the Subcommander and the subordinate behind the chair. Like their leader, they were dressed in a blend of military fatigues and civilian rags. One window, covered with a soiled blanket. No electrical outlets. One table, with a kerosene lamp. He heard shouting from at least two individuals outside, bringing the minimum total of bad guys to six.

◆

"So, was it good for you?" Morgan asked quietly, leaning over and brushing Maggie's hair away from her eyes.

Her first thought was that she would like to have remembered it. She pulled the sheet coyly to her body. "What are you doing in my room, kind sir?" she cooed, her voice reflecting some uncertainty.

Finally, Morgan cackled. "Relax. I slept on the couch." His houseguest joined the laughter.

"You're in a better mood, I see."

"Maggie, I know I can't keep going the way I have. So…" He walked to the window. "I am declaring my independence."

"From?"

He faced her, then looked up at an angle and put his forefinger to his lips. "Hmm. Good question. Where should I start?"

Maggie swung around to the edge of the bed and swigged some of the black go-juice Morgan had brought. Spying her jeans, she stood and wriggled into them, pulling them up over her panties. She and Morgan had known each other too long to be embarrassed, she figured. She tugged at her hiking boots and laced them up.

"Morgan, I can't."

"Can't?"

"Can't spend the day with you. I have meetings with clients all day long. But I'll be done at about six-thirty."

"Great. Can you take tomorrow off?"

She hesitated and let her gaze follow him down the stairs. Uncertain quite how to take the inquiry, Maggie finally followed him down the stairs and into the den. "I guess." A pause. "I mean, sure. It'll take a couple of calls. What'd you have in mind?"

Morgan turned, the smile seeming a bit incomplete without horns and a pitchfork. "I thought I might try to swing a cabin up at Yellowstone."

You could have driven a truck through the hole in the conversation. And Maggie was quite certain her heartbeat was as obvious to Morgan as it was to her. What was he suggesting?

"Cat got your tongue?" Suddenly Morgan was standing very close.

Maggie was beginning to lift up on her toes toward him when she felt her purse being pushed to her stomach.

"Better get out of here and get your stuff done so we can go."

Maggie took her purse and cut her eyes toward him as she moved to the door. "I haven't said I was going yet.'

Morgan followed her to the front porch. She never looked back as she bounced down the steps. She teased, "But I'll think about it." In her mind though, she was already wondering what slinky little thing she could buy today.

◆

In time, a *señorita*, in similar apparel to Morales', but tailored – and cleaner – arrived with a canteen. A very pretty face peeked through the dust. She moved slowly toward Weston, head tilted, eyebrows arched. She dangled the container by its cracked leather strap and, as she practically danced around the chair, rested her forefinger on the top of the foreigner's head.

"So. You are the American *Presidente*?" The English was broken enough that in other circumstances it might have held some amusement.

The hostage's eyes followed as she moved around him.

"I think you do not now look so powered. Are you powered?

The woman straddled the legs of the American as she sat on his lap facing him, trailing her legs on the floor behind her. Without a word she unscrewed the cap from the canteen. One hand lifted the man's chin with the pressure of a wisp of wind; the other placed the opening to parched lips. Then as the water began to roll down Former President Weston's throat, the temptress slammed the vessel into his mouth, the feathery support of her fingers becoming an upward thrust.

Weston lurched backward, throwing his head to one side to escape the rushing water. Gasping, coughing he tried to shake her from his lap.

"Oh, *pobresito*. You no like my *agua*? I have hurt you." The teaser lowered the canteen to the ground beside the chair. She placed her mouth close to Weston's ear and whispered, "Let me make it good."

The three men remaining in the room leered at the full length of the *señorita's* lean figure and grinned as she toyed with the gringo.

She placed one hand on his groin and began to massage him through his trousers. She cupped her hand underneath and lifted gently, squeezing him delicately between her thumb and fingers.

"There, my *jefe*. You are better, I think. Your new friend taking care of you, *si*?" Her words were a soft purr, but her hand became a suddenly clinched fist as she ripped at him with an upward motion. Leaping backward from her place astride Weston, she landed with a flourish of her feet befitting a flamenco dancer. The young woman's open hand shot toward the ceiling and her head flew straight back. The laugh pierced the air and went straight through Weston's agony to his soul.

As though caught up by a whirlwind his tormenter spun around, tumbling nearly to the floor. "*Puta!*" Morales exploded, releasing her from his grip. The young woman continued her frenzied laughter, staring past her leader toward the American. Her grin was finally silenced by the rebel *jefe's* closed fist and she sprawled across the dirt floor, sliding on her back headfirst into the planked wall. On raised elbows, the Mexican woman's black eyes pierced Morales for an instant before moving once again to Weston. She rose, refusing to wipe the red that was dribbling below her nose and from the corner of her mouth. She brushed at her clothes, though, and rose. Finally, her lower body twirled underneath her smiling head, which had returned to the subject of her torment. The performance over, the dark eyes drifted once more over Morales, the corners of full lips curled downward, and she paraded past him to the door.

Displaying what appeared to be a genuine mixture of concern and embarrassment, clinched yellowed teeth showed between Morales' parted lips. "Forgive the girl. Mariana is not as friendly as me," he said, this time in English. He reached and lifted the canteen gently to his captive's mouth, easing the welcome liquid into his mouth.

Returning the cap to the canteen, which he placed on the table, the rebel *subcomandante* lifted both arms ceremoniously toward the door. "You have a visitor."

Weston strained his eyes in an effort to make out the features of the figure approaching from the bright daylight of the open doorway. When his pupils dilated sufficiently to take in the man standing directly in front of him, what the former President of the United States saw was a man of distinctly Middle Easter origin.

"Replace the blindfold, you fool."

◆

Maggie had left Morgan wondering how to spend his day. As upset as he was about the Weston kidnapping, he decided he couldn't just sit around the television until the thing was resolved. Besides, there was absolutely nothing he could do.

He checked the news early in the day, but it was the same reports he had heard the night before. The only difference was that there were a lot more fluff pieces on Weston and Portillo – their political careers, how they had formed such a strong friendship. There were photos of Portillo's widow, and children, which Morgan found upsetting. But after listening to Alicia Weston describe her husband in such glowing terms, speaking of his honor and dignity, Morgan left to try to occupy his mind with other, less disconcerting matters.

Morgan went through the last of the coffee, stretched his arms behind him and walked outside.

Morgan had moved to a small apartment in Jackson Hole upon arriving from D.C. but lived there only eight months before buying the log home in which he now lived. As it turned out, the combination of the government pension he received – courtesy of President Weston – along with the fairly substantial sum of money he had saved from his days as a photojournalist, and the small amount of money he had inherited when his mother had passed away a year before had made it possible for him to live very comfortably. Certainly a home in most of the nicer areas around Jackson Hole proper was priced far beyond his means. Specifically, the exclusive area northwest of the city along the Snake River between Teton Village and the town of Moose, was pricier than he could afford. But the displaced Texan had stumbled onto a ten-acre plot there and he had somehow gotten to it before anyone else and before the couple selling it realized it was dramatically underpriced. Morgan never knew that his friend on Pennsylvania Avenue in Washington had worked behind the scenes for him yet again. So nestled among the ranches of movie stars, CEOs of major corporations, and politicians, near some of the best trout waters in the world, Morgan had begun his post-CIA life. Within a short drive of some of the most scenic landscape in the nation, Josh Morgan began a quiet, private life, catching many of those trout and photographing the animals and natural wonders in Grand Teton and Yellowstone National Parks.

On this morning Morgan chose to stay around his house and accomplish some delinquent tasks. His home was by no means large when compared to those of most of his neighbors, but at 2,900 square feet, it felt like a convention center for a single man, even one with as many diverse interests as he had. The house was built into the side of a small hill. The lower floor included a game room and a mostly-neglected weight room. The main floor contained the kitchen, dining area, den, a more formal sitting area, guest bedroom, and his office, which had actually been another small bedroom. The upstairs was merely a loft with a single bedroom with a spectacular view overlooking the meandering waters of the Snake River. The garage sat aside the main floor of the home to the south.

Many of the exceptional wildlife photographs Morgan had made required no more effort than to take his camera onto the porch that wrapped around the east and north sides of the main floor of his house. He had regular visitors on his property, including moose, coyote, and the occasional black bear. He had never seen grizzlies nor signs of them on his property, though on occasion they were seen in the Jackson area.

On the frequent days when he was in a bad mood, these spectacular surroundings provided some measure of solace. When he was in a good mood like today – a rare event – there was no better place on earth than home.

◆

"It's the real deal."

"So, what we have here is a ransom demand from Mexico?" Wendell Mercer confirmed.

"El Paso, actually," his Chief of Staff corrected. "Made good time. It was mailed day before yesterday."

"Jesus Christ!" Mercer muttered as he moved to the chair behind his desk. He continued to stare at the plain white paper. "And they want...?"

"Three million dollars," Henry James completed his sentence for him.

"I can read, Hank," POTUS barked, looking over his reading glasses.

"Yes, Mr. President. It's sure not much."

"Funny, I was just thinking it's about three million dollars more than he's worth." The laughter that followed made the Chief of Staff uneasy. As much as he liked the man, he was not without his indiscretions, and not just the coldness he sometimes displayed. How he found humor in anything related to this situation was amazing to Henry James. James couldn't know that the incongruous nature of Mercer's response to the situation was his initial relief that the abduction had nothing to do with the recent pact he had made with Saudi President al-Hashimi. But as POTUS put the event into context with the intelligence reports he had received – specifically the assessment that Saudi agents were somehow linked to Mexican rebels – a wave of nausea overcame the man.

Tiny beads of perspiration dotted the President's forehead. He rested his hands on his desk to halt the slight trembling. Time – he had to find a way to buy time to consider what all of this meant. al-Hashimi had every reason to despise Weston, but this was unthinkable. Had he abducted Weston? Was Weston dead? "God, what have I done?" President Wendell Mercer asked himself.

"Who knows about this, Hank?"

"The letter?"

"Yes. The damned letter."

"Just you and I, sir. Well, and the aide that opens and marks the mail. I was going to get it to the Bureau..."

"Let's just keep it between you and me, pal."

"Sir?"

"You have a problem with that?" the President challenged, standing with his hands on his hips.

"Wendell – I mean, Mr. President, this is, after all, evidence of a crime."

"So, you're telling me that you buy the story. Kidnapping for ransom by a bunch of Mexican banditos. We pony up three mil; they cough him up. And we all live happily after. That what you think, Hank?"

Silence.

"So, Hank, who do you think is behind this? You're a bright guy."

The Chief of Staff raised his head to look at his boss. His teeth ground together. He had to fight the urge to unbutton his collar as he felt the warmth rising up his neck to his face.

"Hank, Hank, sit down." Mercer placed his arm on his chief of staff's shoulder. It was an attempt at a fatherly gesture that annoyed James, especially since he was a year older than the President.

The President continued his pitch. "You were in the same meeting I was the other day." The two men sat down on the love seat across the Oval Office from the President's desk. The Chief Executive's voice was hushed. "If the Saudis are behind this, months of work by Secretary of State McGregor, her staff... Hell, Hank, you've invested a lot of energy in this new accord with President al-Hashimi. I've personally got a lot at stake if this blows up in my face. And if al-Hashimi has anything at all to do with this, that's exactly what will happen."

We finally get to the heart of the matter, the Chief of Staff thought. "What do you recommend, sir?"

"Time, buddy, time. We get our friends at NSA to look into this quietly. If we resolve this issue behind the scenes, then we salvage the trade talks, get Weston back... hell, we'll all be heroes. Shit, we get extra leverage over the Saudi bastards by threatening to make any involvement they have in this thing public." He left an opening for James to offer an objection, but in his heart, Mercer knew the man well enough to know that none would be forthcoming.

"So, what do you suggest, sir?" the aide's voice cracked.

POTUS propped his elbows on his knees and tapped his chin with his left hand. "Get Blake over here. He's sharp, and I get the feeling he's a team player."

James stared at his boss a few seconds. "And his boss?"

"Let's keep the circle small for now. Just Blake."

"Langley?"

"Piss on 'em. I don't trust Donleavy. And they're such a cult. If anyone over there gets wind of this, Chris'll know, too."

The President's staffer took a deep breath.

"What's on your mind, Hank?"

"Mr. Pres... Wendell, I wouldn't be doing my job if I didn't suggest alternatives to an issue." He finally worked up the nerve to make eye contact with his boss. "I say we give this letter to the Attorney General. Macy and you go back a longtime. Tell him to get a workup on it – quietly – and..."

The President stood now, towering over his still-seated Chief of Staff. It seemed like someone else's voice. "And you also aren't doing your job if you don't do what I tell you to. I'll expect Blake in my office this afternoon."

"Yes, sir. I'll clear my schedule so I…"

"I don't think you need to be here, James. Just arrange a time and have Mrs. Oakley work the rest of my schedule around it. In fact, forget that. I'll call him myself. That's all for now."

The good look Henry James got of his boss' back told him it was time to take his leave. Walking to his office, he lifted the phone, and pulled up a number from the computerized directory.

"Parnell," came the greeting from the DDI's direct line.

"Betsy, Henry James from over at the House. Got time for lunch?"

CHAPTER 14

"The prick," pronounced Betsy Parnell over the table at McCormick & Schmick's.

"So, you see my dilemma," the White House Chief of Staff concluded. "Christ, Bets. I've never gone behind his back on anything. And he can't find out that I have."

"Hank, I don't know if I can promise that."

"Please. You can act as if you developed the intel from another source. It's plausible. Of course, we won't have the 'ransom' demand to investigate, but we know at its core it's almost certainly a sham anyhow. Probably a ruse to buy the Saudis some time or misdirect us. But it does provide a lead. At least it's some indication where to look to find the real people behind this."

"Okay, I'll try. I have to tell the DCI."

"No, dammit!" Several people at other tables looked at James.

"You know what you're asking me to do, keeping Donleavy out of the loop?"

"No more than what I am doing."

"Yeah, but you volunteered for it. I didn't."

"Betsy," the Chief of Staff pleaded.

"Okay. Okay. But I can't do this alone. I'm going to talk to Ben Reid. He's senior at the Saudi Arabia desk. He's a good guy. I can trust him. I'll have him see if there is a way to tie this into al-Hashimi from his end. If we can cook up something, I'll go to Donleavy with what we get, and your name will stay out of it."

The DDI got up to leave just as the waiter was arriving with the check. "He's getting it," she remarked, with a gesture toward her lunch companion.

◆

Two of Morgan's projects seemed to be perpetually in-progress. The first was improving the attic space over his garage. The second seemingly endless project for Morgan was his half-hearted attempts at remodeling his office. He had been working at it for a couple of months with little to show for the effort. He decided that today would be a good day to resume those projects. He worked for about three hours and decided to break for lunch. He fixed a sandwich, grabbed a handful of potato chips from the bag and popped open a Sprite Zero. With a tired sigh he sat down in his chair to check on the latest news. The only thing worse than knowing what was transpiring was not knowing.

The helplessness he felt in this situation was overwhelming. He had met Weston only the one time, but the meeting had impacted his life dramatically. And now, at a time when Weston needed help, he was powerless. He had thought to call some of his former colleagues at CIA to get the real scoop on the situation, but the truth was that he had had very few real friends there. Furthermore, the elapsed time since his departure had put enough emotional distance between him and them that he would have felt uncomfortable calling them for an update.

The only close friend he had in the Company was Ben Reid, an analyst who had done well at the Agency. He had risen to the position of Senior Case Officer at the Saudi Arabia Desk, and now headed that department. And due to the emphasis on the Middle East in recent years, he had developed a close working relationship with the DDI, reporting directly to her. Ben and Morgan had entered CIA at the same time, albeit along different career paths. Ben was a strange mix of talent and physical appearance. He had attended the University of Michigan on a football scholarship, playing tight end on a national championship team. An African-American – he hated that term; he insisted he was simply an American – six feet eight inches in height, and weighing in at two hundred forty-five pounds, he had the imposing presence that prevented him from blending in anywhere as a field officer. But Reid had a burning desire to enter the intelligence field, so he learned Arabic. Gulf War Part One had convinced him that future threats to his country would be largely from Islamic extremists. The second war and the World Trade Center bombings and other terrorist attacks had proved him right. Analysis was not as glamorous as being a spook, but Ben was happier than he could ever have hoped. And his special language skills had put him on the fast track.

Reid and Morgan met by chance and hit it off immediately. When not on assignment in some far reaches of the world, Morgan would often go out on the town with Ben. And after Reid married his high school sweetheart, Rebecca, they would often have Morgan to their apartment for dinner. They had tried a couple of times to set Morgan up with Becky's girlfriends, but nothing ever worked out. Morgan was far too busy with his work to be able to commit the time and attention required to form a relationship. It was about a year after Ben and Becky Reid were married that Morgan's time at the Agency had ended. He had spoken to his friend only once since then, but corresponded somewhat more frequently via email. Morgan was thrilled when he found out that his friends were expecting. The Reids had a baby girl almost a year ago.

Morgan considered calling Reid to find out what was being said around the halls at Langley concerning the Weston abduction but decided against it. Morgan had important plans for the next couple of days. But he would certainly never be out of touch with civilization. He was sure Maggie would understand having his phone softly chirping alerts in the background while they… well, while they whatever. Yes, he was sure he would know things as soon as they happened.

Morgan left his lunch dishes in the kitchen sink and went to the garage. Never one to push any single chore to a conclusion before beginning another, he donned his protective eyeglasses and climbed the stepladder into the attic. However, upon reaching his perch he merely sat on the partially finished plywood decking. With forearms propped on knees pulled up to his chest, the man recalled the revelation he had sprung on Maggie the night before. The full realization of the impact of his disclosure rushed through Morgan. He removed the plastic goggles and leaned against one of the boxes of memories that had wound up in this loft.

Maggie Loughlin was the first non-agency individual Morgan had told about the events in and related to the Central American island country of Terrador. "If I had known how good it would feel, I would have told someone years ago," he thought. The fact was that there had been no one in his life that he felt he could tell; not until Maggie, that is. He had hinted at a secret past to some of his closest friends, but it was generally dismissed, he believed, as the macho insinuations that were pervasive among American males. Every male who has ever talked to a female in any American bar, it seemed, had been a Navy SEAL, a former pro athlete, or a spy. But in Morgan's case, the mysterious past was true. He wondered now if the occasional discrete references he made were attempts to offload some of the burden he carried.

Even his mother went to her grave without knowing her son's true occupation. He felt she would not have understood and would have been terrified if she felt her son had a dangerous career. Peggy Morgan had been uneasy enough with her son's "job" as a globe-trotting photojournalist because of the situations in which it placed him. Still, in retrospect, he wished he had told her. With no siblings, he trusted nobody enough to confide the details of his real occupation.

Today Morgan felt ten pounds lighter and years younger. He worried about Weston's safety but was able to deal with it in a rational manner. So, in spite of the calamities that still existed around the world, today, he thought, was perfect. He replaced his glasses, grabbed a hammer, and stood abruptly, only to feel the blunt impact of his head striking a rafter. His hand reflexively rose to the pain, dropping the hammer, which crashed partly through the flimsy sheetrock that formed the ceiling of the garage below.

"Well, maybe not entirely perfect," he grumbled to himself.

◆

Fadi Al-Majeed's soul burned violently within him as he spoke with his surrogate terrorist, but his outward appearance painted a calm, even amiable demeanor to Morales. He stared at the rebel leader and folded his hands behind him. "Come," he ordered, and turned toward the door. A dirty guard pushed the door open for the pair, only to receive a cold stare from the visitor and neglect from his commander. The door closed behind the two men.

The Saudi agent led Morales a good distance from the rickety shack where the product of their collaboration sat. The two business partners stood silently for several seconds until the *subcomandante* initiated the dialogue. "I did not think you were to come to Chihuahua, *amigo*. Why the change in plans?"

"That is what I have come to ask you. Why the change in plans?" the Saudi parroted. The blank expression Morales returned prompted him to continue, "The Mexican President?"

The reply began with a shrug and a smirk. "Regrettable, but simply the passionate act of an oppressed patriot."

"The 'passionate' action will create great difficulty in moving the American from your country in the manner we had arranged. And it was foolish to remove the blindfold, my friend."

"It does no harm." the Mexican insisted. "He does not see outside. Even if he did, he would not know where he is."

The Saudi conspirator countered, "But it was necessary to maintain secrecy with regard to our identities."

Morales laughed and slapped his sponsor on the back, "You assume he may be able to escape? Unlikely!"

"Unlikely?"

"Impossible. Escape is impossible, my friend."

The barely contained rage boiled within the Arab as he turned to confront the arrogance. "I take nothing for granted."

He stopped and looked toward the horizon. Morales moved beside him and looked as well.

"You see something, mi *amigo*?" He craned his neck to see around the scrub brush.

"What I see, brother, is the future. You have much to learn if you are to be an effective leader. Your rebellion will fail. Your men will abandon you. Your cause will be extinguished if you do not learn skills and begin to act with discipline."

Morales bristled in his *subcomandante* uniform. "My men are loyal to me. They respect me. They follow my command. Did we not deliver your prize to you?"

Al-Majeed looked down into his face. "I ask again, what of the Mexican President?"

The *SNZ* leader's countenance grew stern as he turned away from his accuser to again face the distant horizon. His chin rose slightly. "And I have given my answer."

"The very lack of discipline I warn you of."

"It changed nothing."

"It changed everything!"

"The man who shot him has been punished!" Morales faced the Saudi agent now and stretched his small frame to its full height before him.

"Because of this fool, the entire process for moving my prize, as you refer to him, out of your country has been compromised. It would have been hard enough to get the American beyond your borders if authorities only believed they were looking for a hostage held by Mexican revolutionaries. The level of security and the intensity of the investigation grew into a giant the moment the operation included an assassination. Every border checkpoint was closed. Even travel along your roads has become risky."

The Mexican rebel considered the ingratitude of this bastard. He had fulfilled his part, yet this pig was lecturing him. Perhaps a full minute elapsed before another word was given and, then, Morales' words were simply, "Did you bring the rest of my money?"

The Saudi intelligence agent's face expressed nothing, but he had just made a fateful decision.

"Yes, it is in my automobile. Please gather all your men, so that they may see my expression of gratitude and join in the celebration of our success. And bring liquor for a toast."

Morales' chest visibly inflated and the ends of his moustache rose with his smile. He clasped his hands behind his back and marched away to summon his band.

"Gracias! I will bring them to you."

Al-Majeed watched momentarily as the gullible fool left to assemble his men. The Muslim walked to the rental car and opened the trunk as the company of dirty revolutionaries congregated in front of the vehicle.

Morales handed Al-Majeed a half full bottle of tequila as he passed and positioned himself in front of the rag-tag bunch and announced with authority, "My men are all present."

"What of the girl I saw earlier?"

"She has gone to Chihuahua… for supplies, I have been told. I think she is unhappy with a… uh, a discussion we had earlier." Morales smiled and cast a look over his assembly of banditos, who erupted with laughter.

"Yes, I saw the results of your… discussion," Al-Majeed informed him. "Very well.

"I wish to thank you and reward you for your extraordinary efforts on behalf of my country and our great leader."

Morales granted a smug bow and translated the tribute for his men. One of the group whispered to another, "I hope he has brought the *dinero*."

President of the United States Wendell Mercer sat alone in the residence area of the White House. He found himself tapping rapidly on the arm of his easy chair, a nervous habit he had managed to mostly control for at least the last twenty years or so. A brandy snifter sat on the coffee table, its contents untouched. Beside it sat a plate with a ham and Swiss sandwich, likewise ignored. Mercer had managed to eat a few of the potato chips on the plate before pushing it away entirely.

He reached for the cognac, raised it to his lips before pausing and slinging it against the wall with a sharp crack. Mercer's sigh was more a gasp and he reached to massage his temples.

"What kind of shit have I stepped in?" he worried, pounding his fist lightly on his forehead.

Al-Majeed stood before the assembly of rag-tag rebels. "It is a custom among my people to celebrate victories and honor your allies with a toast." The Arab made up his comments as he went, realizing that these peasants would not know that his religion forbade the consumption of alcohol.

"It is with gratitude," he continued, "that I honor your accomplishment. My religion requires that the hands be empty of weapons during the toast as a symbol of friendship. So, in honor of Allah, and your God, please place your guns on the ground, line up and face the east." He paused while Morales directed his men. To Al-Majeed's amazement, every one of the twenty-three revolutionaries laid their weapons on the ground or against the front of his auto and lined up facing away from where he was standing.

The Arab passed the half empty bottle of tequila to the man farthest from him, understanding that all eyes would be on the bottle – and away from him – during the "celebration." He walked behind the lineup to the rear of his car, selecting two AK-47s on his way past the assorted weapons.

"The custom demands that we each drink from the same bottle." He almost smiled as the lambs so willingly followed him.

"Please drink, good friends. To our success!"

◆

Former POTUS Weston reacted dramatically at the sound of the automatic weapon fire originating outside the shack. His blood raced, and he prayed his rescue was beginning. Fearing stray bullets, he rocked his chair frantically until he fell to the floor and what he hoped was a safer position.

The gunfire seemed to carry on forever. Moments after it had ceased, he heard the creaking of the rotting wooden door as it opened. The light reflected from the high parts of his cheeks below his mask and into his eyes. He heard the sound of slowly-paced footfalls on the dirty floor, moving toward where he lay. A pair of hands lifted him from the ground and his chair into an upright position. But instead of removing his blindfold, the person spoke, "You seem to have fallen. You have been so much trouble. But you are worth it."

The accent was undeniably Middle-Eastern.

CHAPTER 15

Everson Blake found himself in the Oval Office for the second time in three days.

"Coffee. Mr. Blake? People call you, Ev, right?"

"Yes, sir, and coffee would be great, with cream please." He watched with some amazement as the President of the US poured the coffee himself.

"So, how are things over at NSA? You've been there a while."

"Longer than I care to remember, Mr. President."

The conversation went on like that for five minutes or so, with the Commander-in-Chief asking Blake about everything from whether he played golf to how his daughters were doing.

Finally, Blake himself put an end to the polite banter. "Sir, I appreciate your interest in me, but I suspect you didn't call me over on short notice for small talk."

"To the point. I like that." POTUS saw something in his guest's eyes that he understood. "You're right, but humor me a bit longer." He lifted the blue folder from his desk and, ignoring his vanity in front of the guest, donned his reading glasses. "I'm an avid reader. I had to take a shit one day and was wondering what I could read. I said, 'I know. I'll read Ev's file. Well, maybe that's not exactly how it happened, but let's just say that I am acquainted with your tenure over at the National Security Agency, and at CIA prior to that.

"Seems you have a letter of reprimand in your folder."

Blake looked Mercer squarely in the eyes and never flinched. "That's right, sir. I found myself in the uncomfortable and unjustified position..."

POTUS interrupted, "Right. And nobody in Leavenworth is ever guilty either. Ev, I don't care about any of the circumstances, though I will say that I don't believe for a minute that you were unaware of what was going on with the Salinas operation. It's beyond me how you survived that, but honestly, I don't give a crap if you were knee-deep in it. In fact, there's the strong possibility that you can help me with something."

There was a prolonged pause as Blake considered where the conversation was headed. Finally, "What can I do for you, Mr. President?"

◆

Despite his intentions to refrain from hovering around his television, it didn't take Morgan long to tire of the hot work in the attic of his garage and have his concern for President Weston take over. Sitting in front of the tube was simply the place he had to be. Maggie had called to let him know that she was still on schedule for their getaway.

As Morgan hung up the phone, the picture on the TV changed to the now-familiar overhead view of the area surrounding the damaged railcar. Morgan turned up the volume and listened, hoping for some good news.

◆

Ev handed the note back to the President. "Interesting situation, sir. I see your dilemma. If the truth of Saudi involvement gets out, bye-bye oil."

"Blake, we are just trying to open up avenues for peace in the Middle East," Mercer responded.

"Right, Mr. President. And all the convicts at Leavenworth?" He allowed time for the taunt to sink in before he went on, "And if you pay the ransom and don't get Weston back, you wind up with egg on your face."

Mercer began to think of Blake as a person with whom he could work. "You have sized it up rather concisely. There is another possibility."

"Yes, sir. If you get the former Prez back, and he knows the Saudis are involved…"

"Bye-bye oil."

Blake smiled at the Chief Executive's reply. "Yes, sir."

"So I need your help, Ev."

"What about Henry James?"

"I'm afraid Hank might feel a little overwhelmed by such a daunting task. He seemed, well, uncomfortable with my view on this matter."

"Then what do you suggest, Mr. President?"

The nation's highest officeholder rose and avoided Blake's eyes for the moment. "In the past you seemed to have a talent for creating, shall we say, appropriate paper trails to support a necessary conclusion."

"At least that's what I was accused of. Yes, sir."

"And if I am correct about the extent of your involvement in the Terrador fiasco, you have no qualms about the messier side of intelligence work either." He turned with folded arms to study his visitor's reaction. "Blake, I need this problem to go away." The Most Powerful Man in the World felt a wave of relief in the smile he saw on the Deputy Director's lips.

Blake twisted at one corner of his moustache. "I have always been willing to do whatever is needed to serve my God and my country, Mr. President. And I find no moral conflict in the sometimes-contradictory necessities of satisfying those two ends."

"I'm counting on it, Ev."

There was quietness in the Oval Office, but not of awkwardness or tension. It was the still recognition that a non-verbal contract had just been completed.

◆

Tracy Adams was once again on the air. Though his usual time slot was in the primetime hours from 6 until 11 p.m., in extraordinary circumstances he assumed the lead whatever the time of day. Morgan knew it was without a doubt good for his career, but it was also good for the network that viewers felt that they had the A-team on the job. The anchor turned the story over to the correspondent.

"This is Cameron Neal reporting live from *Cuesta de Muñiz*, Mexico. It seems that a veil of secrecy has enveloped the events of the last twenty-or-so hours. Officials are tight-lipped, offering few insights into the 'what' and 'why' of this amazing affair. Our video recording of the incident has not been returned. Needless to say, we are not pleased with the delay, but as I mentioned yesterday, things are done differently here."

"A little blunt for a news reporter," Morgan observed with a laugh.

"However," Neal continued, "we have now been able to talk to passengers aboard the train. Their eyewitness accounts have shed some light on the assault on the *Águila*. These details seem certain:

"The Presidential Car was not separated from the rest of the train by the force of the explosion that toppled it. Instead it was released – no one is quite sure how – and allowed to roll to the bottom of the hill where it came to rest.

"The explosions – there were actually three – came at intervals after the cars were separated. The first came almost immediately after the attack began and Railcar One had been separated from the rest of the train. The other explosions came some time later and were several minutes apart. It is not known which of the two occurred first, the one on the tracks or the one alongside them.

"Strangely, that is about the extent of the firsthand knowledge of the events by the train's passengers. Shortly after the assault had begun all of us were told to lie on the floors of their cars by the security details aboard the train. So, neither they nor we had a view of the…"

The QNN correspondent's summary stalled and she acquired that cockeyed look reporters get when being spoken to through their earphones.

"Tracy, Mexican authorities have just returned our tape from yesterday's events. We're going to play it for you now. It is unedited. You are seeing it at the same time we get our first look."

Morgan thought it a bit funny how the term "tape" was still used sometimes even though most of the video cameras in use now used hard drives to record digital files of the images they recorded. Old habits die hard, he supposed. He wondered if the reporter was even old enough to remember when actual tape was used.

There was the awkward delay while the digital file was being loaded and the reporter had nothing prepared to say. Finally, new images filled Morgan's television screen.

◆

An hour after Blake finished his meeting with the President, he placed a call to him.

"Sir, just on a lark, I made a check of phone records from a few people's desks and mobiles. One unusual hit. Hank James." He waited but received no reply, so he continued. "He called the DDI, then had lunch with her. I think we have to conclude the cat is out of the bag."

"That fucking little bastard."

"Yes, sir. I would recommend being proactive. Might I suggest that you arrange a meeting with my boss, the DCI, the Vice President, and James? Tell them, that after reconsidering Hank's recommendation, you decided he was right. Use the meeting to find out what they know. Then I will provide SIGINT leading them the wrong way. That should give me a head start.

"You need to ask my boss to have me report directly to you with regard to this matter. Mr. President, I have associates I will need to involve. And I must be able to exercise my own judgement and travel at will."

"Done," came the reply.

"Sir, this could get messy. I'm sure you are aware of that. And as a gesture of your support, I suppose you would call it, I would appreciate your backing on one longstanding personal matter. It primarily relates to the issue we discussed regarding my personnel file, but it could also impact the present situation. There is an individual that I believe could compromise the cover story if the operation concludes successfully."

"Blake, if you are successful in your current assignment, you have my word that you will be immune from any questions regarding your conduct, either abroad or at home."

The promise was followed by a dial tone.

Deputy Director Blake next performed some incidental tasks. He set up signal traffic surveillances on a number of people, from federal agencies in the District to a private residence in Jackson Hole, Wyoming.

Then Blake said a little prayer of thanks that God had given him the sword of righteousness to smite his enemies.

◆

The initial scenes were of the floor, walls, and ceiling of the railcar in which QNN's Barry Dement was being jostled around. The rough movement of the already-running camera was apparent. There was no sound track on the footage. The images that followed were all wide-angle shots from the single position where the video operator had placed the camera before he was forced to retreat to safety.

Neal began to narrate the recording.

"Tracy, nearest the train you can see a mish-mash of steel track extending from the sizable crater in the ground. So, the explosion had obviously taken place by now. Further down the hill you can see the VIP car rolling away from the rest of the train."

Morgan watched with amazement as the train rolled up the far hill, then back toward the camera, and away again, repeating the process until it came to rest at the floor of the valley.

Neal resumed her description. "You can see that some of the attackers have assumed positions behind the major portion of the train. Oh, God!" she cried as one of the men fell over wounded or dead from return fire. It was not graphic, but was real life and sudden.

She collected herself. "It appears that the rest of the attacking force moved away from the train. The car in which the Presidents rode is some distance from the camera as you can see."

The scene unfolded and soon an explosion thrust dirt violently into the sky.

"Tracy, we can now verify from the tape that the explosion away from the car occurred first. It is difficult to determine what caused it. Perhaps after we examine the images, we can get some more information. As you can see the assailants that rode away are out of view of the camera."

More of the video rolled until activity began at the railcar. The footage showed a man running away from the car, to the right from the camera's point-of-view. Then he turned and stopped. Just as he began to return to the train car, an explosion ripped at it, hurling the far end into the air. Though just larger than a speck, what was obviously a body could be seen flying away from the eruption.

Josh Morgan watched the remainder of the "tape" with trained detachment as attackers re-entered the camera's field of view. There, before the eyes of television viewers throughout the world, a man pointed his weapon at the figure on the ground – Cameron Neal identified it as President Portillo. Armed men took what must have been President Weston hostage. As they lifted him to his feet, the video instantly went to static.

The QNN crew seemed not to realize, but Morgan knew that the authorities had reserved everything else for themselves.

"Incredible stuff," understated Tracy. "Exclusive footage from Quantum News Network photographer Barry Dement.

"Cameron, our expert analysts have examined your previous footage of the scene and have speculated that the two charges near the felled VIP car were planted, or buried, and that the one nearer the train had apparently been set off atop the ground. It is not clear from the tape we have just seen. Any word on that?"

"Tracy, we have heard – unofficially, of course – the same conclusions. The damaged track behind the last car of the train obviously prevented the train from backing down to where the VIP car came to rest. And it would seem that the gunfire was an attempt to prevent any security personnel or soldiers from the train from moving to help President Portillo and former President Weston. Whether this was an intended part of the plan or not is not clear."

"Of course, it was planned, moron," thought Morgan.

Ms. Neal continued, "Speculation is rampant about the motive behind the assault…" She concluded her report with no additional revelations.

"That footage is making the rounds," Morgan said aloud.

Tracy Adams picked up the recap. "Thanks, Cameron. We have just learned that President Wendell Mercer will address the nation tonight. These will be his first personal comments about the tragedy that has unfolded over the last day. A statement was issued yesterday about two-and-a-half hours after the incident, but these will be the first public comments by Mercer himself. We understand that those comments will be delivered at eight-thirty Eastern Daylight Time."

Morgan's nose wrinkled and his eyebrows lowered as he thought about the current President. "Took you a day to figure out how to deal with this, I guess," he thought with no small amount of disdain. Some animosity towards the man he upset on Election Day was understandable, he guessed, but over the years Mercer made no effort to hide it. He exhibited a smugness with regard to his predecessor that would have been unbecoming to any man, but especially so for the President of the greatest nation on the earth. "Still," Morgan admitted to the TV screen, "I'd like to hear what the man has to say." He knew that Mercer often withheld important details about high-profile issues until he could reveal them himself. Perhaps tonight would be no different.

Morgan thought about the time conflict between President Wendy's speech and his "date" with Maggie. Surely she will understand if we leave an hour or so later, Morgan speculated.

President Mercer opened the door to the Oval Office and invited his guests in. Then he abruptly excused himself, left the office, and shut the door behind him. The surprised contingent of bureaucrats glanced curiously among themselves.

The Director of Central Intelligence spoke first. "Hank, what is this about?"

The President's Chief of Staff honestly confided, "No clue." I hope to hell he's going to brief all of you about the ransom note, he prayed silently.

DDI Elizabeth Parnell watched Henry James. He was cracking his knuckles. She noticed that the nails on his right hand were chewed to the quick. Then she exchanged a glance with her boss. Donleavy tilted his head discretely toward the fidgety James and raised his eyebrows. His younger protégé shrugged with her eyes.

Security Advisor Edgar Templeton was seated beside the NSA Director. "Stan, where's your boy?"

"Special project, Ed," Grayson returned tersely. "Compiling some intel into a briefing for the President."

Betsy noticed Hank's head swivel abruptly toward Grayson at the mention of the Chief of Staff's boss. She also realized that Vice President Melton-Hendrickson was not present. "Is Ben coming up with anything?" she silently hoped more than wondered.

In the private quarters of the Presidential mansion, Mercer was just washing his hands after a trip to the john when he heard the knock on the door.

"Dad?" Wesley Mercer had the run of the President's home.

"Wes! I wasn't expecting you." Father and son embraced.

"Figured you'd still be in the Office, Dad."

"Supposed to be. As a matter of fact, I have a few people down there waiting for me right now."

"Well, I'll let you get to them."

"No hurry, Son," POTUS explained, flopping onto the couch. "They're cooling their heels a bit. What gets you down to the District?"

"Cassandra had a meeting with Senator Kim on the insurance bill coming up for a vote next week. I came down with her. Promised her a tour of the House when she finishes up."

"Cassandra? Oh, the new junior partner at your firm. So, bring her over. Maybe it'll get you in her pants." The father winked at his son.

"Jeez, Dad."

"Seen your mother lately?"

"Last week, actually. She and Howard are doing fine."

"Old Howard," he chuckled. The Chief Executive rose and pulled down on his tie. "How is the old fart? Hell, a cunt married to a pussy!"

Wes stared at his father and leaned back on the love seat and smiled. But under his breath he muttered, "Damn you."

The White House's resident looked at his watch. "Twenty minutes. They should be pretty pissed by now," Mercer concluded. He slipped his coat back on, primped in the mirror and proceeded to the door. "Guess I should get down there. Stick around for dinner. Cassandra, too. I have to go on TV for a few minutes, then I should be free for a late one – dinner that is."

Wesley Mercer heard his father's laughter fading down the hallway.

◆

The President let out an artificial sigh as he addressed his guests. "Hank brought this letter to my attention. It came in the mail today." The President waited until his guests had each read their copy of the ransom note before continuing. "I believed the demand to be some sort of hoax, and disregarded Hank's recommendation to have it analyzed. But," and he turned to nod at his Chief of Staff, "James was right, in principle."

Henry James finally exhaled.

"In principle?" Chris Donleavy queried.

The Chief Executive stood and walked to the middle of the group. His plan was based loosely on Everson Blake's recommendation but included personal modifications. "Chris, there are multiple issues that will be affected if this demand is legitimate. We all debated the interpretation of certain intelligence last Sunday in this very place. I asked Everson Blake to assess the various viewpoints expressed then in light of new intercepts. Subsequent to my request to Blake, even more communiqués received by NSA shed light on the intentions of the Saudis."

Grayson was stunned at the suggestion that his Deputy was collating intelligence received by the NSA of which he had no knowledge.

"It turns out that there is indeed an operation underway by the Saudi Arabian government – against the nation of Mexico. Their intentions are to disrupt the flow of oil from the recently discovered fields." Mercer studied the faces of the group to measure the success of this lie.

"I have ordered Blake to Mexico to discuss the intercepts, indeed to warn them about this operation." Mercer looked at the NSA's Director. "Blake was the obvious choice since he best understands the content and nature of the intelligence findings."

Donleavy and Parnell turned in unison toward NSA Director Grayson to find him staring at the floor, arms folded tightly against his chest. The CIA representatives then turned their eyes toward one another.

Mercer resumed his monologue. "I have also dispatched Secretary of State McGregor first to the Mexican Embassy to underscore the diplomatic initiatives we have underway and to ask for restraint in reacting to the new information. She will then contact the Saudi Embassy to discuss the extent to which our negotiations will be jeopardized if actions are undertaken against our Mexican allies."

"Begging your pardon, Mr. President." It was the DCI who spoke, holding his hand up like a schoolboy beseeching his teacher for permission to speak. "Wouldn't it have been prudent to first approach the Saudis? With any luck the contact would forestall any operation. In addition, Mexico has many things on their minds right now, and may not be prepared for such discussions."

POTUS placed his hands on his waist and turned directly away from Donleavy. A pause increased the anticipation of Mercer's response to the subtle challenge.

"Mr. Director, it is not in our best interests to disclose our intelligence capabilities to Saudi officials. Furthermore, the business of government goes on despite the disasters that befall nations. The Mexican government will be happy to receive this assistance from us. Finally," – the President turned to face his challenger – "it is in the context of the tragedy in Mexico that the Secretary is visiting their embassy. She is the first representation of condolences from the United States.

"Let me conclude by saying that my orders to each of you are to stand down from any investigation, intelligence activities, or analyses regarding the Saudis' op or the Mexican train situation."

It was a contest to see whether Donleavy or Grayson would object first. The NSA Director prevailed.

"Sir, this is unprecedented. To cease collections…"

"Those are my orders. In addition, you are to refrain from discussions among yourselves or with any other person or persons regarding these matters. I trust we are clear."

And with that, President of the United States Wendell Mercer thanked his guests for their "cooperation" and excused himself.

Henry James and Ed Templeton, the two individuals in the meeting closest to the President were the first to leave and did so abruptly. On his way out, the Chief of Staff peeked over his shoulder at Betsy Parnell. His eyes were glazed, his shoulders were bowed. His briefings folders brushed the door frame and fell to the floor. James stooped to pick them up, paused with one palm flat on the carpet. Then in a single motion he scooped up the entire bunch of papers in a wad, and slowly rose. A quiet "mother fucker" announced his exit.

◆

In her office at Langley, Betsy Parnell sat at her desk, eyes closed, the index finger of her left hand tapping at her left earring in a slow rhythm.

"What's up, Betsy?" Ben Reid peeked into the open door of his boss' office. He followed up, "You feel bad?"

"Absolutely sick to my stomach, Ben. Sit down."

The analyst pulled the chair closer to Parnell's desk and waited.

In time, Betsy spoke. "Ben, I want you to listen very carefully to exactly what I have to say."

"Uh, sure boss." Reid knew something was up and anticipated her disclosure.

"I'm serious, I want you to listen very carefully to exactly what I say and then follow my directions precisely.

Reid wondered at the emphases on specific words.

"The President has ordered me, Donleavy – everyone in the damned meeting last Sunday except Everson Blake – to stand down on any direct intelligence collection regarding perceived operations by the Saudis in North America. Same goes for the attack on the train in Mexico. But you weren't at that meeting, were you, Ben?"

Her associate smiled as he caught on.

"He has told me unequivocally that I am to refrain from discussing these matters with anyone else until told otherwise.

"Having passed these orders along to you, let me clarify my expectations for your general work. I would expect that you continue to assimilate and analyze any intel of a generic nature that comes across your desk and to pass your findings along to the appropriate field personnel. I have every confidence in your work, so I see no reason for you to run every insignificant bit of data past me.

"Do you understand, Ben?"

"Yes, ma'am, I certainly do." The corners of his lips curled slightly upward again.

"Wonderful, now get out of here and back to work. I, on the other hand, am going home and explore my liquor cabinet."

Ben Reid turned into the hallway from the DDI's office. In other words, he interpreted, just keep you out of it.

◆

Maggie bounced through the door to find Morgan sitting in front of his widescreen. Her heart sank a bit as he motioned her to be quiet. She rebounded a bit at his double-take and ensuing reaction.

"God, Maggie, you look incredible! It's just like when we first met."

Maggie extended an arm, placed the other hand behind her newly cropped locks, and spun about in a mimic of a runway model. "I got it cut at lunch today – to celebrate meeting you again." Morgan continued to gaze as she walked to a spot behind where he sat on the couch and propped her elbows on his shoulders and her chin on the top of his head.

"Watch your show," she consented.

On the screen Tracy Adams was in his usual place behind the anchor desk. "Momentarily we will hear from the President about the events that are transfixing the world. We go now to Sandy Thomas, QNN Senior White House Correspondent, live at the White House briefing room."

Thomas had the look of a man ten years his junior. He had moved from field journalism to bureau work. Earning his stripes in London, then Paris, he was in his third year of covering the White House for Quantum News. He had a reputation for fearlessly interrogating anyone, up to and including the President. Yet his approach never came across as adversarial. Consequently, he was extremely popular with viewers. He was relentless in making sure that the question an interviewee answered was indeed the one he had been asked. And he was uniquely successful in that regard. He was unwilling to allow practiced politicians to use his questions as mere launching pads for talking points they intended to follow.

"The President is entering the room, along with Chief of Staff Henry James, Attorney General Stan Grayson, and National Security Advisor, General Ed Templeton," Thomas declared for the viewers. "Quite a lineup of high-ranking officials for the President's address. But more than a display of sympathy, their presence reflects the wide-ranging impact of yesterday's events on the United States itself."

White House Spokesman Art Faulkner announced, "Ladies and Gentlemen, the President of the United States."

President Wendell Michael Mercer strode purposefully through the doors to the press corps' left and made his way to the podium bearing the Presidential Seal. He glanced at his notes momentarily, then looked up and about the room of reporters awaiting his words. His eyes turned slightly downward again, and in the manner that had become a trademark expression for the man, sighed and nodded his head slowly three or four times before setting his notes aside and folding his hands on the lectern before him. This gave the erroneous appearance that the President was going to speak extemporaneously, but in fact he always had the

Teleprompters before him. Tonight, however, the man was genuinely going to address the nation from his heart. And the one thing that was closest to his heart was his approval ratings. So, he spoke unpracticed lines with practiced emotion.

"Let me first extend on behalf of every man, woman, and child in the United States our deepest sympathies to the people of Mexico, and more specifically, to the family of President Francisco Portillo for the tragedy that has befallen them. Mere words cannot convey the deep sorrow we feel for the President's wife, Isabella, and his three children, Jorge, José Lino, and little Margarita. We share your grief, as well as the utter contempt at this act of treachery, unprecedented in modern times, against your husband and father.

"The death of President Portillo is not only a loss to his nation, but to the world at large. An untiring advocate of peace and justice, this great man led Mexico through turbulent times as the architect of the economic and political transformation of his country. President Portillo's efforts elevated Mexico to a place of respect and influence not only in our hemisphere, but around the globe. Under his leadership the ties – no, the friendship – between the United States and Mexico became uncompromisingly strong, and the cornerstone for joint initiatives in peace and democracy far beyond the borders of our two nations. The loss of our friend – my friend – will not be easily overcome but the enduring alliance between his beloved Mexico and the United States will be his legacy.

"The cowardly assault on *el Águila de la Amistad* was an affront to a symbol of the friendship between our neighboring countries, to be sure. But it was also an attack against the freedom of good men and women everywhere, against the right to live and travel safely, against the right to vigorously pursue joy and happiness.

"The strike against the train was also a strike against the United States of America. We consider the kidnapping of former President Weston by this group of terrorists as a declaration of war against us and against all for which we stand. We will use every resource, every asset, every means at our disposal to bring these cowards to justice and ensure that President Weston is returned safely to his family and our nation.

"President Weston carried the standard of freedom and equality throughout the world. Under the banner of peace, he worked vigorously alongside President Portillo to build the strong relationship that exists between the United States and Mexico today.

"We ask every nation, every person in the world to join us in the condemnation of these rebels. Provide no safe harbor, no asylum for the conspirators who carried out this despicable act.

"The strength of individuals is not measured by how we respond in good times. The virtue of a nation is not found in our ability to persevere

142

and do right in times of prosperity. No, our power and our righteousness are found in the resolve to cling stridently to our convictions and to act unwaveringly according to our faith and our consciences when we are under siege by the evil forces of this world. We will survive this calamity, we will overcome this assault against human decency, and we will triumph over the false power of evil in our world.

"And to the perpetrators of this horrible deed we say, the forces of right will prevail. You will not succeed!"

As the President stepped away from the microphone, reporters began clamoring for the first question. But Mercer turned and walked through the doorways which closed behind him. White House Spokesman Faulkner considered the several departures in the Chief Executive's remarks from the words given him by his speechwriter. He knew they would lead to trouble as he returned to the podium. "I would be glad to answer just a few questions," he lied into the microphone, feeling less than "glad" at the prospect of fielding the question that was likely to lead the way. Nobody could say that President Mercer was not an eloquent, powerful orator when he chose to speak "from the heart" as he had just done. But he occasionally misspoke, or worse, used words that provoked certain lines of questioning or tipped off knowledge that was not intended to be revealed. Faulkner tried to avoid Sandy Thomas, but Thomas spoke through the other reporters and forced his seniority and his question to the fore anyway.

"Art, the President used the words 'rebels' and 'terrorists' in his remarks. What do you know about the individuals conspiring to conduct this murder and the kidnapping, and was the President indicating knowledge of an organization behind these acts?"

"Shit!" Faulkner almost said out loud. "You don't miss a thing, do you, Sandy?" he thought. "Why couldn't Mercer have just stuck to his friggin' script?!"

Then aloud, "Sandy. I would warn against reading much into the President's choice of words. I think he only meant to suggest that any act of this nature would certainly be categorized as an act of terrorism. And the fact that it was clearly carried out by Mexicans within their own country against their President would seem to classify it as an act of rebellion. The President's words weren't intended to indicate knowledge of an organization or specific group of people responsible for this attack. We have received a number of contacts claiming responsibility for the attack, but none to which we ascribe any legitimacy. We have received no – I repeat – no word from any source we consider to be associated with this act.

"Next question. Betty?" The questions were asked and answered – after a fashion – for another twenty minutes and the session was adjourned. Journalists scrambled for the door to frame commentary that they hoped their editors and readers or directors and viewers would find to be an interesting and informative accounting of a set of questions and an often unrelated set of answers.

On the way out of the briefing room Sandy Thomas was stopped by one of Faulkner's staffers who offered a coded phrase that signaled the impending leak of "anonymous" information to him. "Don't you ever change your jacket, Sandy?" he said in passing.

"I wonder what he's got for me this time," Thomas thought with a smile.

◆

Josh Morgan leaned forward in his chair in Jackson Hole, Wyoming, and tried to make sense of the jumbled, disjointed questions and statements he had just heard. His instincts were in high gear. The government obviously knew more than they were letting on. And he was even more certain that the answers to the questions after the President's remarks were less than truthful, even more so than usual.

Maggie watched a bit impatiently as Morgan lifted his phone and punched in the number of Ben Reid.

After his on-air summary of the President's remarks for the benefit of his network's viewers, QNN Correspondent Thomas worked in the White House Press Room, reviewing notes, organizing thoughts, and preparing questions for the subsequent interviews he knew he would be conducting. In time, press briefings were distributed to the pool of journalists. As the staff member approached Thomas, she took the envelope from the bottom of the stack and handed it to the reporter. Though he was dying to ascertain the contents, he simply tossed the unopened package into his open briefcase and continued to work.

After a suitable amount of time had elapsed, he gathered his belongings, said a few goodbyes, and headed to the apartment where he lived alone. Arriving there he opened the burgundy-colored satchel and retrieved the white envelope. He poured himself a much-needed rum and coke and sank onto his bed. Thomas tore into the package with the small White House seal in one corner and flipped the pages for the additional document that promised to be there.

After only a few lines of reading the journalist set his magic elixir on the nightstand and resumed reading again, more slowly this time. When he reached the bottom of the page, he swung his legs over the side of his bed and let out a deep breath.

"What the hell?"

Thomas had a standing agreement with Faulkner to postpone reporting leaked information for at least twelve hours. This was one of those times that would be hard to honor the arrangement.

A telephone rang in a cubicle in the headquarters of the Central Intelligence Agency in Langley, Virginia. Five rings and it was routed to voice mail. "Extension 8478," then the beep. The greeting was nondescript – CIA had no sense of humor when it came to announcing the name of the organization at which the call had arrived, or the name of the person whose extension had received it. The voice was that of a generic female, so Morgan couldn't be certain that he had reached Benny's desk. He briefly toyed with leaving a message but dismissed the idea as he considered the ramifications if he had reached a wrong number. He had no illusions about any secrecy attached to his call. As soon as the call rang the number was registered on the computerized PBX system, and before he heard the second ring, it had already been compared to a list of names and numbers and his identity logged.

Morgan turned to Maggie and the look on her face told him she expected the apology that he was about to deliver.

At the National Security Agency's headquarters in Fort Meade, Maryland, an email alert was automatically generated and forwarded to the mailbox in the "To:" field. The text listed incoming calls over the last hour to a number of individuals. The note detailed by target extension the time of the call, whether it was received or directed to voicemail, the calling number, and the name attached to it.

Everson Blake scanned the message; his eyes froze at one entry. He leaned back in his chair and bit at the earpiece of his reading glasses. "Well, hello, Morgan. What a coincidence. I've been thinking about you," he sneered to the email displayed on his monitor.

Then Blake picked up his own telephone and made a call.

CHAPTER 16

The news of the late-night broadcasts was that there was none. No new information, no leads, just a growing number of expert analysts offering their views on what might have happened, who might be behind it, where the former President might be being held, and why it might have been done. The regular news anchors and reporters must have been finding it a tremendous challenge to say the same things over and over again. The same aerial and ground photos of the scene of the attack on the train were being used. Occasionally new eyewitnesses from the train were interviewed on camera, but even their stories were repeats of one another. Like the news correspondents, they saw the initial assault on the train, but were hiding on the floor. They heard explosions and gunfire. Morgan flipped channels in the hopes that one station might break a story with actual facts.

Maggie had long since given up on her romantic getaway with Morgan and was watching the broadcast along with him. But she understood. He had too much emotion invested in the unfolding news story to ignore it. And in a way, she was glad. She hadn't seen Morgan so energized about anything in a very long time. He was focused, intense.

Morgan watched until after two-thirty, breaking occasionally to grab a snack or a beer. His occasional glance at Maggie registered pangs of guilt – and regret – but despite this he was beginning to feel that Weston would not be recovered quickly, and he was gripped with concern about the drama.

Maggie was sleeping on Morgan's bed. He walked in and stood beside her, considering whether to awaken her and crawl under the cover beside her. But he didn't want the first time to seem purely physical, so for the second night in a row, he laid the comforter on his sleeping friend and returned to his couch, with the television still on.

◆

Fadi Al-Majeed had waited until dark before leaving the vicinity of the rebel camp. He had hoped in vain that *la Señorita Mariana* would return, at which time he would dispose of the last witness to the *Zapatista*-Saudi Arabia alliance. But more than that he wanted the cover of dark to make his dash northward. Waiting until well after sundown he began the drive to the US-Mexican border. With security at extraordinary levels in Mexico because of the assassination of a popular President, the Saudi felt it would be easier to smuggle the American back into his own country than to attempt to follow the original plan.

He had made one accommodation to the new plan with a phone call to the Saudi Embassy in D.C. He spoke with a midlevel diplomat. The Station Chief had long since departed the office, but in reality, his involvement was not necessary. The matter at hand was strictly logistical. Within an hour after the telephone conversation was completed, a rented recreational vehicle left El Paso and headed west on I-10 and into southern New Mexico.

The most precarious part of Al-Majeed's intended journey would be the leg to the border. There was the strong likelihood of checkpoints along the Chihuahuan roads and highways. But it was likely, Al-Majeed thought, that the heaviest emphasis would be around Chihuahua and near the border. US and Mexican forces would search everyone at the border crossings on roads of all sizes. Illegal air traffic would be monitored as well, as would locations frequently used by illegal immigrants, he thought the Americans called them.

But the intelligence officer had another way in, if he could just get there. It would add hundreds of miles to his trip, but this was no time to be impatient.

He traveled west on State Highway 16 and circled Ciudad Chihuahua to the south on a small dirt road until joining Federal Highway 45 north and out of the city. Some 100 kilometers later the Mexican equivalent to a US Interstate split. Al-Majeed took the northwest split. The road intersected State Highway 10, which turned sharply north after extending west for fifty-four kilometers.

The entire journey had gone without threat or interruption until the Saudi neared the tiny town of Oñate, just south of Nuevos Casas Grandes. The flashing lights of the roadblock were visible almost two kilometers away. There were no dirt roads to flee to; no places to hide. He had topped a small rise in the road before seeing the red and blue bursts of light, so he knew his presence was as visible to the officials as theirs was to him. Since the traffic was light on the highway, he could not lose himself among other vehicles, and therefore any effort to turn the auto around would be instantly obvious. He took the binoculars he had secured at Morales' hideout and slowed the car. Al-Majeed had seen only one set of lights, but he wanted to be sure. The field glasses confirmed it – a single patrol car. He had really just one chance. He gathered what he needed from the seat beside him and proceeded at the speed limit. He timed his arrival at the checkpoint so that there were no other vehicles present.

The Arab slowed his auto. Despite his blindfold the former US President could detect the alternating red and blue from the patrol car. He listened intently.

The Mexican *policia* apparently was not radioing in information on every car he stopped. Without returning to his vehicle, he approached Al-Majeed's auto, one hand resting the beam of the flashlight onto the driver's face, and his other hand on the grip of his weapon. The obvious surprise of seeing a Middle-Easterner was apparent on his face, but nobody thought they were looking for a Saudi.

Al-Majeed prepared to execute his plan. As he lowered the window Weston began a muffled yell and thrashed around frantically. The distracted law official turned his attention and his light to the commotion in the back floorboard. As a result, he never saw Al-Majeed's already-drawn pistol. The last impressions of his life were two brilliant explosions of light on the periphery of his vision. His chest shook with the dual impacts.

The intelligence officer put one last round into the fallen policeman's head and hurriedly surveyed the highway in front and behind – no other vehicles. He jumped to the fallen officer and dragged him to his car. He returned to pick up the flashlight and pistol. Assuming a position behind the wheel he now saw the two dots of approaching headlights. He drove the patrol car directly behind his owned stopped vehicle, threw open the door, ran to his vehicle, spread his legs and leaned with both hands onto the trunk.

When the oncoming vehicle reached and passed him, the occupant saw a man awaiting search by the local *policia* who had caught him in some transgression. Fadi Al-Majeed maintained the position until well after the taillights became faint red glows, but was prepared to again use the pistol he had liberated from one of Morales' men.

Free to move again the agent scampered to the patrol car. He couldn't determine which switch extinguished the flashing lights, so he began flipping switches until they darkened. He put the car in gear and drove perpendicular to the highway over the Chihuahuan desert for about two hundred meters. With the darkened vehicle adequately off the road he sped back to his auto. He placed his foot calmly on the accelerator and resumed his deliberate drive for the border.

In the early days of planning the kidnapping of the former American President, Saudi Arabia had considered a number of partners. In retrospect, the choice seemed to have been a poor one, but at least the target of the plan was indeed in Al-Majeed's possession. One of the potential partners had been drug smugglers. And even though they were not selected and had no knowledge of the actual plan, they offered assistance in the form of logistics. They had no love for the Americans. Its citizens were simply customers. There was only contempt for the US government because of its interdictions in the flow of their products to the marketplace.

The most creative means of the traffickers in avoiding detection included firing packages of the drugs across the border with bazooka-like devices to waiting associates or using drones and even submarines in rare cases. But for the ease of large-scale movements across the border, one tried and true method had been the construction of tunnels. Some were large enough for a tractor-trailer to pass through though the Saudi's requirements were not so substantial. The United States Drug Enforcement Agency and Immigration and Naturalization Service had discovered many of the covert entryways into the US – but not all of them.

Weeks ago, Saudi agents in the United States delivered the arms and explosives used in the attack on the train to their Mexican partners through one of those tunnels on the New Mexican border with its namesake. Rifles of various types – Russian-made, even some American weaponry – grenade launchers, plastic explosives, detonators, and other essentials were smuggled into Mexico to the *SNZ* revolutionaries. They even provided cell and satellite phones to the surrogate terrorists. The Saudi agents provided assistance in planting the explosives along the railroad tracks and training the rebels in the use of the detonation devices.

Al-Majeed was nearing the same tunnel employed in the flow of supplies for the operation. He had traveled up Chihuahuan State Highway 2 without incident. From there he turned north onto the road to the Mexican town named after General Rodrigo M. Quevedo and its border partner, Columbus, New Mexico. Shortly after making the northward turn, he exited the paved road onto privately owned land. The almost-road was difficult to see even with the nearly full moonlight and the headlights of the vehicle were almost inadequate at picking up the changes in the terrain that could indicate where traffic had traversed the dirt in moving drugs and illegals into the United States.

Finally, after a brutal pounding over the desert earth, in and out of gullies, over and around mounds of sand, the Arab's headlights shone on the facility he hoped would make his trek easier. It had been more physically cruel to his prisoner than Al-Majeed would have preferred – he had been given specific orders to deliver Weston in perfect health – but under the circumstances it couldn't be helped. Al-Majeed promised himself he would be a more accommodating host once he was in the United States. In the hours following the kidnapping, corrupt officials at high places in the Mexican military and law enforcement agencies who were on the payroll of Saudi agents had directed the investigation away from the rebel hideout. He had been fearful that guilt over the unplanned killing of the Mexican President would cause someone in his employ to reveal the plan, but no such betrayal seems to have occurred. No such protection was available to the captor for the remainder of the road trip, but it mattered little at this point. The Arab and his companion were about to enter the jurisdiction of the United States of America.

The Saudi entered the southern end of the tunnel and after a short distance into it, the auto's headlights lit up the sight he had desperately wanted to see. Al-Majeed stopped the car, leaving its lights illuminated. Turning on the flashlight he had appropriated from the Mexican policeman, he walked a short distance ahead where an American Excursions rental recreational vehicle displaying Texas license plates was waiting. Inside were food and water, maps, and other essentials. His colleagues in the United States had done well.

Al-Majeed opened the rear door of the car that had carried him to this point. He helped the American to his feet, removed his blindfold, gag, and bindings. He encouraged him to move around. Finally, Al-Majeed handed the man a bottle of water from their new vehicle and offered him the opportunity to relieve himself behind one of the vehicles. He knew it had been a long, uncomfortable trip.

"You will be somewhat more comfortable for the remainder of the trip. How much so will depend largely on you. But until I have examined the truck more closely, you must take care of your business here."

The pair had driven through the night. Though he knew the sun would be rising soon, the intelligence agent needed rest, and time to think. The tunnel would be the perfect hideout while he collected his physical energy and his wits.

As he prepared to restrain his captive, the Saudi looked at the ex-President. The first comments from his captor in a number of hours were a puzzle to Weston.

The Saudi inquired, "We will spend the day here. How does it feel to be home?"

CHAPTER 17

DAY 7 – THURSDAY

A quick look at the newspaper, then the TV, but still no new information about the former President. The former CIA officer checked email – he had neglected to do so for days. But there were only the usual jokes from his small circle of friends and spam explaining how to get federal grants or announcing new herbal remedies for various ailments – nothing of importance.

Maggie slept until ten and rose in a decidedly good mood, much to Morgan's relief. She had apparently forgiven him for the change in plans from the night before, he realized.

Morgan made a trip into Jackson to get some dog food for Biscuit, run a few errands, then picked up a takeout pizza at Artisan Pizza, and headed home. By this time, it was almost noon. He walked into the house and felt the urge to kiss Maggie, but the two only exchanged smiles. He set the box containing the Italian pepperoni pizza on the coffee table and moved to the refrigerator for soft drinks to go with their lunch. From the television behind him, Morgan heard the now-familiar voice of Quantum News anchor Tracy Adams. "Jeez, what is he? The bionic news anchor?" he laughed.

"No way the senior person is going to give way on a story like this one," Maggie returned. "This is what they live for."

"We have a late-breaking update from White House news correspondent, Sandy Thomas."

The pair sat on the sofa.

"A source in Washington has indicated that a message has been received from the kidnappers of former United States President Trent Weston. The government official, speaking on condition of anonymity, informed me in a confidential phone call this morning that a demand has been received for a ransom of three million dollars for the safe return of the ex-Chief Executive.

"Despite claims to the contrary last night by White House Spokesman Arthur Faulkner, this demand was received yesterday morning. Furthermore, and again this conflicts with statements by Faulkner last evening, a group has been identified as the likely conspirators. Chiapas rebels of southern Mexico, according to this source, are believed by officials in the US intelligence community to be behind the attack that also left several dead, including Mexican President Francisco Portillo. The rebels of the Chiapas area on the Pacific coast of Mexico have been at odds with the Mexican government for a number of years, but a breakdown in negotiations several years ago nevertheless saw the absence of any real violence continue into what amounted to a de facto truce. Apparently that truce is over.

"My source indicated that American officials are not sure whether this action was undertaken by the previously known leaders of the Chiapas forces, or if the attack represents an initiative by a splinter group."

Adams spoke. "Sandy, are US officials convinced that this ransom demand is legitimate, considering the number of phony claims of responsibility that Faulkner indicated they have received?"

"Again, Tracy, this was told to me on conditions that his identity not be revealed, but apparently the demand was received in the mail from Texas. Here is a photocopy of the envelope in which the demand was mailed. An odd, but effective way to make a ransom demand, but the postmark was dated prior to the attack, indicating foreknowledge of the event. It would seem that the method was selected to establish the *bonafides* of their claim. My source did not indicate whether any subsequent communiqué has been received. This is Sandy Thomas, live from Washington."

"So, let's recap," announced the news anchor, turning toward the camera. "In an exclusive report heard only on QNN, it has been learned that US government officials have received a three-million-dollar ransom demand for the safe return of former President Trenton Weston. The demand was reportedly made by a group of Mexican rebels from the Chiapas region of their country and was received via US mail. The note is believed to be legitimate because it was postmarked prior to the actual kidnapping. So, in a stunning revelation…"

Morgan turned down the sound and stared unbelieving at the television set. "All this for a ransom?"

"And only three million?" Maggie joined in. "They could have gotten more for a business executive."

"And gotten it with less complications. This just isn't adding up,"

Morgan said aloud. He stood and put his hand to his face. Pacing, he said, "Think, Josh. What doesn't smell right?" He gently slapped his forehead several times with the heel of his hand.

Morgan organized what he knew about such kidnappings in the context of what he had heard over the last day-and-a-half. He decided that it shouldn't be surprising that the Chiapas rebels have decided to join the kidnapping-for-profit business. After all, it was big business throughout the world, and a common way for rebels to fund their activities. But the puzzle, he thought, was why go after someone as prominent as a former President of the US. It would bring all sorts of unwanted attention. Kidnapping for ransom had evolved into a trade in its own right. Businessmen and women living or working in volatile regions are kidnapped, ransoms are demanded, negotiations are begun by specialists in the field – "Sheesh. Specialists in the field. How ludicrous," Morgan thought – a settlement is reached, the money paid, the hostage is returned. "Strictly business," he said aloud.

"What?" Maggie's face indicated the confusion she felt from the isolated comment.

"I was just thinking how terrorist kidnapping of this kind has become an industry. But, you know, a person of such visibility as Weston. This oversteps the bounds of a business transaction. They had to know that the justice and intelligence officials of at least the United States and Mexico would be all over their asses. So, what would make Weston worth all the grief? You go after a big fish for a big prize," Morgan assumed.

"And you're right, Maggie. Why only three million? Heck, three million dollars is a considerable amount of money, but it would seem they are leaving a lot on the table when the catch is someone like Weston."

Maggie was now in synch with Morgan. "Maybe they wanted the notoriety that grabbing someone of such power would bring."

"Perhaps. But from a business perspective," Morgan answered, "this would make it practically impossible to conduct a profitable business trade in future kidnappings."

"And likely they will all be in prison," Maggie suggested.

"Or dead," was the response. "Especially since they killed Portillo. Why do that? Wouldn't they hold him for ransom, too? No, it can't be for the publicity. So, why take an extraordinary amount of risk only to ask for a ransom that isn't commensurate with that risk?"

"Maybe they just asked for an amount they knew they could get. But what I hear you saying is that an oil executive would have brought maybe as much without nearly the hassle. And they would have been left alone for the most part to do it again and again."

"Exactly, Maggie."

Morgan reached for a slice of the now-cold pizza. "Shoot, maybe they're just *stupido*," he grunted.

The talking heads on the various news networks now had something new about which to talk, at least. Though QNN had scooped everyone on the report, there was still the race to see who could make the most use of the information. Specialists on the Mexican political scene, and the Chiapas rebellion, in particular, were assembled in rapid fashion. They were brought in to pontificate as to what such a move would mean with respect to the informal armistice between the rebels and the government, and to the relations between the United States and Mexico.

The entire history of the Chiapas uprising was told and retold. Graphics were created displaying maps and charts. Some of the analysts even raised some of the same questions that Morgan had but seemed more willing to accept the story at face value than he was.

"By, the way, Sweetheart..." The red was instantaneous in Maggie's cheeks right down onto her neck. She lowered her eyes away from the grinning Morgan.

"You were saying... dear."

Maggie grabbed two empty glasses and escaped to the refrigerator. Her voice was low. "I was just saying that I noticed while you were gone that your 'New Mail' window popped up on your monitor."

"Thanks... Honey."

Maggie turned to call Morgan a smart-ass, but he was now standing right in front of her.

His embrace was different than the "pal" hugs they had exchanged countless times in the past. "I guess I was a bit unrealistic to think I would be able to tear myself away from the news right now. I promise, in a couple of days things will be different."

Maggie laid her head against Morgan's chest.

"Things are already different, Morgan."

The escape to Yellowstone postponed, Maggie Loughlin decided to go to her office long enough to complete a couple of tasks.

Morgan decided to do a bit of research about this Chiapas thing and sat down at his computer to access the Internet. As he logged on, the email notification Maggie had mentioned reappeared. He accessed his email account and noticed he had four messages.

One note was from a cousin back in Texas who was his best friend as a kid. More precisely the email was from Amy, his cousin's wife. She was one of only a couple of people whose email Morgan genuinely looked forward to getting. They often held news of what was going on back home but mostly they gave Morgan the latest on their daughter Allie. In addition to being a straight-A student who was active in all manner of school activities, Allie was a black belt in Taekwondo and this email was news of her winning a National Championship in sparring. Though not her first championship, it was her first as a black belt.

Another email was a fishing report he subscribed to. One was an advertisement for sexual aids – where do these guys get my name? he thought – and the last was an electronic greeting card. Such notes were old fare now but still convenient and clever. All of the providers offered at least some that one could send free of charge. Morgan was certain that the "card" was from his grandfather, who had discovered computers some years ago as a means to fill the loneliness he felt when his Ellie had died. Silas Houston inundated Morgan with joke emails, cartoons, and these electronic greeting cards to the point that it was a nuisance, but a pleasant one. Morgan had other things to do right now and left the emails unopened and turned to his research project.

After a couple of hours reading about the Mexican political situation, Morgan still had the feeling that there was something missing here. The attack on the train didn't fit what he had read or his evaluation of the situation. But if, as Sandy Thomas had suggested, this move represented the emergence of a new faction of the Chiapas movement, then perhaps all bets were off, and you really couldn't analyze the actions of this group based on previous history.

From the other room television news caught Morgan's attention – another breaking news story. With each special report, his hopes rose at the prospect that the information may be about the rescue of President Weston. But as with the previous ones this report held no such news.

As he entered the den Morgan saw a face on the screen that matched the ones that he had been seeing on his computer monitor. A man in military garb and a black ski mask. The man spoke in Spanish, reading from a prepared statement, which was translated by the voiceover.

"The *Zapatista* National liberation Army denies in the strongest possible terms any association with the terrorists that have chosen to attack Mexico and the United States. The *EZLN* does not recognize, in fact, is not familiar with the radicals who defame the name of a great hero of the Mexican people by calling itself the New Soldiers of the *Zapatistas*.

"The *EZLN* has fought a political battle. It has occasionally led to physical conflict, but our war is primarily a war of ideas and for us victory will be found when the rights of the indigenous peoples of Mexico are recognized.

"We condemn senseless violence and the appropriating of a noble cause to include the citizens of another nation."

Correspondent Joseph Li's face now filled the screen. "So, in a remarkable step, a spokesman for the *Zapatista* National Liberation Army has issued a statement denying responsibility for, indeed any knowledge of this group that, according to our own Sandy Thomas, is behind the attack on *el Águila de la Amistad* in northern Mexico.

"It is common for groups around the world to claim responsibility for actions in which they had no part. It is no less common for organizations to deny complicity in acts in which they were in fact involved. While that may be the case with regard to the *EZLN* – falsely denying involvement in the train's attack – I will say that such a move does not seem to be consistent with what we have seen from them in the past."

"That was fast. But it was what I was thinking," said Morgan, returning to his desk.

Morgan was about to close his browser when he remembered the electronic greeting he had received earlier. Opening his inbox once again, he double-clicked the item, and when it had appeared, he placed his pointer over the link in the body of the note and clicked once. The action took him past the greeting card company's homepage to the site where he could access his card. He typed in the ID that had been provided to him in the email and a birthday card opened on his monitor. "Birthday?" questioned the recipient. "My birthday is over two months away." But the front of the card got his attention. In garish colors a caricature of a coyote was silhouetted against a full moon, its head turned up in the familiar pose. "Coyote" had been the code name often used by Morgan when he was with CIA. Very few people at the Agency would know that, and nobody outside the organization.

Morgan jumped slightly as he heard his front door open. He was not accustomed to having anyone come and go so freely from his house.

"Morgan, 's me."

"Come here, Maggie."

Maggie pulled up a chair next to Morgan, instinctively looking at the monitor in front of him. He noticed that she had changed into shorts, hiking boots, and a loose tank top. He smiled, unconsciously took a deep breath, and shook his head slightly before returning to his task.

"What's up?"

"Look at this, Maggie."

Maggie took control of the mouse and navigated the card. She read aloud, "'It's your birthday.' It's not your birthday," she remarked facing Morgan.

He smiled. "Yeah, I'm aware of that, Loughlin."

She scrolled down the screen to the "inside" of the card, and resumed reading, "'Have a howling good time.' That's corny. Sorta funny, but very corny," she gave him a puzzled look, "but it's still not your birthday." She raised her eyebrows and gave Morgan a huge grin.

"Read the personal note." Electronic greeting cards always offered a space to include comments, and sometimes attachments such as photographs.

Maggie cleared her throat playfully. "Josh, Glad you could join me for a few days while I was in Cozumel on business." Her voiced slowed and became softer as she read the email. "Thought you might enjoy one of the photos I took. By the way, the piece of luggage that was stolen there; turns out the company isn't going to do a thing about it. Figures. Oh, well! Love, Carrie."

Morgan noticed the change in Maggie's voice as she read the note from "Carrie." She softly cleared her throat, for real this time.

"Thanks for sharing this with me, Morgan."

He wasn't sure if she was talking to him or not. She remained facing the screen but seemed to be looking past it.

He took her by the shoulders and turned her toward him. "Maggie, I don't know a Carrie."

She turned to him, but her eyes never made contact with his. "I really shouldn't be reading your personal stuff," she said, emitting a fake laugh and starting to rise.

Morgan gently pushed her back into her seat. He raised her chin with a single finger and looked squarely into her blue eyes. "Maggie... I don't know anyone named Carrie."

She paused and smiled with some confidence. "So, I don't get it," she answered. Her voice was a bit more even now.

"Neither do I."

"So, what's the attachment?"

"No clue. I was just reading this when you showed up."

"Yeah, I caught you reading a love letter, didn't I?" Her sense of humor returned with a smile.

Morgan dragged the icon for the attachment onto his computer's desktop, where he double-clicked it. While the file was opening, he offered some explanations.

"I've been to Cozumel a number of times. Been there on some scuba diving vacations; even produced a photo essay for a travel magazine. But I haven't been there in years." He cut his eyes toward Maggie. "And never with anyone named Carrie. I don't even know anyone named Carrie. And it's not like my life has been so filled with romantic interests that I would lose track." Now his attention was fully on the computer.

"So... It's not your birthday. You don't know a 'Carrie.' Looks like you got someone else's card."

"No, it may be mine. What the hell?"

The file had opened to display a high-quality image.

"I remember that *café*. It's the *Café Cuzamil*. Definitely in Cozumel."

Maggie leaned closer to the monitor. "He's cute!" she remarked, pointing at the photo. She smiled and cut her eyes toward her friend. "Do you recognize any of them?"

In front of the *café* along the street were three young adults – a young man with two nice-looking women in their early twenties.

"Oooh! That Carrie. Sweet!" His comment earned him a slug on the arm. After the pair's laughter ceased, Morgan shook his head. "No." He clicked on the "Zoom" icon a few times, increasing the apparent size of the photo several fold. "No, never seen 'em before – any of 'em." He clicked the size down to its original appearance.

"Nice sharp picture, but the composition leaves something to be desired," he continued.

"Always the photographer, huh, Morgan?"

"Occupational hazard." He assumed a deliberately pretentious nasal tone. "Without a doubt the standards for vacation photographs are substantially less than those for publication, but," he recovered his real voice, "this sucks. People should at least read the manual that comes with the camera."

"Two girls in the photo; one guy. So I'm betting the one behind the camera is a guy, too, and you guys are prohibited by law from reading instructions. Aren't you?"

"Funny, Mag. So, it's a vacation. You want the *café* in the shot, I guess, but the pic is out of whack."

"'Out of whack.' A highly technical photography term, I suppose."

"Of course. What I mean is, it's a little too inclusive. Heck, those two men on the upstairs patio of the *café* might as well have been the subjects of this photo." Morgan's mind halted on the last phrase.

"Might as well have been the subjects of the photo," he repeated out loud.

"What did you say?"

"Maybe they are," Morgan countered. A click-and-hold action with the mouse, and a couple of movements created a small dotted frame around the two men in question. Then Morgan placed the mouse pointer inside the frame he had arranged and clicked. The framed area enlarged to a size that filled his computer screen. The exaggerated size caused some loss in quality, but the faces were clear enough.

Maggie and Morgan both leaned forward. Her face swiveled back and forth between the former CIA spook and the screen.

"No, don't recognize them, either." Morgan leaned back in his swivel chair. "I feel like I'm looking at something important, but I can't figure out what."

"Mexico," Maggie blurted out.

Morgan was silent but turned to face Maggie.

She hooked a thumb over her shoulder as though she was hitching a ride. Morgan's eyes followed it in the general direction of the television. His gaze returned to her. He shook his head and shrugged.

"Morgan, this photo was made in Mexico – Cozumel, Mexico. All we've been talking about the last couple of days is Mexico – and the attack on the train"

"Holy shit!" came the whisper, and he spun back toward the screen.

Josh Morgan felt the hairs on his neck stand up as he leaned forward in his chair. He stared at the two men in the photo more intently now. He shook his head again.

"What am I am not seeing?" he complained.

Maggie watched as Josh Morgan's eyes widened and he abruptly pushed himself away from the desk. She observed him sag a bit. His head drooped somewhat, then raised and turned toward her in slow-motion.

"Look at those men, Maggie."

Now it was she who squinted and shook her head.

"Look at the man on the left."

The light clicked on. "He's not Mexican," she realized, though she hadn't made the same connection as Morgan.

"He's Middle Eastern, Maggie." Though the images of the men were in profile, it was suddenly clear. One of the men was Mexican; the other man was an Arab!

"Josh, is that what you're supposed to see?"

Maggie and Morgan rocked back in their chairs.

"Hmm. I get this email with a photo that was taken in Mexico. There is a Middle Eastern man in it. Is that it? Is some Middle Eastern group involved in this thing?"

"But who would send this to you, Josh? And why?" Maggie took charge of the mouse again and scrolled up to the personal note. "What did Carrie say?"

With that question, Morgan's mind struggled to connect the dots. "Coyote – that's me. So, the email wasn't a mistake – it was sent to me intentionally." Maggie's bewildered expression penetrated his concentration. He waved a hand. "Never mind," he grunted. "There is a Mexican-Middle Eastern connection in the train attack. But why did I get this? And who is it from?" He puckered his lips and closed his eyes. "The reference to the lost luggage, and that her employer isn't going to take care of it. Is that it? Wait, 'Carrie' didn't say "employer." She said 'company.'

"Holy…!" Morgan's voice trailed off in a gasp.

Maggie's head wheeled toward Morgan, eyebrows raised, mouth open. "Josh?"

"Some Middle Eastern group is involved in the kidnapping. And CIA – the government – knows and isn't going to a damn thing about it!" Morgan practically shouted the words.

"How…? How did you get there?"

Morgan explained. "The key is company. The Company – CIA! Carrie said her luggage was stolen – not lost, stolen – and she said the company wasn't going to do a thing about it. She didn't say 'pay for it.' The Company 'isn't going to do a thing about it.'"

"What sense would that make," Maggie challenged. "If the government knows, they'll do something. Wouldn't they?"

The answer was slow in coming. "I don't know." A deep breath surged in and out, and he looked at her. "I don't know. What was it the President said last night that caught the reporter's attention?"

"He said rebels…"

"He also used the word 'terrorists,' Maggie."

"The White House spokes-guy answered that, Josh."

"Seemed a little weak to me." Morgan's eyebrows lowered.

Maggie reached over and placed her hands on Morgan's knees. Her face was blank; her lips quivered. "Do you know what you're saying? I know you think the President knows more than he's saying but you still haven't figured out who sent you the email, or why."

Quietly Maggie wondered if her friend's experience with the Central Intelligence Agency had made him a little too paranoid.

Morgan couldn't decide if he had received this information from someone who knew about his bond with Weston, and knew he would want to know, or if someone had sent it to him because they believed he would be able to do something about it.

"Isn't there someone you can talk to about this?"

"The only person would be a friend of mine who is still with the Agency. I'm a little uneasy about calling him, but… Crap, what can it hurt?"

Morgan turned to pick up the cell phone beside his computer to try again to reach Ben Reid. "This guy is the best friend – shoot, the only friend I had at CIA. Benny and his wife, Becky, would have me over when I was in town. You know, home-cooked meals and all that." He punched in half the number he still remembered and continued, "I was his best man, but I haven't talked to him in a while. Why do people lose touch like that? Anyhow, they have a little girl…"

"Morgan?" Maggie watched as Morgan lowered the phone from his ear and rested it to his chest. He pressed the button to clear its display. Maggie stood, took Morgan's hands in hers and turned him toward her. Then she took the phone from him and placed it on the desk.

She watched the color continue to fade from Morgan's face. She cupped his face in her hands and appealed softly, "Sweetheart." There was no trace of jest in her voice this time.

Morgan bit his lip and raised his eyes to the ceiling. "Their little girl's name is Carrie. The email is from Ben."

CHAPTER 18

The border crossing had gone without incident and the atmosphere inside the RV was different for both men. They had crossed from private land in Mexico through the drug traffickers' tunnel onto a private ranch on the US side. They had entered New Mexico and joined State Highway 9 west of Pancho Villa State Park. Driving through New Mexico consisted of frequent long stretches of desert terrain. The summer days were almost unbearably hot, but the nights were much cooler. The inside of the camper was relatively safe from unwelcome eyes, which was the Arab's chief concern since he was holding one of America's former Presidents hostage. Fadi Al-Majeed was improvising. The original plan called for placing the American pig aboard a Saudi yacht in Playa del Carmen, Mexico, and sending him on his way to Saudi Arabia. He knew that he would be taking his prize to another port now, one in the United States. He just didn't know which yet.

Former President Weston was riding in a swivel captain's seat that sat slightly aback the two front seats, without a blindfold, without a gag. Hidden from view there was little chance that the highly recognizable American political celebrity could do anything to attract attention. So the host allowed his guest more freedom. All things considered Al-Majeed was pleased with his creative solution to the travel problems. It was comfortable, if slow, and would be an inconvenience more than a hardship to his passenger. He was to deliver his prize alive. Secondly, not only was he to hand Weston over alive, but unharmed. The former President would be displayed on television sets worldwide. He needed to appear as having been treated with respect and with regard for his well-being. The Mexican surrogates had roughed the man up some, but nothing visible, and nothing from which he would not recover in short order.

Of course, some restraint was necessary, so the Saudi agent tied his companion's ankles, ran the cord to his wrists and secured them as well. He ran a rope behind Weston's seat and tied each end snugly to the one connecting his hands and ankles.

Al-Majeed had driven far north through Deming and Albuquerque. His route was determined by two major considerations. First, he felt he needed to put as much distance as possible between him and the Mexican border.

Secondly, the Arab decided that, although it added hundreds of miles to whatever his destination might be, he would drive exclusively on America's Interstate Highways or other large national roads. There was safety in numbers, and on these giant highways his vehicle would be lost among the countless others that traversed them around the clock. He always drove the speed limit, never over, never under. He did nothing that would make him stand out, or present the risk of being stopped by the ever-present patrol cars.

He purchased fuel from service stations that offered twenty-four hour pay-at-the pump service to avoid any more contact with people than was necessary. The foreign agent was using credit cards left for him by the same colleagues that had provided the RV. His current legend was still Saudi, but a different one than he had used to get into Cozumel. He had a full set of papers declaring him to be legally inside the United States, but they were, for the most part, useless to him. He knew that, if he was stopped, his traveling companion would be recognized, and who he was, or where he was from would be the least of his worries. The accommodations on board the recreational camper eliminated the need to stop at motels. He planned to travel as rapidly as possible once he had determined to which Gulf of Mexico port he would direct the yacht. Until then he would travel about seven to eight hours each day.

Meals consisted mostly of sandwiches made from items left on the truck for him by his counterparts in the US.

The rented vehicle was near Albuquerque. Al-Majeed hoped to make it through New Mexico's largest city and a bit farther before stopping for the night. He had started late in the day since he had driven through the night before. On this night he would interrupt the journey just long enough for a few hours of rest, and then begin driving in a more normal routine through the daylight hours.

It would be a long trip, so conversation, even with the American President, would have added spice to the journey. The opportunity to hurl taunts at this war criminal would be a bonus to the Arab, an added benefit to the job he was assigned. But the old man had refused to participate. He had not said a word the entire distance from the Mexican border.

"I suppose you're taking me home," the President finally spoke, having noted from road signs through his limited view out the RV's windows that he was in his home country.

162

The Saudi agent let loose a genuine laugh. "You face your destiny with humor. But, of course, you are incorrect. The idiot Mexican infidels who liberated you from the train made it necessary to change plans. But going home? That was never part of the equation."

"Saudi?" the American questioned.

"I am."

"So, what are your plans? I assume you are trying to get me to your country."

"Correct again."

"Execution or prison."

"We will see."

"There'll be hell to pay."

"That's the idea."

◆

What to do? It was nearly midnight. Morgan had been out of the game for a long time. He had no resources, no contacts. Besides, why would he think he would really be able to accomplish anything as an army of one? He had no idea where to start, and the people who would have such information were apparently disinclined to do anything with it. The measures that Benny took to get this information to him made it clear that he would be unable to provide any direct assistance. Morgan truly had no one to whom he could turn for help. And the very thought of a solo operation scared him shitless. "Crap," he thought, "the idea of being involved in this at all is out of the question."

He sat looking at the printed copy of the photo that Benny had sent him. Before deleting it from his computer he had printed and poured over the "birthday card" to make sure he had not missed any clues. No, nothing else had been there, he reassured himself now. He held the photo in his hands hoping that something would leap off the paper, but, of course, nothing did.

Morgan concluded that he had three possible locations in Mexico linked to the kidnapping – Cozumel, Chiapas, and the area east of Chihuahua where the train had been hit. His first thought was to go to Cozumel and try to establish some leads there. But he had this growing sense that he didn't have the luxury of time that it would take to travel to a number of locations in his quest for clues. There had to be something that could eliminate a few steps, shortcuts that could get him closer to the former President, he prayed.

"Wow, I sound like I'm actually going to try to do something." He stretched and rubbed his eyes.

Maggie had gone home for the night. She had decided to work from

Morgan's house for the next day or two rather than go into her office. So she would spend the night at home, gather some clothes and her computer and return early the next morning to keep Morgan company at this difficult time. She didn't know Morgan was beginning to consider other plans.

Before heading to bed Morgan decided to take a quick look at some of the video he had recorded during parts of the news summaries. He fast-forwarded through a couple of real-time hours of digital media on his DVR, trying to get a sense of something that might be important. Suddenly Morgan pressed the "pause" button and reversed the image slowly. The "Play" button returned the video to the section that had caught his attention.

When Sandy Thomas broke the story of the ransom note he had displayed a photocopy of not only the letter taking responsibility for the abduction, but of the postmark on the envelope. Morgan paused the playback. In addition to the date the letter was mailed – the proof that it had been mailed prior to the kidnapping – there was one other piece of information. Morgan got down on his knees in front of the television. He stared at the screen for several seconds before he made it out. He thanked God for the clarity of the frozen frames on the DVR recording. In spite of the relatively small size of the envelope on the image, he finally recognized the print: "MAILED FROM ZIP CODE 79905."

CHAPTER 19

DAY 8 – FRIDAY

Fadi Al-Majeed steered the American Excursions rental onto the exit from Interstate 40 in Moriarty, New Mexico. Moments later he pulled into a small RV campground and awakened the office clerk. It was just after midnight. He requested a campsite at the rear of the complex, telling the clerk that it would be quieter away from the highway. The Saudi pulled the camper into the drive-through site. He untied his hostage's legs to let him visit the bathroom on the RV and stretch his legs. He had stopped previously to replace the gag. The process of registering in these camping facilities was a critical point in the ongoing process. The proximity of so many other people would no doubt tempt his guest. Leaving his traveling companion in the vehicle alone while he paid for the campsite provided at least some opportunity for the former President to draw attention to himself, so it was necessary to fully restrain him during those times.

The brief release of his captive to relieve himself was also risky. Al-Majeed was on full alert during this period and would not allow the American to even close the bathroom door. The man was so recognizable, and the news of his capture so widespread, that the simple act of revealing his face to someone through the window could end the operation that had taken so long to plan. And Al-Majeed would never know he had been compromised until the police arrived.

Weston always tried to prolong the times when he was at least partially free of his bindings. This instance was no different. He hoped to create some sort of disturbance to alert someone, anyone. But once again, he was unsuccessful.

Even for an experienced intelligence operative, periods of time with minimal sleep took its toll on his disposition. Tonight was a night when Al-Majeed released his anger at the American and at the changes that the foolish *Zapatistas'* actions had necessitated. Though Weston's efforts at creating a scene were unfruitful, the Arab had had enough. He slammed the American onto the bed forcefully. Weston realized that he might provoke his adversary into creating a scene of his own.

The intelligence officer jumped on top of the former Chief Executive and pulled his taped mouth to his face. Al-Majeed smiled through clenched teeth.

"You waste your time trying to make others aware of your presence here. You, my friend, will face your end soon. You led the Great Satan in its oppression of all Islamic people throughout the world. During his life my great President al-Hashimi withstood your bombs, your soldiers, your missiles. He leads our country in defiance of your sanctions. Allah has delivered us from your evil. And he has delivered you into our hands."

"Shout, you bastard. Dammit, shout your friggin' lungs out," Weston pleaded silently. He struggled to move. He pushed. He resisted as much as possible, considering the restraints. The only goal in his life right now was to provoke this hypocrite into something that would alert someone. But the man never complied. Despite the intensity of his emotions Al-Majeed's voice never rose above a whisper as he continued his controlled rage.

"Where is your god now? Is he to be found? No! Allah has triumphed. You have asked what your fate is to be. You will be delivered to my great leader in our powerful country. There you will be displayed before the world. All will know that we are mighty and you are weak. They will see that our god is powerful and that he is bringing you to answer for your sins against his children.

"You will be tried as a war criminal. You will be executed. The world will respect Saudi Arabia. We will have our place in the order of the world. President al-Hashimi's greatness will be made manifest."

Weston's eyes widened above the silver tape over his mouth. "You're mad!" they said.

◆

The prayer was heartfelt.

"My God, Thou art mighty and powerful and the righteous judge over all the world. I thank thee for thy loving kindness and grace. Thy justice rules the heavens and the earth. Thy strength is ever-present; thy mercy knows no bounds.

"I thank thee, my Lord, for delivering thine enemies into my hands. For their past sins and their present iniquities, thou hast anointed me to perform thy will and exact thy judgement on their evil hearts. I thank thee for choosing me as Thine instrument to prepare the ways for my President and my nation. And I praise thee for allowing me to avenge mine own injuries. Thou art my sword and my strength. In my Savior's name, Amen."

Everson Blake kissed his wife and they rose from their knees.

"Tell the girls I'm sorry to miss Sunday dinner with them. I'll call and let you know where I am."

With that he took his briefcase and the travel mug of coffee and walked through the door. He had a murder to monitor.

◆

Morgan was awake an hour before the alarm went off. He stretched his arms and yawned. He rolled over and pulled the pillow over his eyes, begging himself to go back to sleep. Finally, he rose and sat on the edge of his bed. "Go to bed late; make up for it by getting up early," he mumbled. "Makes a lot of sense, Morgan."

It took a minute to summon any energy and a couple of attempts to get his weary body to stand, but once done he hobbled to the bath room. "You look like crap," he said to the mirror. "Might as well get busy, though," he acknowledged to himself.

He walked barefoot down the stairs and into the kitchen where he flipped the switch on the coffee maker to "brew." Biscuit bounded through his pet entry in the side door.

"What in blazes are you so happy about?" his master griped. But Biscuit had a way of flipping Morgan's instant-on switch. Soon they were rolling in the floor. "Good thing you like Maggie, pal. I think you're going to be seeing a lot more of her."

A shave, shower, and brushed teeth later, Morgan was sitting in front of his computer looking at the home page for the United States Postal Service. A couple of links and he was at the zip code lookup page. He typed in "79905" and clicked "Search." The answer appeared on the screen: El Paso, Texas; 4400 East Paisano Drive. "A place to start, Biscuit," he told his companion.

That was the only information he needed, so Morgan refreshed his coffee cup, turned off all the lights in the house, and made his way to the front porch swing with Biscuit. Through most of his life he had never been a morning person, though his work in the employ of CIA mostly required that he work long hours that began early in the day. But when he moved to Wyoming, even in his darkest days that had just now begun to be erased from his mind, Morgan loved rising early. The soft light emerging over the horizon moved him in an almost religious way. Even in the cold of winter, he spent most mornings in this very place until the rising sun lit the section of the Snake River that he could see from his house. In the summer it happened at an early hour, but this day was cloudy and would prevent the show.

Josh Morgan sat a few moments desperately trying to conjure a solution, or at least someone on whom he could offload the discoveries he had made. He was not the cavalry any more. It was still dark when the ex-CIA officer lifted himself off the swing and proceeded into his home.

"C'mon, Biscuit," he commanded. But the Golden Retriever stood at the edge of the porch, staring intently toward the drive leading away from the log home. "Biscuit!" It was a little sterner this time.

"Oh, knock yourself out. You know where your door is." Morgan knew there were all manner of things to interest the dog. Deer, elk, coyotes, even the occasional moose or black bear wandered across the property, and, so far, his furry friend had shown the good sense to stay out of harm's way. He shut the door behind him.

He checked his email to see if he had received another note from his friend in D.C. Nothing. Morgan wanted to discuss this with Ben, but he had gone to great lengths to disguise his identity and the nature of the intel he had disclosed. Morgan knew he would prefer to keep it that way.

Outside Biscuit was barking with relentless canine passion. "The people having breakfast down at Nora's can probably hear you, buddy," the owner wanted to tell the dog. He strained through the glass storm door for some glimpse of whatever was agitating Biscuit.

Ben Reid stood quietly looking at Carrie in her crib. Rebecca would shoot him if he woke her, but he often worked late and left early. So he started to pick her up anyway.

A sleepy voice behind him said quietly, "Don't you do it." Two arms wrapped around Ben's chest and a head snuggled on his back. "She'll be awake soon enough anyhow, and I'll be chasing her all day."

Ben reached around him and pulled his wife beside him, leaving his arm on her shoulder and pulling her tight. "She's a doll, isn't she? I can't believe she's going to be a year old in a couple of days."

"She is sweet." Rebecca Reid looked at her husband looking at their daughter. "Okay, Ben, go ahead."

The words had barely left her lips before Ben was lifting the baby into his arms. Even at the early age, Carrie exhibited the mannerisms that transcend age. Awakened from her slumber, she yawned and stretched. She was slow to clear the tiny cobwebs from her mind, but once she did, she rewarded her daddy with an enormous smile.

The family moved to the couch in the den and sat together, Rebecca sleepily laying her head on Ben's shoulder and Ben bouncing his reason for living on his knee.

"I sent Josh an email last night."

"Mmm. Hear back?" a still not alert voice asked.

His head shook while he gurgled at a smiling face. "No, probably won't anytime soon. I asked him his thoughts on the train attack and gave him some of mine. I'm sure it's just eating him up." It wasn't exactly the truth but close enough that Ben didn't feel he had outright lied to Becky.

As suddenly as only a baby can manage, the smile morphed into a frown.

Just as quickly, Ben handed her over to Mommy. "Your turn."

"Thanks."

"My pleasure," and he grinned again. He pulled a squirming baby and a groggy mommy into a tight little bundle with himself. "God has been so good to me."

"To all of us, Honey."

The moment was one of those that hung suspended in time as if energizing itself with the clarity required to become a perfect memory.

Finally, Ben rose and grabbed his things. "Gotta run, sweetie." He tickled Carrie on the chin.

Rebecca followed him to the door. "Think you can get off early tonight? It's Friday, you know."

"Babe, things are hopping. What did you have in mind?"

"Oh, I was thinking we haven't had a 'date' in quite some time." Rebecca Reid arched her eyebrows several times rapidly.

Ben laughed over his shoulder as he walked to his car. "Ooh, baby. You don't have to ask me twice."

He drove away waving, as his wife bounced their daughter's hand up and down at Daddy.

◆

He couldn't see what Biscuit had cornered down the drive, but Morgan knew whatever it was, it had him pretty upset. A bear? he wondered. He walked into his bedroom. Leaving the lights off to maintain his night vision, he opened the drawer of his nightstand and removed the Sig Sauer P226 he kept there. Next, he reached under his bed for the small but extraordinarily powerful diving light he always kept there in case of power outages.

Finally, he returned to the front door. Morgan was ordinarily protective of the wildlife that visited his property. He hadn't hunted since he moved to Wyoming. But he certainly didn't want anything to happen to his canine best friend. Simultaneous to his opening the door, he heard a yelp of pain from his dog, then silence.

"Biscuit!" Morgan screamed, throwing back the door and stepping onto the porch. "C'mere boy." He whistled and flipped on the lantern and shone it down the sloping landscape toward where he had heard Biscuit. Caught in mid-stride by the sudden light was a man dressed in black, barely distinguishable in the darkness of the fading night. Morgan and the man both froze. The trespasser assumed a position that defined his intentions. Though Morgan couldn't see it, he knew the man was aiming a gun. Morgan dove downward, thrusting his fingers through the narrowing gap in the closing door. At the same time, he heard the whiz above his head, the glass on the door exploded and sprinkled down on him. There was no sound.

"Suppressed!" the intended victim thought incredibly. He hurled himself through what remained of the shattered door and into the house. The element of surprise evaporated, the assailant was running at full speed up the grassy hill toward the house. Morgan could hear the man's steps. Fear gripped him, and he quaked in his place with no plan coming to mind.

Finally, Morgan raised his .40 caliber semi and fired a pair of rounds somewhere toward Eastern Wyoming just to give the man something to think about. He thought he heard the thud of the man hitting the ground in an evasive move. But Morgan realized that he was close – very, very close. He seized the opportunity to move.

The former CIA officer felt certain the intruder would not enter the front door but was uncertain where he would attack. Morgan crawled to the bar extending from the kitchen counter. It appeared to be out of the line of sight from the door and windows. He puffed loudly and uncontrollably. He raised the gun toward the door but maintained nothing resembling steadiness. Morgan knew that at most he had ten rounds left in his weapon. He had fired the two shots for cover. But had the magazine been fully loaded to start with? he wondered.

He began to hear – no, feel, really – the uninvited guest moving around the perimeter of the house. "Shit! Shit! Shit!" The whisper escaped with a tremble. Since Morgan's home was made of logs, at least whoever was stalking him couldn't simply fire through the walls. And unless he came through the already broken front door, he would have to open or break another window or door, or simply fire through one. That was more likely, Morgan decided. But which one?

Morgan heard, he thought, the gunman moving along the wall of the house that faced the garage. So he would probably look in the window that was almost directly above Morgan. He looked down the hallway that was across from his position on the floor. It might work, he told himself. If he could just time it right. Morgan listened through the partially open window above him. His heart pounded in his ears so loudly that hearing anything else was virtually impossible. But he realized the same thing he was counting on to save him might let him know when to act. At the end of the hallway was the guest bathroom. Its mirror faced out the open door toward Morgan. He squinted as he focused on the mirror. Finally, against the barely discernible twilight emerging despite the morning clouds, Morgan thought he could make out in the mirror the reflection of the cautious silhouette of a figure beginning to peak around the frame of the window above him.

Morgan pointed his light directly at the mirror and turned it on, instantly bouncing the light back in the general direction of the window, and his assailant. As he had hoped the figure turned fully toward the mirror and fired through the window at what he didn't realize was merely a reflection. Morgan dropped the light and raised the gun over his head with both hands and blindly fired backwards through the now-broken window. Knowing it was almost certain that he had missed the man, Morgan swiveled on his knees, then sprang to his feet to fire again. He saw the surprised attacker stumbling backward. Morgan aimed quickly and pulled the trigger.

It was only then that he understood that the Sig's slide was racked into an open position from his previous shot, that it had been his last round. The realization brought a swift and profound panic.

CHAPTER 20

In the same instant that he was certain his life was about to end, Josh Morgan realized that the gunman was continuing to stumble backward. He was stunned as he realized that he had hit the intruder with his first, and only, shot.

But even as he felt the relief of escape, in the periphery of his view Morgan saw the red pinpoint of a laser sight streaking across the wall toward him. Morgan fell clumsily into the kitchen as the impacts of fully automatic gunfire from a second attacker immediately began tracing the red light in its path along the wall.

The additional gunman had approached the house from the north while the first had moved from the east. The unknown intruder moved in the opposite direction as the original one and had fired through a window in the northwest corner of the den. Morgan burst through the kitchen door and outside toward the garage. Crouching on the run to pick up the automatic weapon lying beside the first attacker, he noticed the heavy bleeding from the chest wound caused by his desperate shot.

His first instinct was to turn and fight, but common sense prevailed as he rightly concluded that he was no match for the professionals that were assaulting him. He fled to the garage and ducked inside the doorway. He immediately turned and pointed the H&K MP5 at the southeast corner of the house where he expected to see the gunman appear. Seconds passed; his hands began to tremble; his breathing failed to steady. He knew he had guessed incorrectly.

Curling around the frame of the garage door toward the southwest corner of the log home he spied the black-clad man just beginning to cross the gap between there and the garage. Morgan pulled the trigger. A three-shot burst sent the man diving back to the house and cover. Almost immediately his gun appeared around the edge and sent a spray of bullets both into the exterior of the garage and flying through the open doorway past Morgan, the clacking of the mechanical apparatus of the gun louder than the suppressed fire.

The former CIA officer dashed to the door at the back end of the garage to guard against his assailant moving to that location. Arriving there, he fired another burst through the doorway toward the house's corner. Another long burst rained on his position. He braced himself against the wall. It occurred to him to wonder how much ammunition he had remaining. Scanning the assault weapon Morgan was relieved to find that the second magazine taped to the one currently inserted into the gun was completely full. He determined how to remove the magazine currently supplying the bullets and looked into it.

"Almost empty," he cursed. He replaced the magazine and fired until it emptied, hoping it would persuade his adversary that he was out of ammo. Hurriedly he extracted the empty magazine, ripped the tape holding it to the second one, and flipped it away. Attempting to place the new magazine in the gun, he dropped it. With a metallic crack it hit the concrete floor and fell into the exposed area of the open door.

"Idiot," he proclaimed himself. He eased his head around the edge of the wall to peak at the attacker's position. Now Morgan was praying that he would not take the bait. If he assaulted Morgan's position in the garage, Morgan would have no way to return fire. Fortunately, the gunman had reacted cautiously and remained in place. He was, however, still holding his weapon around the corner, and peering carefully as well. He must have seen the magazine hit the floor, Morgan thought, but perhaps suspected Morgan was setting a trap with the act of dropping it.

"Lucky he doesn't realize I'm just a clumsy ass," Morgan grimaced.

The tension was increasing as the fading night was giving way to the gray canopy of an overcast day. But Morgan was much calmer than he had been. Adrenaline had taken over, and though his pulse was racing, he was approaching the situation with much more clarity. Reaching to his left he retrieved a small hoe that hung on the wall of the garage. He was just preparing to reach with it for his ammunition when he realized that the desperate action might convince his attacker that he was indeed unable to fire and encourage him to rush the garage. Morgan knew that he would never be able to load the gun in time and quietly leaned the hoe against the wall of the garage. A bolder act was required.

Taking a long, deep breath he thought through his plan. With his back against the wall, both figuratively and literally, Morgan closed his eyes and rested his head backward. With a single urgent move, he spun into the open doorway and pointed his empty submachine gun at the location of his enemy, then just as rapidly lunged back to his hiding place. The expected gunfire ripped around Morgan, but he had anticipated the other man's reaction correctly. Although he had fired at Morgan's exposed body, he had himself ducked to the safety of the corner of the house. So, when Morgan rushed into the doorway the second time, the attacker was unprepared. Morgan literally fell backward out of the doorway and sat with his back against the stacked logs making up his garage, and frantically stabbed the retrieved magazine in the weapon. Chambering a round, he held the gun around the edge of the portal and fired a burst, if only to let the man behind the other gun know he was back in the game.

"So, why the hell are you after me?" Morgan's voice broke as he shouted.

Around the corner of the house, the intruder maintained his passive expression and his silence, attending only to the requirements of his assignment.

Morgan used his sleeves to wipe the sweat from his face and stared at the Jeep he kept in his garage. "Why couldn't I be one of those that kept a spare key in my vehicle," he lamented. And despite the fact that he learned how to hotwire a vehicle at the Farm, he was out of practice and quite sure he couldn't pull it off in an adequately brief amount of time. He gazed past his Jeep and a smile creased his face. Morgan's eyes followed the relatively steep slope down the length of his drive and decided that gravity might be his best ally. He crouched and moved quickly to the driver's side of his Jeep and placed the manual transmission floor stick in neutral.

Returning to his original position beside the door, he shouted to the attacker. "Ready to surrender?" He felt almost embarrassed as soon as the words left his mouth. "Idiot," came the muted self-rebuke. The silence was exactly the reply he anticipated.

Morgan braced his back on the pine log wall, placed both feet on the front bumper of the Jeep, and prepared to push. He thought, "Are you sure this is a good idea, Morgan?"

Breathing an inaudible sigh, the prey turned the selector switch to full auto and pointed the barrel so that the bullets would at least make it through the open doorway, though he knew there was no way they would pass anywhere near the predator. Morgan fired a long burst of nine-millimeter rounds and, to his surprise, expended the last of his ammo in the effort. He pushed mightily against the vehicle.

Barely able to bridge the gap between the garage wall and the bumper, Morgan strained his legs against the stubborn vehicle. Slowly, the Wrangler began to roll backward and out the garage. Its momentum established, Morgan rushed around the side of the Jeep, and flew up the stepladder into the attic. He took the few steps on the partially finished decking to the front of the garage where he could view through the narrow slits in the vent on the face of the garage above its door. He could also view downward through an unfinished air vent in the ceiling of the garage into its interior below him.

"This had better work," he told himself.

The Jeep escaped the open doorway of the garage and moved the few additional feet necessary to reveal itself to the attacker. A quick flip of the selector to full auto sent an intense burst of bullets toward the driverless vehicle.

From his place in the attic Morgan heard the frantic footfalls and, peering through the slots in the vent which rested beneath him on the ceiling to the garage below, he saw the black figure bursting through the garage and out the vehicle entryway.

"Run, you sorry bastard," Morgan urged. As soon as the man was far enough away from the structure, he would race from his hiding place into the house for the rifle he always kept by the fireplace. All he could reasonably hope for was one good shot before his attacker reached the Jeep and discovered that he wasn't in it.

But as Morgan shifted his view to and through the vent in the front wall of the garage, horror struck him. As he watched the Wrangler rolling wildly down the gravel drive, he saw, turning onto the drive from Moose-Wilson Road was a red Ford F250 pickup.

"Maggie!" he gasped.

◆

Across the country Ben Reid was on his way to CIA headquarters in Langley, Virginia. The quickest way to get from his home in Lee's Corner, Virginia, was to simply make a beeline to the Capital Beltway, Interstate 495, until he arrived at the Old Georgetown Pike, where he would turn east and straight in to CIA. Sometimes Ben wanted a little variety. It helped clear out the early morning cobwebs, or provide some time to prepare for the day's work. The drive up Reston Parkway to Fox Mills Road, then to Lawyers Road, was the route he chose today to break the monotony. It was a good morning for Reid. Carrie was rarely awake to see him off to work, but with Rebecca's permission, she was today. The proud daddy was occupied with the thought of his daughter's imminent first birthday. She had just begun to walk in the last couple of weeks and was jabbering things that could occasionally be mistaken for words. Ultimately his thoughts turned to his communication the night before. Did Morgan get the email? More importantly, did he get the message?

Reid had every confidence that Morgan would decipher the cryptic note. But when he did, what would he do? Ben had no idea, but if anyone could think of some way to get help to Weston, it was Morgan.

This drive to Langley from Ben's home was quite pretty in places, passing over many of the small creeks and rivers that coursed their ways to the Potomac. Another bonus was that the gridlock was less severe than the common-sense route. There were a couple of stretches along the drive where he could pick up some steam, in excess of the posted speed limit. It was a fun place to test the acceleration and handling of his new Ford Mustang.

Ben was nearing one of the bridges that spanned the tributaries when a car suddenly cut him off. Reid breathed a mild curse and jerked the wheel to the right and hit the brakes. As he angled for the shoulder of the road and his best hope of safety, another vehicle hit him from behind, creating the momentum which propelled his car toward the earthen embankment and the river below. The Mustang's airbag deployed from the impact so Ben couldn't see where he was heading. But his last vision had been of the approaching ravine. The changing attitude of the car as it became airborne confirmed his fear that he was plunging over the edge.

"Oh, Carrie," he thought, as his car impacted two-thirds the way down the sloping ledge. The rear of the car actually struck first, due to the steepness of the dirt wall bordering the river. The front end slammed down next, just as it reached the water's edge. The sudden loss of impetus threw the rear around and rotated it so that the red car crashed into the water on its top. Windows shattered at the car's initial impact, so the vehicle began to sink immediately.

Though seriously injured, the driver was alive. But that would change soon. Unconscious and unable to extricate himself from the disappearing Mustang, Ben Reid drowned strapped securely upside-down in his submerged car.

◆

Maggie negotiated the turn into Morgan's drive. She screamed hysterically as she caught the sight of a dark green and tan missile hurtling toward her. Despite recklessly swinging her truck, she wasn't able to avoid the collision. The Jeep clipped Maggie's left rear fender, sending it careening to one side and into a small stand of trees. The angled collision with a small aspen spun it with a violence out of proportion with its relatively slow speed and rolled it up on one side, the bottom of the vehicle facing Maggie.

Meanwhile Maggie's torso flew sideways as she swerved the pickup to her right, slinging her head into the glass of the truck's door. It only took her a moment to stop her truck, tumble from the door, and storm toward Morgan's now motionless Jeep.

"Josh! Josh!" she shrieked, trembling as she contemplated what she would find in the Jeep.

Maggie stumbled around to the far side of the Jeep but when she reached the Wrangler, no Morgan. In fact, nobody at all. She surveyed the area. Perhaps he had been catapulted from the overturned Jeep. Quivering with a mixture of fear, relief, and befuddlement, she turned her attention toward the garage from which the vehicle had come bounding. Maggie saw, in the dim gray light of the early morning, a black figure frozen in the open doorway of Morgan's garage. In his hands she recognized the unmistakable silhouette of a gun.

In the attic Morgan was in near panic for the first time since the ordeal began. He looked downward through the ceiling vent where his black-clothed adversary stood motionless almost directly below him, facing the end of the drive – and Maggie! The man appeared to be indecisive as he contemplated how to deal with the unexpected development. Now that it was obvious to him that Morgan had to still be near the garage, the man's head pivoted in small staccato motions, swiveling from Maggie to the house, to the garage interior, and back again.

Morgan knew that the hit man's dilemma was whether to deal with Maggie or his original target. Morgan's pulse quickened. He could only think of one response. In a single motion he jumped from the plywood floor onto a section of sheetrock between the rafters, at the same instant discarding his useless weapon. The creaking of the wood under his weight alerted the man below. Both his eyes and his gun were turning upward as Morgan crashed through weak ceiling material toward him. Morgan's left arm slammed against one of the two-by-six-inch ceiling joists between which he was falling, but the rush of adrenaline made the pain barely noticeable.

His impact with the intruder, though indirect, sent the attacker reeling into the side wall of the garage. His H&K weapon hit the concrete floor and slid out the doorway. Morgan tumbled backward but did not completely fall. He lunged for the weapon, but the other man swung his legs, knocking Morgan's from under him. Morgan flew to his feet at the just rising attacker, the momentum sending both men against the solid log wall. The man in black reached for a handgun. Morgan grabbed the hand with both of his and slammed it into the wall, but failed to dislodge the Glock semiautomatic. With his free arm the assailant swung his opponent around. Morgan clung desperately to the weapon and pulled the man off-balance with him.

The two men wrestled on the floor and the nine-millimeter weapon slid away from both. As each tried to rise, the attacker delivered a punch to Morgan's stomach and another to his jaw. Stars flew for the defender as he fell once again to the concrete. He managed to grab the other man's ankle, tripping him. Morgan scrambled to his feet and toward the figure, reaching him just as his outstretched fingers were touching the black pistol. Morgan pulled the hand away, but again received a blow, an elbow to the jaw. He fell violently to the garage floor, yet managed to maintain his grip on the black sweater of his enemy.

They rolled out the gaping doorway. Morgan's adversary stood first, pulling a knife from its scabbard on his torso. Suddenly there was the scream of a revved engine from where Maggie had stopped her truck down the drive. Simultaneously there was the roar of sand and rocks spewing against metal. The attacker looked toward the Ford; Morgan did not.

By the time the man spun back with the knife toward his target, Morgan had retrieved the submachine gun dropped by the man when Morgan had first crashed through the ceiling. The villain recoiled abruptly as Morgan unleashed the nine-millimeter rounds into his body. Before gravity could pull the man's body into its clutches, Maggie's red missile blasted into him, crushing him between it and the outside wall of the log garage.

The energy immediately fled from Morgan and he slumped to the ground, sitting and staring at his victim, pinned upright between the red Ford and the wall. Morgan's gaze turned to Maggie, who was hidden behind the material of a deployed airbag. He stood and rushed to her door as she was pushing the emptying bag away from her. She turned her head weakly toward the open window of her truck.

"Hi, Morgan." The words were barely audible. Josh Morgan slung open the door to the vehicle and pulled Maggie to him. They slumped to the ground in front of the garage. Maggie burst into tears as her friend held her face tightly to his chest.

"Maggie, Maggie. I'm sorry. I'm so sorry." He lifted her tear-streaked face to his and brushed her hair away from her eyes. "Are you okay?"

The reply came in two forms. The confused, blank stare gave way to a thin smile. Then her head bobbed. Maggie buried her face in Morgan's arms, and again the tears flowed.

◆

Near Langley, Virginia, vehicles braked and pulled to the shoulder of the road, turning on emergency flashers. Cell phones made frantic 911 calls. Men searched for the best way to scramble to the river partially hiding the crashed Mustang. But up the way two vehicles continued their progress away from the scene of the accident. Inside one of them two men exchanged smiles. Then the passenger flipped open his mobile phone and placed a call to Everson Blake.

◆

Morgan and Maggie finally summoned the energy to stand. Morgan escorted Maggie into the house and seated her on the couch. He offered a shot of whiskey, but she just wanted water. She clasped the glass with both hands and took small sips.

"Are you okay?" he asked for the thousandth time.

"I'm fine. You?" she finally realized to ask.

"Yeah, yeah. I'm okay. Heck, this happens to me all the time." He smiled, or tried to, and continued, "I'm sorry, Maggie, but I've got to take care of this." He left Maggie to survey the battlefield.

He went to the first attacker he had shot and found him to be very dead. He went through his pockets but found no identification of any kind. The "uniform" had no tags or markings. Morgan was not surprised. These were not burglars looking to support a drug habit. These were professional operations personnel. Morgan thought, this is from my past. But why now? He looked again at the dead man lying beside his house.

"Who are you?" he asked, almost expecting a reply. The pool of blood under the man's chest had stopped expanding, and much of it had soaked into the grass.

Morgan moved to the man still pinned between the garage and Maggie's truck.

He pushed the dead man with both hands. "You son of a bitch. You goddammed son of a bitch. Why?" The words were unfettered and at full pitch. Morgan propelled his closed fist into the jaw of the lifeless body. Then he grabbed him by the black sweater and unleashed a string of expletives. He shook him forward and back, as if trying to wake him to answer the questions tearing at Morgan.

A hand, then a second, tugged at his sleeve, gently.

"Josh."

He turned and embraced Maggie. As he did, she concluded silently, "He's really pissed."

The next hour or more was frenetic with Morgan performing some of the necessary tasks and shouting instructions to Maggie to do others. The front end of Maggie's truck was crushed, Morgan hoped he could start it. He twisted the key. The engine turned over but chugged to a stop when Morgan yanked the gearshift lever into reverse. The truck rolled back, however, just enough to allow the attacker's body to crumple to the ground.

Josh Morgan knew he couldn't call the authorities. He had neither the answers to the inevitable questions nor the time to deal with them.

Maggie interrupted his frantic pace and Morgan noticed she couldn't take her eyes off the crushed, bullet-riddled, blood-soaked body of the attacker. He placed an arm around her shoulder and led her away from the grisly scene.

"I know Blake had something to do with this. Apparently, he hasn't moved on from this either. And my 'insurance policy' is sort of indisposed." He returned to his work.

"But what about when he gets back? Blake has to think he might be rescued."

Morgan turned his lowered head toward Maggie. He paused, faced her, and backed away a step, leaning against the truck.

Maggie saw the light click on in Morgan's mind as he tilted his head toward where the bodies lay.

"What if Blake knows he's not coming back?" Morgan's face went instantly white as he accepted that as a possibility.

"Oh, shit!" he said and began to work even more wildly. I've gotta do something."

"I know. I knew that yesterday. Let's get back to work."

Morgan righted his Jeep, towed it up the drive with his tractor and, after some effort, forced it into the garage beside where he had also moved Maggie's truck with the John Deere. Then, for the first time in more than an hour, he paused to rest.

"I can't find Biscuit," he told Maggie. "He cried out when he found the guys on our land. I found a spot with a lot of blood."

"Cried out" had a more human connotation than whined or yelped, but that was how Morgan thought of the Golden Retriever. "I know the bastard shot him." With no more words he returned to his work.

"Josh, you have to notify someone. This, this is a crime."

Without answering, Morgan continued wrestling with the bodies.

Morgan clinched the steering wheel of the tractor desperately and glanced above him at the raised bucket in which two bodies now lay. He was just pulling the lever to tilt the oversized shovel and deposit the corpses onto the loose dirt of his in-progress trout pond when a familiar voice shouted to him from behind over the engine's idling. Morgan wheeled to see the unexpected and unwanted visitor, turned off the diesel engine and climbed from his vehicle and waved.

"Hey, Morgan!" Deputy Sheriff Scott Taggart continued, "Was driving by and saw you heading down the drive."

"Hi, Tag," Morgan returned, moving as rapidly as he felt he could toward the deputy without appearing suspicious.

"Haven't got that pond finished yet, I see." He continued moving toward Morgan.

"No… I seem to spend too much time playing," Morgan said, reaching his friend and delivering a handshake with warmth he didn't feel. He desperately wanted to continue the conversation where they stood, but the deputy proceeded to the barren area in front of the green and yellow tractor. Shit, he silently muttered at Taggart's back. He hurried to catch up.

"So, how's the new tractor? She's a beauty." Taggart crawled onto the seat. "I sure could use a new one, too, but, you know, a deputy's salary." He turned to Morgan and smiled. "Mind if I fire her up?" It wasn't really a question. The deputy turned the key and the diesel roared to life.

Morgan felt the weakness creep upward from his knees through his entire body. His breathing stopped as he watched his guest fondling the controls of the giant toy. "Let me show you the pond," he blurted and stepped to the front of the tractor directly below the shovel.

"Jeez, Josh, I coulda dropped the bucket right on your sorry-ass head," Tag warned, and finally killed the engine.

As the deputy stepped from the tractor, shaking his head, his radio crackled to life, giving Morgan the reprieve he desperately needed.

After a brief conversation and a quick "ten-four," Teton County Sheriff's Deputy Taggart said, "Well, pal, duty calls. Gotta go do that 'serve and protect' thing. Let's go fishing soon."

"Yeah, we'll do that." Morgan's answer was lifeless.

Taggart finally looked up the hill and saw Maggie. He shot a last look over his shoulder and flashed a knowing smile to his fishing buddy. "You devil," he laughed. And with that he returned to his county-owned SUV and pulled back onto Moose-Wilson Road.

Morgan waited a safe amount of time before returning to his tractor and dropping the two corpses unceremoniously onto the dirt. He hurriedly stabbed the shovel at the soft ground, systematically increasing the size of the makeshift grave. After he had convinced himself that the depth was adequate, he moved the tractor to the dead attackers, lowered the edge of the loader to the ground, and coldly pushed the pair into the hole.

The surging Mexican economy had a widespread and profound impact on international commerce that necessitated upgrades to many of the country's airports. The city of Chihuahua's *Aeropuerto Internacional General Roberto Fierro Villalobo* had expanded its operations dramatically and received flights from most of the major airlines. The Deputy Director's American Airlines flight wasn't scheduled to arrive in Chihuahua from Washington Dulles by way of DFW International until 1:00 p.m. Blake used the onboard mobile telephones for the third time to check voicemail on his private Agency mobile telephone. While that phone was secure, he knew that he couldn't guarantee the phone he used to retrieve the messages would be. So, the messages were to be brief and, to the uninformed listener, benign.

Blake hoped to hear one simple phrase: "Hey, pal, I got those tickets to the Nationals game." The message would seem to refer to the local professional baseball team but in truth would indicate that the operation had succeeded. If the mission had failed, the message would have merely said, "Hate to disappoint you but I wasn't able to come up with the tickets."

What puzzled Blake was that there was no message at all. It was still early, but it was a simple in-and-out. More than that, this operation was personal. It was a gift from God, he believed. But there was no message, and he had another two-and-a-half hours on this stupid plane. The NSA officer had called once on the first leg of the flight, and twice more during the brief time since departing Dallas-Fort Worth. He was very near to losing his temper, even though with Blake one would hardly notice the event in any visible way. He shifted in his first-class seat yet again, earning another impatient look from the woman beside him.

Blake turned his head one way and then another looking for the flight attendant, who, of course, in first class was never far away. Ev knew he was drinking too much but he desperately needed another. He wiped at his brow repeatedly with his handkerchief. In between times he held the white cotton cloth at his mouth, occasionally chewing at one corner of it and twisting at one side of his moustache. Blake's nerves were almost always like steel, but he didn't like flying, he didn't like anything that smacked of fieldwork, and mostly he didn't like waiting for this confirmation.

"Where is the stewardess?" he muttered. At that moment the flight attendant turned the corner from her station. Blake held up his glass and pointed to it.

Momentarily the American Airlines employee arrived at his seat with the refreshment.

"You certainly like Dr. Pepper, don't you, sir?"

◆

Fadi Al-Majeed was unaccustomed to driving such an unwieldy vehicle. And the pouring rain wasn't helping matters. Such torrents were rare in the American Southwest in the summertime, but the black clouds had followed him like a plague since hitting the highway. He and his hostage had left Moriarty, New Mexico, around noon and were making poor time.

"You wonder at my rage at you last night, don't you?" the driver asked his passenger by way of the mirror above him. "It is the same as my great President's and my country's rage toward America. Last night you provoked me, and I responded in a logical way. Throughout the world you have flaunted your sins. You have oppressed Muslims everywhere. You have taken the side of Zionists and have rained your power on us. Do you not expect us to respond also in a logical manner? We have God on our side. Allah and his angels protect us. The Islamic peoples of the world are rallying now as they have throughout history and are uniting against you infidels. It is the proper acts of Muslim brothers against the attacks of children of Satan. The Great Satan has unleashed this holy war upon itself.

"Your policies and attitudes toward the holy children have brought you to the face of justice. I am a part of that face. The thousands of children of Islam you have killed in my country and others are also part of that face. President al-Hashimi is part of that face. It is the face of Allah. Israel and the new Zion are suffering the fate you have set before yourselves. You suffer because you create suffering. You will die because you have killed.

"Do not wonder at my acts against you or my brothers' acts against your country. It is the justice of a holy nation and our Jihad."

For the first time since he was abducted, Trenton Weston believed he would not survive the ordeal.

◆

With Morgan's Jeep and her truck both out of commission, Maggie Loughlin was behind the wheel of Josh Morgan's Denali in front of the Jackson Hole Airport terminal just north of the city. She had both hands on the wheel and stared downward. Morgan gazed straight ahead as he went through the details. His voice was barely audible.

"Find some place to stay. I'm sure you're safe. They shouldn't know anything about you, and besides, it's me they're after. But just in case, stay away from my house the whole time I'm gone. I mean it. Don't go there to check my messages; no checking the mail. Nothing. Understood?"

The auburn hair shook as her head bobbed gently.

"Okay then. I'll try to let you know where I am whenever I can, but I may not be able to."

The photojournalist stepped out and retrieved his photo gear bag and small backpack. Maggie's gaze was still fixed on the floor of the SUV. Morgan set his bags on the curb and leaned into the passenger-side window.

"Don't worry. See ya soon, Mag."

The blue eyes turned to face him. Her cheeks were soaked.

"I love you, Josh."

Morgan couldn't speak. He only smiled and nodded and pushed himself up from the truck. The truck eased away from the curb. Morgan watched momentarily. He wanted to shout after Maggie. Instead, he snatched his luggage and started for the terminal.

CHAPTER 21

Betsy Parnell returned the handset to its cradle. Tough lady though she was, she wept openly. Benjamin Reid had been a friend more than anything else. She had been to his home, had shared dinner with him, Rebecca, and little Carrie.

"God, he loved his family," Betsy told the ceiling.

The CIA Deputy Director for Intelligence considered what she would do. Of course, the first task was to call a meeting of her staff and deliver the tragic news. She wondered if any work would be accomplished that day. Her team was incredibly professional, but Ben had been a standout, and immensely popular among his peers. Parnell couldn't allow the entire group to go home, but perhaps she could do without a few. She would, of course, have to remain in her office. There was much to be done. And much she was curious about in light of the President's decisions.

The President... The DDI had asked Ben, albeit it surreptitiously, to look into what was going on between the Saudis and the SNZ. Had he found out anything? She knew he had worked late. She went to Reid's cubicle and, using her master passwords, accessed his files.

Parnell quickly made her way through his work log and found the path to his notes about the situation. "Thank goodness you're organized," she thought, but flinched when she realized she couldn't speak of Ben in the present tense any longer.

Betsy used the mouse to drag his files onto a file transfer icon and sent it to her own computer via Reid's network software. She returned to her office to retrieve the transmission. It was then that she noticed an electronic note Ben had sent to her the night before. She double-clicked on it.

"Boss, smell a rat with EB. BR." That was it.

"'EB' – Blake," Betsy deduced and opened some of Reid's files. The "Case Notes Log" was a software "notepad" on which Ben kept a diary of activity regarding a project. The DDI scanned some of the notes Ben had recorded the previous night.

"20:12   NSA friend says EB out indefinitely.

"20:39   Flight information – EB to Chihuahua.

"20:51   Mexico Desk – re: ransom note – nothing. But source inside *EZLN* told them heard of new org forming. Leader – Geraldo Morales, name only, no details. Number of men left Chiapas in cars – destination unknown.

"21:47   Morgan called, I'll fill him in. Would want to know."

That was the last entry. "Morgan," Betsy wondered. "Who the hell is Morgan?"

She returned to Ben's desk and checked his "Sent" folder. Nothing to a Morgan-anyone, or anybody-Morgan. "Who are you, Morgan?"

Parnell decided she would take care of the matter of informing her department of Ben's accident. Then she would look into Ben's last notation more closely.

◆

Despite her promise to Morgan that she wouldn't return to his house, Maggie remembered that her computer with all her business records was in her smashed pickup truck. She felt she had no alternative but to pick it up. She surveyed the property from the end of the drive before continuing to the garage. She and Morgan had done a remarkable job of cleaning the property. Morgan had completely removed the shattered glass door and moved it to the garage. She had swept up the glass. It was as if nothing had happened there – except for the bullet holes in the walls of the garage. The sight of them brought the scene flooding back. Maggie had watched in horror as the Jeep, fueled by gravity, sped toward her. Then Morgan and the attacker fighting up the hill. It was like a hallucination, but her fear and anger were real.

The woman walked to the back of the garage and entered through the walk-through door. Retrieving her belongings from the red Ford she hurried back to Morgan's truck. She started the engine and put the stick in reverse. She was just beginning to turn the truck around when they caught her eye.

"Oh, my!"

CHAPTER 22

Morgan's flight to El Paso lasted just over five hours. It took creative scheduling to keep the journey even that short. American Flight 2246 got him to Dallas-Fort Worth International Airport at 6:00 p.m. Central Daylight Time. A hurried taxi ride to Dallas Love Field enabled him to just make his Southwest Airlines flight to El Paso International, where he arrived at 7:30 p.m. MDT. The post office was obviously closed now, he regretted, so he would have to begin his investigation in the morning. Morgan rented a car and headed off to find a place to stay. He had opted against making reservations in advance since he was traveling under his own name. He had no resources for a cover I.D., so he had decided there was no use telegraphing his movements any farther in advance than he had to. The ex-spook didn't know who the bad guys were. He also paid cash for everything to avoid using credit cards, which were easily traceable. Of course, every cash transaction required a credit card for a deposit, but they were only "swiped" and not submitted for payment unless he failed to pay.

Morgan wished he could call Maggie, but even when he told her he would try, he knew he would not.

Before finding a motel room Morgan decide to find 4400 East Paisano Drive.

◆

The Saudi was barely able to contain his frustration. He had intended to drive many more miles this day, but the weather had prevented it. He had only made it as far as Vega, Texas, a small town west of Amarillo. For his part, President Weston was thankful for the delay. He needed the time to formulate his own battle plans. Years before, a courageous group of Americans had prevented terrorists from adding to the worst terrorist

187

tragedy in the history of the United States. Knowing their own fate, they had regained control of an airliner and flew it into the Pennsylvania countryside, rather than let the terrorists who had seized it use it as a weapon. They had sacrificed their own lives in order to save others.

Former President of the United States decided he could do no less.

◆

At that moment in Chihuahua, Mexico, Everson Blake sat in his rental car, now using his own secure mobile phone. Still no response from the team he had dispatched to Wyoming. He "hung up" his telephone. His chest heaved with the substantial breath he took. The NSA manager propped his chin on his fist and looked out the window of the car. He dialed another NSA extension.

"Blake. What have you got, Terry?"

On the other end of the line was Terry Henderson, one of the analysts reporting to Blake.

"Sir, we've had some unusual intercepts, past and present. We went back to some of our recordings. Since you had us looking at Cozumel, we were checking hits there first. We filtered two mobile calls from there to San Cristobal, Chiapas. The talkers were pretty careful; no useful information."

"So, do you have anything I can use?" Blake bristled.

"Oh, I think you're going to like it, sir. I can tell you first that your location appears to be a better choice than you thought."

Blake assumed the former President had been moved from the Chihuahua area, but could think of no better place to begin his search.

"How so?"

"Sir, we started matching calls to the same mobile number. Obviously, we can't triangulate in Mexico like we can in some places. It's a matter of where we can intercept air or what we can trace on landline…"

"Henderson, the point."

"Sorry. The point is we have found some interesting calls involving the Cozumel unit – not calls it originated, but calls it received. There were calls routed through switches that clearly identified the fact that it went to Chiapas, basically the same area it had called from Cozumel. But it then made some calls from the Chihuahua area over the last several days. So the same phone has been in Cozumel, Chiapas, and Chihuahua. But here's the kicker. A couple of days ago – let's see, yeah – Wednesday there were three calls to that number in a space of only a few minutes. We pinned down a few things from the switching records. The calls were never answered. They were routed to some area east of Chihuahua. And they all originated from the same number, an apartment in Chihuahua."

"Address," Blake demanded. Henderson complied.

"Sir, unless I involve other people... What I'm saying is that I don't have the skills to break out the recordings myself. I could ask..."

Blake barked, "No others are to be involved. We'll go strictly by locations of the communications. At least for now.

"All right, then."

"'All right, then?' That's it?" the analyst thought. 'Thanks.' 'Great work.' 'Well-done.' Any of those would have been nice."

"I need a couple of other things." The Deputy Director gave the details and hung up without another word.

◆

In a small motel at the edge of El Paso, Josh Morgan was, he decided, praying. Not an especially religious man, he nevertheless held to a Christian faith he had acquired as a young teenager. His first thoughts were of Maggie. He was thankful that she had been kept safe in the attack that morning, and he prayed that God would continue to watch over her. Morgan also asked God to be with and protect the former President and return him safely to his home. It wasn't until his very last requests that his own name came. He asked that he be able to help, and thanked God for protecting him from the gunmen that day. But he was in way over his head and scared out of his mind and needed divine help.

It never occurred to Morgan to ask God to keep him safe as he proceeded. He figured there were more important matters.

◆

"Hi, sweetie," Blake spoke tenderly into the phone. "Your mom said the two of you had a pretty successful shopping day." Beaming the entire time, Daddy listened to his oldest daughter ramble on in the completely incomprehensible way that teenagers did.

"You know, I'm having second thoughts about this college thing. Seems like a community college and living at home would be the best solution, at least as far as I'm concerned." The NSA Deputy Director delighted in the "Oh, Daddy" that followed. A few minutes more with Toni, a brief conversation with his youngest, and suddenly, Everson Blake's day didn't seem so bad.

◆

Elizabeth Parnell had suffered through a long day at CIA headquarters. She had received word of the loss of a friend and colleague. She had relayed the information to her staff, which had been received with great despair.

She attended to functional and organizational matters, including the emotional task of assigning people to carry on Ben's responsibilities.

Betsy had spent the mid-afternoon visiting with Rebecca Reid, listening and consoling with genuine empathy. She watched as the new widow rocked her infant girl.

But now she was back at work. She stopped in Ben's cube again and had a thought. She walked into the next cube where Sam Devlin was still working.

"Hi, Sam."

"Hi, Director Parnell. Tough about Benny."

"Yeah. Real tough. Say, did Ben ever mention anyone named Morgan to you? Don't know if that's a first name or a last."

Devlin leaned back in his chair with one hand behind his head, the other tapping his pen on his desk.

"No. Doesn't ring a bell." You might ask Angie Brooks. She's known Ben – knew Ben – a lot longer than I did. I think she's still here. She just got back after going over to see Mrs. Reid, I think."

"Yeah, me, too. Thanks."

Brooks was indeed at her desk but wasn't working. Her eyes were moist and she was simply sitting in her chair, clutching a box of tissues. The sight seemed to demand that the DDI knock.

"Hi, Angie. How you doing?"

Seeing the Deputy Director, she began to shuffle some things around her desk.

"Ms. Parnell, I…"

"It's okay, Angie. I haven't felt much like working myself. You knew Ben pretty well, I guess."

"I really knew his wife better. I went to church with the two of them."

"I hate to bother you, but does the name Morgan ring a bell with you. I think he was a friend of Ben's."

"Sure, Josh Morgan. He was best man at Ben and Rebecca's wedding. I was her Maid of Honor. Rebecca had this idea of getting Josh and me together. Why do you ask?"

"Oh, it's not real important. Do you know anything about him, where he lives, when Ben might have seen him?" DDI inquired.

"No, but you could ask Rebecca."

Parnell had thought of that but didn't think it was appropriate today. "Sure, I'll do that," she replied, turning to walk to her office. "Sorry to have bothered you. Why don't you knock it off for today? It's awfully late."

"Thanks. I think I'll do that," the junior analyst said, immediately beginning to shut things down.

Betsy was a few steps away when she heard Brooks' next comment.

"Josh was really sweet, but I just couldn't see myself dating a Company man."

The Deputy Director came to a dead stop and turned.

"Excuse me?"

"I didn't think it would work out."

"No, what did you say about a Company man?" she urged.

Angie never looked up from gathering her things, but said, "Oh, he was a field guy. I wasn't supposed to know, I'm sure, but Rebecca told me." She raised her head toward Parnell. "But that's all I know."

Elizabeth Parnell was sure her jaw was dragging the floor. She stood without a sound while Angie Brooks turned off the light over her work surface and stood to leave.

"Thanks, Angie. Get some rest," she finally said.

"Thank you, ma'am, but I think I'll go back to see if Rebecca needs anything. Goodnight."

Parnell's mind was racing. She returned to her office and pulled up the file on Josh Morgan. She got all the personal information, and some summary data about his career.

"Curious," she thought. "An awful lot of 'restricted' details." She typed in her password. The instantaneous reply was "Access Denied."

"What the...?" She retyped her password. Same message.

"I'm a friggin' Deputy Director. Nothing is 'restricted' from me." Parnell stared at the computer screen, as if waiting for it to reconsider, but it did not.

"Shit," and she went back to the non-restricted details. "A Murtha officer?" she saw, referring to the amendment regarding journalists and espionage. She had personally never heard of a photojournalist NOC. Even though technically the President could approve it, it just wasn't done. Then she saw another word that raised her eyebrows.

"Terrador." On her way up the Agency ladder she had seen much of the intelligence surrounding the Latin American op but had never needed to know anything on the operations side.

The highest-ranking woman in CIA history looked at her watch. It was still early enough to visit Rebecca Reid.

◆

It would be his first address to his nation as President, and José-Eduardo Herrera felt inadequate to the task. His love and loyalty for Portillo ran deep. It was no small matter for him to have put aside his own presidential ambitions to run alongside any man. But he grew to believe that Portillo was the right man for this era in Mexico's history. It didn't damage his ego to admit that he was not in the man's class. Herrera knew that he would be a good President, but his friend had been a superior one.

The new President's words would be carried around the world. The beginning of his administration would be witnessed by televisions audiences, who would, fairly or not, pass judgement on him by what he said this night. Herrera began his remarks.

"Fellow citizens, *los Estados Unidos Mexicanos* has suffered a great loss. Violence has taken a father, a husband, a statesman, a friend. But while enemies of our way of life have taken a great man, President Portillo would insist that he is not an indispensable man.

"Yes, we mourn the loss of our President, but we are not defeated. Yes, we will miss the leadership he brought to our nation, but we are not helpless without him. The greatest tribute we can pay to our fallen leader is to persevere in his death. He has led us to greatness as a nation. But he has also prepared us to carry on, to work with our hearts and souls, and hands and minds, to fulfill the promise of his life. The spirit of Mexico, the idea of Mexico, lives on in each of us. We must toil tirelessly; we must strive relentlessly to achieve the full extent of the greatness President Portillo has brought within our reach.

"We pledge unconditional support to our friends in the United States of America. The Mexican people not only offer our sympathies for the kidnapping of their great President Weston, but declare our resolve to right this act of evil, by locating this friend of Mexico, and returning him safely home.

"Every resource of our government and every breath of our lives are committed to justice and peace.

"We accept the word of the *Zapatista* National Liberation Army in denying a role in this attack. Our investigation indicates that this is a new faction of radicals that separates itself from the spirit of Emilio Zapata by its conduct and by its spirit.

"Zapata cried 'land and liberty.' But these terrorists violate his great dignity by devoting their lives to 'extortion and violence.'

"There will be no quarter given to terrorists on our soil, whether they act from abroad, or from within. We must give our full measure of commitment, our unwavering sacrifice to ensure peace, safety, and prosperity for all Mexican people.

"The borders of Mexico are on guard. Every city and highway, every village and back road are being watched. We have assembled a net through which these enemies of Americans and Mexicans will not slip. There will be no escape for these traitors to our nation. The snare will close until they are found. The full power and authority of two great nations are being energized to achieve justice. Mexico and the United States are cooperating at every level. These terrorists will be found.

"We pray for God's peace and His might and dedicate ourselves to the assurance that this will not stand."

◆

"You're really kind. I'm so sorry to disturb you right now."

"It's okay Betsy. I'm glad to help. Ben really liked you, and he loved working for you. Anything I can do." Rebecca was slightly more in control this evening. She led her late husband's boss to his home office.

Betsy Parnell turned on Ben's home computer.

"Good boy," she said upon seeing that Reid had used the same passwords at home as on his work computer. She expertly sped through the path to his email software.

"Microsoft Outlook. Good." Near the top of the list of "Inbox" was a receipt from Blue Mountain Greeting Cards. Ben had sent a birthday card to Morgan. Parnell quickly copied all the email files onto a flash drive, excused herself and returned to Langley.

At her office, the DDI looked through every note she had transferred from Reid's home computer. There weren't many. Ben obviously moved a lot of emails out of that software to other folders soon after he got them. The only memo at all having to do with Morgan was the 'birthday card' note.

She opened the email and read the birthday wishes first. The first thing she saw prompted her to click open Morgan's file again.

"Clever, Ben," she said when she confirmed her recollection that "Coyote" had been the photojournalist's code name. But, as she scanned his file to refresh her memory, she saw that Morgan's birthday was in September.

Parnell looked at the email, back at the personal info, then back to the card again.

"Ben, you would have known when you best man's birthday is. What have we really got here?" She looked at the free text her colleague had added. "Sounds more like a love note. Carrie? Why did you sign it with your daughter's name?

"What's the photo?" She opened the attachment.

The DDI abruptly pushed back from her desk.

"Shit, Ben! You know better!"

With the knowledge she had of the details of her meeting with Mercer, Parnell assessed the note and uncovered the real message in a heartbeat.

"But why did you tell this guy, Ben?"

◆

Nearly two thousand miles away, a man sat in a rented camper as the captive of a Saudi intelligence agent. Weston was very important to Josh Morgan. But he was expendable to the current President of the United States.

◆

At the La Paloma Apartments in Chihuahua, Ev Blake and his associate were hard at work. Mark Sanders had a chiseled physique and the lightly scarred skin of severe teen-aged acne. As a Navy SEAL he had distinguished himself with his cunning and his resolve. And because he had shown not the slightest qualms about wet ops the five-foot eleven inch, two-hundred-and-four-pounder had caught the attention of CIA. He was no longer employed by the Agency but still free-lanced and had been an associate of Ev's during the Terrador days.

"Quite a contradiction in style" the muscle said, holding both an exceedingly short white dress in one hand and camouflaged military-style BDUs in the other.

The brains just grunted as he sat at a desk flipping through letters. "Member of the *SNZ*. Definitely a player," Blake concluded.

The pair continued rifling through the belongings of the resident, Mariana Lopez.

Mark Sanders remarked, "She's gone, Blake."

"Yes, I think you're right, but this helps." He grinned as he turned to his associate and waved a two-page letter. "Ever been to Playa Del Carmen?"

CHAPTER 23

DAY 9 – SATURDAY

Morgan was up earlier than usual, but there was no reason to skip breakfast. The post office didn't open until eight-thirty on Saturdays. He desperately wanted to call Maggie but didn't dare. So he finished his Grand Slam at Denny's and returned to his motel room. He had poured over USA Today while eating. Now in his motel room he watched QNN, Fox, CNN, and MSNBC. Like the newspaper, they offered little in the way of new details about the missing former President. Morgan was disappointed that the story seemed to be growing stale from a journalistic point of view.

He checked out of his room and left early in order to be at the post office when it opened.

◆

A number of Saudis were just beginning their workday in Washington, D.C. For their colleague on the other end of the phone in the RV Park just off I-40 Business in Vega, Texas, it was an hour earlier and the start of another day in which he would transport himself and his passenger toward their respective fates. Al-Majeed knew that in his destiny lay not only the pleasure of Allah and the rewards he would bestow on his faithful child in heaven, but, more immediately, the earthly gratitude of the Holy Islamic Republic of Saudi Arabia and Muslims everywhere. He would be a hero to all the nations of Islam.

And he knew that the American President awaited an equally certain destiny based on his own choices in life. The only thing left to resolve was by what route the Saudi would transport the infidel to his judgment and he had finally made that decision.

The Head of Mission at the Saudi Embassy in Washington offered his congratulations on the success of the mission. He realized there were complications, but the fact that the former leader of the Great Satan was in custody had both surprised and elated him.

"Allah be praised, my friend. Your plan has been executed and we are another step closer to winning the war against the American infidels."

"You are kind, brother, but do not consider the war won. We have won but one battle. The fight continues," Al-Majeed said to his countrymen with feigned modesty.

"But it is a major battle that we have won," insisted the diplomat.

"It is, to be sure. Now we must adapt if we are to preserve this victory. There have been events that require adjustments in our plan. Since it is no longer possible to complete the business transaction in the way we had intended, here are the modifications we must make."

The Saudi agent recited a laundry list of needs to his associates in the District of Columbia.

"It is understood. We will begin immediately. The will of Allah be done."

The conversation ended but the phones were soon spreading the news of the changes requested by the intelligence officer. As the recreational vehicle resumed its progress eastward on Interstate 40, the new details regarding the North American portion of the operation were being transmitted to various points in the United States and to a private phone in Riyadh.

Most importantly, in a matter of minutes a 225-foot yacht of Saudi Arabian registry, *Al-Amânah*, dropped its mooring near Playa del Carmen, Mexico, and began to steam north.

◆

CIA's Deputy Director, Intelligence, was frequently in her office on weekends. Usually she was reviewing ongoing projects, but not like this one.

She called the office of DCI Donleavy, who had been the Deputy Director of Operations at the time of the Terrador op. Of course, he was there this day as well.

"Hi, Bets. I heard about Ben. I'm sorry."

"Thanks, Chris. The reason I'm calling is, I ran across a name in some of Ben's files – Josh Morgan. What can you tell me about him?"

The pause was so long that Betsy wondered if they had been disconnected. Finally, Donleavy spoke. "Why do you ask?"

"Remember our meeting over at the House, the instructions we got?"

"Non-instructions is more like it. But, yeah, I remember. What of it?"

"Ben Reid was looking into it."

"He wasn't supposed to…."

"No, actually, Mercer told you and me not to look into it any more or talk to anyone about it. I just never told Ben to quit his work."

"Damn, Betsy," he started, but he stopped. "No, I'm with you. So, what's this about Morgan?"

"I think Ben told him about the President's decision to hold off action."

"Crap, Elizabeth." Donleavy was like her parents, the DDI realized. It was "Betsy" until he was pissed. Then it was "Elizabeth."

"Why the hell did he do that?"

"Nobody was going to do anything, so what did it hurt? Morgan was a journalist, so I'm guessing Ben was leaking it to him in the hopes of there being some publicizing of the facts, and some public pressure brought to bear."

"No, it's more than that. Josh Morgan would want to know everything about Weston."

"Why is that? Oh, and Ben also made a note about suspecting Blake is up to no good."

"Weston, Blake, and Morgan. Sounds like old times. Come to my office." Then the line went dead.

The former Chief Executive of the United States pondered his dilemma. He knew he would never allow his country to be humiliated by yet another intelligence failure, one that would allow a country to parade him in front of the entire world as a war criminal. What Weston couldn't comprehend was that not a single US agency had discovered the plot, even if it did begin on Mexican soil. It was further astounding to him that the Saudi had not been interdicted at some point along this journey, except for the bumbling patrolman Al-Majeed had shot. All personal feelings aside, the man was not sure his successor in the Oval Office had the team around him to thwart the plan but was willing to give him the benefit of the doubt. What he was certain of was that if he made it all the way to Saudi Arabia, Mercer had neither the foreign policy expertise, nor the political will to properly resolve the issue. Weston wondered how the crisis would affect the current President's initiative at re-establishing some degree of relations with the Middle Eastern dictatorship.

Weston also speculated as to how much time he had. His personal actions would unfold along two paths. There was no doubt that an attempt at escape would occur first and would, in fact, negate the need for the second if successful. And he knew that whatever plans he developed would have to be able to be acted out within the context of the vehicle in which he rode. The ex-Commander-in-Chief could not hope for a stroke of luck. He couldn't consider scenarios that required daylight versus night, good weather versus bad. No, he had to design alternatives that he could act on any place, any time, in any situation. He began to study every detail of the interior of his delivery vehicle.

◆

Parnell spent about twenty minutes in the DCI's office during which he told her everything about the Terrador screw-up and the rumored relationships among Morgan, Blake, and the former President.

Back at her desk she was still trying to get her mind around what she had heard. "An op gone bad. Morgan ultimately turns the situation around, virtually single-handedly. Blake gets a reprimand, but a lot of people think he was dirty in the thing. And a rumor that Weston intervened on Morgan's behalf.

"Practically an espionage soap opera," she decided.

She checked Morgan's last known address in Wyoming, got his number, and called. His voicemail finally picked up.

"Morgan. Leave a message."

Creative greeting, Betsy observed sarcastically. The beep came.

"Josh, this is DDI Betsy Parnell. I was a friend of Ben Reid's. Call me, please." And she gave her direct number.

◆

On his mobile phone the Deputy Director of the National Security Agency was hearing the results of his request from the night before. He had anticipated what he was hearing but was nevertheless disturbed.

"No activity on Morgan's phone except some inbound. No answers. You'll find one caller interesting – the CIA DDI."

That bit of information stunned Blake. "Interesting. Go on."

"No credit card activity. But his driver's license was recorded on a car rental company's computer."

"Where?" Blake demanded matter-of-factly.

"Budget Rentals, El Paso airport," reported Terry Henderson. His credit card number would've been recorded for a deposit, but he paid cash. Looks like he's trying to make it hard to track him, but it's not working. Anyhow, I backtracked and got his name on an American Airlines passenger manifest. He arrived in El Paso early yesterday evening."

"Anything else?" asked Blake.

"Nothing. No activity on his mobile. Looks like we won't know anything until he uses a card, returns the car, uses his cell, something."

"Well, it's not what I wanted to hear, but good work," Blake said before he disconnected.

"'Good work?' That's a switch." Henderson considered with a smirk as he looked at the telephone headset he had just removed.

Blake walked through the scenarios in his mind. "How could they have missed him?" he wondered.

"What?" asked Blake's traveling partner.

"Morgan is on the move. He's in El Paso."

"Maybe he wasn't at his house yesterday."

"No," Blake answered, "they would have called to report that. Well, at least he's behind us."

Sanders was astonished. "Behind us? You saying he's gonna try to do something? By himself?"

"I'm saying exactly that. You didn't know this guy. He has, let's say, a connection with the former President. He's naïve, but very bright, and resourceful. The problem is that he has a misguided sense of right and wrong. Morgan is incapable of understanding what is in the best interests of his country. His loyalties are misaligned. That's why the hit – rather attempted hit. Been wanting to get around to that for some time, but, well, there were obstacles."

Sanders listened to his boss' laundry list of grievances against the former spy. A thin smile creased his lips. "Jeez, and here I thought it was just personal."

Blake's lips never changed, but his eyes betrayed an obvious delight. "Oh, it is personal."

◆

Morgan carried his cameras and wore an old press badge on a lanyard around his neck to fully characterize his cover as a photojournalist.

"Frankly, I'm surprised no one has been here yet. I called the FBI." The postal clerk spoke with the Mexican accent that was characteristic of a large number of US citizens in El Paso. "I saw that the letter went to the White House from our zip code and called right away. Well, right away after the Mexico thing."

Morgan snapped photos of the building the people, the street outside, and documented dialogue with a digital voice recorder. The best thing about his cover is that he needed to make no effort at hiding the fact that he was collecting intelligence. He cared little about the images. He was looking for information.

"I understand the letter originated here, but what other information can you provide? The real key is who mailed the letter."

"I know who mailed the letter, *Señor*."

Morgan blinked a couple of times. "You know who mailed the letter? How can you remember from the thousands of parcels that come through here? For all you know, it may have been dropped in a night slot."

"I remember this customer," assured the clerk, using his hands to make the universal gesture for a shapely figure.

"A woman?"

"*Si*. My wife would kill me for what I was thinking about her."

"Describe her, please," he begged, holding the recorder to the man's face.

"Hispanic. My height." Five-seven, Morgan judged.

"White dress, just barely covering the goods." The clerk exhaled a muted whistle.

"Black hair, perfect skin, and…" The postal employee cupped his hands largely, about twelve inches in front of his own chest.

Morgan smiled. Despite the graphic description, there were very few concrete details that would be helpful. The one useful element of the portrait the man painted was that there was nothing covert about the woman. So other people – men – would have likely noticed her.

"One other thing – which way did she go?"

"South. I'm positive." Another smile.

◆

In Jackson Hole, Maggie was staying at the home of her coworker, Curtis Jones. His friend Tim Simpson was there most of the time.

She couldn't resist calling Morgan's home. She knew the passcode to Morgan's voicemail. She had seen him dial it often enough. Maybe he would leave a message for her there, thinking that she would, against his wishes, go there to look in on things.

"Morgan," Maggie heard. "Leave a message."

She tapped the code on her phone's screen.

"Hello. You have two new messages." The drab, generic computer-generated voice was annoying, but better than the overly-pleasant female voice on some mailboxes. "I will replay two new messages."

The first was a telemarketing recording that droned on for over two minutes. Maggie didn't know how to fast-forward the recording.

Finally, the second message began. Maggie wasn't prepared and had to scramble to find pen and paper. She hoped she got the number right. She hung up the phone and sat quietly. She wasn't sure what the message meant, but her instincts told her one thing.

"Josh is going to want to know about this."

◆

Wendell Mercer sat in the private residence of the White House, scanning daily briefs. The television was tuned to CNN, though the volume was muted. He glanced up in time to see his own face staring from the screen. He restored the sound and saw footage of former President and Mrs. Weston aboard the Mexican tourist train. The anchor, Abraham Stein, segued to his guest, as Mercer returned to his reading.

"Madam First Lady, thank you for joining us at this difficult time."

The President's head popped up from the pages.

"Mrs. Weston, how are you holding up?" asked Stein.

"It's been a test of my faith, to say the least, Abe, but I've got a number of strong and wonderful people around me, providing support. The outpouring of concern from the American people has been incredible, too, and I would like to thank them for it."

Alicia Weston's eyes were red, her hair uncharacteristically mussed, and the blue dress wrinkled. It was an understandable departure from the usually immaculate attention she gave to her appearance.

Stein continued, "Have you heard anything new about your husband?"

"Nothing at all. I heard the reports of the ransom demand on the news along with everyone else. It seems clear that the people who did this consider it an act against the United States rather than an attack on an old woman and her husband. So I suspect any communications will occur between the terrorists and our government.'

"You're saying that you received no notice from the government about the note; you heard the reporter break it?"

"That's correct."

"What have you heard from US officials, Mrs. Weston?"

"Really, not very much… I'm sure they are busy with the investigation," knowing the veiled accusation was hardly veiled.

"Bitch," Mercer muttered.

The interview continued with the obvious questions and more obvious answers that now counted as journalism. At the end of the dialogue, one inquiry caught Mercer's attention.

Stein asked, "How satisfied are you that government officials are proceeding with all due diligence to resolve this issue?"

The short but noticeable pause communicated more than the actual response.

"I'm certain President Mercer and the various agencies are doing everything they can."

"Don't count on it, Mrs. Weston," President Mercer said to the television screen. Uncharacteristically, it was more an apology than a taunt.

◆

Fadi Al-Majeed was glad to have the conversation, or, more precisely, the chance to further wax philosophical about his religious and political beliefs.

President Weston had been largely unsuccessful in acquiring any useful information. He was ready to try a more adversarial approach. "So where are we heading?"

"You have asked many questions today. Are you so fearful for your fate?" the Saudi inquired.

"There is nothing you could tell me that would shake my faith in the one true God." The gauntlet was thrown.

"You god is a myth. Allah will be gracious to his children. The world will laugh at your desperation when you cry to a god who does not answer, a god who does not live. You will be President al-Hashimi's example of the utter failure of your misplaced faith."

"Are you so certain? During my presidency I met many true Muslims who were dedicated to peace and goodness. They are the true disciples of Allah and will find their reward in his bosom. They will be the ones rewarded by Allah…"

"What do you know of Islam?! You cannot know what it is like to be set upon by the mongrels of the world." It was the first time since they had been together that Weston had heard his captor shout. The enraged Arab continued, "Your world is a house of lies, of blasphemies. Your words are the hypocrisies that bring you closer to your destiny."

"My destiny lies in the kindness of my God. I have prayed and he has answered."

The foreigner did not respond verbally, but his eyes glared into the mirror above him at his bound hostage behind. His eyes were lit with a quiet knowing but it was not passed on to Weston. The captive still had no useful information, nothing on which to estimate his enemy's – and his – timetable. Through the windshield he could see the blurred images of passing road signs. He knew that they had proceeded through Amarillo and were not far down Highway 287, which he guessed they would likely follow to the Dallas-Fort Worth area, though he could not imagine that the Metroplex would be the place where they would end their journey. So it seemed likely that he would merely pass through his adopted home. He would pass so close to his Alicia but would not see her. Mr. Weston hoped that, somehow, Mrs. Weston knew he was thinking about her, and how much he loved her.

Phase One was firm in his mind, but he had no inkling yet of what Phase Two would entail.

◆

Even Morgan was amazed at how easy it was to find men – shop owners, construction workers, and others – who had seen the mystery woman. He quickly traced her route to a bus stop. He was even able to estimate a time. He already knew the date from the postmark.

A call to the city transit office and an introduction led him to the name of the bus driver. The weekend manager wouldn't provide the name of the driver but agreed to call him at home and have him call Morgan if he would entertain a conversation.

Morgan looked for a number on the payphone he was using, but none was there. Morgan felt he had no choice but to give out his cell number.

The call came quickly. Morgan got the home number of El Paso transit driver Francis Washington. The man's memory was as vivid as the postal clerk's has been, stating how he was afraid he would wreck the bus because he continually looked in his mirror at the woman seated in the third row on the right side of the bus.

Finally, the piece of data Morgan was looking for. His target exited Washington's bus and headed for the footbridge over the Rio Grande into the Mexican ciudad of Juarez. Details fell into place quickly. Morgan guessed correctly that the object of so many men's lust had gone into the bus station just across the border.

"Chihuahua," Morgan finally learned. The temptress had gone to Chihuahua.

Morgan returned to the El Paso airport and booked a flight to Chihuahua. While waiting for his plane the retired spy lifted the handset of a pay phone and called Maggie's office. He was going to be pissed if she was there, but he decided this was the safest way to get a message to her.

"Image Quest," the male voice greeted.

Morgan was caught off guard by getting a real human's voice.

"Curtis?"

"Speaking."

"Josh Morgan."

"Maggie's at my place," he blurted. His boss had told him almost nothing about what had happened at Morgan's house, but he knew something had shaken her, that Morgan was on some kind of a mission, and that his friend was in love with Morgan. That was all he needed to know.

Morgan let out a deep breath at finding that Maggie had gone somewhere other than her home.

"Is she okay?"

"Unsettled but mostly okay. She's tough."

Morgan wondered how much Curtis knew, but decided he trusted Maggie's judgement.

"Tim is staying with her today," Jones told his caller.

"Thanks, Curtis. Really."

Jones gave his number to Morgan. "She would love to hear from you."

Morgan disconnected the call and looked at the coins in his hand. No time to get more change and he didn't want to use his cell. The intercom had already announced boarding for his flight. He would just have to make it quick, he decided. He dialed the number he had just received and deposited the required amount at the prompt. He had one dime left.

"Have to make it real quick."

A voicemail greeting proceeded, using precious seconds of the coin call.

"Beep, dammit," Morgan urged. When it did, he started his message. "Tell Maggie…"

Tim and Maggie had decided not to answer the telephone until they identified the caller, and both were huddled over the outdated electronic device. As soon as Morgan's voice began, the woman grabbed the phone with both hands.

"Josh," she recognized.

"I'm okay. Only have a minute," he told her in verbal shorthand.

"Then I have to tell you something. I checked messages at your house and…"

"Maggie!" He didn't ask how.

She talked right over his attempt to interrupt. "Somebody named Betsy Parnell called."

"The DDI?"

"That's what she said. She gave this number…"

"Hold on." He wasn't prepared for this. Nothing to write on or with. He grabbed his digital recorder and pushed a button.

"Go," he said, shoving the machine against the earpiece. As he listened, he heard Maggie start, and the voiceover of a recording asking for more money. Maggie continued, and as she finished, the line disconnected.

Morgan heard the final boarding call for his flight. No time to call now, he realized, and moved toward the gate.

◆

"Are we ever going to eat? It's well after noon and I would like to eat."

Al-Majeed cast a glance at his hostage in the rearview mirror of the rented American Excursions motor home.

"Does Allah forbid me eating? A steak sounds good," Weston continued.

"We will eat." The Arab turned into a roadside rest area soon afterward.

"Here is your meal," he snorted. It was bread with vegetables. "And your special drink." Weston had persuaded him that a soft drink would be allowed. At the last service station, he had bought his passenger a Pepsi Cola. He opened the can and set it before Weston with his plate. He untied the rope from the man's feet and hands, permitted him a visit to the bathroom, and watched him eat.

The Middle-Eastern man hardly took his eyes off his guest, but each time he did, Weston worked at the pull-tab on the can, thanking God that the Arab had bought the drink in a can instead of a bottle. It took only two attempts to pry it free. With his next swallow he finished the drink and placed the empty container in the sack that served as a trash bin. He hoped his Saudi host would not inspect it.

Soon both men were in their traveling positions and beginning the next leg of their journey. Weston managed a better grasp of the tiny piece of aluminum he had palmed and broke it in half. One of the pieces had a quarter-inch jagged edge. It would have to do. He began to scrape at the rope that connected his hands and feet to the seat pedestal. It could hardly be called sharp. Abrasive was a more accurate description.

The ex-President held no hope of freeing either his hands or his feet, but cutting the one connecting rope would at least unbind him from the seat on which he rode. He prayed that the evening ride would be a long one.

◆

Two men departed their plane in Cancun. A drive of about sixty kilometers lay ahead of Blake and Sanders. The Deputy Director of the National Security Agency sent his associate to get a rental car while he dialed Terry Henderson's number at NSA's Fort Meade headquarters.

"Talk to me, Henderson," Blake began immediately.

"Hi, boss. Okay, here's the latest." He summarized the developments since he last spoke with his boss.

"All calls to Morgan's house are short, indicating they are probably messages. So we started running a string on any calls originating from the Jackson Hole area. He got one call from the home of a Curtis Jones. Jones works at some place called Image Quest. That store is owned by a Margaret Loughlin.

"Her phones – business and home – show up a lot on Morgan's phone details. Looks like there is some relationship between her and Morgan. Odd thing is that there are no calls from her home over the last day.

"There was one interesting call to Jones' home, from a payphone at – get this – the El Paso airport. Gotta be our boy. Curiously his home phone records don't show a single call to that number – ever. My guess, Loughlin is holed up at Jones' place."

"You're probably right, Henderson. Go on."

"Back to our boy. He's in Chihuahua."

"Dang. What about the Saudi?" the NSA manager demanded.

"Just getting to that. There have been a number of calls from the Saudi Embassy over the last several months to the El Paso area, southern New Mexico, Chihuahua, and Chiapas. In the last day or so, there have been two inbound calls from a mobile matching those locations. First call was from a small town in Mexico. Immediately after that call, a call went back out to El Paso to a place that rents recreational vehicles. The second call was from a small town in Texas. The phone call had hardly ended before a land-to-sea call was made from the embassy. I haven't made the recipient yet."

Blake made the connection. "There is a Saudi yacht in Playa del Carmen – the *Al-Amânah*. We suspect it is implicated. The call was probably to it. Some overheads would be useful."

"I'll get it done, sir."

"What else?" said Blake.

"The only other thing is that there has been no apparent communication between our target and the CIA pukes. No indication that he returned the DDI's call."

"So, he's doing all this on his own?" Blake was astonished.

"That's it, I think, Director Blake." His subordinate reviewed his notes. "Yes, sir, that's all for now."

"Give me Morgan's flight information."

Henderson detailed their target's itinerary.

"Good job, Terry. Your efforts will pay off when I get back to NSA." The line went dead.

Terry Henderson leaned back in his office chair and took off his headset. "Well, it's the fast track now, Terry," he congratulated himself.

◆

Blake took a seat in the Cancun airport and waited for Sanders to return. The man brought his index fingers to a point on his chin. How did this thing fit together? Blake was both alarmed and impressed that Josh Morgan was making such progress. But what did Morgan think he could do? He will need help at some point, but seems to be flying solo for now, Blake assumed.

He closed his eyes and slouched in his chair. His thoughts returned to the primary mission. "What is the Saudi up to?" he pondered. "He obviously has Weston and is moving him himself.

"The calls to the Saudis, and the subsequent return calls. Assume the call from Mexico was from him. A call was placed to El Paso. Were they sending help? Could he be moving into the United State? In an RV?

"What if he has changed his plans? Okay, then he has crossed the border at El Paso," he guessed incorrectly. "Be a major feat to get across under the circumstances. But assume he has. And the call from Texas? If that was him, he's heading east, probably to the Gulf coast somewhere. And

if the call from the Saudi embassy was to the *Al-Amânah*?"

"Heck," he said aloud in his strongest language.

Sanders was just arriving and, hearing Blake's "expletive," smiled thinly and said. "Don't lose control, Ev."

"We have to go, Mark."

CHAPTER 24

Sometimes things go poorly; sometimes they proceed as if with divine intervention. Josh Morgan thanked God that his current efforts seemed to fall among the latter. The fact that the woman he trailed had taken such obvious delight in flaunting her sensuality had created a trail of breadcrumbs right to her apartment. He stood near the door and surveyed his surroundings. Gringos stood out in this neighborhood in Chihuahua.

Confident he was not being observed. He slid a credit card into the crease between the door and the frame.

"At least I can use this for something," he remarked at the rectangular piece of plastic.

Closing the door behind him, his first reaction was, "What a dump." Then he realized that the room had been searched previously without regard for the tenant's property. Morgan feared his predecessor had already taken anything of value, but he explored the room anyhow.

He shuffled through the clothing that lay everywhere and saw the skimpy white dress in the pile. "Bingo," he smiled.

Outside the door he heard the metallic tinkling of keys, followed by the clicking of tumblers in the lock as one was inserted. Morgan rushed to position himself behind the door just before it opened. The entrant paused and shrieked her alarm at the sight of her domicile. Morgan flung both arms around the woman, and kicked the door shut.

Mariana Lopez swung her body around violently, bringing the two crashing onto the bed. One of Morgan's arms came free and the woman seized the opportunity to swing wildly, raking her long fingernails across her attacker's face. His other arm came free. Mariana tried to lift herself from the bed, but Morgan managed to regain a grip on one of her arms.

She spun around, surprising Morgan by counterattacking and the pair tumbled back onto the bed, then to the floor. The Mexican woman stunned

Morgan with a knee to the groin and smashed a fist into his eye. Without judging himself, Morgan finally swung at the woman's face. Even though his hand was open, his opponent went reeling off of him. Still she fought back vigorously.

Mariana again seized the initiative, throwing a lamp at Morgan. It slowed abruptly as it hit the extent of the electrical cord, but still hit its target as he rose from the floor. Now the woman lunged for the door. Morgan dove, clipping her ankles just enough to send her headfirst into the wood. He yanked a blanket from the bed and jumped toward the addled Mariana, covering her flailing fists and upper body with it. He straddled the Mexican's body and placed his left hand where he knew her neck would be. For all intents and purposes the fight was over. Just one thing remained.

Morgan raised his right hand, stopping it at its highest point. He closed his eyes briefly and took a deep breath. He whispered, "Shit," and brought his fist crashing into the blanket. The figure it covered went limp.

◆

The first foreign dignitary that Herrera contacted as President of Mexico was President Wendell Mercer of the United States, and as a courtesy, he spoke in fluent English. It was a skill both he and his late colleague shared.

"Mr. President, let me first express my sincere regrets at the tragic abduction of President Weston. My nation is prepared to cooperate fully with any law enforcement representatives you choose to send to Mexico." To himself, the Mexican President wondered at the meager response by the northern neighbor to this point.

"Thank you, President Herrera. My nation mourns with you in the loss of President Portillo. He was a courageous warrior for peace and will long be remembered for the leadership he provided in bringing your country to its current prosperity."

"Thank you, President Mercer."

POTUS resumed, "I would like to clarify my position with regard to the crime involving the murders of your leader and numerous members of the security details and the abduction of Weston. My feeling is that this was an act committed on Mexican soil and we respect your jurisdiction regarding the investigation. We will not interfere with your law enforcement officials in the conduct of their duties."

On the other end of the phone, Herrera was dumbfounded at what he was hearing from his American counterpart.

"Having said that," Mercer emphasized, "let me assure you that we have been utilizing every arm of our intelligence agencies in an attempt to intercept any communications that might occur outside your borders. Of course, we would not consider any surveillance of electronic signaling in

Mexico for fear that it could be construed as overreach."

"I assure you, Mr. President, we would make no such assertion, and would, in fact, welcome your direct assistance."

"I appreciate your comments, Mr. President, but I understand that it is a diplomatic rather than a practical response. After a proper amount of time I will announce an independent investigation by the United States to be directed by our agencies. I believe we would be in agreement that both President Portillo and President Weston would understand the political importance of allowing Mexico full rein in conducting the initial inquiry into this treacherous act."

"On the contrary, sir, I believe that they would support the cooperation that they worked so hard to establish between neighbors."

"Again, I understand the political nature of your assertions and your generosity in speaking, but you have my personal assurance that we will not hold you to those promises.

"Thank you for your courtesy in calling. I wish you well and pledge the continued support of the United States as you embark upon your administration. We will continue to keep you apprised of our intelligence intercepts, and I am confident you will keep us informed of your progress as well. And I trust you know that I will keep our conversation confidential, as I know you will."

POTUS clicked the button that disconnected the speakerphone and the Mexican President, who sat motionless with the handset still to his ear. Slowly he moved it to its cradle, squinting straight forward the entire time.

"'Continue' to keep us apprised? He hasn't begun to apprise us," the former Mexican Vice President said, returning to his native Spanish. He considered the rambling politi-babble and the abruptness with which Mercer had cut him off.

"What was that about? Since when would cooperation be an infringement upon our jurisdiction? Does he not care of the plight of his predecessor? Weston might be dead before Mercer does anything."

◆

In Washington, D.C., Wendell Mercer pushed his chair away from his desk and massaged his temples. He unconsciously moved one of his fingers and bit at his fingernail, something he hadn't done since his first Presidential campaign.

He slammed a finger first on the speakerphone button and then the one that speed-dialed the SecState.

"Good day, sir." McGregor said cheerfully.

"How is the dialogue coming with the Saudis?"

"Sir? I, uh, have the report for our regular Monday meeting."

"Give me a friggin' summary, Sue."

"Well, sir, I have to report that progress has slowed somewhat. I believe I emailed you yesterday that they have canceled the meeting scheduled for Tuesday. My department hasn't confirmed a reschedule yet. These things, of course take time."

"Let's cut through the crap. What's your take?"

"Yes, sir." She gulped silently. "Frankly, Mr. President, I believe the pending agreement may be in jeopardy and..." The Secretary of State stopped when she heard the dial tone.

Mercer hurled himself out of his chair and toward the window. He stood with hands on his hips and stared downward at great length.

"Dammit, Mercer. Fucking dammit. What the hell is going on? What in the frigging hell was I thinking?

He buzzed his Chief of Staff. "James, find me Everson Blake." That was the entirety of the one-way conversation.

Down the hall, Hank James replied to a dead line. "What's the matter, you bastard? Things not going well?" Then he slammed down the handset just to make himself feel better.

◆

Mariana woke up restrained, in part by the cord of the same lamp she had thrown at her assailant. Hands and feet tied, mouth gagged, she looked at the gringo sitting on her bed, rubbing the scratches on his face.

Morgan had desperately wanted to run, but knew he needed this woman's knowledge. To his astonishment, in spite of the racket from the room, nobody inquired. The *policia* did not arrive.

Morgan studied Mariana's eyes. They were wide, intense, and moist. He wasn't sure if what he saw was defiance or fear, but there were definitely hatred and contempt.

"Feeling's mutual, lady," he said, not caring that she probably had no clue what he meant.

"*¿Habla Inglés?*" he asked, and received nothing in response.

Then he moved within six inches of her face and startled her with his command of Spanish. "You bitch. You better understand who is in charge here. Whether you live or die depends on whether you decide to cooperate or not. *¿Comprende?*"

Finally, a nod.

"I am going to remove the cloth from your mouth. You scream, you die." Morgan paused and stared at the woman. Then he grabbed the end of the scarf and yanked forcefully, making his point, and trying to solidify an image as a lunatic gringo capable of anything to get the info he wanted. It worked, he saw as she flinched back from where he hovered over her.

Morgan sat on the edge of the bed and sized up his adversary. She was without makeup and her clothing disheveled, but a wild beauty shone through, making it instantly apparent why she had turned so many heads in El Paso. "I wonder if she realizes that her teases led me here," Morgan considered.

The interrogation began. "What is your name?" he continued in Spanish. "Ofelia Guerrera."

Morgan's hand shot to her throat. "I have no time for lies, and I am short of patience already. Now what is your goddammed name, bitch?"

"I am Ofelia Guerrera," she maintained.

Morgan released the hand from her throat, but his other roughly thrust an envelope onto her face. He shoved her head back before retracting his hand to a short distance from her face.

"Do you think I am stupid? Do you think I cannot read? While you were out, I went through some of your mail. Read the address!" he shouted.

She saw the envelope in front of her and her head dropped.

"Now, one more time. What is your name?"

Her head did not rise. "Mariana Lopez," she said meekly.

"We gringos have an expression: three strikes and you're out. That, Mariana, was strike one. Do not treat me like a fool." Morgan returned to his seat on the bed, unconsciously rubbing his own injured face. Mariana's eyes brightened at that and she sat a little straighter.

Her intruder accused, "You mailed a letter in El Paso."

She considered lying but instead, "Si." The response was muted through her clenched teeth. "How could he know that?" was her instant thought.

"Where do I find the American?" The suddenness of the critical question widened the *señorita's* eyes once again.

She feared his reaction to the truth. "I do not know."

The inquisitor slammed both fists onto the bed. "Wrong answer, goddammit. That is strike two, you whore!" he exclaimed, thought he somehow believed her. "You walk a dangerous path!"

The beautiful revolutionary sobbed in waves now. "I do not know. I beg you to believe me. I do not know where the man is."

Gotcha, Morgan thought, seeing her break. But he rose and circled her, eyeing her intensely, disguising his confidence that she would now give truthful answers.

"I do not know. He was at Morales' camp yesterday, but he is gone now."

Morales, Morgan seized the name. He told himself, "I'll save that for later. For now, "Who knows where he is?"

"Nobody knows. They are all dead." Her voice quaked and the tears increased.

That was an answer Morgan didn't expect. The rhythm of his

questioning faltered momentarily.

"Who's dead?"

The words began to explode from her mouth. "All of them. All of them. They were shot – in the backs. They were all lying on the ground. He didn't..."

The photojournalist kicked a nearby trash can for effect. "Get to the point!"

The girl – that's the way she appeared to him now – shuddered as he roared.

"Are you talking about the men who attacked the train?"

Her head bobbed.

His knees buckled as a possibility rushed to his mind. He held his breath, but bluffed violence as he asked, "Is the American... dead?"

"I do not think so."

He breathed again. "Take me there." It was more a request than a demand this time.

Her voice softened as well, but the quivering continued. "I cannot." She shook her head, gently at first, but increasing in tempo and vigor. "I do not want to die."

The ex-intelligence officer held one of the Mexican's own kitchen knives to her throat. "*Si?* Then you must take me there." He gave her time to think.

"*Si.* I will take you," she surrendered.

◆

An inquiry with the harbormaster confirmed what Blake already knew.

"*Señor*, I do not know where the boat is going, but she is gone from Playa del Carmen"

Blake and Sanders returned to their auto and sat in the parking area. The henchman waited for his boss to speak.

Finally, Blake said, "I was right. We have been wasting our time. Weston is being taken to the United States."

"Well, we had to come here and check it out, Ev."

"We're having to move too fast. We can't just sit around and wait on intercepts."

Sanders spoke logically to reassure the man, "Yeah, and it's not like you have access to all the resources of US intelligence for this op. Hell, not even of your own NSA."

It was true, Blake admitted. He had to keep this operation quiet. His only resource in the Agency was Terry Henderson. He had selected him because he was an ambitious brown-noser – anyone other than Blake would have said "kiss-ass" — that would do whatever he was told. And the people at CIA? Blake's thoughts turned to the call Parnell had made to Morgan. Apparently, they never spoke, but what was she up to? President Wendy was going to tell them to keep their noses out of the investigation. It would seem he didn't have the control over his people that he thought he did. So why was Betsy trying to get to Morgan? Maybe she was trying to discourage him from acting. It was pretty obvious Ben Reid had somehow gotten info to Morgan. That's why he had to go, too. Perhaps the DDI was trying to undo what Ben had started. No, she didn't like the President any more that Blake did, so she wouldn't be intimidated by his orders.

Blake pulled at the corner of the black hair above his lip. Finally, he spoke again, "We need to figure out where that boat is going." He dialed his secure mobile.

"Extension 1809," came the voice at the other end.

"Henderson, have you ordered the sat photos yet?"

"Ordered, yes. Received, no."

"ASAP," Blake snorted. "Use my name. Heck use the President's name. I don't care what you do, but I need that information today."

"Yes, sir."

Henderson depressed the button to disconnect. "The President?" he wondered. "What the hell has he got to do with this?"

The rusted out old truck chugged out highway 18 east from Chihuahua. The American man and the Mexican woman rode in quiet tension. Morgan drove with the large kitchen knife on his lap while Mariana gave directions. Her ankles were tied to the frame of the bench seat and to her hands.

The first kilometers out of town were without words until Morgan asked in a calm tone, "Why did you want the American?" He didn't feel he needed to maintain the crazed persona any longer. Mariana had been broken.

"We only wanted the money."

"Money?" the driver continued in Spanish.

"Morales agreed to turn over your President to the Arab for money."

First things first, Morgan warned himself. "Who is Morales? The *jefe* of the *Soldados Nuevos de Zapata*?"

The black hair waved as she spun her head around with her mouth gaping. The name was not disclosed in the letter she had mailed, yet this American knew. "*Si. SNZ.*"

Next, he hoped to learn the identity of the man in Ben Reid's photo. "What Arab?"

"The one from Saudi Arabia. I do not know his name. He gave us arms, explosives, phones, and, of course, money. All he wanted was the President."

"Why?"

"*No se.*"

Morgan stared at her.

"I am telling the truth. I do not know." Mariana was calm and compliant.

"Morales – how did he meet the Saudi?"

"I do not know how they made contact at first. But they met recently in Cozumel."

"Did he kill your *companeros?*"

"I think so. He must have. He was there when I left yesterday."

Morgan jumped on the realization. "Was the American there, too?"

"*Si.*"

There was a longer period of silence this time. Finally, Morgan asked, "Why did the Saudi kill Morales and his men?"

"I do not know," Mariana acknowledged. "Maybe he intended to all along. He was unhappy that the Mexican *Presidente* was killed."

"So that was not planned?"

"No. An act of defiance in the battle."

◆

Blake was waiting for the greeting on the machine at his home to end when his wife interrupted the recording.

"Hello."

"Hi, Honey. I decided you weren't home. I'm glad you are." He listened politely while Mrs. Blake filled him in on her day. His turn finally came to talk.

"I feel really bad about missing church tomorrow, but it can't be helped. Tell Smith that I brought my Bible Study Guide with me and I'll prepare as though I was going to be there." Then the husband listened to more of the latest news from home.

"Oh, and I can't remember. Is it next Sunday that Reverend Gaston is coming over for dinner? Uh-huh... Great. Okay. Gotta run. I love you." And the happy couple hung up their phones.

◆

At the Mexican woman's direction Morgan finally turned onto a dirt road, then onto mere dirt. Weaving around the small hills and dodging the scrub brush, Morgan followed the girl's instructions, but hardly needed them. Fresh tire tracks – from the trip she said she took there that morning

— were clear enough. Nor did he need her to tell him where the hideout was. The buzzards circling overhead pointed the way. He was curious how the rebels were able to spirit the ex-President here after the train attack without being detected.

When he pulled into a small open area in front of a wood and metal shack, Morgan saw a line of bodies, all men, lying in various positions in the sand. The dead wore various combinations of military garb and ordinary work clothes. His companion turned her face down and the shudders were obvious throughout her lean figure.

Outside the truck Morgan beheld a spectacle unlike any he had seen since he witnessed, with camera, revolutionary battles in Central America. The bodies were riddled with innumerable wounds that could have only come from automatic gunfire. The corpses were, for the most part, in a loose line. There was a broken tequila bottle near the end of the line.

The ex-spy moved to the shack, picking up an AK-47 from among the weapons littering the area. He glanced through the doorway, squinting his eyes into submission in adjusting to the dim light. Convinced there was nobody home, he still entered gun first. The furnishings were sparse, but in the center of the building sat a single chair, with loose ropes lying on the ground.

Nothing of use, Josh Morgan thought. "Except now I know for sure Weston was here."

He exchanged the machine gun for an American-made forty-five caliber military pistol that was lying near one of the bodies and returned to the truck. He placed the key in the ignition, then halted before starting the truck. One unasked question occurred to him. He faced his companion.

"Who broke into your apartment?"

Mariana looked at him, eyes red, but dry, the dirt on her face creased from the many tears. "It was surely the Saudi."

Morgan held the steering wheel with both hands and looked around at the grisly scene again. "Why would he need to go there?" he pondered. "He would like to kill the Mexican woman, but would he take that kind of risk? Especially while he had President Weston. This whole area is an incredibly risky place for him to be." No, he concluded, it probably wasn't the Saudi. And although Morgan might not know exactly who invaded her apartment, he almost certainly knew who had sent him.

An earlier question returned. "How did you get the American here, and how did they not find this hideout? They must have been searching every meter of land around here."

"The *Zapatistas* first rode their horses and vehicles in various directions away from here. I waited for Morales in this truck and just drove here. Your President was tied and in the water barrel in back. He had a tube to breathe through. The top was nailed shut. We came to a roadblock – a local policeman. Water was obviously sloshing out the top of the barrel, so he did not look there. We were prepared to shoot him, if necessary but he was very accommodating. I was dressed quite... nicely." Even in these circumstances, her ego blazed through, Morgan saw.

"Once we were here the *Federale* coordinating the search kept people away from here. He only had to mark the map that this area had been searched already."

"He was a *Zapatista?*"

"He was just a greedy man." Her smile returned.

"You said Morales met with the Saudi in Cozumel. Would he return there?"

"I do not know his plans," Mariana said in her first lie to her abductor since they left her apartment. He must not have seen the notes discussing the yacht, she knew.

The former intelligence officer considered the geography of Mexico. The Saudi, if driving to Cozumel, would have to journey around the Gulf of Mexico, which would take him perhaps days to complete since he would have to take significant precautions. Maybe he had a private plane. He certainly couldn't take a commercial flight. His hostage was recognizable – and hot merchandise.

No, he didn't go back to Cozumel at all, Morgan knew. But he had nothing else to go on.

Morgan turned his attention to his captive. The bruised cheek he inflicted through the blanket during the scuffle in her apartment was swollen and a deep purple. Even if he hadn't a tinge of regret for having hit her, it was another matter entirely to kill her in cold blood, regardless of her role in kidnapping his friend. Yet they were in the very middle of nowhere. Morgan was sure that she would not be found for some time. He lifted the kitchen knife from its place beside the seat of the truck.

Mariana's eyes burned and she struggled with every fiber of her being at the restraints. He waved the knife slowly, dramatically, in front of the *señorita's* face, and yellow liquid spread across her pants and onto the vehicle's seat. Morgan took some satisfaction at the fear manifested on her face.

The tip of the blade rested against Mariana's throat. The former CIA officer finally spoke. "It is your good fortune that I do not have it in me to kill you. If I were like you or your *revolucionarios*, I would slit your throat right now and be done with you."

"But I can't." And with that he tossed the knife out the window of the truck. Mariana's whimpers were hardly different than a grade-school-aged *chicita*. He took no delight in her panic, but neither did he feel the slightest remorse at her predicament or what he was about to do. He drove about two minutes in the opposite direction from the rebels' camp and the dirt road he would soon travel.

Opening the door, he explained, "The knife is where I threw it, about one kilometer from here, at the hut. It will be difficult, but possible, for you to walk there. I saw water outside the shack, too. You may make it back to the road to Chihuahua." He reached to untie her binding from underneath the seat, then across her to open the door. "Even in your filth you should have no problem getting a ride. Maybe it will be some benevolent person, or possibly someone who will violate you and make you sorry you were ever born. Either way, I don't care."

She pleaded, "I will die out here."

"I could kill you now and save you some misery," he offered.

"I will do anything. I will give you anything."

"You have nothing I want." As he delivered the insult, he pushed her forcefully. The black-haired woman twisted and managed to get her feet on the ground first, but still fell to the dirt with a thud. Morgan cringed. This disturbed him a bit, but he had to assure that he would be safely out of Chihuahua before she could notify anyone. He knew there was the possibility that Mariana could warn someone in Cozumel of his arrival, but he was convinced she would not. He had a fair amount of confidence that her revolutionary days were over.

Driving away he looked in the side mirror and saw Mariana Lopez already struggling to her feet.

◆

The rented motor home was traveling on I–35, south of Denton, Texas, and approaching Dallas. The Saudi operative had indeed done as Weston had hoped and driven for an extended period in an attempt to make up for the time lost the day before. For nearly seven hours the vehicle had continued without stopping. And careful to cease his efforts whenever the driver peered at him in the truck's mirror, the US political figure had used the pop-top to scrape diligently at the line that bound his restrained hands and feet together and to his seat. That he had never dropped his tool had been something of a miracle to him. And finally, the rope was severed. Weston trapped the line between his knees as it was about to give so that it would not drop to the floor. The timing could not have worked our better. The vehicle was north of the city of Lewisville, which was heavily populated and in which the Interstate was well lit. Weston thought if he could lunge for the side door and spring it open, he could hurl himself outside before his captor could act.

The desperate hostage said a prayer for success – or a quick end. He had no illusions about his chances. He suspected these things never worked like they did in spy novels or movies. If his escape resulted in his death, at least it would spare his beloved country the humiliation of seeing him put on display as a war criminal. Mercer would not have to endure the uncertainty of how to deal with that situation. When Weston finally made his move, it would be a bonus if someone got the license number and the Saudi was apprehended.

Former President of the United States of America Trenton Lewis Weston took a breath and contemplated just how he would get to the door and open it. He was prepared to make his move whenever the Saudi began to exit the Interstate for any reason. It was very late at night and Weston's heart accelerated to a pace beyond its already frantic rate when Al-Majeed began turning onto an off-ramp, probably to get gas at the station ahead. Then his heart leapt to his throat when he realized the station was closed. The lights were dimmed and there was not another vehicle there. Whenever he could, his driver stopped at stations that were closed but had 24-hour self-service. The passenger realized that if they stopped without anyone else around, his plan would be futile. He could not wait until the vehicle stopped fully. The Saudi needed to be occupied with driving to enable Weston a head start out the mobile camper. He steeled his resolve. "God, please!" The prayer raced instinctively through his being. There would be just one shot.

The American jumped to his still-bound feet and bunny-hopped across the floor. The vehicle was swerving as it proceeded down the ramp. And the severed rope did not slide as smoothly as he had hoped from the one around his feet. The resistance on his feet from the tension of the line on his seat caused him to stumble toward the back of the cabin of the RV and away from the door. With hands and feet bound Weston struggled to regain his footing. The driver yanked the wheel to the right and hit the brake pedal violently. He slammed the stick into "Park" well before the vehicle stopped rolling, grinding gears, and locking the tires. The motor home slid across the shoulder onto the grass along the road.

Al-Majeed dove headlong for the American, who had managed to get to his feet and was moving again for the door. Weston's tied hands were on the lever and just beginning to pull when the smaller, but younger and more solid attacker hit him roughly on his left arm and chest. Both crashed across the dining table and onto the floor. The older man thrashed and kicked and threw his arms and head and feet at the Saudi, until a single blow from the Arab's fist sent his head reeling onto the floor of the cabin. His mind went blank, his body still immediately.

Fadi Al-Majeed was frantic. He struggled to rise as he heard the first voice begin to call to his vehicle. He hurriedly lifted the unconscious American onto the bed and pulled a blanket over him. He jerked the door to the rear berth shut. There was pounding on the door and it began to open. The Saudi rushed to confront the person attempting to enter.

"Hey! Hey in there! You all right? Hello?" The voice from just outside was loud and anxious. Its trembling was obvious and soon it was joined by another, and then a third voice completed the chorus. The door to the camper swung open and the beam of a powerful light shone in, to the driver's seat and toward the back. It crossed the approaching Arab, and jerked back toward him, and the piercing light rested on his face. His eyes slammed shut from the penetrating beam, and his head shot to the side. His hands rose instinctively to cover his face.

The first of two men jumped into the camper. "Buddy, you okay? What happened?"

CHAPTER 25

The personnel at the Saudi Embassy were wrapping up the late-night conference call with their leader.

"Are we clear on our actions?" the distant voice of Holy Islamic Kingdom of Saudi Arabia President Yasim al-Hashimi asked his audience.

"We are," answered the Station Chief. "We will contact the American Secretary of State in the morning."

"Very well," al-Hashimi permitted. "You will inform her that there is no need for further dialogue. Negotiations are no longer in our national interest, you will say. You will not provide any additional comments."

Another voice assumed the Dictator's speakerphone. "Our President al-Hashimi has concluded the meeting. He thanks you for your devotion to your country." And the line went dead.

Abou Shakra dismissed the group. He lingered with the Mukhabarat Station Chief. "The President shares our optimism for the successful completion of the mission," boasted Nagim.

"It would appear so," the Head of Mission responded with equal enthusiasm.

"Do you think he would have embarked on this mission had he known the Americans would initiate these discussions?"

The smile of delight foreshadowed Abou Shakra's reply. "Of course. He could have aborted the operation at any point if it suited him and was contrary to his political plans. The talks with the American harlot McGregor and the infidel Mercer were never of any consequence. Besides, what we might have gained from the negotiations, we will achieve through our current plans. When the world sees our strength, they will recognize our leadership of the Muslim nations. Our Kingdom will be revered as the world power that we are. Their pathetic attempts at sanctions will be abandoned. Trade will be restored. The world will know our resolve and will fear us."

◆

A second, younger man scampered up the steps and into the RV. He did not speak but looked around in anticipation of seeing injuries.

"I said 'Are you all right?'" the Good Samaritan repeated.

"Yes, yes, I am fine," Al-Majeed assured him. "I, uh, I must have fallen asleep. I was exiting the highway, and the next thing I know, I was waking and also seeing the grass around me. I did not know what to do and put my foot on the brake too strongly. But I am fine now." Thinking on your feet was a must for intelligence officers.

"Pal, you're hurt," came the voice from a third head sticking through the door.

The Saudi reached to his face and felt the thick liquid dripping from the gash under his eye. He realized, with a curse, that the would-be escapee had butted him with his forehead.

"No, I am fine. Thank you. I would really just like to be on my way, please."

The third man's head disappeared from the doorway, then reappeared to speak. "I don't think you're gonna go nowheres, fella. Ya got a flat on one of your tires out here."

The Arab was speechless. He had not familiarized himself with the various details of the rented vehicle. The ray from the light returned to his face. He could barely see past the glare to the man holding it, but even without seeing he could feel the distrust that some Americans had of Middle Easterners, in light of the two Gulf Wars, the righteous acts they referred to as terrorism, and other difficulties. The Saudi reminded himself to be cheerful. He smiled and began to talk amiably to the men. He explained how stupid he felt at having the accident. He spoke of his "brother" who lived in Dallas, whom he was visiting from New Mexico to take camping. He thanked the men for their concern and explained that people's willingness to help one another was the thing he most admired about "his" adopted country. His chattiness worked to allay the helpers' suspicions about him, and soon, much to the liar's chagrin, they were all offering to help change his tire. Bobby Joe, the third man to stop at the scene of the "accident," was an auto tow truck driver. Al-Majeed truly needed assistance, but what he really wanted was for the crowd to disperse. There was an unconscious man in the back that might come to at any time.

Al-Majeed excused himself from the tire-changing party and re-entered the camper. He stared with hatred at his traveling partner. His actions had greatly complicated things. He was still out, and he began to worry about whether he had struck the old man too severely. He feared hitting him again but needed to ensure that he remained hidden from the Texans cheerfully providing assistance outside. He would not be able to explain any rustling noises that the American bastard would surely create if he awoke. It was with a mixture of fear and pleasure that he delivered another blow to the back of the man's head.

Al-Majeed exited the vehicle and found the men had almost finished changing the tire. But as he turned to thank them for their help, unwanted flashing blue lights illuminated the area. The Texas Department of Public Safety patrol car slowed to a stop behind the RV. The officer had seen the congregation of headlights and slowing traffic around the off-ramp and had come to investigate. The Saudi did not have his weapon – it was inside the truck – and, besides, he realized, there were far too many men around. The bouncing light of the approaching patrolman brightened as he came nearer.

"What's going on here?"

'Hey, Harold."

The ray of light spun toward the familiar voice.

"Hello, Bobby Joe," the officer returned. His demeanor appeared to the Arab to be greatly improved at the sight of an acquaintance. "What the hell is going on?"

"Oh, tourist trouble," he laughed and moved to shake his friend's hand. The Saudi noticed that the patrolman's right hand, which had been resting on his holstered pistol, now rested casually at his side. The tire-changer continued, "This fella here got into a bit of trouble with his RV. Says he dozed off and hit the shoulder a little hard."

The light turned and rested squarely on the "tourist's" face.

"Don't think there was no other damage. I think he's good to go now." The light held its position and the Saudi squinted.

"'Zat right?"

Al-Majeed's pulse had quickened and he felt a dampness under his arms. He had been in far more precarious situations in his intelligence career but never with so much at stake.

"Yes, sir. I suppose I tried to cover a little more ground tonight than I should have. But, thanks to these kind gentlemen, everything is fine now."

"You appear to be cut," the officer suggested, as he turned his light to the RV and began to walk around it.

Al-Majeed followed him and attempted to portray the right combination of embarrassment and confidence. "Oh, it is nothing. The scar will be a souvenir of my trip to Texas," he joked. The two men completed the rest of the trip around the recreational vehicle in silence.

"Can I see your driver's license and rental agreement for the RV, please?" the Public Safety officer requested.

"Of, course," the Saudi said and moved toward the door. He had no idea what he was going to do. Even though he had the papers, he realized that, in a single oversight regarding his forged documents, the rental agreement would not have been changed to reflect his current alias but would show the names of the associates who had actually rented it for his use. Consequently, he was totally unprepared for this eventuality.

Bobby Joe interceded, "Hell, Harold, he's had a rough enough time of it. Why don't ya just let him be on his way? Ya know, show a little Texas hospitality. I'm sure he's just gonna pull over at the first spot and bed down for the night. Ain't that right?"

Al-Majeed didn't want to seem too anxious, so he continued toward the camper's door, where he paused. "Yes, sir," he said with a shake of his head. "The Lord has been very good to me tonight," he admitted, changing his terminology to suit the listeners. He waited at the step with his hand on the knob.

Patrolman Harold finally relented, "Okay, but you get stopped and get some rest. Understand?"

"That's exactly what I will do," the RV's driver agreed, and he meant it.

He shook hands with the helpers and stepped into his vehicle as they and the few onlookers began to disperse. As he moved to the driver's seat he repeated, "Allah has indeed been good to me tonight."

◆

In Cancun, Mexico, Everson Blake was fuming. Inability to get a flight out was not the problem. He could have pulled strings. He simply didn't know where to go. Without the feedback from Henderson, the NSA officer would be wasting additional time if he randomly picked a destination. He had considered heading to Houston. It would be a relatively short flight, and at least he would be back in the United States. But Cancun's airport originated flights to many of the major cities in the States. Once he knew where the Saudi yacht was heading, there was a very good chance he could fly directly to that port. So he and his sidekick had checked into a hotel.

Sanders went to the restaurant. Blake didn't feel like leaving the room and had told him to bring something back for him. In the meantime, he was drinking a Dr. Pepper and eating peanuts from the mini-bar in the room.

His mobile rang. "Yes?" was his way of answering.

"Houston area, boss. I'm ninety percent certain." It was Henderson. "And she's smoking, too. Around twenty knots, looks like."

Blake's lips snarled. "I could have been there already," he wished. "But no, I made the right decision under the circumstances.

"When?" he queried.

"She's still better than 400 miles out. ETA is a little before midnight tomorrow, if she can keep her screws turning at this rate. That's the scoop on the yacht. But that's not all. Josh Morgan is heading your way."

"What?" the Deputy Director exclaimed.

"For real. He's booked to Cozumel in the morning."

"Flight info," Blake barked, scrambling for a pen and paper.

His minion complied.

The NSA officer entertained the hope that the Saudi had killed his hostage and was merely making a run for it. But the fact that the *Al-Amānah* was heading for Houston seemed to indicate otherwise. If the Saudi agent was alone, he would find it fairly easy to slip through any nets to make his escape. Especially since the United States intelligence agencies' official position was that only Mexican radicals were involved in the kidnapping. Nobody was looking for a Saudi national. No one but he and Morgan, that is. No, he was certain that the old man was unfortunately still alive and that the plan was to get him aboard the yacht somewhere around Houston.

Blake walked onto his balcony and took in the moonlight shining onto the Caribbean Sea. "Pretty clever," he admitted, "taking Weston through the United States. Don't know how he got across the border. But if he did that, getting the old fool back out aboard the boat would be a piece of cake." He stood, tossing nuts in to the air, catching them in his mouth. He had successfully caught twelve in a row when Mark Sanders walked in carrying a Styrofoam box that smelled like enchiladas. He laid his boss' dinner on the coffee table and joined him on the balcony.

"Any word?" he inquired.

Blake turned and smiled broadly. "God is being gracious to me, Mark. Apparently, the boat is headed to Houston, where it will pick up Weston from the Arab."

"Holy shit." Sanders didn't share his partner's religious beliefs or his aversion to colorful language. "That'll make it easier for us. I didn't know what we were going to do when we thought the boat was going to be in Mexico. But we can get anything – hell, anyone – we need back home. This is freaking great. I'll make the reservations for first thing in the morning?"

"No. A change in plans," the Deputy Director countered. "Get us a hop to Cozumel in the morning, and a flight from there to Houston later in the afternoon. We have plenty of time to get to Texas, but there are some arrangements to make." He rattled off a list of tasks to his crony.

Walking back onto the patio, he thanked God for making his path easier. "Okay, lucky thirteen," he said confidently. He tossed a peanut into the air, tilted his head back and opened his mouth. The morsel bounced off his cheek and onto the concrete veranda, and then off the patio, where it fell the six floors to the ground.

CHAPTER 26

DAY 10 – SUNDAY

Morgan sweated through the overnight stay in Chihuahua, but his delay was uneventful. The first flight out made it possible for him to arrive in San Miguel, Cozumel, by late morning.

Cozumel was one of Josh Morgan's favorite places. He loved the laid-back atmosphere that survived in spite of the extensive commercial development in recent years. But he was there on business. From the *aeropuerto* he took a cab directly to the *Café Cuzamil*.

Morgan spoke with several waiters and showed each the printed copy of the photo that Ben Reid had sent him. Not one of the *café's* employees remembered either man in the picture.

Morgan had not showered in over a day. He had hardly eaten over the last two. So, after his friendly interrogation of the *café* staff, he sat at a table and ordered a Diet Coke and lunch. He had just swept the first bite of fried fish into his mouth when an American man in his mid-twenties slid back a chair and sat down. The former was too tired and too frustrated to be annoyed. He chewed the fish and studied the unwanted visitor carefully.

The man smiled and pushed long, sandy hair behind his ears. Morgan finished chewing his food. In time, he simply said, "Do I know you?"

The guest gazed skyward, rubbed his chin facetiously and said, "Hmmm. No. No, I'm pretty sure you don't." His eyes returned to Morgan's and he grinned. "But you'll want to."

Morgan set down his fork and leaned back in his chair, tossing his napkin onto the table. "Oh, and why is that?"

The young man looked down at the piece of photo paper lying on the table and turned it toward himself.

"Well, for one thing, I take pretty good pictures." He rotated the paper back toward Morgan and gave a tilted smile. "Don't ya think?"

Morgan sized up the young man. He rested both arms on the table and maintained a quiet gaze across the table.

"Elizabeth Parnell sent me" were the words that broke the silence. "Shall we walk?"

Morgan nodded once. He left *dinero* on the table. Both men rose and the former CIA agent gestured to let the current one lead the way. He felt like asking the traditional sentry challenge, "Friend or Foe."

They walked across Avenida Melgar to the sea wall and found a spot away from other "tourists."

Morgan finally ended his own silence when he asked, "What do you want?"

"I should ask what it is that you want."

"I want the men who took President Weston to return him. Period." He made no effort to be covert. He folded his arms and stared into the dark eyes of the young man. His intensity was apparent to anyone who cared to watch. "Now you."

"I just want to talk," the young spy said. He lowered an open hand toward the seawall. Morgan waited and looked around the area. He unfolded his arms and sat.

Both men stared straight ahead from the whitewashed wall.

"So, you like the island?"

Morgan's head turned slowly toward the other man and stopped there. His counterpart, startled, returned the gesture. Their eyes locked in one of the more traditional testosterone challenges. The younger man finally "blinked" and turned away.

The "winner" spoke. "I don't know who you are; rather, I don't care who you are. And I don't feel like playing spy games. So cut to the chase."

"Whoa. Lighten up. I'm on your side."

"Are you?"

Now the young man's eyes zeroed in on Morgan and dropped any pretense of tradecraft. "Well, the DDI is. Me? I don't think I like you very much, but, yeah, I want the same thing you do. Something really sucks about this kidnapping. It smells and I don't like it."

There was another period of silence. Morgan resented the feeling he had that the young spy reminded him of himself at that stage in his career.

"What's your name?"

"You can call me Bill."

"Okay – Bill." Morgan offered his first smile to his counterpart.

The apparent beach bum continued, "So here's the scoop. There was a yacht in Playa del Carmen over on the Yucatan flying the Saudi flag. The name is *Al-'Amânah*. Supposedly some rich oil sheik here on vacation. It's just a guess, but I suspect it was here to pick up another passenger. But best info says it didn't happen." The young man turned his gaze to Morgan again. He tilted his head and arched his eyebrows. Morgan glanced briefly at him, then turned away once more.

"You said 'was' at Playa del Carmen. Where is it now?"

"Can't say with absolute certainty, but recon shows it rounded the Yucatan Peninsula, and is on a bearing of three hundred fifteen degrees. Looks like Houston."

"Houston?" Morgan stood and turned to the blue Caribbean waters. "What sense does that make?"

"Bill" remained seated. "Don't know for sure. But if we're right, it means that Weston has been moved from Mexico back into the States. And since they're arranging transportation, this isn't a kidnapping for ransom."

"I know," Morgan replied. Now the younger man stood beside him.

"There's another thing. Parnell said an analyst was looking into a possible connection between the abduction and our friends in the Middle East."

"Ben Reid."

"That's him. He thought the Deputy Director of the NSA was up to something. Blake's apparently in Mexico, too. POTUS told DDI that he was here to exchange intel intercepts with the Mexican government, but Reid, then Parnell, did some checking. Flight records put him first in Chihuahua, then to Cancun."

"Up from Playa del Carmen?"

"Yes. Is he trying to rescue Weston?" Bill asked.

"Don't think so," Morgan returned.

Another pause. Then, "Are you saying he's in bed with the Saudis?" Bill's eyes were wide and directed at Morgan.

"No, I don't think that's it, either."

"What are you saying?"

◆

The Saudi had found a roadside park campground shared with eighteen-wheelers immediately after the incident of the night before. Now he and his hostage were preparing to continue their journey southward. Weston had slept almost comatose throughout the night. He had hardly moved; hardly made a sound. The Saudi worried that he might have seriously injured the American – or worse. He had prayed to Allah for his recovery and Allah, he believed, had granted it.

"President al-Hashimi will not like your appearance. But he would like it less if you were dead, and less still if you escaped. It is, as you Americans say, the lesser of evils." Fadi Al-Majeed sat on the chair usually reserved for his hostage, who was on the bench beside the dining table.

The face of the former leader of the United States was covered with scratches. There was a cut under his chin. One eye was swollen severely, and underneath it was black and purple with traces of yellow. The captive had not spoken since he woke, wouldn't eat, wouldn't drink. He had not awakened until nearly 10:00 a.m., and since that time had simply sat and stared at Al-Majeed. The Saudi felt a grudging admiration for the old man's escape attempt.

"You should drink your water. You have bread before you. Eat."

The American finally spoke through swollen lips. "I will not have your food or drink."

"As you wish, but I believe you will change your mind."

The Arab left Weston on the bench seat. He tied the man's hands behind him. He secured his prisoner's ankles more closely together than on previous days and tied them to the supporting post of the dining table.

"You may sit or lie down. I do not care which. My work is almost complete. By tonight we will end our road journey. By tomorrow night, you will be sailing to my country to meet your fate."

The Saudi intelligence officer moved to his place behind the wheel and started the RV's engine. He looked into the mirror at Weston and grinned.

"You almost made it out of the truck, old man. But I would have had to kill you rather than let you escape."

The reply was barely comprehensible through the puffy lips. "You will not deliver me to the son of a bitch you work for. I will be rescued, and you will die."

"You do not believe that, or you would not have tried to escape."

"So at least I know," Weston thought. "End of journey tonight. Sailing tomorrow night. Port city within driving distance today. Probably Houston area. Maybe New Orleans or some small port in between.

"Clarity," the former leader of the free world decided, "is an elusive thing. And it can pick a helluva time to show up." He smiled and thought of his wife. He wondered how she was holding up. Alicia was the reason he hated thinking in the terms that he was. She was an important part of the reason he was so resolute. He could not let her worry at his situation. In his mind he felt closure would be easier for her than watching the events unfold with the rest of the world. Weston wanted to be able to reconcile his death with some sense of purpose.

The flight had been scheduled for 10:40 a.m. Everson Blake held little confidence in the commuter planes or regional Mexican airlines, so he had opted to catch the Continental flight from Houston as it stopped in Cancun before continuing on to Cozumel. Its location near the gulf coast made Houston a prime candidate for summer rainstorms, though they were usually in the evenings. But this day a morning downpour had backed up traffic at Bush Intercontinental Airport. The downstream effect had Blake squirming at his seat, tapping on the plastic arm and glancing repeatedly at his watch. He called for an update from Henderson but there was no new information. The only interesting item was that the President's Chief of Staff had called to inquire how to reach him. Henderson seemed quite anxious to get that message off his shoulders, but Blake had decided he had no need to talk to the President or his errand boy and would call them if and when he felt like it. He tugged at his moustache and compared the small clock on his wrist against the one mounted on the wall in the waiting area. One-thirty.

"Hell, Ev, if we had known this was gonna happen, we could have taken the ferry and been there by now."

The NSA Deputy neither answered nor looked at his partner, who resumed looking at the Mexican-language newspaper, as though he could really read it. He looked up again.

"Want something to drink?"

The NSA Deputy sniffed as he answered, "What I want is for the plane to get here." He rose to check the availability of a commuter shuttle but was interrupted by a brassy voice over the loudspeaker announcing the arrival of the flight. He wheeled around abruptly. He snatched up his sport coat and brushed by Sanders on the way to the doorway that led to the tarmac. The Deputy Director knew it would be several minutes before he could board. Nevertheless, he took his place at the head of a line that wasn't even beginning to form yet.

Sanders remained seated and shook his head. He could take his leisure and be on the plane every bit as fast as his boss.

"Damn, Blake. You are one anal son of a bitch. But you're the one with the contacts." The ex-SEAL turned his attention back to the paper.

◆

Secretary of State of the United States Susan McGregor sat in her office looking at her telephone. She knew that the capstone of her career as the country's chief diplomatic officer had just vanished without so much as a legitimate explanation. Beyond the professional and political implications to herself, there remained the matter of telling President Mercer that his own legacy had been preempted. McGregor was a take-charge person else she wouldn't be where she was. But this was one task she had to resist delegating. The President was not going to be happy.

SecState summoned the courage and dialed the White House. Mrs. Oakley answered and announced McGregor to her boss.

"Mr. President," she got right to the point, "I'm afraid I have some disappointing news. The Saudis have withdrawn from negotiations." She winced and braced herself for the verbal blitz that was sure to come. The pounding of her heart increased with the extended silence that followed.

"Did they give a reason?" the President finally asked. His voice was subdued and, Sue thought, held no trace of surprise.

"No, sir, at least nothing specific. The Head of Mission only indicated that his directions from Riyadh were that further pursuing any new initiatives was not in the interest of the people of his nation at this time. When I pressed for more information, Mission Chief Abou Shakra only repeated, verbatim, the same statement. I'm sorry, sir."

Another period of silence. "Thanks for letting me know, Sue. I know you did your best. We can follow up tomorrow. I'll have Mrs. Oakley set up something. Goodbye."

The Secretary held the phone to her ear for several seconds, ignoring the dial-tone. Her hand finally moved to lay the handset down. She looked down at the two pages of notes she had prepared for the call. On it were the questions she had anticipated from Mercer and her planned responses. She set them aside and folded her hands on her desk. Her boss hadn't asked any of the questions. He never raised his voice or suggested a failure on the part of her or her staff. The Secretary had never known him to be so gracious in the face of such a serious disappointment – not when there was no camera present, she corrected herself. She searched for the right word to describe his reaction. Understanding, she decided.

"Imagine that. 'Mercer' and 'understanding.' Now those are two words that don't often come up in the same sentence."

◆

Josh Morgan sat in the terminal of the Cozumel airport. Seats to and from the resort were hard to come by on short notice, but the DDI had pulled some strings, anticipating he would want to head for Houston. He wondered if he was being played, taken out of the action. But time was short, and he had no better information to act on. "Bill," for all his smart-ass cockiness, seemed on the level. At least Morgan's gut told him he was. The story he told did not contradict anything that Morgan knew or suspected.

He watched from the departure lounge as arriving passengers exited the plane that he would soon board. There would be the usual intermission between arrival and departure while crews replenished drinks and snacks and cleaned the aircraft. He observed with some jealousy the men and women who were arriving for a temporary reprieve from their daily lives. Children bounced along behind some of them. The former intelligence officer envied them that they were largely unaffected by the events transpiring all around them. He held his watch up and checked the time. He would board in about fifteen minutes and be in the air toward Houston in about twenty-five. He let out a deep breath.

"I have no freakin' idea what I am going to do if I catch up to this guy."

◆

Terry Henderson sat at his desk at Fort Meade looking at his computer monitor. "Oh, crap. Blake's gonna shit!"

◆

Blake was in his seat on row nineteen. He hated flying coach. He had flown nothing but first class or private jets for as long as he remembered, but he had no choice in this case. He was reaching to press the button to turn off his mobile phone when it rang. He dropped the phone onto the floor of the plane, lunged but the seat belt he had already fastened jerked him back into his seat. He fumbled trying to unfasten it, but eventually managed to gather up the telephone and attempt to connect the call. No one there. He waited a couple of moments and dialed his voice mail. He found that he had one message.

"Henderson. Boss, your guy is on a flight that is leaving Cozumel at two o'clock for Houston."

The Deputy Director looked ahead to see the flight attendants preparing to start the video monitors that had replaced the sample oxygen masks and seat belts that until recently had been used for the in-flight safety demonstrations. They were about to shut the door, he realized.

"Wait!" he shouted.

There were puzzled, panicked looks on faces of the flight attendants and every one of the eighteen rows of passengers staring back at him.

"I have to get off! Don't shut the door." He jumped to his feet, slamming his head into the overhead compartments. Two rows behind him Mark Sanders was as confused as everyone else about Blake's actions, but followed his lead. The sight of two men springing to their feet alarmed the entire cabin of people, but nobody challenged him. He charged up the aisle, shouting at the aircraft personnel to leave the door open. An Air Marshall stood and ordered Blake and Sanders to stop. The two men responded to the command by turning to face a man with a very real gun pointing at them.

A few minutes later, verification of Blake's ID got him and his companion out of the interrogation room. "National security," Blake had told them, and he was convinced it was.

His identification also got him a seat on the next flight out of Cancun to Houston.

◆

"Mr. President, I have called Blake on his office phone. I have called him on his mobile phone." Henry James continued, "I have talked to his admin, who directed me to an analyst working with him on a special project. He wouldn't give me the number of the secure mobile phone Blake is using."

Wendell Mercer slammed both palms onto his desk in the Oval Office.

"You inept bastard. What are you saying? I am the goddammed President of the United Fucking States. And some low-level functionary won't do anything but take a goddammed message? The little shit." POTUS shoved the phone toward James. "Get the little shit on the phone this goddammed instant!"

Mercer threw both hands into the air wildly and bolted up from his chair. He leaned one hand against the windowsill and dragged the other through his hair. He lowered his gaze and rubbed his temples with both hands, while behind him Hank James tried to maintain control of his quivering fingers long enough to dial Terry Henderson's number at NSA.

"This is out of hand," the President mumbled. "It's a goddammed nightmare. What the hell was I thinking?"

"Sir," was the only word the Chief of Staff spoke as he pressed the speakerphone button.

"Extension 1809," announced the young-sounding voice.

"Who is this?" Mercer demanded.

"I am not allowed to give that…"

"This is the goddammed President. Now who the hell is this?" he insisted.

At the other end of 0the line, Henderson was jerking his feet off the trashcan beside his desk and sitting at attention. He stammered and looked around the cubicles near him as if anyone would be able to tell him if this was really the President, and what to do.

Mercer's voice fell from a shout to a more moderate volume, but the intensity caused the recipient of the call to tremble.

"Son, you know that my Chief of Staff called you this morning looking for Everson Blake," the Chief Executive said icily. "So, you should know this is indeed the President. If you have any concern for your career, you need to give me that number now."

The President got his answer.

◆

Josh Morgan glanced out his window at the deep blue of the Gulf of Mexico below him. There was the occasional speck that represented an oceangoing cargo ship or possibly a cruise liner.

He worried through the next steps to take. It was clear to him that he could not approach any federal official – FBI, CIA – with what he knew. He had no sense of whom he could trust. He was feeling more certain that he wasn't up to this task. Morgan felt a measure of pride at what he had accomplished. He believed that he had not only performed admirably, but that he had been the right person for the job. There was also the feeling like it was old times. It had been an uplifting experience in a way, resurrecting his self-confidence and eradicating the fear that had dictated his life for such a long time. But it was time to turn it over to the cavalry. Problem was, Morgan didn't know who the cavalry was.

He contemplated his limited options. There was a significant downside to every choice. The plot was too far along to risk undermining it. The climax was near, Morgan knew, and the impending conclusion left no margin for error.

The smile started small, then widened and was ultimately accompanied by a satisfied sigh. "Of, course," Morgan concluded silently. "The simplest solution."

◆

Even though she was one of a very small group of individuals that could rightfully be called seconds-in-command at CIA, Elizabeth Parnell had never burst into her boss' office unannounced – until now.

"Chris, I'm sorry, but this can't wait."

DCI Donleavy was leaning back in his chair with the phone in one hand and the earpiece to his glasses in his mouth. He stopped in midsentence and stared at his DDI shutting the door behind her and marching to his desk. He did nothing for a moment until he finally said, "I'll call you back." He grappled with his phone trying to put it in its place, never taking his eyes off his visitor.

"Okay, Betsy. What's going on?"

Parnell buried her face in her hands. When she finally looked up Chris Donleavy watched the crimson flush of her face disappear into an ashen gray. She leaned forward and practically whispered, "I think they're trying to kill him."

"What, Betsy? Who's trying to kill who?"

"Weston? Mercer has sent Blake to find Weston and kill him." She reached out and grabbed her superior's hands. He glanced down at this unexpected act. "I can't believe he would go this far…"

"Whoa, whoa. Calm down." The DCI looked around his room as though checking for eavesdroppers that couldn't possibly be there. "What are you saying? What are you talking about?

"I told you I had Ben looking into the Saudi-Mexican connection when he died… Jesus." Another thought entered her mind. Her eyes were glassy as if she had suddenly forgotten where she was. Donleavy walked around his desk to sit in the chair beside hers.

"Betsy, slow down."

Her voice quaked as she resumed the tale. "Ben was still looking into this thing. I told you he thought Blake was up to something, and I also told you about Josh Morgan, that Ben had sent him a note."

"Go on," he suggested, though he wasn't sure he was going to like what he heard.

"I tried to get in touch with Morgan, but just got his voicemail. He never called back. Just on a hunch I had someone look into whether he had booked any travel. He went to El Paso first, then Chihuahua, then Cozumel. Since he appeared to be on the right track, I decided to give him some help. I had Roadrunner check into what could be going on in that area that might have to do with the Middle East. He found out that there was a yacht of Saudi registry in Playa del Carmen that had just left and headed north. Overheads pointed to Houston. Blake was in Playa del Carmen, too."

"I'm sorry, Betsy. What are you saying?" the DCI implored her.

"I think Blake and Morgan are both looking for Weston. And since Morgan is probably the good guy in the equation, I decided to have Roadrunner find him, and fill him in on what we know. It's pretty obvious there is a Saudi-Mexican connection. Whether Weston is on the boat – or will be – I don't know. But Morgan and Blake have both zeroed in on that area. On a hunch, again I had Roadrunner snag a ticket for Morgan to Houston, and…"

"Betsy," Donleavy interrupted, "what did you say about killing someone?"

"Roadrunner just called in. He said that Morgan thinks that Blake is out to kill Weston." The fire was back in the DDI's cheeks.

Chris Donleavy dropped his associate's hands and stiffened in his chair. "What makes him think that? That's absurd. Why would Blake want him dead?"

"Not just Blake, Chris."

Donleavy returned her stare. Momentarily his mouth opened. "Oh, no. No, Bets. That doesn't make sense. You can't…" He paused. "Maybe

Blake's trying to negotiate something with Saudi Arabia. Maybe he's just running interference with Morgan. Maybe the President just needs Morgan to butt out. I just can't bring myself to think that…"

"I don't want to think that, Chris, but it makes sense in a way. Mercer has this hard on for Saudi Arabia's oil. But then they go and snatch Weston. Who knows what they have in mind? But if any of their involvement becomes public knowledge it's a tremendous embarrassment to Mercer. Or worse, his complicity could amount to treason. But say we rescue Weston… He tells his tale, same result. That's why Mercer called us off. If Weston's dead, the kidnappers get the blame. And then it's just a mess to clean up."

"Even Mercer would never go to those lengths." The Director of Central Intelligence sat limply now, except for his hands, which clenched the arms of his chair tightly. "Oh, Jesus," he finally whispered.

CHAPTER 27

Once Morgan arrived at Terminal E at George Bush Intercontinental Airport, he made his way through secure corridors and across a sky bridge to the Federal Inspection Services area to clear Immigration and Passport Control. Fortunately, though his globetrotting days were over, he had had the foresight to enroll in the Global Entry Trusted Traveler Network Program when it first became available, so he headed directly to one of the program's kiosks. Though there was still a line, it was much quicker than going through the lines to deal with an immigrations officer.

Immediately upon disembarking their plane and prior to visiting the kiosks in Immigrations, Blake and Sanders settled beneath the first set of monitors displaying information about arriving flights. Blake was on the phone with Henderson getting the number of the flight Josh Morgan had boarded. The NSA deputy Director was more than a little miffed that his subordinate had neglected to leave that on the message, and though to a lesser degree, that he himself had not called before boarding his flight in Cancun. He hung up the phone and guided his eyes through the myriad of inbound flights on the monitors hanging from the ceiling.

"There it is!" he said, pointing at the display. Sanders' eyes followed his associate's finger.

The two men rushed to the line of people waiting their turn at the kiosks.

Next Josh walked quickly downstairs to level one with the two bags he had carried with him on the plane along with the Global Entry receipt he had received at the kiosk in Immigrations. Despite efforts by all parties involved to expedite the process, clearing Customs remained more of an ordeal than he had hoped.

"Crap," he muttered aloud as he took his place at the end of a long line of other international travelers.

While he waited his turn, Morgan considered his intended course of action. The local police seemed like the alternative that carried the least risk. Once he determined the location of Weston, or the place to which he would be taken, he would simply call the local police. Regardless of the involvement of federal agencies, local law enforcement officials would have to act on the tip, wouldn't they? Even if they checked with national authorities, they couldn't ignore the possibility of a crime being committed on their turf, he thought. Yes, there might be an attempt by some federal office to call them off, but they would have to follow up.

Not far across the Customs exit area, passengers were streaming in from Immigrations, among them were travelers who had been aboard another Continental flight that had originated in Cancun. Two men were enraging many of their fellow passengers, pushing their way through the crowds of people who believed themselves to be in every bit as big a hurry.

Sanders sped ahead. He arrived first at the luggage carousel identified on the arrival monitor as the one to which Morgan would have to go to collect his bags, had he checked any, and moved among the diminishing group of people waiting to collect their belongings. He didn't know Josh Morgan and was not sure he would recognize him from the photos he had seen. But he was just as certain that the man wouldn't recognize him either. His eyes scanned the people, comparing their faces to the photo sent by Henderson to his smart phone. None of them matched.

Everson Blake was panting as he arrived at the baggage claim area. He wiped his brow with his handkerchief as he slowed to a more comfortable pace. Across the baggage conveyor he locked eyes with Sanders, who shook his head side to side and shrugged.

Blake took in every face. No Morgan. He reviewed the crowd. Then, almost directly behind Sanders, some twenty yards further, the NSA Deputy Director saw Josh Morgan, third in line, waiting his turn to speak with the Customs Officer at the desk at the head of his line.

The Deputy Director caught Sanders' attention again and dipped his forehead slightly and pointed with hands and eyes toward their target.

"There!" he said.

Sanders wheeled around to where his boss pointed but not recognizing Morgan, turned back toward Blake.

"There! Near the head of the line!" he barked as he rushed past Sanders who fell in behind him. Both trotted toward the Customs Exit area.

The line behind Morgan was surprisingly short, with only four additional people behind him. As they reached the line of people, Blake's first thought was to flash his NSA credentials and push past them but identifying himself would almost certainly lead to the involvement of the federal agents throughout the room and necessitate dealing with his prey through official channels. So instead, he decided to defer that action unless it became absolutely essential. Blake had less formal plans for Morgan.

Josh absentmindedly looked behind him and staring back at him just a few people behind was the face that had haunted him from the pages of Time only a few, long days earlier. He tried in vain to blink the image away, but it remained. There was the same crooked grin that lifted one side of the bushy moustache. It was the kind of smile that held a sinister tone because, despite being a smile, it had a total lack of emotion. Morgan's pulse quickened as he wondered why Blake hadn't just moved ahead to apprehend him.

"Personal," he realized.

As he considered how to proceed, he was left to realize that if he tried to shortcut the Customs process, he would be detained. Blake would surely step in and take custody of him. But whether he did or not, it would be game over for him and President Weston would be left to meet whatever fate was intended for him. So he waited impatiently in line, as apparently Blake was willing to do.

The person at the desk finished up and the one immediately behind him moved to take his place. Josh moved forward. Of course, so did Everson Blake. Looking back again, Morgan tried to avoid direct eye contact with his pursuer but found it impossible.

Finally, after what seemed like an interminably long time, he heard, "Next." Josh stepped forward.

The ex-CIA officer tried to behave calmly to avoid appearing suspicious to the Customs Officer and though he felt like he was unsuccessful, in relatively short order, the Customs official slid his passport back and dismissed him simply by saying, "Next" to the traveler following him.

What Morgan hadn't noticed during his turn at the desk was that the Customs officers had opened a new line to accommodate the overflow of people waiting their turn. Somehow Blake and Sanders had asserted themselves to the head of that line and were even now being processed for exit.

Morgan tried to push through the people waiting for the revolving door exit to the lobby but before he could get there, a hand seized his shoulder.

"Don't be in such a hurry."

Morgan turned and was face to ruddy face with a man about his height, but who was bulkier. He smiled what one would have thought was a pleasant greeting for an old friend. His features were unremarkable enough, except the eyes, which suggested a dangerous potential. The almost-black embers communicated a seriousness that conveyed a warning that he was a man not to be trifled with. He crossed his hand over his jacket and shot his eyes downward to where they suggested a gun lay at the ready.

"Really. I insist," Sanders told him.

Morgan stared back at the man with equal intensity, though he said nothing. His head pivoted to see Blake at his side. He turned to face him fully and for the first time in years, he was not afraid of the man. The two foes stood toe to toe, neither moving, neither blinking, neither saying a word. Blake's smile faded just as one began to appear on Morgan's face. The Deputy Director's eyes finally turned away. After a pause he looked again into Morgan's face.

"Ben Reid is dead," he said matter-of-factly.

The remark got the desired effect. Morgan's eyes widened and his brows stretched at his skin. Then his body sagged, and his eyes turned down.

"It was an... accident," Blake offered with feigned sympathy.

Morgan raised his eyes to Blake's again and saw the twinkle of a man consummately proud of himself. Rage boiled with sadness inside the man who had just lost a dear friend.

"Car wreck, I heard. Thought you'd want to hear it from me," Blake taunted. "Too bad about his little girl. She is turning one year old – tomorrow I think."

Morgan stepped abruptly toward Blake, but a large hand stopped him. The other hand was reaching inside a sport coat. The head belonging to the hands was tilted to one side and the inner tips of the eyebrows slanted downward at an extreme angle.

"Make no mistake about it, Morgan. I will shoot you, right here, right now, if I have to," the ex-Special Ops warrior growled.

Morgan remained silent and shifted his stare back to his adversary of so many years ago.

Blake hated the silence and filled it with his own voice. "You've been a busy boy. El Paso. Chihuahua. Cozumel. By the way, we just missed each other there. I had to hustle to get here for our reunion." He started to walk. Sanders' hand prodded Morgan along beside him to the ground transportation area with its line of rental car booths. Sanders walked to an attendant at one of them. Blake stayed with his now captive and began to lead him to the exits.

"I understand you had some visitors a couple of days ago." His head turned to look for a reaction. Morgan maintained his straight-ahead glare, but finally spoke.

"Were they the best you could scrape up?" He stopped and let his eyes follow Blake. "They're dead, you know. Buried 'em on my property, as a matter of fact. Good fertilizer."

Blake's jaws tightened at the disclosure. He reached up and twisted his moustache. He had certainly suspected the two-man team was dead but was unnerved at the news, nonetheless. He managed to regain a small smile. He paused about halfway to the doors to wait for Sanders.

"Good. I'm… relieved you weren't hurt. You are quite resourceful, it would seem. So, it would also appear that we are looking for the same lost item." His eyes cut toward Morgan.

"Yes, but only one of us wants to bring him back."

Deputy Director Blake reached for his pocket so quickly that Morgan flinched backward.

Blake laughed loudly. "Phone." It was set on vibrate.

"Yes."

Sanders returned from the rental car counter and moved with Morgan to the exits. Blake lagged behind slightly with his phone to his ear. At the other end of the line, the somewhat meek voice of Henry James spoke, "Hold for the President."

Everson Blake's eyes shot toward Sanders. He raised his hand toward him like a traffic cop and walked a short distance away.

◆

In the White House, President Wendell Mercer motioned his Chief of Staff out the door of the Oval Office.

"Blake, what the hell is going on? This is going far beyond what I had in mind."

Blake asked, "What *did* you have in mind, sir?"

The question froze POTUS.

Blake attacked. "With all due respect, sir, I am doing what we both knew would be done. Your misgivings are not unexpected and quite natural. But I certainly see no reason to abandon the operation."

The President's words were a whispered growl, filled with dread and urgency. "Listen, Blake, if you proceed, you are on your own with this now. Get back to Washington and we'll think of some plausible way out of this. I am sure Saudi Arabia is setting up for some negotiated return for Weston in which they will get some major concessions from us."

"Sir, you've already given them everything they could possibly want, including recognition."

"Goddammit, Blake. Get your ass back up here. It's over. I order you to abort and get back to Washington. I could have you arrested. You'll never convince anyone that I was involved in this."

"Mr. President, you have misjudged a great number of things. First, I believe you have no clue what the Saudis are really up to. Secondly, you act as though I am under your command with regard to this. I see this as more an… equal partnership. I am doing what you wanted, of course, but I am also putting some things back in place, things of a more personal nature.

"The fact that you have developed cold feet is of no consequence to me. Your illusion that you will not be implicated is naïve, to say the least. I have any number of recordings from which I could make a compelling case of your involvement."

"Don't overestimate yourself, Blake. I have said nothing specific. And my White House phone is as secure as they come."

"Yes, sir. But the conversation we are having right now is being recorded from my end. I believe you've defined your role rather explicitly." He could feel the President's agony in the silence.

"Mr. President, I understand your difficulty in dealing with this. Even with your lack of morality you are probably suffering from a crisis of conscience. It is important that you learn, as I have, that there is a certain dispensation from God in dealing with issues related to your country and to a greater good. What we are accomplishing is for the long-term benefit of the United States. If, at the end of the day, you benefit, and I benefit, then that is a blessing from God for our willingness to do the difficult things for our nation."

In the Oval Office, the nation's Chief Executive continued to hold the phone to his ear in disbelieving silence. Since he had become President, nobody except his ex-wife had ever hung up on him.

◆

Blake walked backed to his partner and their new captive, sliding his phone back into his jacket. The tips of his moustache lifted with satisfaction at the telephone call. He continued past the waiting pair, who fell in behind him, and led them through the doors from the lobby area.

Morgan understood that his prospects for getting out of this alive had dimmed considerably since Blake had found him. Blake had essentially confessed to his attempted murder, and the murder of Ben Reid. There was no way Morgan would be left alive to testify.

He knew he would have to make a break, but he had no doubt of the resolve of the muscle behind Blake's brains. He further knew that if he didn't make a clean getaway, Blake could flash his NSA ID at any time, and simply cart him away. He wondered where they were going. It was crowded. A good opportunity should present itself.

As they walked, Blake's ex-special operations companion once again moved his hand and surreptitiously tapped his jacket with his hand and glared at Morgan to threaten with his gun. This time Morgan simply responded to the action with a slight smile.

"How big an idiot do you think I am?" he wanted to say.

The three walked through the revolving door, Blake in one compartment, Sanders snugged tightly in the following one with his captive. The door expelled them to the sidewalk where the VIP concierge would deliver the Lincoln Town Car. Morgan set his bags down. He knew he couldn't get into a vehicle, or all bets were off. Until then, he thought, he was almost certain he was safe.

When Sanders covertly threatened Morgan with his "gun" the most recent time, it occurred to him – it should have the very first time, he realized – that the man was bluffing. He would have never made it past security, no matter whether he was with NSA or not. And Morgan was pretty sure he wasn't.

The three men stood on the sidewalk. Hardly any conversation had taken place since Blake had returned from his phone call. That changed.

"Margaret Loughlin. I assume you're close," the Deputy Director stated. "I understand she's quite attractive."

Morgan felt his knees nearly buckle but said nothing.

"You put her at risk," Blake taunted. He watched the paleness consume his younger rival's face. "Yes, we have her under close surveillance. If you cooperate there is at least the chance that she will come to no harm."

Morgan knew he hadn't concealed the horror in his eyes. Was Blake bluffing? He felt his throat tightening, constricting his breath. Blake was ruthless, to be sure. The attack on his home had proved that. Morgan was confident that there was no way in hell that Blake was going to let him go, but Maggie? The bastard might kill her just for spite. But if Morgan went quietly the former President would die – or worse. At this point his own safety was moot; Blake already had him. So it came down to trading Weston for Maggie. There was no good way to resolve this. Honor versus love. "Damnation," he complained to himself. "Why me? How did I get involved in this?" He decided there was no way to assure Maggie's safety, so he chose to do what he could for Weston.

"You already intend to kill Weston. If I cooperate, you'll kill me, too." He faced Blake. "Hell, this is personal now. Do whatever the hell you want to Maggie," he lied. His eyes revealed the hatred and contempt he had for the man he studied, but it was what was beyond Blake that seized his attention. An airport courier was parking his motorcycle along the curb, leaving it idling, and heading toward the doorway with his documents.

"As you wish. You must set priorities, Morgan. You have to act on your convictions. It is unfortunate that when all this is finished, you will have failed everyone you care about."

Morgan could feel the pressure of his blood growing. Nausea was sweeping over him. Blake was right, he knew. He had to act on his convictions. He had to make a dramatic decision, and it would indeed impact any number of people. And Morgan had to decide without the luxury of time or consultation. Worse, the very lives – or deaths – of people he cared about hung in the balance. He turned again to the courier who was just entering the terminal. Facing Blake, he felt the brush of Sanders directly behind him where he knew he would be keeping a wary eye on him. Somehow, Morgan had to find a way to snatch hope from a no-win situation. He agonized at the thought that there might not be a way.

He locked his eyes on Blake's and read in them that he had to act. Josh Morgan tightened his fist and swung his elbow furiously behind him catching Sanders flush in the side of the head. Upon feeling the crack of his arm against the face, he snapped his head forward and felt Blake's breaking nose on his forehead. He raced past the staggering Deputy Director and sprinted for the motorcycle he had been watching. Astride the bike, he leaned forward and rolled his right wrist back forcefully. The motorcycle was smaller than he would have liked and lacking in power but still it launched forward. The front wheel strained to rise, but Morgan's forward weight held it skimming along the ground. The driver wrestled fiercely to control the machine, steered sharply to the leftmost lane to avoid his nemeses. Blake was hunched over, holding a handkerchief to his profusely bleeding nose; Sanders was darting around a cab just pulling to the curb, attempting to intercept their escaping prisoner. He lunged, but just missed Morgan.

The fleeing man knew he had a head start, just not how much. It would only be a matter of seconds until the concierge delivered Blake's car. To complicate matters he had just stolen a motorcycle and wondered how long until airport security was also on his ass. Shit, he had to make the most of the time. He wove among the cars on his way to the airport exit. If he could just make it that far, he might have a chance. There were a number of booths ahead, most with green lights illuminated.

The barrier arms of the exit lanes were so close to the concrete barriers that even with the small-sized motorcycle, Josh wouldn't be able to squeeze through. And if he tried to force his way up between the lines of waiting cars, he would likely be detained at the booth.

"I'm sure whichever one I pick will be the slowest," Morgan predicted. There were two cars ahead of him in the lane he selected. He swiveled his head to see a white Lincoln Town Car speeding through the traffic. He could barely pick out the silhouettes of two passengers. The first car in his lane moved ahead and through the gate. "One more," he said, hoping his urgency would somehow convey itself into speeding up his lane. "Oh, shit! Money." He stood, straddling the bike, and fumbled through his pocket for money. He snared his money clip and yanked a fifty out. He looked again at the rapidly approaching Town Car. It moved to the rental car lane and arrived just as the final car obstructing Morgan's exit proceeded through the gate. He moved ahead the one spot to the window where the attendant stood. Morgan looked to the right and made direct eye contact across four lanes of departing vehicles with Mark Sanders. The glare in his eyes told Morgan everything he needed to know of the pair's intentions toward him.

Leaning forward from the passenger seat to look past Sanders, Ev Blake displayed an equally ominous stare from either side of a swelling, bloody nose.

CHAPTER 28

"Thank you for seeing us on a Sunday evening at such short notice, Mr. President."

"Not at all, Chris. Betsy, how are you?" The President shook each of their hands rather weakly, Christopher Donleavy observed. He examined Mercer further. He appeared somewhat distracted. Even his posture seemed a little loose. His bearing usually reflected self-confidence, more an arrogance, the DCI opined. Today he looked as though he was ill, or maybe he was beaten down by something. "That would be something new for President Wendy," Donleavy mused.

"What brings you over? You said it was urgent."

Donleavy turned toward his associate for moral support before proceeding. He hoped the scowl on her face wasn't as obvious to the President as it was to him. "Sir, we have an issue relating to President Weston and Saudi Arabia – and, we believe, Everson Blake." He studied POTUS' face for a reaction. It never changed. And Mercer didn't reply. The lack of response was intimidating as the head of the United States' intelligence community resumed.

"Sir, I know you told us – ordered us – to discontinue our investigation into the Saudi connection with the former President's disappearance..." He broke off in mid-sentence to offer his boss the chance to interject. He almost hoped the President would become argumentative. An escalation in the tone of the dialogue might raise his adrenaline level and give him more courage to attack with the awkward accusations he was here to make. But DCI Donleavy was astonished at the reaction from the President. Not only did he retain his passivity, the man lowered his gaze away from his guest. "Guess I've still got the floor," Donleavy thought. He looked at Parnell again and observed a degree of puzzlement equal to his own.

Over the next several minutes Chris Donleavy, with contributions from

DDI Parnell, summarized both what they knew and what they believed about the abduction of Former President Trenton Weston. They withheld the details about Josh Morgan's involvement. They also stopped short of an accusation that Blake intended to see that Weston did not survive the ordeal.

Donleavy waited for denials and outbursts, neither of which came. Wendell Mercer simply sat behind his desk, eyes turned toward the window. He rested his chin on the hand of his left arm, which rested on the right one folded across his chest. Without turning to face the CIA directors, he mumbled an accusation. "You have no idea what this about."

Mercer swiveled his chair and stood. He walked toward the pair. He paused, and when he faced Donleavy and Parnell directly, the DCI saw the glimmer of fire in the man's eyes that he had expected from the start.

◆

"What the hell are you doing?"

Morgan turned to the attendant. "Huh?"

"I said, what the hell are you doing in this lane? Couriers don't pay. And you're holding up traffic."

Morgan was stunned, but not inclined to argue. As he twisted the grip to accelerate his bike, he turned again to assess the progress of Blake and Sanders. They were just handing over the rental agreement. They could have simply run the exit and flashed NSA ID when stopped. But they would definitely be stopped, and it could make the difference between catching him or not, the motorcyclist knew. "They must figure the stop would cost more time, so they are playing it safe," Morgan figured. He rocketed forward, worried about his pursuers and wondering what the attendant had been talking about. Morgan soon realized that his bike was clearly marked with a vendor pass. He had, after all, taken possession of his transportation from a courier. Morgan looked in the bike's mirror. He had about a quarter mile jump on the bad guys.

Outside the airport, Morgan felt he had a fighting chance. The danger of being apprehended for motorcycle theft seemed less imminent, and the speed limit increased dramatically. He had no idea where he was going but he wanted to get there fast. The underpowered bike was losing ground to the two men behind. He sped along the road exiting the airport toward Interstate 45 South. If he had seen a suitable place to pull off or hide, or escape across terrain where the car couldn't follow, he would take it. But the cycle wasn't exactly equipped for off-road travel.

Bush Intercontinental was not far off the Interstate and Morgan thought he might lose the tail if he could get into heavier traffic where they might have to slow down and he could use the bike's smaller size and maneuverability to an advantage. He crossed the overpass and zoomed south down the onramp toward the eight-lane freeway. Screeching tires told him that Blake and Sanders were closing in.

The Director of Central Intelligence watched the spirit reemerge in the President of the United States and steeled himself for a confrontation. Mercer posed before his visitors from the Central Intelligence Agency. Donleavy thought it apparent that the man had resurrected some of his usual resolve and knew that he had just made some sort of decision. No matter, the DCI told himself. He would not be bullied by Mercer in this matter. He had additional ammunition to fire, and it was powerful.

POTUS stood with his hands on his hips. "You have no idea what this is about," President Mercer repeated. "There is much more to the story than you know. Blake is out to kill Weston."

The heads of the DCI and the DDI flinched in unison and both their jaws literally gaped at the revelation.

As the President related his astonishing confession, his listeners sat stoically. Mercer added his spin to the story, insinuating, though never specifically saying that Blake had decided on his own to kill the ex-President. He contended that he had given Blake virtually free reign but insisted that he never considered the possibility. He saw the pair's disbelief in their eyes but didn't care. Mercer's stomach wrenched as he realized that he would indeed be accountable for his own complicity. He decided he would deal with that later. The President completed the admission and asked Donleavy, "What do we need to do?"

Morgan and his pursuers were some distance from downtown Houston, so the traffic was not as heavy as Morgan had hoped. In fact, it was very light considering the capacity of the road. His flexibility in losing his attackers was limited because their ability to follow was almost unlimited. The 100CC bike was simply not powerful enough to run away from the Lincoln. Morgan weaved his way frantically to keep vehicles between him and the white car that would ram him if it ever got an unimpeded line.

The frantic speed seemed exponentially higher on the motorcycle. Morgan had expected, based on his many visits to Houston, that the highway would have held many more autos, even on a Sunday, and given him more of a tactical advantage. He still faced the other danger adding to the two men racing after him – the police. By now the motorcycle theft would have certainly been reported. If he were to be stopped for speeding, the patrol officer would soon determine that his bike had been stolen from Bush Intercontinental Airport. But at least a police officer wouldn't kill him on the spot. Morgan wasn't so sure about the two men in hot pursuit. For all he knew, one of them might have had a weapon dropped in their rental car surreptitiously. He had to keep the pace up.

Morgan constantly scanned the side of the road. He needed to get off the Interstate, by means of a legal or illegal exit, in a way that Blake and his henchman couldn't follow. He would have already made a break off the highway, but the entire stretch was under construction of a utilities trench. Morgan knew that as he approached Loop 610, which circles the downtown portion of the huge city, traffic would begin to stack up. But he was also sure he couldn't wait that long. He darted in and out of the cars that were present. Cars began to weave in and out in front of him. Somehow through all of it, Sanders found a path to stay right with him. Morgan simply could not put distance between himself and the white Town Car.

Morgan was in the next to leftmost lane of the four that made up the southbound side of the highway. He continually scanned ahead for opportunities to evade his pursuers. It was clear for about a hundred yards in front of him. The next lane to the right had one car, a Honda Accord, and he was gaining on it rapidly. "Everybody is moving a lot slower that I am," he realized. Ahead of the car in the lane furthest right a late seventies model Chevy pickup was going even slower still. Morgan slowed to let Sanders pull closer, so the speed of the rental car was greater than his. When he was only about three car lengths behind the Honda in the next lane, he leaned and jerked the bike behind and past it to the rightmost lane.

"Come on with me, dickhead," Morgan snorted. And as he wished, the man did just that. He accelerated the stolen Yamaha toward the Chevy truck that remained in front of him in the far-right lane. "I hope you're not looking too far ahead of me," he said as Sanders' car swung from its original lane, behind the Accord, just as Morgan had. And also like him, the Lincoln continued over to the outside lane. The pickup there was dead ahead of Morgan and coming up awfully fast. Morgan waited until the last possible moment and cut away to the narrow rougher shoulder and accelerated. Suddenly Blake's driver found himself right on the bumper of the black Chevrolet pickup. He got a real good look of the pickup's tailgate, but somehow managed to slam on the brakes and swerve his vehicle to miss hitting it.

"Shit!" Morgan exclaimed, seeing that his "pick" had failed. The bike was whining at an incredible pitch, its engine straining at the demand being placed on it. Morgan looked anxiously past the shoulder of the road. There was still no place he could safely get off the pavement, at least not one where his companions couldn't follow. The concrete barricades of the high-occupancy lane in the center prevented him from escaping across the median. He moved back to an interior lane. He glanced at his fuel gauge. At least he saw he was in good shape with gas. In the rear-view mirror, he saw the white car, undaunted by its near miss and gaining ground again.

Morgan surveyed the Interstate ahead for another opportunity to shake his tail. Both vehicles were in the next to left lane when Morgan saw a chance for an instant replay of his previous tactic, but with an added twist. In the rightmost lane was an older Nissan Altima, going considerably slower than the flow of traffic. His view of the situation just ahead of that car was encouraging.

He tried to coax a bit more speed from his Yamaha, then blasted all the way into the right lane. The difficult part of setting picks with a motorcycle instead of a car was that it wasn't large enough to adequately obstruct the attackers' view. But this might work, he thought. "Let's see if you can do it again," he telepathed to his followers. He pulled much closer to the Altima than he thought was safe as he began to slow down to match its speed. The car in the next lane was moving up, giving the appearance that Morgan was now boxed in behind the Pontiac. As he had hoped, Sanders began accelerating for a run at him. As the white car picked up speed and distance, Morgan bailed onto the shoulder.

"Come on, you bastard," he actually yelled, and, though there was no way he could have ever heard the shout, Sanders did just that. But instead of a slower car, this time the pick was set by a stalled Chevrolet Impala, motionless on the shoulder. Morgan twisted the bike's throttle as far back as he could. The small engine of the motorcycle was not very responsive at these high speeds, but it gave him the burst he needed. The boost accelerated him past the moving Nissan and he narrowly averted disaster by squeezing back in front of it, coming within five feet of the left rear light of the stalled Chevy.

The Town Car slammed on its brakes as Morgan looked over for the inevitable crash – that wasn't. Sanders jerked the wheel, Morgan saw, and steered the car off the road into the ditch alongside. Though he clipped the fender of the motionless Impala, he incredibly maintained control of his car, and found his way back onto the highway. Morgan had put some distance on the trailing vehicle, but it was not enough. The superior horsepower of the automobile soon had it gaining on him once again.

"Almost out of moves, buddy," the motorcyclist bitched to himself. He looked ahead again for any opportunity he could seize to free himself of this nuisance. There was one last trick in his arsenal. The former spy stayed in the right lane, praying that his stalker would make up enough ground for this to work. If he began to slow too obviously, his trackers would sniff out his tactic. The Lincoln approached, closing the gap at a steady rate. The amount of traffic was beginning to pick up somewhat as they grew nearer to the heart of the metropolis. Morgan wanted Sanders close, but not close enough for a collision. The man had closed significantly, but the motorcycle rider thought he had enough room.

As he raced forward just near the entry point of an onramp, he pressed hard on the foot- and handbrakes of his bike, locking the tires up with a screech and puffs of bluish smoke. As he slowed to a nearly complete stop, and with Sanders racing toward him with no intention of stopping, Josh Morgan swung the rear of the bike around and yanked the handgrip backward, rocketing the cycle into forward motion again. He angled to his left and shot up the onramp beside the string of startled drivers waiting their turns to enter the Interstate. Below him the chatter of the Lincoln's anti-lock brakes could be heard over the motorcycle's whining motor. The significant weight of the car provided sufficient momentum to carry it far past the mouth of the ramp. But even if Sanders had been able to stop in time, there was simply no room for a full-sized automobile to negotiate the single lane of the ramp against the flow of traffic.

The white car pulled to a stop on the limited shoulder of the road. Both men slung their doors open violently and jumped out of the vehicle. Glancing back briefly to measure his success, Morgan saw Sanders pound the top of the luxury car, then kick at the tire before spinning around with his fist in the air. Blake remained absolutely in character, refusing to give in to his rage, and instead, stood with his left hand on the top of the open passenger-side door. His eyes traced Morgan's path up the line of cars and on to safety.

The fox raced on to live another day. The hounds fell hopelessly behind and could only wait for another chance to hunt.

"Maybe we can catch him," Sanders shouted above a passing recreational vehicle's engine, knowing better.

"We can't," Blake corrected.

"Any idea where he might go?"

"Well, we're both looking for the same thing, so I'm sure we'll meet again soon," the disappointed Everson Blake said. "We just have to make sure we get there first. If we do, then when he shows up, we'll have all our ducks in a row.

The two men calmly returned to their seats and tried to make their way back onto an increasingly crowded highway.

◆

Fadi Al-Majeed's head rotated as he looked curiously at the animated actions of two men standing beside their automobile on I45's shoulder. As the white car faded from his view, the Saudi's eyes shifted to where his hostage was lying. "We are nearly there, my friend."

◆

The logical thing would have been to get the hell out of Dodge, but Morgan's life had been nothing close to normal for days now. Reaching what he believed was a convincing distance for someone attempting a getaway, he slowed the bike and reversed his direction. Getting back on Blake's ass would be difficult, at best. But the NSA bastard had substantial intelligence on Weston's movements, it would appear, and Morgan had none.

He drove the Yamaha along the service road, squinting at the traffic stretching into the distance below. He might never find them, or worse, he might find them right behind him. It had been over six years since Morgan had tried to tail someone. It was never a skill he had needed to rely on in CIA. He usually walked right up to his targets, arranged a meeting through an intermediary, or occasionally even made an appointment. As a photojournalist many of the people he spied on were often glad to see him. But moving surveillance was a skill taught at the Farm. He hoped he remembered the lesson.

The elevated frontage road provided a commanding view of Interstate 45, but the lower speed limit prevented him from gaining ground on the line of vehicles below. It was early evening and traffic was backing up a bit, perhaps because it was nearing downtown Houston or possibly there was an accident ahead. Either way the pace was slowing enough that the pursuer was more optimistic of his chances of acquiring his mark. There were an incredible number of white autos in the procession. A white car was about a half mile ahead, but Morgan looked more closely and discovered it was a Chrysler. A white Cadillac slammed on its brakes in the growing traffic jam. The better part of a mile up the highway a white car was easing onto the off-ramp.

"My motorcycle needs a little more pep," Morgan wished. "My motorcycle. Right," he reminded himself that he had just committed felony theft. "I hope to hell this all works out." But he knew he couldn't think of that right now. He eased up to a closer spot in the line of cars on the frontage, careful to keep several between him and the white car he was gaining on. "Heck, yeah," he wanted to shout as a white Lincoln Town Car slid into place a dozen cars ahead of him. Its occupants were two men – Blake and Sanders.

With their roles reversed, Morgan proceeded with the necessary caution to stay out of sight of his quarry. He noted curiously that Sanders drove as though he hadn't a care in the world, never even applying any tradecraft to his driving. He never doubled back, never made sudden changes of directions. "Either he is overconfident that nobody would be following him," Morgan speculated, "or he just doesn't give a shit." The car made the turn onto Loop 610 and headed west to circle the downtown area.

The two men's car exited the Loop approximately on the west side of downtown Houston. Morgan followed. The car turned into the Galleria Westin's parking area. Morgan held back and pulled his bike into a space behind the hotel's shuttle, where he watched the two men exit the car. Even from this distance he could see the bright red on Blake's white shirt from the blood that had found its way out of his broken nose.

"If I could have, I would have done more than that, you ass," Morgan harrumphed. As he spied on the two men, a voice broke his concentration. He turned to see one of Houston's finest standing at his side.

CHAPTER 29

"Yes, ma'am?" she heard the caller ask. Langley had texted Roadrunner with a prearranged message that instructed him to call in and the call was transferred to the DDI.

"What do you know about the Al-'Amânah?" she inquired.

"Only what you gave me, that it appears headed for Houston."

"Nothing else? Okay," Parnell told him. "Here's what I want you to do."

Betsy Parnell reflected on her orders to the young CIA officer. More than the fact that the Agency operating on US soil in this way flirted with all sorts of illegalities, she was suffering a major moral dilemma at putting her young officer in harm's way. She hated resorting to this, but she still didn't trust Mercer.

◆

Morgan felt the perspiration leap from his pores as he stared at the patrol officer. He didn't know how long she had been behind him. He had never thought to check to see who was following him while he was following Blake. The officer could have been driving right behind him and his stolen vehicle and he wouldn't have noticed.

"Sorry, sir," offered the fifty-ish police officer, "you can't park here. It's for the hotel shuttles only." She smiled politely and that was that.

"Yes, ma'am," Morgan managed to say. He put the bike back in gear and rolled slowly forward. At about the same time, the valet assumed his seat in the Lincoln Town Car and was moving toward the parking garage. Morgan made a mental note of the license plate number and kept on driving.

The only things Morgan had with him after Blake and Sanders intercepted him were what he physically had on his body at the time – his money clip, passport, and mobile phone. The phone was fully charged. Morgan had made no calls on it for fear of being tracked down, or worse, leading anyone that might be looking for him to Maggie. In fact, he had turned it off to prevent been located by its signal. "Well, he thought, "Blake knows about Maggie, and he knows where I am. No reason to worry about that now."

When he turned the smart phone on, the display indicated several voicemails from Scott Taggart. No time to check those now and, anyhow, Morgan had some idea what they might be about. He started dialing Curtis Jones' number to warn Maggie about the danger she faced. He paused and tapped his chin with his phone. "But what could she do? How would she take it?" Morgan worried. He ran through the various scenarios. Maggie was resourceful, he knew, but she would be in way over her head.

"Shit. What am I gonna do?" He looked upward in thought, as if seeking divine guidance. And whether divinely inspired or not, he settled on a plan. He punched different numbers into his phone and pressed "Send."

"Taggart," the familiar voice greeted him.

"Tag, it's me – Morgan."

"Where the hell are you?" The question was almost a shout.

"Tag, I…"

"I dropped by your house to see you yesterday. Quite a mess. Bullet holes everywhere. A trashed-out truck in your garage. And has your phone been turned off? What the hell is going on, Josh?"

"I need your help, Tag."

Scott Taggart was curt. "I need answers first, Morgan."

"I understand," and over the next ten minutes Morgan gave his sometimes-fishing buddy the CliffsNotes version of the events at his house. He included only the story of the attack and that it involved some activities in his past. He didn't provide details of his life as a spy or what he was currently doing.

"Jesus, Morgan. You buried them under your tractor? What were you thinking? I'm gonna have to turn this one in. Hell, you're gonna have to turn yourself in."

"I will, Tag, when I get back. I'm in Houston. Listen, I need your help. And to help me, you're going to have to trust me."

"I don't know how I can. You said they were in the bucket of the tractor while I was there?" His voice betrayed disappointment and hurt as much as it did a lawman's take on a possible crime.

"Scott, the thing at my house. It's not over." Morgan paused and began to feel the tremors of the fright that was welling up. He began to ramble.

"Maggie's probably in danger. It's serious. She won't know how to deal with it, and I need you to take care of her. The man behind the attack at my house is here in Houston. He says that if I don't cooperate, then Maggie... Well, he said he has her under surveillance and something will happen to her."

Taggart couldn't keep up with the tale. "Why can't you just 'cooperate' with him?"

Morgan raised his voice, "No, dammit, I can't. There's too much at stake here. Are you going to help me or not?"

Both men felt that level of intimate tension that only good friends can experience. Finally, Morgan spoke again. "Please, Tag," he pleaded.

Morgan drove a few blocks away from the rental car agency and pulled the Ford Explorer into a parking spot. He walked back to the agency and cranked the stolen motorcycle. If the cops found it there, they would go inside and, within two minutes, have his name – his real name. He drove the Yamaha to and past the Explorer by several more blocks. He wiped down all the areas he might have touched during the time he had the bike. After all, his prints would be on file with the government and an inquiry into them would set off all sorts of alarms. Then he tossed the keys behind a nearby bush so nobody – well, nobody else, he reminded himself – would steal the bike. Finally, Morgan retraced the route back to the Explorer and drove to a convenience store. He went inside and got a soft drink, a pre-made ham sandwich, and a bag of Cheetos. He unscrewed the cap from the bottle and ripped open the bag and stuffed a few of the orange puffs into his mouth. He dropped coins into the slot of a pay phone, careful not to touch anything with his bare fingers. Cheetos left fingerprints that could be identified without the need for print dust. He dialed the number and waited for the answer.

"Houston Police Department."

He returned the greeting, "Hi, I wanted to let you know where a motorcycle is. It was stolen." He gave the location of the bike and the keys and got away from the payphone in a hurry.

◆

Despite his protestations to the contrary that morning, Trenton Weston was sitting up, eating bread and drinking water. His "camping partner" was in a decidedly good mood now, leading the ex-President to realize that the man's role in the operation was nearly accomplished. He listened without comprehension as his captor spoke on his mobile phone in Arabic. Al-Majeed pulled at the side of the curtain to assess the situation in an RV Park.

"We are in a campground in Alvin, Texas. It is off the main highway and should be quieter as we wait through the day." He listened to the reply from the other end of the phone.

Upon hearing the only words he understood in the stream of Arabic – "Alvin, Texas" – the American looked up from his meager meal and mumbled sarcastically, "Tell your friend that Nolan Ryan is from here."

Al-Majeed offered a bewildered look at him and returned to his phone conversation and his native language. "It is south of Houston and very near the rendezvous point. You have made the arrangements?" He paused for the answer, then reached for the pen and notepaper. "Very good. Gulf Mariners Marina. Very good. Near Freeport, Texas. Yes. Address?" He scribbled frantically. "Time?" Then finally, "Thank you, my brother... Yes... Allah, be praised."

It was difficult to tell through his captor's accent, but Weston heard what he thought was "Freeport" and possibly "Gulf Mariners Marina."

The Arab pressed the "End" button on his mobile and penned the last details. He swiveled the chair toward his guest and began in English, "You should know what is to happen to you.

"Tomorrow night we will complete our journey together. My associates, only kilometers from your White House, have made arrangements to transport you to our nation on *Al-'Am̂anah*. I will deliver you to my brothers on it and you will be on your way to your judgement."

"What the hell is Al-'Am̂anah?"

"It is a very big boat belonging to a Saudi Sheikh. The name means..." Al-Majeed paused to consider a suitable translation. "'The trust,'" he revealed to Weston. "That is as close as I can find in your language. It represents the moral responsibility to all the things that Allah has ordained for his children. It is a word, I suppose, that means our 'duty.'"

The Saudi studied the befuddled look in the eyes of his captive. "You wonder what that means to me. Al-'Am̂anah is why I do this? I have a family that has suffered because of the arrogance of the Great Satan. My wife and our two sons are safe and protected because of my service to President al-Hashimi. But my brothers and their sons and daughters and wives are not so fortunate." Al-Majeed noticed the intensity increase in Weston's eyes. "You think I could not have a wife and a family? I am not so different than you. But my love for them, for my country, and for Allah is great. I will give my life to provide them the same freedom and security that you American pigs take for granted. And if I give my life, then my rewards will be great. Allah is great and protects his children. To do his will on earth is my duty."

Weston flinched as the Saudi moved to the bench seat beside him and placed his face near his. "This has been far too easy. I feared that when we moved inside America, there would be many encounters with your federal police, but it has not been so. The only opposition to our movements came from you." Al-Majeed poked his prize on his chest. "Nothing has come from the outside. Your country does not care for you, I think. I believe I am – what do you say in your language? – home free."

Weston managed a smile to imply confidence, but he shared the man's sentiments. This had been far too easy. He was shattered at either the incompetence or lack of resolve by his government.

◆

Everson Blake didn't take notes. His near-photographic memory made it unnecessary. Terry Henderson was about to go home for the evening and was giving his boss the latest intel.

"Sounds like the yacht is heading to a marina near Freeport on the gulf coast south of Houston."

"Name?" Blake demanded holding the ice bag on his nose.

"'Gulf Mariners Marina.' I don't know where it is, except that it is off of 288 on the Gulf of Mexico. All I got was information that the yacht made a marine telephone call to that facility, so I'd say it's safe to assume that the boat is heading there to pick up your target." Henderson still didn't know what the operation was about. He just knew that Blake had a real hard on to track down Josh Morgan and a Saudi agent, and that this yacht was his likely rendezvous.

"We'll find it. Where is the Saudi?"

"No idea. He's gone quiet on us," the young protégé admitted. Henderson had not yet received word on the last call from Alvin, Texas to the Saudi Embassy.

The NSA Deputy Director was about to hang up when a thought occurred to him in regard to Mercer's call earlier. "Terry, why don't you take tomorrow off?"

"Thanks, sir. Are you sure?"

"Yes. And don't stay around your house. I need you out of pocket. Do you understand? Lose yourself." Then he turned to Sanders and they discussed what arrangements they would need to make.

The white Lincoln Town Car was on the second level of the Westin's parking garage. Fortunately, there was a spot not too far from those reserved for valet parking. Morgan parked the Explorer and tossed the wrapper from his now-devoured sandwich in the floorboard along with an empty bottle and other trash. He crawled into the back seat and tried to get comfortable. He washed down a couple of No-Doz tablets with some bottled water he had picked up earlier and settled in for his surveillance.

CHAPTER 30

DAY 11 – MONDAY

At two hours after midnight, a valet from the Westin Hotel arrived at Blake's car and drove it down the ramp toward the exit. Several parking spaces away a dark blue Ford Explorer remained perfectly still. In the back lay a dozing Josh Morgan.

The back seat of the Explorer was the acme of discomfort, but the stress and fatigue made it possible for him to sleep anyhow despite the caffeine pills. He reached up to the ache in his neck even before he was completely awake. His eyes flickered at the lack of recognition of his surroundings. Suddenly he seized the thought that had been rattling just below his consciousness. He eased forward from the position he had slouched to and peered at the parking space across and down from his. He stared for a moment, then sat up abruptly and rubbed his eyes with both hands and shook his head. Morgan looked up and down the rows of automobiles.

"That's got to be the right space, but…" The place where Blake's car had sat was empty. Morgan eased the door open and swung his stiff legs onto the pavement. He moved his eyes deliberately around the garage. No movement. He checked the time. 2:08 a.m.

"Well, there shouldn't be any movement at two-friggin'-o'clock in the morning," he sneered. "Nice job, Morgan; asleep on the job." He moved toward the empty space and cast his gaze about it as though the Lincoln would magically reappear. "How the hell could I do that?" He ran to the wall at the edge of the garage. He looked out onto the street. Getting his bearing he rushed to another side from which he could see the hotel entry. As he watched, the Lincoln pulled up the covered drive to the lobby's doors. The valet stepped out and held the vehicle's door for Sanders who took the driver's seat. Morgan froze, turning his eyes toward his own car, then back to the scene below. He decided to determine which way the man headed before running to his SUV.

"The Loop. He's heading for the Loop." Morgan bolted for his rental and jerked it into gear. Tires squealed as he rounded the corners in the garage's ramp in a desperate attempt to reach ground level. He braked urgently at the exit. A sleepy-eyed attendant took the twenty-dollar bill Morgan thrust at him. A scolding for the reckless driving accompanied his scowl and his slow pace of handling the transaction – right up until Morgan blurted, "Keep the change." With that the arm flew up and the Explorer's tires broke traction. Morgan accelerated toward the street and made the right-hand turn toward Loop 610. The distance to the Interstate bypass was only a few blocks and Morgan saw no evidence of any taillights. He continued along Westheimer to the light and yanked the wheel right and onto the frontage road. Still no cars ahead. Even in Houston the traffic is relatively light in the wee hours of the morning. He had to guess so he opted for heading out onto the Loop.

He pressed the gas pedal and began assuming the same pace as the cars on the highway and merged into the flow. There were enough cars on the Loop that Morgan couldn't identify all the cars ahead of him. He surpassed the speed limit, but still wasn't gaining ground on many of the cars. He drove for about five minutes and was about to give up the chase. He knew he could go back to the Westin and watch for Blake to leave, but his gut told him that Sanders had to be doing something critical to their mission to be out at the early hour. In the orange glow of the highway lights, about a mile ahead, a white car of some type moved to exit the Loop. "If that's not him, I'll head back to the hotel." Morgan decided.

Approaching the off-ramp, he signaled the right turn and slowed his SUV. Morgan reached the frontage road but couldn't locate the white vehicle. Slowing considerably, he pivoted his head frantically at each cross street. At the intersection with South Braeswood Morgan looked right and was turning his head left before the comprehension hit him as to what he had seen. Jerking his head back, he saw a white automobile heading away from him about a half mile away barely lit by the street lights. He slowed and moved to pursue. He still wasn't sure it was his quarry, but it was the only possibility he had. "It's either him or it's not. No use tipping my hand." He slowed to avoid gaining ground on the car. There was almost no traffic; a tail would be obvious.

The car made a right turn. Morgan covered the distance to the intersection and determined that the car was still proceeding before he turned the same corner. After only a half-mile the car slowed to make another right turn. "He's checking his six," Morgan speculated, and so continued past the intersection, turning his head away from the receding car. After he had gone a couple of blocks, he slowed a bit and watched his rearview mirror. Three blocks to his rear, an unmistakable Town Car crossed South Rice yet again. Morgan made a parallel turn and waited thirty seconds before resuming. But a traffic light turned red, forcing him to stop again. As he considered running the light, the white car crossed ahead of him on Chimney Rock Road.

"Where's he heading, Josh? Where's he heading?" The pursuer watched his quarry turn right. Morgan turned a street earlier and shortly afterwards made a left to return him to South Rice, and his original course. To his relief the Lincoln did likewise ahead of him. The follower slowed his speed to let the gap widen between him and his target. The cat and mouse routine continued for nearly twenty minutes. Morgan believed he was passing the scrutiny of the leading driver but couldn't be sure.

In time Sanders turned into a 7-11. "Odd time and route to be going out for a newspaper or a pack of cigarettes," Morgan thought sarcastically. He continued past the convenience store and pulled into a nearby used car lot. He killed his lights and engine and watched. His adversary parked at the side of the building. Seven or eight minutes later Sanders emerged with a small sack of his purchases, Morgan assumed. But instead of returning to the Lincoln the man opened the door to a black Dodge cargo van. Sanders drove away from the store and in five minutes he was back on Loop 610, followed by a blue Ford Explorer.

Trailing Sanders was easier now that the route was confined to the Interstate. Morgan followed him south, then east, on Loop 610 as he circled Houston. South of downtown the two vehicles exited on State Highway 288 south toward Freeport. Forty-five miles and fifty minutes later the black van passed the small town of Clute and exited southeast onto State 332. Morgan was unfamiliar with this part of Texas, but he knew it led to the Gulf coast. The Saudi yacht was headed this way, Morgan had been told. Maybe he was about to find out where.

About a half-hour after passing through Clute, Mark Sanders completed the remaining several miles of his winding route, drove through the entrance to the Gulf Mariners Marina, and slowed his van to a crawl. There were few boats in the obviously new marina. Some had motors, others had masts, but none approached two hundred feet in length. He looked at the notes that Blake had scribbled for him.

"Right goddammed place," Sanders confirmed. "But there's no fucking way a boat that size is gonna dock here." He drove closer to the gate that was intended to keep out the uninvited, but which stood wide open. Blake's colleague circled slowly around the parking lot. "Something's fishy,"

Sanders concluded. "Either our intel is bad, or we've interpreted it wrong."

Another pass around the parking lot and he pulled over to call Blake.

"What is it?" a sleepy and obviously upset Deputy Director, NSA, said harshly into the phone.

"Me, boss. I'm at the marina. Ain't no way in hell this boat is gonna use this marina."

Blake tried to think away the cobwebs. "And you're at the right place?"

"No doubt about it, Ev."

"So, you made the swap – got the stuff?"

"Yeah."

A long enough pause that Sanders wondered if Blake had dozed. Finally, he said, "Okay, come on back to the hotel. Henderson says the yacht can't be there until tomorrow night anyhow."

"Tonight," Sanders corrected.

"Right. Tonight. Come on back and try to get a couple of hours sleep. Maybe we can track down Morgan. With any luck, this thing will all be wrapped up by tomorrow."

The click annoyed Sanders. "Yeah, well good fuckin' night to you, too," he griped.

◆

Morgan watched from his spot some distance from where the black van had made a couple of circles around the parking lot. He parked near a racing sailboat that sat on a trailer and watched as Sanders abruptly left.

"So why did we come out here?" he asked the departing van. He waited until the vehicle was a good distance ahead before he resumed tailing. Then he stopped his truck. The little tremors in his gut told him that this had to be an important place.

"Think, Josh. You followed them because you thought they had better data," he said as if speaking to another person. "Maybe Sanders was just casing the joint. Maybe this is the place. If that's right, there's no reason to go all the way back to Houston with him. I can just wait here."

Morgan surveyed the marina as his adversary had only moments before. "But the boat's supposed to be one big sucker. I don't think it can get in here." But he decided to trust his instincts anyhow. He pulled to an open parking space among the trailered boats and the vehicles that probably belonged to the owners of some of the relatively few boats that occupied the slips.

"This is going to be the place to be," Morgan decided with conviction. With that he drove to find a convenience store for some coffee, snacks, and drinks. Returning to the Gulf Mariners Marina he parked in what he hoped would be a strategically advantageous place and crawled into the back seat, feeling that this time he could sleep for a while without screwing up anything. He set the alarm on his phone for two hours later. Within minutes he was snoring again.

CHAPTER 31

Teton County Deputy Sheriff Scott Taggart was uncomfortable, and pissed. It was before five o'clock in the morning. Unless he was going fishing somewhere, he was never up at this hour. And he hadn't stayed up all night since he was in college. He sat in his own Jeep just down from Curtis Jones' small brick house. Opening his thermos bottle confirmed what he hoped he was mistaken about. He tilted it up over his cup and – nothing. Tag wiped the drop or two from the rim of the bottle and licked the liquid from his finger. "Crap," he muttered as he replaced the lid and tossed the stainless-steel container in the back seat.

The deputy arched his back and placed his hand between it and the seat. "Jeeps sure weren't made for comfort," he griped. But if Morgan was right about Maggie being in danger – and Taggart wasn't sure he was – then a Sheriff's department vehicle would be too visible to enable him to be much good to her. He was putting his career on the line. Were there really two bodies buried on his friend's property? And what was behind the wild tale Morgan told him, anyhow? Deputy Taggart knew his friend had been moody, maybe even weird over the last year or so, but a story with this much… intrigue, he recalled the spy novelists' term for it? "Freaking ridiculous," he bitched again.

"My back is aching. I seriously need to piss. I'm hungry, and I haven't slept all night." Taggart stretched again and continued talking to himself. Josh Morgan had been a good friend for a few years and deserved the benefit of the doubt. The bottom line, the lawman decided, was that he probably should trust him, but…

"This is BS. I am not doing this." He reached for his keys.

◆

Perhaps his mind was subconsciously reacting to his earlier failure, but, for whatever reason, Morgan found it difficult to sleep more than a few minutes at a stretch. By six o'clock the sky was brightening with the impending sunrise and he was unable to go back to sleep at all. And not knowing what, if anything, was going to happen here, or when it might occur, he knew it wasn't wise to resume trying. He sat up, remaining in the back seat in order to be less visible, and checked the surrounding area.

The Gulf Mariners Marina was pretty much way the hell away from much of anything else, Morgan realized. The nearest towns were very small. He wondered if any of them even had police or fire departments. Freeport would, but it was about half an hour away. The remoteness was probably one reason why Gulf Mariners was chosen for whatever it was that would – or might, he corrected – happen there. The facility was obviously very new. The great majority of the boat slips weren't occupied yet. The ones that were mostly held sailboats. The dock nearest the office had a line of identical powerboats. Even the empty slips had dock boxes installed already. Morgan guessed it was probably a service of the marina management to help entice lessees to store their boats there. Individual gates shut off each dock from unauthorized visitors. The former spy squinted at the nearest one. It appeared to have a keypad. Boat owners will have the combination, he speculated. The benefit of daylight allowed Morgan to more or less confirm what he had decided the night before: this marina couldn't accommodate a ship the size of the Saudi yacht.

"So how does this place figure into Weston's kidnapping?" Morgan considered. His heart sank as he realized again that it may indeed not. He simply had no better leads. "Sanders came here for a reason, didn't he? But what was it?"

◆

The full-size white Ford van rolled slowly down the avenue on the southwest side of Jackson, Wyoming. The magnetic sign attached to its door advertised that its driver worked for "City Plumbing." He checked the address on the paper attached to his clipboard. The "plumber" scanned the house numbers.

"312… 314… Three-sixteen." He depressed the brake pedal completely and put the lever in "Park." The thirty-something year-old man sat momentarily, looking first into the driver-side exterior mirror, then the one on the passenger side. He studied the vehicles lining both sides of the street. Finally, he reached for the keys and silenced the engine. Another quick look up and down the street and the plumber picked up his cell phone. His right hand traced the number on the job sheet, while his left thumb punched the buttons on the device.

The telephone inside the house completed its fifth ring and the machine clicked on. "Hi. This is Curtis. Maybe I'm not home. Maybe I don't want to answer the phone. Either way, you're going to have to leave…" The caller hung up before the greeting was completed. He expected that the residents were home and not answering. He reached into his tool bag and retrieved the nine-millimeter pistol. The man continued to survey his surroundings as he screwed the cylinder into the gun whose report it would suppress and returned the assembly to the bag. Preparations complete, the man from City Plumbing opened the door of the van and walked toward the house.

Morgan watched as one man arrived to open the marina office. Shortly afterward a second man arrived and disappeared into the office as well. He walked out shortly and moved from one dock to the next, unlocking and opening the gates. He paused occasionally and sipped from his cup. Finally, the man returned to the small building. Morgan noticed a sign that said, "Ship's Store." "They could have binoculars," he knew. "And a pair sure would come in handy." But if this was to be a place where actions would play out, Blake would be here and, in fact, might be here already, Morgan considered. "Better sit tight," he concluded.

The former intelligence officer turned his cell phone on. He had kept it off virtually the entire time he had been away from Wyoming. He had not checked voicemail. He had made Maggie promise not to call him.

"Maggie." Morgan smiled, then he winced. "God, I hope she's alright." He decided he had to call her. The phone at Curtis Jones' house rang five times and his machine picked up.

"Curtis. Maggie. It's Josh. Pick up."

Inside Curtis Jones' house two men and one female exchanged worried looks around the answering machine where they had gathered. The first caller had hung up before leaving a message. And now the phone was ringing again. The machine welcomed the caller and then beeped.

"Curtis. Maggie. It's Josh. Pick up." Maggie's hand was starting for the phone when the doorbell rang. A larger hand reached out to stop hers. Three pairs of eyes widened and darted around. In the background Morgan simply said he would call back. Curtis moved quietly to the curtains covering the large window facing the street. He leaned his head against the wall to align his right eye with the crease of light at the edge and looked at the porch without moving the fabric of the window covering. He studied the man before the door holding a bag and a clipboard. He recoiled reflexively when the doorbell rang again. Now he turned his attention to the van parked in front of his house.

Jones turned to his two companions, mouthed the word "plumber" to them, and expressed his uncertainty with a shrug. Maggie looked at the man standing beside her. He registered his vote by shaking his head from side to side. Maggie turned back toward Curtis and duplicated the gesture.

All three sets of eyes jerked toward the knob on the front door. Maggie began to quiver as the visitor began to attempt to open the door. The man at the window moved, too loudly he was sure, toward his two houseguests. They exchanged a few hurried whispers. Tears began to leak from Maggie's eyes, and she put her hands to her face, unable to move otherwise. A hand grabbed her forcefully and dragged her to a place in the bedroom. Curtis surged for his place behind the kitchen counter. Releasing his hold on Maggie, the third person hid in the open doorway to the bathroom off the hall leading from the den.

Even in the bedroom Maggie could hear the clatter of lock picks, first inside the doorknob, then in the deadbolt. Three quaking people listened to the creak of the door opening and the soft click as it hit the limit of the door chain. Maggie peered through the bedroom door to where Curtis was hiding. The sound of cutters snipping the metal restraint elicited an exchange of panicked grimaces between them. Maggie was sobbing now, vainly trying to muffle the noise by covering her mouth with both hands. She slipped completely out of view into the bedroom and into the closet.

The creaking resumed along with the sound of cautious footsteps on the entryway tile. The door clicked shut and there was the soft rustling of a hand shuffling inside the bag. Then the steps started again, muted by the carpet in the den. Curtis' blood rushed through his head, throbbing at his temples. Though his eyes were closed, he rolled them back. His hands shook. His entire body did. Jones tried to hold his breath, knowing it would become a loud gasp if he exhaled. Finally, he held back his middle finger with his thumb. Applying pressure against the thumb's resistance, he hesitated before letting it go. The finger thumped against the wood to the cabinet door with a crack. Curtis squirmed, creating a muted indication of his presence behind the counter.

In the den the intruder froze, except for his head, which spun toward the kitchen. Slowly, in synchronized movements, the plumber raised his silenced weapon and turned to face the source of the noise. As he began to take his first step toward where Curtis Jones was hiding, he heard the ratcheting of a hammer being pulled back for action. The accompanying words were, "Freeze, asshole!"

A flurry of possible actions raced through his mind, but, in the end, the plumber knew his fate was fixed by the gun pointed directly at his back.

CHAPTER 32

Teton County Deputy Sheriff Taggart poised himself to shoot at the slightest provocation. He watched the man begin to raise the hand holding the weapon over his head. "Drop the gun!" he demanded ferociously. "Now, goddammit!" The plumber stooped slightly and dropped the nine-millimeter to the floor.

"Now the bag!" There was a thud as the satchel hit the floor.

"On the floor! Now! Stretch your damned hands toward me." The man kneeled, then lay down as commanded.

Tag looked across the room at Jones and smiled. "You did good, Curtis. Pick up his gun." Curtis Jones picked up the weapon and held it expertly on the prone figure.

Maggie stood behind the Deputy and smiled through her sobs. Taggart handed her his pistol and seized the handcuffs from his belt. As he knelt beside his prisoner, putting a knee on his back and pulling his arms behind him, he told his gun-wielding partners, "If he so much as breathes hard, shoot his ass."

Maggie didn't smile as she said, "I may shoot him anyhow." The captive raised his head just enough to see the intensity of two dark blue eyes looking over the barrel of a gun at him.

Tag let out a chuckle and shook his head as he snapped the second of the metal bracelets shut. "Damn, if Morgan wasn't right."

◆

The NSA's Deputy Director studied himself in the car's mirror while waiting for Henderson to answer his phone. His reflection revealed a red nose with broken skin, two dark purple spots on either side of its bridge, and his displeasure with himself for having told Henderson to take the day off without arranging a way to reach him. Henderson's voicemail came on the line.

"Terry, I need some information. If you check messages, call me."

"Sorry, Blake," Sanders bemoaned, "but that's the straight scoop. No way that boat gets into that marina."

"Yeah, and I told Henderson to lose himself today." He shook his head.

The two were interrupted by Blake's mobile. His eyes shot to his phone screen, expecting to see Henderson's number on the display. Instead he saw the area code and exchange of the White House PBX. "No time for this," he snorted.

President Mercer hung up. There was the blush of embarrassment and he smiled weakly at his Director of Central Intelligence.

Donleavy found the man disgusting, but he respected the Office. While the man deserved to be treated with utter contempt, the President should not be disregarded. So he found himself interceding in the awkwardness of the moment. "Perhaps he was just in a bad cell," he reassured.

Mercer's eyes averted the DCI's. "I... I just don't know how to track him down." He sighed. "I don't know how to stop this."

"We've got the FBI on it. He checked out of the hotel very early this morning. We found his rental car at a Houston convenience store, so we know he changed transportation. That's all we've got. In the absence of other information, we have no place to go," the DCI lamented.

"What about that kid over at NSA?" the President queried. He was beginning to regain some semblance of his Presidential presence.

"Henderson? Can't find him. The Bureau is looking everywhere." America's chief spy was frustrated with the situation and with the President. Mercer's behavior had not been just criminal; it had been immoral, and Donleavy considered that far worse.

POTUS looked up from the document he was reading. His face had a presumptive look. Donleavy had a worried countenance that could only be exacerbated by his boss' words. "Time is running short, you know."

The remark lit the DCI's fuse and he blurted, "Well, whose freaking fault is that, you know?"

◆

"So, what's the plan?"

"Maybe go right to the source," replied Blake, who held up his phone.

A call to Directory Assistance and a connection later, the other end picked up, "Gulf Mariners Marina."

"Yeah, I'm supposed to make a delivery to a yacht of Saudi Arabian registry, and I seem to have lost the information about the port it is going to arrive at," Blake prompted. "Can you tell me if this is the right marina?"

"Saudi Arabian yacht?" the voice on the other end of the line responded with a laugh. "Don't think so but let me find out. Hey, Clark, know anything about a Saudi yacht?"

Another voice spoke, "Hi, this is Clark. What do you need?"

"I'm in a world of trouble if I don't remember where I'm supposed to make this delivery. There's a Saudi boat, a big fucker, supposed to dock somewhere in the bay."

Sanders' mouth fell open. In the years that he had known Blake he had not once heard him utter a curse. And if he had had to predict which one might eventually cross his lips, the F-word would have been his last choice.

"Buddy, I don't know anything about an Arabian boat. The only thing even remotely resembling it was a guy I took a call from yesterday. Heavy Middle Eastern accent. Wanted to rent a boat from us," Clark declared.

"Rent?" Blake asked the marina manager.

"Yeah, wanted something capable of getting some distance offshore – to make a delivery or something."

Blake's mind ran the possibilities, then said, "Thank God. They must have decided to deliver to the boat out in the bay. What boat did you rent him?"

Clark paused and looked at his Assistant Manager as if he had a clue as to the content of the telephone conversation. Finally, he turned back to the caller. "What the hell. Let's see." He looked at the activity log. "Jezebel."

"Excuse me?" Blake countered.

"The Jezebel. That's the name of the boat we reserved for him. Corny, I know, but the people that rent boats seem to expect that it – I guess I should say she – should have a name. So 'Jezebel.'"

Blake grinned at Sanders and gave him a thumbs-up. "Thanks, pal. You've really saved my ass."

Sanders shook his head. Two curses in two minutes. He might get the hang of it yet, Sanders thought.

Blake hung up the phone and turned toward his associate, who responded with a taunt. "Colorful language."

Blake thrust his finger in Sanders' face. "Shut up!" He stuttered, trying vainly to think of something else to say. Finally, he spewed forth his next words. "Just… just shut up!"

◆

Terry Henderson didn't know how he wanted to spend his day, but at NSA, days off were hard to come by and, after all, Blake had told him to get lost. He found himself at the White House, of all places. He knew he wouldn't get in on the tour on such short notice, but he thought this would be a good day to see some of those things that people who lived in D.C. never got around to visiting. Henderson wandered around Lafayette Park, visited St. John's cathedral, then found a payphone at one of the shops nearby since he had left his mobile at home. He figured "get lost" meant exactly that. He dialed his voicemail number and retrieved his messages.

"Jeez. Make up your mind, Blake." He depressed the switchhook, deposited coins, and dialed Blake's number.

Only a couple of miles away, an FBI functionary called his boss. "Henderson checked his messages and we traced it. You're not gonna believe where he is."

Blake didn't recognize the number but thought it might be his subordinate. "Yes," was his greeting via his mobile phone.

"Me, boss."

"Never mind, Henderson. Get off the phone." He hung up.

In Washington, Henderson stared at the phone, and continued talking to the man who had just hung up on him. "Blake, you are one weird-ass jerk." He dropped the phone on its cord and shot his middle finger through it to his boss. He walked to a bench in the park and sat down. He leaned back and stretched to chill and to capture the maximum amount of rays on a glorious summer day. "I sure wish to hell I knew what was going on," he said to no one.

Across the street from Lafayette Park in the White House, Secret Service Agents were scrambling. They walked toward a specific store a block away, scanning every person they met in an attempt to find their target. One agent walked through the park, casting his eyes about for a specific NSA employee. He passed a bench where one person was catching some late afternoon sun but kept on walking. Then he spoke discretely into his sleeve.

Josh Morgan resumed his surveillance from the Explorer after relieving himself into an empty plastic Gatorade bottle. No sooner had he resumed his stakeout than a black cargo van appeared. It was identical to the one he had tailed the night before. He strained to see the license plate. "Hi guys."

◆

Terry Henderson heard a chorus of voices yell at him, "Freeze! Federal agents!" He scrambled in no specific direction, throwing his hands skyward, his head rotating back and forth at the agents pointing guns at him.

◆

One primary pier extended along the shore of the marina, from which the individual ones stretched perpendicularly to provide the docks for the boats.

"He certainly is casual about his work," Morgan said of the man unloading his equipment from the van. Morgan watched as Sanders walked the docks, moving matter-of-factly from one boat to another. He paused at one point, seeming unusually interested in a line of Xebec brand boats, named after the three-masted ships often used by pirates in days past. All were identical except for unique names and large consecutive 10-inch numbered decals. Sanders glanced at one of the Xebec Piratas specifically, though without stopping.

Next, he walked off the dock and down the shoreline farther from the office to a place behind a dumpster that would shield him from view from the office. He began unloading scuba equipment and a bag of unknown contents.

"What the heck...?" Morgan questioned. "I wish I had binoculars," he continued, straining for a better view, but primarily concerning himself with remaining invisible to the pair he watched.

He watched as Sanders assembled his scuba gear. "Doesn't this place have security?" Morgan wondered. He marveled that a man could simply don diving equipment and walk through gates into a facility such as this. But that's exactly what Sanders did.

The ex-intelligence operative sat back and contemplated what his eyes were telling him. "If Blake knows what he's doing, then that boat is involved. And there seems to be only one logical conclusion. If the yacht is too big to come to Mohammed, then you take Mohammed to the yacht. The Saudi is going to deliver Weston to the ship, and he's going to use that boat. What does that mean for me?"

◆

Terry Henderson sat in a chair surrounded by a contingent of FBI and

Secret Service Agents. "I want an attorney," he said, endeavoring to project some appearance of composure. Nobody replied. The entire team of agents stared at him as though they were waiting for something. The assembly suddenly parted with a chorus of "Sir" and "Mr. President." Terry's only thought was, "Oh, crap."

He stared at the vacuum between the men in suits and, sure enough, Wendell Mercer walked directly toward him.

"I believe we spoke on the phone recently," the World's Most Powerful Man barked at him. He moved directly in front of the seated NSA employee. He leaned forward, resting his hands on the arms of the young man's chair. He placed his face a mere eight inches in front of Henderson's. "Now, Son, you wanted a lawyer. Well, I'm a damned lawyer. And you are going to answer my questions."

◆

Mark Sanders fell backwards into the water, holding his mask and regulator in place with one hand, and the bag of "goodies" with the other. He collected himself at the surface and quickly descended. "Shit, I hate diving around docks – all this fuel filming at the surface," he recalled. The ex-SEAL dropped to a depth of about twelve feet and checked his position. The route would be easy to determine, the diver knew. All he had to do was swim south beneath the dock he entered from, swim under two adjoining docks, and turn left at the third one. The boat he was looking for was in the seventh slip on that dock. "No problem," he thought. He kicked his fins and was off.

Sanders reached what he knew to be the right boat but decide he should confirm it. There was no need to surface. The refraction of the water made the names on the transoms of the identical boats clearly visible to the diver. He read the name of the boat he hovered beneath. "Jezebel," he recognized.

Aquanaut Sanders ascended to the hull of the Pirata 2861 Bay Cruiser. He opened the mesh bag and retrieved the contents. He raised the instrument and held it firmly against the underside of the boat. He pressed one button, bringing the LED on the device to life. Another button pushed and held, and the red numbers displayed 01:30:00. He assessed the condition of the package he had delivered and slowly reestablished a depth of twelve feet. Reversing his previous course, he returned to the low section of the dock where he had entered the water. The ascent and egress were accomplished in short order. Once he was on the pier, Sanders removed his gear and made a nonchalant trek to the van.

"Amazing," Morgan thought. "A guy walks to the water in full gear, jumps in, and is never questioned." He shook his head.

Morgan continued his surveillance as the diver stowed his tank and other equipment in the back of the van. As he finished packing his gear, Ev Blake appeared from around the van.

"Done?" he asked Sanders.

"Piece of cake."

Blake pitched him a towel he had liberated from the hotel and waited while he dried off. He inspected the marina's parking lot again. A few vehicles had come and gone, but mostly the ones that were there when the two arrived were still in place. "Must be people out on their boats," Blake deduced.

The pair moved inside the van. "So how does this work?" Blake asked Sanders.

"There are two ways to detonate." He displayed a wireless detonator. "I enabled the receiver on the boat package. We wait for the Saudi and Weston to board the Jezebel; I throw this toggle and press this button and the timer begins its countdown. And – bingo – the charge goes off ninety minutes later. The other possibility is here." He pointed to the transmitter's "B" channel, consisting of a second toggle, covered by a plastic cap that opened on a hinge, and button. "We need to, we can blow the thing instantaneously, just by flipping the toggle and pressing this. Certainly, the optimal choice is to let him get out to sea, away from curious eyes. But... it's nice to have choices."

"It works underwater?"

"Sure. No deeper than it is. Less than three feet." He said to Blake, "You know, you ordered up a ton of explosives, boss." Of course, he was speaking figuratively, but he might as well have meant it literally. The plastic explosives would render the Jezebel and everything and everyone aboard pieces of debris floating on the Gulf of Mexico.

Blake twisted the corner of his moustache. "I wanted to leave nothing to chance." He gazed at Sanders as if to ask if there were any more stupid remarks.

◆

Morgan had been sick to his stomach since he attempted to reach Maggie. He turned on his mobile phone and dialed Curtis Jones' number again. His heart stopped as someone answered the phone immediately. A female voice asked the question, "Josh?"

"Maggie?"

"Josh, this guy came... he had a gun... he broke in... Tag was here..." Her tears took over.

"Maggie, are you okay?"

"I'm fine." She tried to continue but couldn't.

"Tag? Curtis?" Morgan begged.

"They're fine. We're all okay. When are you coming home?" Maggie's voice was soft and hopeful, but she anticipated an unwelcome answer. Morgan's delayed response reinforced her fears.

"It's not over, Maggie. I have to finish this thing."

"I understand," but she hated that she did.

Morgan gulped in an attempt to get past his conflicting feelings. "As soon as I get a handle where the final act is going to go down, I'm gonna call the cops in and just keep my head down. But I have to honor what I owe Weston. He set me free, Maggie, but you saved me. I love you, Maggie. I'll be home soon. I promise."

"I know, Morgan. You turd," she laughed. "What am I gonna do with you?"

"Live happily ever after, I hope."

"Pretty corny, Morgan." She paused and closed her eyes. "But I hope so, too."

"See ya, Maggie."

"See ya, Josh."

The Deputy Director was mortified. The previous day was the first Sunday since... "Gosh, I don't remember a day of worship that I didn't talk to Ellen," he thought with regret. Blake had been away on Sundays before, but he always called home and said a brief prayer with his wife. He called her and apologized. It was accepted and they talked to each other on the phone while they talked to God.

Knowing Maggie was okay was an incredible relief. The bonus was that he could now contact the local police and let the authorities take over. They could stake out the boat and pick up the Saudi. "And I can go home," he rejoiced. He searched on his phone and got the number for the Freeport Police Department. The Google hit provided a link to call the number.

Momentarily a female voice spoke, "Freeport P.D."

Morgan didn't speak.

"FPD. Hello?" she repeated.

"Wrong number," Morgan blurted, and ended the call. His world had just become infinitely more complicated.

"The cavalry comes and saves the day. Blake sits back and survives the operation – again." Morgan realized that he had nothing on the NSA bastard. The thought of him walking on this one was unacceptable. "No," he convinced himself, "Blake is going down this time." He rubbed his weary face with both hands. He turned his head to look past the docks and over the jetty at the sunlight glistening on the water of the Gulf of Mexico. "I don't know how it gets done, but he can't get away with another murder."

At that moment Josh Morgan knew the whole deal was up to him.

◆

The sun had set and there was a dark purple horizon to the east. The recreational vehicle stopped just short of entering the marina. Al-Majeed inspected the area. The orange-pink glow was disappearing behind him. He smiled with pride as he anticipated a successful conclusion to a complicated operation. It was a tenuous moment, the last link of a chain that would lead to glory for Saudi Arabia and al-Hashimi. He moved the lever back into "Drive" and proceeded slowly toward the piers. "And for me," he appreciated.

Josh Morgan's eyelids drooped. He was tired and hungry. The meager snacks he had picked up were wholly inadequate as meals. He had pissed in the plastic bottle to avoid getting out of the truck. The only thing that made him feel like he was on the right track was the fact that Blake and his henchman were sitting in a black van about a hundred yards distant. Morgan witnessed vehicles come and go but didn't see anything that appeared out of the ordinary. He would have thought he missed something except that the bad guys across the parking lot hadn't moved either. The thing that really pissed Morgan off was that he didn't know what he was watching for. And he suspected the pair in the Dodge van did.

Morgan watched a couple dock a sailboat and walk to the parking lot. The young man leaned his date backward over the hood of his Camaro and place a passionate kiss on her before opening the door for her. He slapped her ass playfully and she turned and shook a dainty finger at him. Slamming the door behind her, the sailor jaunted around the front of his vehicle to take his place behind the wheel.

Morgan's attention wavered from the yellow sports car momentarily as a recreational vehicle entered the lot and parked at the far end. He resumed his voyeurism and noticed that the young lady had lowered her head in the general vicinity of the driver's lap.

Josh Morgan laughed softly. "Oh, to be young and horny." He wished he could have wandered over and bang his fist on the Camaro's trunk. He wanted to see the reaction of the boy. His eyes raised to a point away from the yellow love nest to see a man walking from the RV toward the marina office.

Forgetting to be clandestine, Morgan sat bolt upright in the back seat of the Ford Explorer. "Middle Eastern," he recognized.

CHAPTER 33

In the black Dodge at the Gulf Mariners Marina, National Security Agency Deputy Director Everson Blake's moustache curled up at the tips at the recognition of the Saudi walking from the RV to the adjacent building. He tapped a sleeping Mark Sanders on his forearm.

"Huh?" he exclaimed as he stiffened up in his seat.

"Look," Blake demanded, turning over the binoculars to his colleague.

Sanders blinked his eyes a couple of times and leaned forward, raising the Nikons. "Gotta be our guy."

"'Spect so," Blake replied. "But we'll see soon."

The former SEAL was wide-awake now. "Morgan ever show up?"

"I have watched every vehicle that's come and gone from this whole marina. He's not here," the NSA Deputy gloated.

"We lost him, you think?"

Blake's eyes cut toward his partner. "Or maybe we scared him off. But I just can't believe he gave up." He unwittingly moved his eyes around the parking lot again. "So, it was a recreational camper. Pretty clever."

Al-Majeed moved casually toward the marina office. Acquiring the keys to the boat that had been rented for him, he walked toward the piers, eyes inspecting his surroundings, accompanied by the marina manager. His feelings were an elixir of nervous anticipation and religious fulfillment.

"Praise Allah," he thought as he walked across the dock toward the twenty-eight-foot Xebec. The ten-inch black vinyl stick-on on the bow configured a number six. The artwork on the stern identified the vessel as the Jezebel.

"Odd how the Americans name their boats after women, probably harlots," the Saudi mused silently.

Morgan was confident that this was the man in the photo his late friend had sent, the man he was after, but if he moved prematurely, he would reveal himself to Blake and Sanders. He watched the Arab examining the boats and saw him pause in front of the number six boat. The Arab stepped gingerly onto the boat, led by the man from the marina office. Morgan thought, "Orientation to the boat."

The ex-spook considered his options. The easiest and most logical course of action was to get close to the camper when his quarry was back inside it, wait for the man to come out again and try to get the jump on him there, assuming he was alone. Unfortunately, that exposed him to Blake and his sidekick. They could simply saunter up to Morgan and take him. They could even take him out from a distance if they didn't care about being discrete about it. No, he had to do this in a way that got him to the Arab and President Weston but that kept distance between him and Blake and maintained the element of surprise for as long as possible. He knew his old nemesis was unaware that he was there because he would've taken care of him by now. And he also had to get some idea of what Blake had in mind. If the Deputy Director elected to walk straight up to the RV, Morgan would have no alternative but to rush the vehicle and take his chances with a surprise attack – an unarmed surprise attack, he amended. However, he was fairly confident that wasn't the plan. Otherwise, why would they have placed explosives – presumably – on the boat? That would seem to mean that they wanted to resolve this matter at some distance.

He decided that he could only wait and hope further surveillance would present a solution. But in the meantime, he settled on the only real choice he thought he had. It made more sense than the other plans he had considered and that was unfortunate because it made almost no sense at all.

So Josh Morgan looked over the distance between him and the boat and began investigating the potential paths to get there.

Ten minutes later he saw the marina employee leave the boat. The Saudi lingered another five minutes or so before stepping off the boat and ultimately disappearing into the mobile camper. That was Morgan's opportunity to open the door to his truck and kneel at the ready. As he crouched beside the truck, he thought again of the various approaches to the boat. And he wondered what in the world he was doing.

"Well, I'll never get on the boat once he's on it," Morgan realized. He wished he had a weapon. More accurately, he wished he had an army.

He moved before he could talk himself out of it, running between two lines of trailered boats near which he was parked. The path took him to the first wooden dock from which the other piers extended. He almost tumbled as he crouched behind one of the dock boxes, the fiberglass lockers where boaters stowed much of their gear. They were stacked beside the dock, he supposed, waiting for installation. Casting a wary eye toward the RV, the knowledge registered heavily that President Weston was inside. Through the curtained windows Morgan could see the silhouette of a single person moving about inside.

"Looks like he's alone. At least that's one thing in my favor."

He scrambled farther down the pier, pausing for cover behind another fiberglass box. His breath was coming in gasps now, not because of the physical effort, but because he was scared shitless. He wanted to quit. He wanted help. But here he was. Morgan examined the camper again, then propelled himself quickly down the wooden walkway. He was near the end of the line of boats and trailers that he knew obstructed Blake's view of him. The former field officer sucked in two quick, deep breaths. He was pretty sure that Blake wouldn't tip his hand by pursuing him as he made for the boat. He repeated to himself that it seemed fairly obvious he wanted to blow up the vessel with the captor and hostage on it.

"The boat I'm about to get on. Sheesh."

Grabbing one last breath, Morgan shook his head in disbelief that he was about to do this. "Fuck you, Blake," he thought as he dashed for the end of the primary dock and turned the corner toward the slip where the Jezebel was docked, and where he knew Blake could see him. "I hope I've figured right."

"I'll be...," Ev Blake exclaimed.

"Damned," Sanders added.

Sanders reached for the van's door handle to pursue.

"Wait, Blake commanded. This could solve the whole mess. I don't know where he came from, but he doesn't know we're here," the NSA Deputy Director assumed wrongly. "There's no rush."

Sanders offered a puzzled look at his boss, then shook his head in recognition. He waved the detonator at his boss. "Right," he agreed. "The Saudi takes care of him, then the big bang ends the story." Sanders set the wireless detonation device in the utility bag just behind his seat and raised the field glasses for a better look.

Blake continued for his partner. "If he somehow whacks the Saudi, we blow the boat here. I would like to see this boat get out of the harbor and go with the original plan. But if we have any doubt that Morgan has been taken care of, we push the button. Messy, and visible, but that's the way it goes." In his habit he reached and pinched the corner of his moustache, rolling it between his thumb and forefinger. "God is good," he praised. "He has delivered the enemies of my country into my hands for vindication."

Sanders didn't look at his associate as he responded, "And you get to settle a personal score, too."

Everson Blake grinned broadly, returning the glass to his eyes. "Yes, that, too. That, too."

Morgan crouched behind the dock box, puffing. He didn't hear anybody milling about the marina. He knew he had been lucky so far. It was almost midnight on a Monday so the number of people around the area was less than it probably would have been on a weekend. What commotion he heard was faint, coming from the very distant privately-owned boathouses, he supposed, and not from the docks where the sailboats and rental boats were kept. Suddenly, Morgan heard a door slam in the area of the marina office. Two men spoke and he heard what he believed to be a key ring jingling.

"See you tomorrow, Clark," offered the first voice.

"Yep. Have a good night. Say 'hi' to Jenny. Oh, shut those gates, would you?" Clark requested.

The Gulf Mariners Marina Assistant Manager complied. "Will do. Goodnight. You gave the guy the code, didn't you?"

"Sure did. See ya."

"'Night."

Footsteps approached up the dock from where Morgan crouched. They halted only a few feet from his hiding place. The man whistled, Morgan heard. Then there was the sound of a metal security gate clanking shut at the entry point to the rental dock. "Holy shit!" Morgan whispered to himself at the realization that, had he waited to move, he wouldn't have been able to get past the locked gate. He settled to his hands and knees and sneaked a peek around the edge of the fiberglass box that shielded him. Still no movement from the camper. Morgan waited until the marina employee moved on, then crawled backward and raised himself to a crouch.

"Could just wait and try to ambush him here," Morgan supposed but decided he might find something to use as a weapon on the boat.

Morgan performed a final assessment and made his move to the Jezebel. As quietly as his need for speed allowed, he ran down the walkway between the boat and her sister vessels and jumped onto the swim deck and moved forward into the cockpit. Once there, he opened the fortunately unlocked door to the cabin. The boat shook back and forth from his movements, immediately creating waves that emanated from its waterline.

"God, please let him wait awhile," Morgan prayed, knowing that the ripples needed to settle, or they would give away his presence.

The lights were still on in the interior of the Jezebel from the orientation that the marina manager had given his renter, allowing Morgan to evaluate his options. It didn't take long. There weren't any. The cabin had no real galley. Just an oven, stovetop, and sink. He opened a drawer and found silverware and cutlery, but knives meant close combat. He preferred any alternative to that, but he took an eight-inch paring knife anyhow. There was a fire extinguisher of about twenty inches. "Same problem," Morgan thought. "The guy is bound to have a gun."

"Gun," he thought. His eyes shot around the cabin. He had no hope of finding a gun on a rental boat, he knew; at least not a firearm. But there was one gun he was certain would be aboard if he could just find it. He moved slowly to minimize rocking the boat. He opened drawers; he looked in stowage lockers. His eyes locked on a small compartment at the side of the ladder leading up to the cockpit. "That's where I'd keep it," Morgan told himself. He moved cautiously and opened the small door. The reward was the sight of a flare gun and a box of flares. He seized it and examined the mechanical aspects of a device he had never held before. He wasn't sure he had ever seen one. There were twin buttons on either side of the frame of the gun. Morgan pulled at them and the barrel fell forward on a hinge. Inserting one of the twelve-gauge shells into the opening – he wished they had been loaded with buckshot instead of some pyrotechnic signaling concoction – the former spy pulled the break-over section back, hearing it click into place. The two additional shells went into his pocket.

Josh would like to try to jump the Saudi as soon as he got on the boat, thinking the element of surprise might give him an advantage. But then he would have to deal with Blake back on shore. No, his best chance was to delay until the boat was at least beginning to get underway before making his move.

"Now how to hide?" Morgan pondered. It was, after all a relatively small boat. The bathroom – head, Morgan corrected himself – had a door. On the starboard side of the companionway steps leading back to the cockpit, the passageway to the berth that was in basically the center of the interior only had a curtain. Inside the sleeping area was a closet with a door, but it was far too small to hide in. So he was coming to the conclusion that he had just two possibilities, the head and the berth. He looked for other options. He didn't like the ones he had.

Former President Trenton Weston watched from his position on the bed in the rear sleeping area of the rented camper. Al-Majeed gathered the few items that he would take with him to deliver Weston to his Saudi colleagues. The Arab smiled at him before dropping to the floor and offering praise to his God. Weston had long since ceased to fight at his bindings. They were snugged so tightly at his wrists and ankles that every time he strained at them, he felt the pain of cuts. Knowing what lay ahead for him had allowed him the luxury of formulating contingencies with more specificity. The only thing he knew for sure was that he would never permit himself to be delivered to the Saudi dictator. The images of an American President being subjected to a trial and possible execution would prove divisive and humiliating to his country.

His best hope for escape was to consider escape impossible, at least in the standard definition of the word. Hog-tied as he was, Weston knew he would be a cumbersome object for one man to lift from the water. His limited mobility made swimming impossible. And when he reached the yacht the Saudi had alluded to, the ex-President knew he would be watched by more than one person. The decision was made; the only elements undetermined were when and how to execute. The logistical requirements were simple: open sea away from the marina, and sometime before the transfer was completed.

Weston heard shuffling as his abductor rose from his religious pronouncements and turned to face him. "We will go now," the kidnapper told him.

"You going to carry me?" Weston asked.

The smile he got was hardly friendly. His enemy walked deliberately toward him, seized him by his feet and pulled him roughly forward, until he cleared the bed and hit the floor with a thump. He flipped him over on his face and told him, "Yes, I am. There is no denying that you would take some sort of action if I let you walk. I also know you would prefer to die than go with me, so threatening you with a gun would be useless. So, yes, I will carry you." He ripped a length of duct tape from its roll and pressed it over Weston's mouth and pulled the ends behind the American until they met. Al-Majeed pushed firmly against the entire course of the silver strip around the man's head.

Next, the Arab's preparations took him outside the vehicle. He opened one of the several storage compartments embedded in the exterior of the rented RV and slid out a trunk about three feet by three feet by four feet in size. Moments later he was stuffing Weston into the oversized plastic box and latching the metal clasps. Looking about the interior of the camper he assured himself that his use of it was complete. Al-Majeed backed down the steps of the camper, dragging the trunk behind. He held one end, but the other end slammed onto each step in succession and then the parking lot pavement. He shoved the door shut but didn't bother locking it. Moving to the front of the RV he took one more look around the area before him and proceeded.

The blue chest scraped loudly as the man dragged it across the lot, unavoidably loud in the quietness of the night. He wished he had been provided with one that had wheels. The Saudi worried that someone might hear, but surmised that a man pulling a trunk filled with supplies to a boat would not cause suspicion. The metal security gate came next and the Arab looked at the slip of paper he had been given in the marina office and tapped the four-digit combination onto its keypad. A metallic click indicated that the lock had released. As the trunk rattled across the wooden planks of the dock, Al-Majeed's eyes continuously darted around his surroundings. They immediately fixed on the water surrounding the Jezebel, from which a series of small ripples radiated. The Saudi moved his attention to the dock near the Jezebel. It was clear. Al-Majeed expanded his inspection. His hand reached for the handgun in his jacket pocket.

Across the parking lot two interested spectators watched the unfolding scene. "You get the combination when he opened the gate?" Blake asked the man with the binoculars, though he hoped they wouldn't need it.

"Think so. 5-3-5-9 best I could tell." Sanders maintained his surveillance of the boat, which generated a smile beneath the field glasses. "Blake, he's sniffed out something," he noted, handing the optics to his boss.

Blake watched the Saudi as he examined the boat's exterior. "I think he's got him. Our work may be about done, pal." When he lowered the binoculars, his teeth showed clearly underneath his brushy moustache.

Al-Majeed reached into another pocket and pulled out a Mini-Mag flashlight. He twisted the end and the lightbulb illuminated. The beam went to the water near the boat first and the Middle Easterner looked for bubbles that would indicate a diver. "None," he said in his native language. Next, he directed the flashlight at the cockpit of the boat before moving down the walkways on each side of the twenty-eight-foot vessel. With a necessarily long, high step, he boarded from the port side and used his new position in the cockpit to illuminate the underside of the pier surrounding the Jezebel.

Still nothing. The Saudi turned his attention to the boat itself. He turned off his light and cast his view down the open hatchway. The gun was now out of his pocket. Al-Majeed's eyes bounced around the part of the cabin that was visible from the cockpit. Al-Majeed leaned partly into the opening, leading with his gun. He peered straight down the companionway steps. A few short steps down and he was finally in the salon. He looked first under the table between the settees at the bow. He turned toward the aft section of the boat's interior. Straight before him about amidships, below the cockpit, was the sleeping berth with only a cloth curtain to provide privacy to anyone who might be there. It was partially open. Al-Majeed stepped quietly toward it and yanked it back so forcefully that it ripped partially from its guides along the underside of the deck. Seeing nothing there he spun around toward the bow again. Still nothing. Surveying the salon, he rested his eyes on the only other hiding place he could see and the only place that had a door.

The door to the head opened outwardly, he saw. The Arab pointed the gun toward the currently shielded interior and yanked back on the knob. Springing the door open he prepared to let loose rounds from his silenced weapon, but...

"Empty," the spy uttered. Completing his investigation with another scan of the boat's interior, he replaced his gun to his pocket. Fadi Al-Majeed felt no embarrassment at coming up empty-handed. He had been in the intelligence game too many years to ever feel foolish at over-cautiousness.

The part of the boarding process that required the most brute strength came next. The Saudi moved to the dock and grabbed one end of the trunk, stepped back onto the Jezebel and lifted and yanked at the metal handle and forced one end of the plastic box onto the boat's relatively small swim deck about dock height. A sustained backward pull and the end of Weston's container came along, narrowly fitting through the opening of the transom and along the steps that led upward to the sitting area astern the center cockpit. The intelligence agent sat on the boat's bench seat to collect himself. He rested his forearms on his knees for several moments before rising again. Backing down the first two steps of the ladder leading below, he pulled the trunk toward the hatch and onto its side with its top facing him. Releasing the snaps allowed the top to spring open and Weston fell partly out. Al-Majeed raised the open lid and manhandled his captive the rest of the way out of the container. Once on the deck the former President was sufficiently out of the way to allow the Arab to push the trunk away from the hatch. Clutching Weston under the arms he backed the rest of the way down the steps.

"You are heavy, old man." The prisoner's butt cleared the opening and dropped, pulling his tied legs along. His feet clattered down the steps and both men tumbled to the floor. Weston's fall was cushioned somewhat by the body underneath his. Al-Majeed scrambled to his feet and reflexively put some distance between him and the American. After a moment he dragged the ex-leader of the free world into the sleeping quarters and lifted him onto the bed. Finally, he retreated to the salon where he sank onto one of the cushioned seats around the table for what he believed was a well-deserved rest.

◆

Four miles off the Texas gulf coast the *Al-Amânah* throttled back its engines for the first time in over two-and-a-half days. The captain began steering the yacht in slow orbits around a precise set of coordinates almost due south of Freeport.

◆

Everson Blake had their only pair of binoculars now and was studying the situation aboard Jezebel intently. "He's re-emerged from the cabin."

"Yeah, I see." Sanders didn't need the glasses for that. The two men watched from the black Dodge as the Arab stood at the wheel. A second after seeing the puff of white smoke from the Xebec's exhaust, they heard the engine as it chugged to life. The "captain" moved around the edge of the boat releasing lines, preparing to cast off. "He must have got him," Sanders decided.

Blake stared at the distant boat and then lowered the glasses. "I don't know. He looks too calm."

Sanders countered, "Maybe. But he's a pro. Listen, we know Morgan is on the boat. He went below. The Saudi's back up, so the little shit obviously didn't get him. Pretty clear to me."

"Maybe."

"So, what do we do?"

"Throw the A-switch while I think."

Sanders reached for the wireless detonator in the seat behind him. Throwing the toggle labeled "A" and pressing the corresponding button would start the timer aboard the Jezebel on its backward count from ninety minutes. While Sanders groped for the device Blake continued to size up the situation aboard the Xebec through the Nikons.

From outside the van a voice interrupted their concentration, "Hi, guys. What's up?" Two heads jerked synchronously toward the cheerful speaker. What they saw was a smiling twenty-something-year-old pointing a Sig Sauer P226 at them.

CHAPTER 34

Roadrunner stood just out of reach of any potential response. Beyond where the door could swing into him but close enough to see what was happening in the cab of the Dodge, he taunted the men, "You guys kinda fell asleep, I guess. This was way too easy. Now… I'd like to see two pairs of hands on the dash in front of you." He flashed his eyebrows and spoke with an intensity that belied his age. "Pronto, you sorry shits.

"Now I'm sure you have guns so, one at a time show them to me. You first." He motioned to Blake since he was farther away. He didn't want the activity of the driver to screen some action the passenger might take. "Thumb and forefinger only."

Everson Blake reached slowly inside his jacket and lifted his handgun as directed as though he were holding a mouse by the tail.

"Now toss it to the back of the van."

Blake did as he was told.

"Now you," he ordered Sanders. Sanders duplicated his boss' actions, likewise tossing his gun toward the back of the cargo area where it landed with a thud.

◆

The critical part for Morgan was determining when it was safe to emerge from his hiding place. Cramped quarters or not, the only way he would know for sure that Al-Majeed was occupied and he could exit was when he heard the boat's throttle engage and feel it begin to move back from the slip. The downside was that he didn't want to get out on the open sea. There was still the matter of Everson Blake. Morgan was sure Blake wouldn't leave until he knew the plan was executed. If there was some sort of bomb attached to the bottom of the boat, and he was sure there was,

Morgan guessed that the device was timed to get the boat away from the marina. Otherwise Blake would have blown it already. "Weston's on board; so am I," assessed Morgan. "All his eggs are in one basket." His gut told him, though, that the NSA officer could probably detonate anytime he wanted, and would if he suspected anything was amiss. He tried to avoid shifting. "This is really uncomfortable," he complained silently.

The engine was purring. In time Morgan felt – no, sensed would be more accurate – that the boat was adrift in the slip. Almost immediately he felt a slight bump as its hull touched the dock to port. Ten seconds later he felt the lurch, and the accompanying heightening of the pitch of the engine, as it was geared to reverse. The hidden man understood that he had to move now. He pushed at one side of the hatch above him and soon a patch of light from the cabin was visible. A continued effort slowly raised the cushion up on edge. He shoved it away and rose quickly, but quietly. The storage compartment below the portside couch of the two on the sides of the table in the "V" formed by the bow of the boat had been uncomfortable and extremely difficult to get into, but it had done the trick. When he had allowed the lid to close on top of him, Morgan could only hope that the cushion atop it would fall into place in a way that wouldn't suggest it had been moved. He had lain silently with the flare gun in his hand in the event the hatch was opened.

He stood up awkwardly to the extent that he could, bending around the salon table, holding the flare gun like the semiautomatic he had at home. He stepped out from around the table onto the sole of the salon. His eyes never wavered from the companionway that led to the cockpit.

Morgan moved toward the aft berth. "He wasn't lying on top of me on the couch, so he's got to be back there," he figured. He held the improvised weapon at the ready and pushed the drooping curtain aside. As he did, the light spilling in from the salon spread across the prone figure of Trenton Weston.

Weston rolled over to view his visitor and the surprise was obvious above his taped mouth. He didn't know who this man was – he had only met him once in his life – so he wasn't sure of his intent. Morgan raised a finger to his lips and felt foolish as soon as he did. He chided himself silently, "What the hell is he gonna say, dumb ass. He's got duct tape over his mouth." He pulled the galley knife from his back pocket and leaned over to the man. He sawed at the hand restraints first, the dull knife struggling to cut through the cord. The knife finally broke through. Morgan freed the ex-President's feet next. Finally, he reached behind the man's head and grasped the silver tape. Cutting it apart from where the ends overlapped one another, he leaned back around and gave Weston his best "I'm sorry" look and ripped the tape abruptly with both hands. Though not substantial, the pain was immediate as the sticky material ripped at the older man's skin and hair, pulling some out in the process. President Weston winced but never uttered a sound. His eyes initiated the smile, which then spread to his lower face as his mouth opened through the red rash that remained from the adhesive gag. He mouthed the words, "Thank you."

"Sir, are you okay?" The barely audible query felt like a stupid question before it came out – the man had some serious bruises and a cut – but it was appropriate to inquire anyhow.

It took him several seconds to recognize his rescuer and finally speak. "Josh Morgan. You're a long way from Wyoming." He smiled again and placed a hand on the younger man's shoulder. "I'm fine, son."

Morgan knelt at his friend's feet. "Sir, he's about to drive us out of here if I can't stop him. Stay below for now, but if I can distract him or disarm him, you get overboard as quick as you can. Can you move?"

"I'm fine, Josh. I can help…" Weston insisted.

"Mr. President, you have to get off this boat. People have to see you safe. No arguments. I've got it this." His wink was an attempt to display confidence, but he had very little. He was pretty certain Weston didn't buy it anyhow. Morgan looked to a hook on the inside of the port hull. Retrieving a life jacket, he handed it to the man he had just set free. "Put it on and be ready to move." As he turned, out of the corner of his eye, he saw the ex-President nod and begin to don the orange vest.

The Jezebel was moving forward. Morgan didn't know how far they had moved in the two or three minutes or so it had taken to get out of his hiding place and cut Weston free.

◆

In the parking lot Everson Blake and Mark Sanders stared at the departing boat while Roadrunner stared at them. Blake turned his head slightly to steal a look behind Sanders' seat at the bag containing the transmitter. Then he lifted his gaze toward the man outside. "Who are you?"

Roadrunner replied with a quiet "Beep! Beep!" He knew the two men wouldn't understand the joke. He followed up with a "Does it matter? Now get your eyes forward. I've been here a while. I followed you right in." He looked at the man behind the wheel. "You're not very good. Not sure what you've got planned but I betcha don't like Morgan being on the boat. I say let's just give him a chance to do his thing while we visit."

Blake watched the Jezebel moving away. The NSA officer's stomach churned. Everything he had worked toward for the last week had cleared the end of the rental boat dock and turned to port. A few hundred yards further and she would pass through the opening of the marina then past the jetty and finally the small barrier islands into the open sea – and out of range of the transmitter. He still had hope that the Arab would prevail against whatever Morgan had in mind and that the boat would continue on with the ex-CIA officer dead and the former President subjected to whatever the Saudis had in mind. That seemed to be the better of the outcomes if Blake couldn't resolve his immediate dilemma, he decided. But that wasn't acceptable.

No, he decided, that boat has to be destroyed now.

The boat's speed was next to nothing. The Deputy Director guessed the skipper didn't want to risk being stopped for violating the 5 miles per hour speed limit in the marina.

Roadrunner was curious as to the object behind the driver's seat that was of interest to the man in the passenger seat. He held the compact .45 firmly and leaned a little closer to the open window. The CIA officer told Sanders, "Hand me that bag – very carefully." The man moved his right hand slowly to the floor behind him, simultaneously lowering his left to the handle of the door. He lifted the bag toward the window. As the young man outside took one step forward to receive it, in a single motion, Sanders lifted the handle and shoved at the door. The now too-close CIA spook caught the full force of the opening door and spilled over awkwardly. The Sig Sauer slid away from him as the bag dropped to the pavement and expelled its contents over a wide space. The van's driver tumbled out of the vehicle and onto Roadrunner. Ev Blake also jumped from the van, rushing around the front to the side where the detonator would lie.

◆

On the Jezebel Morgan was leaning around from the aft berth and looking up to the cockpit. He saw the Saudi's lower legs as he stood behind the wheel. Morgan moved fully into the salon and lined up with the companionway ladder. Approaching from below would mean a tactical advantage to his adversary. If he pointed the flare gun at him, he would simply step aside. Morgan considered whether he had a better option than what he had planned and decided he didn't.

◆

On the parking lot Sanders and Roadrunner were rolling on the asphalt. The younger man threw his right leg upward and into Sander's groin, simultaneously throwing him aside with his right arm. Lifting his butt Roadrunner scooted backward on his hands and feet and away from his attacker. He grabbed at his weapon as Sanders recovered and lunged for him, throwing him brutally onto his back again. Roadrunner's head cracked back onto the hard surface, dazing him momentarily and giving the bigger man the advantage. Sanders fell deliberately to the side to gather in the black handgun still lying on the ground. The smaller man regained the initiative and pushed his hand upward, jamming his knuckles into Sanders' throat. The man coughed forcefully and slumped but placed his hand firmly on the barrel of the gun lying facing him on the ground.

Leaving it to his partner to deal with the young man, a few feet away Blake was franticly shuffling through the bag. Unsuccessful there, he began to examine the articles that had spilled from it, but couldn't find the detonator. His eyes alternated between the receding boat and the items scattered on the ground.

Roadrunner yanked Sanders back toward him by his collar with his right hand and threw his left arm around his neck. Hand on the wrong end of the gun, the man dropped it to secure the handle to fire it, but his opponent had pulled forcefully enough that he could no longer reach it. Sanders grasped the arm about him with both his hands. He slammed his head backward into his opponent's face. Minimal damage was done. He tried again but Roadrunner turned his head to the side to avoid the impact. He squeezed tighter. Sanders rolled over quickly and shook loose one of the other combatant's arms. Then he shed the remaining arm and struggled to his feet. Roadrunner did the same. As his adversary bent to retrieve the weapon, the CIA officer lowered his shoulder and rammed Sanders in the side of his ribcage, driving him away from the pistol. Sanders tried to clamber to his feet once again and received a knee to the side of his head for his efforts. The dark sky flashed bright to the stunned man as he spun around and struggled to remain on his feet.

The young spy lunged and seized his weapon from the pavement, turned toward a blindly-charging Sanders, and fell sideways to the hard surface. He raised the automatic and fired twice without aiming. One shot missed. The next round exploded through Sanders' left shoulder, spewing blood, and shredding tissue and flesh.

A few feet away Ev Blake's head spun to take in the sight of his partner being shot by their assailant. His search turned from the detonator to a third gun that had also been behind the driver's seat.

◆

Upon hearing gunshots from the shore, Josh Morgan broke for the ladder with the signal flare gun pointed forward. He climbed the ladder in two bounds and prepared to shout at the Saudi.

Fadi Al-Majeed gazed with increasing excitement at the not-too-distant exit from the marina toward the bay that would lead to the open ocean and a successful conclusion to his operation. From the marina parking area, he heard the unmistakable reports of a large-caliber weapon. He snapped his head around, quite certain that he was the target. In the darkness of the midnight sky the Saudi agent was barely able to make out the silhouetted figures of two men struggling with one another. His hand was moving on the throttle when a figure appeared from the cabin of the boat.

Morgan let out an unintelligible scream as he reached the top of the ladder, stumbling into a near seated position. He slid forward, spinning around on his butt to face the man behind the wheel. He lifted the unorthodox weapon toward Al-Majeed and prepared to use it if necessary. The Saudi's hand pushed the lever forward, surging the Jezebel so abruptly that Morgan fell backward, hitting his head on the transom. But the spike in forward boat speed also startled the boat's skipper enough that he too tumbled backward, and his hand, still on the throttle, yanked the lever into reverse. Morgan recovered slightly from the unexpected increase of boat speed and raised his head in time to see the Arab crash into the pilot's seat and tumble to the deck. The reversing engine slowed the boat. Without rising Morgan charged at the falling adversary, hitting him just as his feet slid from under him and he hit the floor. Feeling the boat stop and begin to back up, Morgan brought his fist to the face of the Arab, then reached, twisted the key, and killed the engine.

◆

Mark Sanders' momentum continued to bring him toward Roadrunner. The young man slid to the side and the wounded man just grazed him as he fell to the ground with a grimace. Thinking he had injured his opponent more than he had, the CIA operative turned toward the second man near the van. Roadrunner raised his gun toward Blake. In a blur, Sanders' good arm shot up and into the younger man's gun hand. The shot exploded skyward.

Leaning into the van Blake stretched across the driver's seat, groping in vain for the gun. The man's heart raced as he came up empty-handed after two attempts. He crawled over the seat for a clearer view of the rear floorboard and immediately saw Sander's pistol in the glow of the vehicle's dome light. His hand found the grip. Blake turned clumsily, lost his balance and found himself wedged awkwardly between the two front seats. Finally, he turned with the gun, still in an almost-seated position, and lifted it toward the two men now wrestling again on the pavement.

Bleeding profusely from his left shoulder, Sanders sat on the CIA officer's chest and right arm. And though one was nearly useless, Sanders had both hands on Roadrunner's left hand, slamming it repeatedly onto the hard surface. His attempts to dislodge the gun were to no avail. The man on bottom heaved his chest once, then again, ultimately creating enough space beneath Sanders to free his right arm. He slammed the bottom of his fist into the side of the man's head like a hammer. Sanders toppled from his position, senses reeling from the blow. As Sanders fell away from him, the young spy pulled his gun hand from the grip of the fallen fighter and discharged three shots rapidly and fatally into the already-wounded man.

Sanders only felt the first shot, which ripped through the ribs on the left side of his chest. The impact of the bullet with bone flattened and fragmented it, sending a spray of soft and hard metals directly through his heart, ripping it apart. Where the second and third shots impacted hardly mattered. Sanders fell face first onto the black asphalt of the marina parking lot.

◆

Al-Majeed used Morgan's distraction with the key to shove him backward and off of him. He surged toward the ex-intelligence officer and swung repeatedly at him, connecting only with a single punch. The hard right, however, dazed the American briefly. The Saudi reached into his pocket for his gun. Morgan swung his leg into the inside of one of the knees straddling him, buckling it and bringing his enemy to the deck. The gun, only partially secured, fell from the man's pocket and underneath the table on the port side of the cockpit. Morgan raised the flare gun toward the Saudi and squeezed the trigger, but without pulling the hammer back. His surprise at the absence of a discharge created a momentary distraction that allowed Al-Majeed to recover and kick the orange gun from Morgan's hands and overboard.

The two men dove in unison for the real gun, but their hands knocked it away. Morgan was the first to get to his knees for a second attempt. The Arab shoved his foe's head upward into the bottom of the cockpit table. Morgan's lids half closed and he sank to the deck in a momentary stupor directly atop the gun. Morgan regained his wits as the Saudi was pulling on him to expose the weapon. A punch to Al-Majeed's throat checked the effort. Morgan shoved the tips of the fingers of his left hand into the right eye of his enemy, sending him spinning away in pain. Morgan snared the handgun. The Saudi held his eye with one hand as he lay on his back. As Morgan struggled to gain control for a shot a foot slammed into his chest.

The force sent him backward through the companionway. His left hand grabbed for the rail alongside the ladder. The instinctive effort swung his feet around and prevented a headfirst fall but didn't check his descent entirely. He and the gun fell to the sole of the salon area below. Without the gun Al-Majeed had no choice but to follow.

◆

Roadrunner kicked Sanders' body off of him and spun his head toward the van to locate his second opponent. His magazine emptied, the field officer's heart stopped as he caught the view of Blake aiming a gun directly at him. The hand that was holding his gun rested on the ground. He held his breath as the subtle action of Blake cranking back the hammer became obvious. Eyes filled with rage, Blake's squeezed his index finger.

Click.

Blake's head shot down toward the gun. Then he realized that Sanders hadn't charged the weapon with a round. He pulled the slide at the top of the semiautomatic to its limit and released it. It sprang forward and rammed a bullet into the chamber as the NSA DD fell intentionally into the cargo area of the van.

Roadrunner rolled to his side and slammed a new magazine into his Sig. In a frenzy he swung up his gun and got off two wild rounds.

Blake leaned forward in a kneeling position for a shot out the door, but his adversary wasn't there. He rose a bit and fell purposefully onto the passenger seat, desperately searching for a place to move. A head popped up in the Dodge's rear window and Blake fired two shots ineptly through the door and then the window.

◆

Morgan never made it to his feet before his Saudi opponent fell onto him from the open hatch. The confined space in the cabin made effective fighting techniques difficult, but the battle was more of a street brawl anyhow. Neither man had any idea where the gun had landed. Morgan felt the force of Al-Majeed's fist as he pounded his face with three successive blows. The American managed to reach through the punches to grab the lapels of the Saudi's jacket and pull him close. But the effort only brought the Saudi near enough to butt Morgan's head with his own. Morgan was able to turn his head slightly and catch the blow on his cheek instead of his nose. The men thrashed about, struggling for advantage.

Al-Majeed retained his superior position and raised his fist to strike again. Morgan was able to toss him marginally to one side. As he tumbled, the Arab fought to launch another punch when a piercing pain seared into his left shoulder blade. He collapsed to his right and was astonished to see the American President standing beside him, wearing an orange life vest, holding a galley knife. Al-Majeed's momentary stagger a second earlier had caused the President's attempt to strike at a glancing angle, lightly ripping muscle but not penetrating deeply. Still, the man held the knife and was preparing for a more damaging strike. The Saudi spy kicked at the American's legs. The older man staggered with the impact and dropped the bladed weapon to catch his fall. Al-Majeed reached for the knife but was restrained by Morgan.

"Get out! Dammit, get out now!" the young American shouted at the older one. He placed his arms under the Arab's and pinned them back over his head. "Please! Go! Now! Get off the boat!"

Weston took a step toward the ladder but halted and looked back at his rescuer and saw him grasp the gun that he had located on the floor just behind his head. "I'm right behind you! Now, get off the damn boat!" The ex-President limped up the ladder. He paused at the cockpit and gave one more look below. Finally, he climbed to the starboard side of the boat and jumped.

CHAPTER 35

Roadrunner never figured to get into a gunfight. There were four rounds left in his magazine as he analyzed his position. He crouched at the back of the van that was rocking with the occupant's movements. Suddenly the CIA operative heard the whack-whack of feet hitting the pavement outside the passenger-side door. He leapt to the vehicle's right side prepared to shoot, but Blake wasn't there.

"Shit!" he said under his breath.

The CIA officer listened for footfalls, heavy breathing – anything. But he was rewarded with nothing. He stood to peek through the rear windows, holding his gun before him with both hands. Seeing no one, Roadrunner began to back away from the vehicle.

At the front of the vehicle Everson Blake also backed away from the van. He positioned himself beside a trash bin and peered around it and spied his foe moving away from the truck to the rear. The NSA officer pulled his head back. He looked both directions for the best route to attack from. At this point escape was not at the top of his list. He managed a furtive glance out toward the Jezebel, which he saw floating unpowered at the end of the docks. He elected to make his way behind a decorative row of shrubs toward a line of small sailboats resting on trailers.

Roadrunner heard the rapid steps of his adversary running and moved along a path parallel to his. He watched a line of boats, occasionally catching sight of shadows. He moved forward. The intelligence officer cursed himself for maintaining the offensive. "I should just hit the road." But he pressed on. He wasn't sure how his counterpart was doing on the boat and he sure couldn't let this guy complete his mission, whatever it was.

◆

Morgan felt the rough squirming of Fadi Al-Majeed on top of him. The Saudi spy braced his feet against the door to the toilet area and pushed, the sudden thrust sending him lurching forward. The action broke Morgan's grip and he dropped the gun he had just recovered. With great difficulty in such limited space, Morgan rolled the Arab over until he was on top of him. The former CIA officer let loose with punches that were more personal than they were protective. A blow to the face followed a chop to the throat with the edge of his hand.

In desperation Al-Majeed flung his hips upward, bucking the American from his perch. As he did, he yanked him by his shirt and threw him over his head. Morgan tumbled forward enough that the Saudi agent was able to crawl away and snatch the knife that had been dropped by the American President. He swung around to face the man who still lay on his back below him, arms at his side. The Saudi raised the knife above his head and shouted "*Allahu Akbar!*" as he dove forward, preparing to bring the knife down. The sight of the felled American's right hand coming from beneath his back held no alarm for the attacker until the recognition apprehended him that it held his gun.

Al-Majeed watched in virtual slow motion as Morgan lifted his hand purposefully toward him. The close environment of the boat's cabin amplified the explosions of the pistol's discharges. Fire and smoke rocketed in rapid succession from the barrel and the feeling of a sledgehammer hitting his chest bewildered the Saudi with its suddenness. His arm collapsed forward with the galley knife, but the action was no longer under his control. Before he landed atop his killer his eyes rolled back and his last breath of life escaped him.

After he fired the gun Josh Morgan raised his arms to brace himself from the body flying at him and to attempt to deflect the shimmering blade in the man's hand. The breath was knocked from his lungs with a harsh gasp at the impact. The knife gouged a rough tear on the outside of his left biceps. He sucked vainly to resume normal breathing. His chest heaved at the weight on top of it, but his lungs failed him. Morgan lay there several seconds before his breathing returned to a semblance of normalcy. He pushed the Saudi's limp body aside and struggled to his hands and knees. His head dropped; the energy to rise failed him. The pain in his chest and abdomen from the assailant's collision with him was unrelenting and sharp. The pangs transformed into waves of nausea that exploded violently, spewing from his mouth onto the sole of the Xebec's salon.

◆

The Deputy Director of the NSA moved away from the line of boats along which he was running, reversed course for about five yards and paused behind one of them. On the other side of the trailers the man he was trying to kill continued at a half-trot past him.

"Too aggressive, kid," Blake delighted in telling himself. He moved in behind his adversary as he heard the footfalls pass. He stepped directly behind Roadrunner at a distance of fifteen feet and shouted, "Hold it." Everson Blake wanted to look into the young pretender's eyes. The man stopped, raised his hands, and turned to face the victor.

Blake's smile didn't match the severity of the look in his eyes as he held his gun on the young man. "'Beep, beep,' yourself."

As he watched the young man's lips start to curl up at the edges, Everson Blake sent a bullet through the uppermost portion of the right side of his chest. The man's body wasn't fully on the ground before Blake had turned and was running to locate the detonator.

◆

Morgan felt some relief. He could breathe again, but he had flashes of weakness circulating through every part of his body from the vomiting. He moved up the ladder slowly, bringing both feet to each step before attacking the next. The former CIA officer paused upon reaching the cockpit and placed his hands on his knees, still holding the pistol in his right hand. He tucked the gun in his pants' pocket and struggled with great difficulty to fully stand.

◆

Blake rummaged through the items on the ground desperately, but still could not locate the wireless transmitter. He dropped to his hands and knees and lowered his head to look underneath the van.

"God damn it!" Blake shouted, cursing for the second time in his adult life, and using the Lord's name in vain for the first. He pounded his fist onto the black surface of the parking lot, anguished at the injustice of the moment. Finally, he raised his head skyward and cursed at God for letting him get so close to success, only to deny it to him. The Deputy Director lowered his face from the audible scream and, exactly at eyelevel on the floorboard of the van, was the detonator.

He gasped at the realization that God had restored him the opportunity to complete his crusade. Detonator in hand he rose and walked toward the docks.

The Jezebel, Blake observed again, seemed to be dead in the water. Her stern bumped against an empty slip on a far dock. "I don't know what happened over there, Morgan, but it doesn't matter now."

Blake flipped up a plastic cover over a toggle switch and a button marked "B." With a complete absence of emotion he pushed the switch forward, lighting a green LED. He gazed with satisfaction at the motionless vessel. He pressed the button.

CHAPTER 36

DAY 12 – TUESDAY

Fire and pieces of the Jezebel erupted into the midnight Texas sky. The echoes of the explosion rattled around the metal boathouses in the marina. Black smoke boiled up, backlit by the inferno on the water and from the blazing remnants of the boat still falling from the sky. Fuel flowed away from the spot with the glow of multicolored tongues of fire licking at the surface of the water. Pieces rained down for several seconds. Flames sprang from wooden planks of the dock nearest the point where the boat used to be. Melting, burning fiberglass landed on two small boats close by, setting fire to them as well. Every boat, every dock rocked violently from the surge of waves emanating from the site of the explosion.

Everson Blake, NSA's Deputy Director, didn't smile, but he had never felt the sense of personal service to his country and individual vindication that he felt at this moment. There would be obstacles to absolution from these acts, but that's what President Mercer was for.

Scant moments before the explosion, Morgan had realized that his life remained in very real danger. With a surge of strength from his panic, he had dived headlong into the salty water and began to swim with adrenaline-fueled urgency. He had made it over twenty yards from the Jezebel, far enough to avoid the direct, mostly upward force of the explosion. But the sonic pressure through the water from the detonation had stunned him and the large series of waves that emanated from the focal point of the blast sent his mind reeling. The force of the furious movement of the water away from the eruption had thrust him headfirst into a piling of the dock he had been near, addling him completely. Josh Morgan's consciousness began to slip away.

As he started to sink into the turbulent water, a hand reached him and pulled him up. Trenton Weston had reached a dock and sheltered himself behind the metal supports that held it up. Though he had also been shaken violently by the explosion, the protection of the structure of the pier had shielded him from the direct force of the blast. And while it made swimming difficult against the rough waves, he had managed to cover the relatively short distance between him and Morgan.

Everson Blake's self-congratulation was interrupted by movement in the water at the edge of his field-of-view. He moved nearer the wooden walkway that ran the full length of the front of the individual piers where the boats were docked. In the water, approaching the second dock to his left, Blake saw the silhouetted outlines of two figures in the water. One had a flotation vest around his chest and was pulling another slowly along but being helped by the surge of the diminishing waves from the detonation.

The Deputy Director couldn't determine the identities of the men but began to move toward them. The walk became a trot, which gave way to a full run as the man rushed to get to the pier to intercept the swimmers.

Beginning to regain his wits, Morgan did his best to achieve an efficient sidestroke. He asked Weston, "You okay?"

"Am I okay? You're the one who almost got blown up!"

Both men breathed in large gasps as they reached the underside of the dock and held on for support.

Weston spoke again. "I can hardly hear, but other than that, yeah, I think I am," he answered. "Thanks, Josh."

"Don't thank me yet. It's not over. Someone had to set off the fireworks, and I suspect we'll see him real soon. Oh, shit. Like now." Morgan couldn't see the face of the man running along the dock in the scattered illuminations of the mercury vapor lights and the flaming film of fuel on the water, but he knew who he was. The man on shore was reaching the security gate at the end of the pier where it stretched out from the main wooden walkway. Morgan pulled the former President far under the overhang of the dock.

Morgan leaned close to the man's ear and whispered, "Please, no arguments. Stay right here until I come back for you."

Weston answered truthfully, "Josh, I've had it. I'm too worn out to go anywhere." He reached up and held the side of Morgan's face in a single cupped hand, exactly like the younger man's dad had done when he was a child. The former CIA officer responded by putting his hand behind the head of the man that had done such much for him. He leaned his forehead to the ex-President's for a moment. The he looked squarely in the eyes that were visible even in the darkness under the pier. "I'll be back, sir."

"I know you will, Josh." He sounded more certain than Morgan was.

Blake stood at the gate and pressed the keypad, hoping that the marina used the same combination on all their docks.

"5-3-5-9," Blake said quietly as he pressed the numbered buttons he recalled from Sanders. A brief pause and... no click – only a beep. He entered the numbers again with the same result. He began to fear that the gates each had different numbers.

"Or Mark got it wrong."

He pressed "5-3-5-8." Nothing. His next attempt, "5-3-5-7," also failed. Near panic, Blake realized he might have to find a way to get to the water and swim to his targets. And with all the commotion, he knew people were going to gather and his short window of opportunity close.

"5-3-5-6" brought the click of the lock releasing. He threw the gate back powerfully and sprinted the first few yards down the dock. The Deputy Director retrieved Sanders' pistol from where he had placed it in his jacket after dispatching Roadrunner and placed both hands on the grip. He covered the wooden dock in an almost crablike manner, walking sideways a few steps to his left before turning his body around to continue the same direction, but in a rightward posture. He stopped and listened for the sounds of movement, either in the water below or on the wooden planks of the pier.

Not twenty-five feet from Blake, further down the dock, Morgan hung just out of the water on one of the cross members supporting the pilings of the pier. The top of the dock was only four feet above the surface of the water. Morgan could tell that Blake had stopped, and where. As the man shifted his body weight slightly, the soft moan of creaking wood betrayed his presence, if not his exact position.

"How are you going to get out of the water without being seen, Josh?" he asked himself silently as he glanced around in the deep shadows beneath the dock. And as the precarious nature of his perch sank in, he worried, "And how long do you think you can hang on here, buddy?" He was still addled from the explosion.

There was a line running from the deck cleat of the boat just in front of him, but if he grabbed it, Morgan knew, the boat would rock and give away his location.

Suddenly he heard what sounded like soft splashing further down the dock. It lasted about a second.

"Weston!" he cursed silently. "Nice diversion, but Blake's going to get down there fast enough to locate the ripples and know exactly where you are." Morgan climbed slowly up the braces against the pilings once he heard the footsteps above him bolt away to zero in on the source of the splashes. He poked his head over the edge of the dock but couldn't see anything because of the presence of a large dock box. "Well, then he can't see me either." Morgan pulled himself up the side of the pier, careful to avoid rocking the boat, and leaned in a crouch against the fiberglass locker. He reached into his pocket and recovered the pistol he had carried from the boat.

This dock was only half occupied, almost exclusively with sailboats. The masts stretched toward the dark Texas sky, swinging back and forth with every disturbance to the boats or the water around them. Morgan poked his head around the locker that concealed him. He saw that Blake had walked the full length of the dock and was working his way back, pacing the walkways between the boats and even surveying the empty slips.

"No flashlight. That must make it hard." Morgan continued to analyze the Deputy Director's movements and capabilities. The tip of his gun was bouncing from boat to water to dock box. "It doesn't appear he found Weston. No gun shot, at least."

Morgan looked around, to the extent that he could, for any means to gain an advantage over Blake. He extracted the magazine from the weapon he held. He had been surprised during the attack on his house by his near-empty pistol. He didn't want that to happen again. To his relief the magazine was nearly full.

Everson Blake was at once enraged and excited. He had failed in his original plan, but now he had the chance to rid himself of the two men who had nearly upset the direction of his life. It was no longer about resuming contact with his Central and South American colleagues. It was only about payback. The Deputy Director hated that emotion in himself. Throughout his adult life Blake had consistently made the logical and moral distinction between his faith and his profession. The Bible was full, he knew, of men who had found God's favor though they committed what others would have thought to be egregious sins. Yes, Blake was sure that God gave special latitude to men who served and honored him. The Lord understood the need to use unorthodox means to enforce His will in an imperfect world. Now the NSA officer's hands trembled with anticipation. He had stepped through the rationale of the situation and was certain that the two men he had seen were Morgan and Weston. The Saudi would have had no reason to leave the boat. He didn't know or care how Morgan had somehow disabled the Arab and escaped to the water with the old man. Blake offered a silent praise. His gracious God had delivered up both Morgan and the former DCI/former President to him. He would administer God's justice to the infidels. And the President of the United

States would provide his legal cover for whatever actions were required. God was indeed good.

Blake advanced with caution, listening, looking. He knew that the splashing he heard had come from just about this point under the dock, but he couldn't find the source. The boards that made up the dock were tightly laid, with almost no gaps to look through to the water below. Complicating matters more, whatever turbulence the splashing might have caused was indistinguishable from the swells still present from the blast.

It was impossible to see where his targets hid. The stalker dared not lean over the edge. There was the possibility that Morgan had a weapon of some sort, and the two-inch thick slats of the pier at least offered some protection from both detection and a gunshot. And the fact was, if Morgan was armed, it appeared he was in no better position to see Blake than the reverse.

The NSA Deputy realized, though, that time was running out for him. The marina was new and virtually empty, yet there was little doubt that somebody would have called authorities about the events of the fifteen or so minutes since the first gunshots. He needed to act soon.

Morgan eased his eyes past the edge of the white fiberglass box for another view of his rival. Blake was facing directly away from him, so he took the opportunity to survey the portion of the dock nearest him. He spotted a coil of loose rope near the next dock box before he ducked back to safety. The box Morgan was hidden behind was mounted about twenty inches from the pier's edge. He shifted his position and began to crawl along the narrow ledge to the rope. The fit was extremely tight and the going slow.

"Sheesh," Morgan griped as he squeezed along. The boards were hard on his knees and his balance was tenuous as he twisted his torso to fit in the confined crawlway. His back was rotated so severely to negotiate the distance to the rope that his face was against the white surface of the locker. Morgan steadied himself with his left hand and solidified his balance by running his right hand above him along the edge of the lid of the box.

The former intelligence officer paused to maintain his equilibrium. He struggled to position his hands securely. The gun was back in his pocket to allow maximum dexterity for his movement. As Morgan resumed his forward motion, he also tilted his head to try to get some sense of what Blake was up to. His left hand slid from the edge of the wooden platform.

Blake was unnerved by the ability of his quarry to remain silent and invisible. Finally giving in to the necessity for speedy action, he walked alongside a Beneteau sailboat. The NSA officer hopped over its twisted wire lifelines to the deck where he hoped the shallower angle might offer a better view of the underside of the dock. He was frustrated to find his ability to survey was only marginally better than before. The hunter made a tactical decision. Moving to the stern of the boat, he tucked his gun into his jacket and stepped over the transom onto the boat's swim deck. He sat down and exhaled in an attempt to purge his apprehension. Sliding into the water as covertly as he could, Blake pushed against the boat's hull to propel himself to the understructure of the dock. Pulling himself along the framework toward the central portion of the pier, he froze instantly and reached for the gun that had belonged to his partner.

Not fifteen feet ahead of him, silhouetted against the faint lights bouncing on the water, a man's form hugged a central piling of the pier. Blake's eyes shot around for the second man. He wondered if his prey was submerged, poised to attack. Finally assured that the first man was alone, Blake raised the weapon and began to squeeze the trigger. Then he reconsidered. He commanded softly, "Pull yourself to me. This way. Slowly."

Josh Morgan was breathing so hard that he nearly completed the fall he had narrowly avoided. His left elbow was on the dock. The fingertips of his right hand strained to maintain their hold on the top edge of the dock box. He gingerly raised himself to a point where he could reestablish some security with his left hand. He collected himself and turned his head to determine whether he had caught Blake's attention. What Morgan saw was the mast of a distant boat tilting back and forth.

"Blake's on the boat," he surmised. Taking advantage of that fact he scrambled without any attempt at stealth and reached a new hiding place with the coiled rope that he had gathered in. He stole a glance down the dock. Blake was nowhere in sight. Morgan dropped cautiously halfway over the side of the dock and fumbled for a foothold on the braces. His toes found a resting place and slid down the angle of the cross member. Morgan's body sank quietly into the water. Hanging an arm over a metal beam at his elbow he organized the rope. He tossed it over one of the docklines holding the boat next to him to the dock.

Examining his rope Morgan tried to remember how to tie a bowline knot to connect it back to itself and form a loop. "Oh, well," he decided. "If you can't tie a good knot, tie lots of 'em." He used one of his fishing knots and got the job done. The line secured to the boat's dockline, the man settled completely in the water and began to weave himself and the rope through the structure of the dock to its other side.

Everson Blake kept an adequate distance between himself and the life-jacketed swimmer trailing behind him.

"Now move away from the back of the boat," he ordered Weston.

Giving himself a margin of safety from any threat from the ex-President, he climbed onto the sailboat, using the rudder as a foothold. The Deputy Director stepped into the cockpit and moved back, alternating his gaze between Weston and the dock space. "Get on the boat."

Weston paddled his way to the boat. "I'm a little older than you. I don't think I can get up there."

"Then you'll die right there. It really doesn't much matter to me. All you are now is bait."

Weston believed him.

Blake saw a swim ladder on the transom separating him from the swim deck. He loosened the latch and unfolded it over the deck and into the water for his captive.

"Now climb up."

Morgan fed out line as he continued toward the far side of the pier from the boat whose dockline his line was attached to. He hoped he had enough. It would be close, he noted as he started the climb topside behind a dock box identical to the one alongside which he had previously perched on the opposite side of the wooden walkway. Just as Morgan pulled himself up, his balance failed him, and the end of the rope dropped toward the water. He lowered himself quickly and saw that it hung tenuously on one of pieces of the metal framework. He seized it. He shut his eyes and gritted his teeth. Blake's prey grunted a curse at himself and, tying a knot in the end of the line, wedged it in the intersection of two small beams near the surface of the dock. Morgan returned to the top edge of the dock and sat dripping behind the dock box, where he thought he heard voices.

Blake prodded Weston with his gun as the pair moved along the ramp next to the sailboat they had just left. When they reached the central walkway of the dock Blake ordered, "Sit down."

Weston was beyond the pointed barbs and sarcasm that had marked his encounters with the Saudi. He was ready for the ordeal to reach whatever conclusion was fated. He merely collapsed to the dock.

The man with the pistol walked a short distance up the dock from the former leader of the United States.

"Morgan!" Blake held both arms straight above him and waved the gun. The way he rotated to take in the entire surroundings reminded Weston of a ballerina wannabe. His theatrics were heavy with the intoxication of the imminent successful conclusion of a years-long goal.

"Morgan! I know you hear me!"

There was a pause as he anticipated a response from his hidden foe.

Morgan sat at the only juncture of the dock where opposite slips each contained a boat. He reached over the edge of the dock to retrieve the rope from where he had wedged it. He gasped as he saw it dangle against the line attached to the boat in this slip nearest him. "Don't rock *this* boat, idiot." Morgan calmed himself and lifted the rope again. It was too short to pull all the way up, but he was able to get it far enough to wedge between two planks in the pier.

A shout at the far end of the wooden walkway broke his concentration. The voice called out his name.

"Blake. Shit."

The distant voice continued, "I've got your pal. Come. Let's talk this over."

Josh Morgan's chest heaved, and his head fell back against the white box. He was paralyzed. What he knew for sure was that as soon as he showed himself, Weston was dead, and he would be next.

Blake waited for an answer. Then he shouted again, "Morgan! Your time has run out. You just don't know it yet." His eyes moved along the few boats at the dock. The Deputy Director called again, "Show yourself!" He paced back and forth in front of Weston, the tempo of his movements quickening with each unanswered shout. He spun around and faced the man he had captured, then just as quickly reversed his position. The scream this time was primitive and possessed a depraved, guttural quality. Blake's frustration exploded, manifesting itself in a rush toward Weston. The Deputy Director dropped to his knees beside the former President and pulled him by the collar, driving the end of his gun barrel brutally against the man's temple.

"You'd better get your boy to answer!"

Trenton Weston pushed against the cold metal and cut his eyes toward Blake. "Do it, you son-of-a-bitch!"

Deputy Director Blake thrust his face toward Weston's. "I will!"

"Do it!" The pitch increased with the volume.

"Don't push me!" His shrieked, his voice breaking as he pulled the hammer back.

"Pull it, goddammit!" Weston screamed.

Blake's finger began to apply pressure to the trigger. Weston squeezed his eyes shut and steeled himself.

CHAPTER 37

"Blake, you bastard!"

Nothing moved but Blake's head. He twisted it down the dock toward the source of the voice and removed the gun from Weston's head. The wildness in his eyes settled into a calmer, more rational coldness.

Weston let loose a rush of air and his body shuddered. The immediate relief was of uncertain duration, he knew, but relieved he was.

Blake strained to see where Morgan was hidden. He heard the voice again. "I've got a way to escape, Blake. You do anything to Weston and I'm out of here. You have to get both of us, you know, or you're toast."

The Deputy Director knew Morgan was right about his needing to eliminate both men, but doubted his assertion that he could get away. Suddenly the mast of one of the boats nearer the far end of the dock began tilting slowly to and fro. The moustache lifted as Blake realized what he was seeing.

"Gotcha!"

He stood and moved a couple of feet from Weston and extended the gun at him. He peered down the gunsight at the seated man. Weston straightened his back and held his chest out and stared bravely at the gunman. Blake held his pose briefly before easing the hammer forward. He grinned over the gun.

"You can wait. I want him to see this." The NSA man pulled back his arm and with a sudden motion, slammed the automatic weapon across President Weston's face. The man slumped to the wooden platform.

Everson Blake spun about and launched into a sprint toward the still tilting mast. His heartbeats quickened, not as much from the exertion, but the excitement. He slowed as he neared the wobbling sailboat. The charging Director softened the impact of his steps and brought his gun up with both hands. He shuffled a bit closer, sliding his steps sideward until he was directly in front of the rocking vessel.

Blake's eyes scoured the white Catalina. He leaned his head from side to side and took a step forward. He lifted his arms before him in a triangle with his torso.

Josh Morgan held his ground at the corner of the dock box, but ceased the gentle tugging at the rope that ran under the wooden deck to where it was tied to the springline of the boat across the dock from him. As he released the line, slack replaced the tension on the boat's springline. The former CIA officer raised his weapon deliberately toward the back of the National Security Agency's Deputy Director.

Blake leaned toward the sailboat that held his attention, directly away from Morgan.

"Morgan!"

"Yes, Blake," he almost whispered.

He heard an almost girlish wheeze come from Blake's lips and saw the jolt of shock wrench through his body at the sound of Morgan's voice. Blake's hands rose cautiously to about shoulder level. Morgan figured that was the automatic response when someone held a gun on you whether you were instructed to, or not.

"Don't shit your pants. And don't turn around. Just put down the gun." There was no relief yet. And no assurance that this thing was over – not until that gun was out of Blake's hand.

"Blake, you put that damned gun down – no, better yet, throw it in the water."

Blake's mind struggled to find some way out of the situation. "How did the moron get behind me?" he wondered. "How? I walked right in front of him." His breathing was rapid and uncontrolled. He considered the odds of successfully getting off a shot. "Never happen," he realized. Jump into the water? "Too far away." A weakness washed over him. His knees were failing him. He actually felt himself shaking.

"You don't have it in you to shoot me," he said to plant doubt. Morgan's reply registered an almost electric shock in him.

"Counting the guy tonight, I've killed three people this week."

Blake lowered the gun slowly and Morgan placed his left hand over the one already on the gun's grip and extended his arms. He took aim and prepared for a desperate move from the man in front of him. But as his weapon descended to about waist-level, the Deputy Director flipped the semi-automatic forward. It fell through the still rippling surface of the water with a splash.

Blake turned to face Morgan.

Morgan stood and stepped toward the man who had brought such misery to his life. He motioned with the gun toward the end of the dock where Weston was propping himself on his elbows. Blake followed the nonverbal cue and began a slow walk toward the dazed former President. Morgan fell in behind him.

"Mind if I lower my hands?" Blake asked him.

"Keep 'em up. It's a good look for you," the man with the gun observed.

NSA stopped and turned around slowly. Ex-CIA stopped and backed away with a more deliberate grip on the automatic. "Keep moving, Blake."

Blake raised his hands a bit higher, stiffened his fingers, and tilted his head. "Easy, Morgan. Just had a question. What are you going to do with me?"

"Not up to me, but I'd guess you're going to jail for a real long time."

Blake threw his head back in a muted laugh and lowered his hands. He leaned forward slightly. The gesture indicated a confidence of some secret knowledge. "I really don't think so. I have, you might say, a 'Get Out of Jail Free' card. So, I ask again, what do you think is going to happen to me?"

Morgan didn't reply but was suddenly aware of a chill overtaking him.

"Cat got your tongue?"

Blake laughed more loudly this time. "Should've shot me when I was armed." He sat down on one of the many dock boxes and folded his arms.

"What do you really have on me?" he demanded. "You think you have a lot? Tell me, what do you really know for a fact?"

Morgan entered the debate. "I know you were trying to kill President Weston. And you sent some guys to kill me. And Maggie."

"Really?" he said dryly. "What evidence do you have that any of those people worked for me? I believe you've taken care of all your witnesses. And here? I was trying to rescue Weston."

Morgan bristled at the lie, "Oh? You roughed him up pretty good."

Blake leered back at him, "I'll find some way to explain that. Maybe I was just breaking up a Saudi plot and didn't know what Weston's connection was with the agent."

"No one will believe he can be implicated in anything. Pretty weak." Morgan was confident Blake would never connect Weston with anything like that, but he didn't like where this was going. Blake was probably right. He really had no hard evidence against the man for anything serious. And he realized, all other witnesses were dead. Nobody besides him had heard the bastard threaten Maggie. And did he threaten her? All he said was that what Morgan was doing put her at risk? And while he all but admitted to killing Ben Reid, he never said anything that would hold up in court.

Blake broke Morgan's thoughts. "People will wonder what your role was in all this, too, you know. What federal agency do you work for? Who put you on this op?"

Morgan's head snapped back at the question.

"Maybe you were involved in this plot. You have a history of being implicated in foreign assassination attempts and all sorts of illegal activities. And here? You were interfering with a federal agent in the performance of his duties. I was the one compromising a foreign plot. You stopped me. How will that look? Weston misunderstood my role and tried to alert you to my position as I tried to apprehend you. I had to shut him up until I captured you. And why didn't you just call the police?"

Morgan thought, "Yeah. Why didn't I?"

In the distance he could see the flashing lights of emergency vehicles, probably from Freeport, coming to check into the gunshots and the still-burning remnants of Jezebel at the marina. Blake nodded his head in that direction.

"They are going to take us both into custody. We will explain our stories with our own interpretations. They will believe me.

"In time your role in the Terrador thing will come to light, as will the fact that your friend cowering at the far end of the dock covered up that illegal operation. That's how it will go down, you realize.

"That is, unless you and I come to some sort of an agreement – here; right now. That's your only way out of this. Otherwise, your life and those of the people you care about are worth nothing."

Josh knew that nothing Blake was babbling about concerning the present circumstances would play, except perhaps in the context of the Terrador debacle. Weston had never been involved, but it could easily be interpreted that he was.

The lights and sirens drew increasingly closer.

"Josh" – Blake was growing increasingly confident – "let me give you the bottom line. I am going to be back in my job within the week. Inside a couple of years, I'll have the top job. But that's of little concern to you, I suspect. Let me tell you what is.

"I will have the capabilities – and the will – to always be looking over your shoulder. You may go to jail; you may die. I don't think Weston has the clout to cover for you anymore. You think you have an insurance policy? I'll put my current President up against your former President. And I believe that my relationship with God Almighty trumps any play you might have?"

Morgan's smile couldn't be helped.

"God?" repeated the former CIA officer flatly. "God is somehow on your side and watching over you?"

Everson Blake's face hardened, exhibiting genuine surprise and even offense at the skepticism of his faith suggested by Morgan's tone.

Morgan went on. "You've been involved in running drugs, laundering money, murders, assassination plots. God blesses you for that?"

Blake stood so abruptly that Morgan jerked the gun up.

"You don't know anything! God's power is made manifest in ways that unbelievers don't – can't – understand. There is a harsh judgement that must extend to all those who would stand against the Almighty and His faithful. I am the tool of God against sinners. The worldly riches of unrepentant souls must be taken from them. It is distributed to the chosen, such as I am.

"As for my activities on behalf of my country, God demands that severe measures be employed to ensure that our nation prospers and is returned again to godly ways. You are an unbeliever, Morgan, and have no understanding of the ways of our Lord."

"Actually, Blake, I have a very deep faith. I just seem to know a different God." To the ex-field officer, Blake's religious proclamations were no different than the fanatical rants of Islamic extremists. It was at this very moment that Josh Morgan fully and finally realized that NSA Deputy Director Everson Blake was undeniably insane. And his madness was made even more dangerous by the power that the man wielded.

"Start walking so I can check on President Weston."

Blake turned and took a couple of steps in the direction of the man still sitting in a heap on the dock. As he did, he spoke over his shoulder.

"God will grant me the time and the opportunity to see you in your grave in the very near future, Mr. Morgan."

"You've miscalculated, Blake. I've grown used to having you in my life. There is nothing you can do or say to worry me anymore."

Blake stopped but didn't turn around, and sneered, though Morgan couldn't see it. He emitted a quiet, sinister chuckle.

"No? You're a weak, frail infidel who is crippled by your inability to set moral arguments in their proper perspective. You have a singular, though misguided sense of honor and duty. You can never understand that ethics are defined by the situations you find yourself in. And the actions required to prevail as a child of God are deserving of special dispensations. I don't separate my faith from my career. They are interminably intertwined.

"But I can assess the range of God's limits on my actions according to the needs of the moment. Can I kill an infidel? Yes, I can. Can I seize the money of drug lords, and use it as a believer? Yes, I can! But you, on the other hand have a moral dilemma. Your sense of honor is inflexible. And in the narrow context of your definition of it, you will always choose to do the honorable thing."

Blake finally turned to face Morgan. He pushed harder, convinced he was gaining absolute power over his adversary.

Weston watched the confrontation between the two men outlined against the marina lights, facing each other halfway up the length of the dock, but couldn't understand the muted conversation.

Josh Morgan looked at the face smiling back at him. The tilted moustache, the greased black hair, and the cold, coal-black eyes.

Everson Blake said, "There is just the one alternative. And I need an answer."

Morgan fixed his eyes firmly on Blake. "You, sir, are a hypocrite – and an asshole."

Blake's countenance changed into complete rage. "I swear on the name of my God…"

Josh Morgan interrupted, "You know what, just say 'hi' to him for me."

Suddenly seagulls sprang from their roosts throughout the Gulf Mariners Marina from where they were just returning after the explosion of the Jezebel. A heron rose from its fishing hole, screaming its primordial roar as it gained altitude. Tiny ripples emanated from the hulls of the few boats as they quivered in the water. The sound thundered dramatically among the buildings and the vessels. The report intruded on the night and the concussion announced the deed in the sudden fright of the hidden creatures of the darkness.

Josh Morgan recoiled to the dock, dropping the gun, and leaned back on his palms. His head dropped back until the stars of the coastal sky filled his view. The ex-CIA officer turned his eyes toward the expanding pool of blood on the wooden planks.

Blake had not completed his final offer of compromise to Morgan when the bullet slammed into his heart. He clutched both hands to his chest, looked briefly down at the blood oozing between his fingers, then raised his head in wide-eyed disbelief. His eyes rolled back, and the pallor of his skin immediately began to ashen. His last breath escaped as an incredulous, "God?" as his knees buckled and he crumpled to the dock with a thud.

Former President of the United State Trenton Weston rose to his knees, straining through the fog beginning to rise from the water and that clouding his mind. He peered at the single figure striding purposefully toward him.

"Oh, Josh, what have you done?"

"What was necessary, sir," a somber Josh Morgan replied.

CHAPTER 38

DAY 14 – THURSDAY

In the early evening Maggie Loughlin's eyes were misting before Morgan's plane ever touched the ground. It had taken almost two days of debriefing and explanations, but he was finally coming home. He stepped from the walkway carrying only a small bag of belongings that he had been provided to last until he got home. He had lost his suitcase and photo bag when he escaped from Blake in the Houston airport.

The two barely managed to remain upright as Maggie fell toward Morgan with an incongruous blend of forcefulness and weakness. They embraced and kissed and embraced and kissed again. Several moments passed before any words were said. When they were, they were simply, "Let's go home."

"Deal," Maggie gushed. "I have a surprise for you."

Maggie made the left turn into Morgan's drive. His eyes moved immediately toward the trout pond. The tractor had been moved, and a hole freshly dug. Maggie read his mind.

"Apparently someone from Washington called the Sheriff and told them to come dig them up. Tag called me and said everything was okay and to tell you to just come down there when you were up to it."

"Tag," Morgan whispered. He looked straight ahead and shook his head as he considered what his friend had done.

"I owe him everything, Josh."

Morgan turned his head and smiled at Maggie. Her eyes were still wet as he brushed back her hair. "We owe him everything."

Morgan left the small bag of clothes in the truck and headed for the porch. The sight of the bullet holes in the garage and along the front of the house surprised him. That day seemed forever ago.

The couple walked arm-in-arm into the den and Maggie threw her arms around Morgan's chest and pulled him close. "Is your life always like this?" she teased. He couldn't resist giving her the standard answer to her standard question.

"Not at all. Usually it's worse.

"So, what's the surprise?"

Maggie dragged him toward the utility room that was just off the kitchen. "He came walking up when I came back here after taking you to the airport." She stopped and let Morgan walk in first. There in his bed, in bandages, lay Biscuit.

"He lost a lot of blood, but the vet said he's going to be fine."

For the first time in a very long time, Josh Morgan felt completely at peace. He pulled Maggie down to the floor with him and the three exchanged hugs and kisses

.

EPILOGUE

DAY 15 – FRIDAY

President Wendell Michael Mercer thought of the meeting as the beginning to an uneasy truce. Former President Trenton Lewis Weston simply thought of it as uneasy.

Secretary of State Henry James handed briefing folders to both men. Mercer opened his and set it on his lap. Weston set his on the love seat beside him and crossed his arms. His cuts were bandaged, and he still carried the deep bruises from his ordeal.

The President stared momentarily at his visitor, then closed his folder. He sighed, bobbed his head slowly, and launched into his prepared statement. His eyes began to mist.

"Thank you for your visit, Mr. President," he said to the man who once sat in this office. I wanted to speak to you to underscore the depths of my profound sympathy at the catastrophic events surrounding your abduction. As my predecessor, you certainly understand the extraordinary measures required in maintaining the fine balance between the nation's wellbeing and one individual's safety. The tragic actions of Everson Blake will never be fully comprehensible to me, but you have my assurance that…"

"Bullshit," Weston said in a very un-Presidential tone.

"I beg your pardon."

"Cut the crap. You disgrace the Office. I have spoken with Director Donleavy, Deputy Director Parnell, Director Grayson, and your Chief of Staff."

James lowered his head as his boss' gaze shot toward him.

The former occupant of the Oval Office leaned forward and continued. "Among us we have developed a very accurate account of the 'catastrophic events surrounding my abduction.' And a recommendation – more precisely, a demand. If you think you can lay your bullshit spin on me – don't! I was there. Remember? So, let me tell you what will happen next."

Three Months Later, The Henry's Fork of the Snake River

"Nice tight loop, Mr. President." Morgan complimented Weston on his newly acquired flycasting skills.

"Thanks. Maybe I'll catch on. And could you just call me Trent?"

Morgan tilted his head and showed an "Are you serious?" look. "Actually, no, sir. I really don't think I could do that," he said soberly.

Weston smiled and continued to watch his dry fly drift with the current. "Thanks for having us up here, Morgan. It's a great place. And it's just what I need to start getting things together again."

"Yes, sir. It's the best place in the world for that."

Nearly fifteen minutes passed before another word was exchanged. Morgan broke the silence. "Sir, can I ask you something? How do you deal with the sense of betrayal you must feel? It must be heartbreaking to know that the President of the United States was ready to write you off, sacrifice you for the sake of his own political agenda."

The former President gazed down and spent several moments working over his artificial lure.

Finding the right words, he finally said, "In my mind, I have to look at it from another perspective. My view is that it wasn't the President who did this; it was Wendell Mercer. There's a difference." He walked alongside his rescuer and friend. "It was a situation where I had to separate the man from the Office.

"All of us who have held that office are, after all, just people. When we act in the capacity of that position our responsibility is to separate ourselves from both the best and worst of our own intentions. We're supposed to work for the people – period." Weston let out a long sigh and sat on the grassy shore of the river. Josh sat beside him.

"When we try to use the power to advance our own needs or prejudices, even the most noble ones, we're in danger of abusing the trust that has been given to us.

"If I don't make the distinction between the Office and the person who holds it in this case, the disillusionment would be too much to bear."

"I see your point, sir," Morgan conceded.

Weston continued his catharsis. "But it would be a lie to say that I wasn't discouraged greatly at his ability to hide his personal actions from the scrutiny and intervention of others who are supposed to be responsible for that. I'm certain some other heads will roll."

"Is this all that will happen to Mercer? He just gets to resign, for 'health reasons,' no less. No charges? No trial?" Morgan asked President Weston, who waved his hand as if to brush aside the concern.

"The nation doesn't need that. And besides, for him, resigning may be the most extreme punishment he could suffer."

More time passed.

He set his rod down and leaned back. "Betsy Parnell came through in the end – sending Trevor O'Bannon to Houston."

"Yes, sir, she did."

"How is 'Roadrunner' doing?"

"I understand he will need another operation but will be fine and back to some form of active duty in another couple of months or so, though it'll be considerably longer before he's back in the field," Morgan was pleased to report.

The companions stood and fished in silence for a few minutes.

"There is at least one good thing that came from this ordeal, Josh. It reaffirmed an element of my faith. I have always believed that life has a balance to it. Whenever evil manifests itself in one person, good overcomes it by inspiring another. An honorable man brings a moral presence to a crisis."

Morgan shook his head in agreement before catching the steady gaze from the ex-President. The former CIA officer flushed at the realization that his friend was speaking of him. He turned away and fumbled at changing the fly on his line while attempting to speak. Finally, he began to stammer a few words.

"I've never specifically thanked you for your assistance after Terrador. You invested in me, made a commitment to me when you didn't even know me. And you did so at a time when I had screwed up royally; and had very nearly made an already bad situation worse."

"Like I say, an honorable man. Josh, maturity comes with age, but honor and self-discipline come by choice. You were – and are – a good man. You deserved better than you were getting after the Terrador operation."

"Well, your commitment to me is what made it possible to try to resist Blake. I owed you everything."

"Then I suppose we've come full circle."

"Sir?"

"Now I owe you everything."

Trenton Weston sent a graceful cast in the direction of a rising trout. As his fly moved with the flowing water, he spoke with a genuine compassion.

"I've never asked you, Josh. What did you get from this whole ordeal?"

Morgan reflected on the question a few moments and discovered a moment of clarity.

The Wyoming sun sparkled on the riffles in the clear water on a perfect October afternoon. Alicia Weston and Maggie Loughlin talked and laughed on the bank as Biscuit ran toward them, returning from a sprint across an open meadow. Secret Service Agent Jack Johnston and his new partner, Jeff Coulter stood watch over the small group.

Trenton Weston waited patiently until Josh Morgan gave his answer.

"Redemption."

A rainbow trout rose to the fly Morgan offered. The battle lasted only a brief time as the fish struggled at the pressure of an unseen presence. The fish fought with courage and, when it was near the limits of its exhaustion and overcome with fear from the fight, it was rewarded for its perseverance by a hand that set it free to challenge another day.

The End

ABOUT THE AUTHOR

Rod Johnson is retired from the financial services industry and lives in north Texas with his wife Amy and daughter Allie. *Half of Faith* is his debut novel. Watch for other Josh Morgan novels!

Follow Rod on Instagram and Facebook @JoshMorganPublishing www.rodjohnsonauthor.com.